The Long Song

Also by Andrea Levy

Fruit of the Lemon
Small Island

The
LONG
SONG

Andrea Levy

A FRANCES COADY BOOK
Farrar, Straus and Giroux
New York

Farrar, Straus and Giroux
18 West 18th Street, New York 10011

Printed in the United States of America
Originally published in 2010 by Headline Review, Great Britain
Published in the United States by Farrar, Straus and Giroux
First American edition, 2010

Library of Congress Cataloging-in-Publication Data
Levy, Andrea, 1956–
    The long song / Andrea Levy.
        p.   cm.
    "A Frances Coady book."
    ISBN: 978-0-374-19217-4 (alk. paper)
    1. Slavery—Fiction.   2. Jamaica—History—19th century—Fiction.   I. Title.

PR6112.E889L66 2010
823'.92—dc22

2009043181

www.fsgbooks.com

1   3   5   7   9   10   8   6   4   2

For Amy, Ivy and Beryl

The Long Song

FOREWORD

THE BOOK YOU ARE now holding within your hand was born of a craving. My mama had a story—a story that lay so fat within her breast that she felt impelled, by some force which was mightier than her own will, to relay this tale to me, her son. Her intention was that, once knowing the tale, I would then, at some other date, convey its narrative to my own daughters. And so it would go on. The fable would never be lost and, in its several recitals, might gain a majesty to rival the legends told whilst pointing at the portraits or busts in any fancy great house upon this island of Jamaica.

It was a fine ambition from a noble old woman for whom many of her years were lived in harsh circumstance. This wish demanded respect.

Unfortunately for my mama, she then proceeded to convey her chronicle to me at some of my busiest hours. Indeed, that sweet woman never seemed to grow too tired to seek me out: early morning, at the heat of midday, or late, late into the night; following me about the house while I was in the process of dressing or washing; whilst I waited for a meal to be brought; as I chewed; as I pushed the plate away; as I was deep in talk with my wife; even at my place of work as several of my men waited, curious for my instruction. It shamed me to find that I did not have time enough to give it heed—that on most occasions I feigned listening to her yarn when, in truth, not one word of it was entering my ear or my mind's eye. Oh, how often did I nod to her when a vigorous shake of the head was what was required? I will not here go into the trouble that this caused within my household, but be sure to know there was plenty of it. No, let us pass with pleasure on to the solution that was eventually found.

A chapbook—a small pamphlet. My mama's words printed upon paper, with the type set down in the blackest ink for ease of reading. Upon its cover there could be the ornamentation of a sturdy woodcut— a horse or cart or bundled sugar cane (for I know a man who can render these with such skill as to trick your eye into believing you were gazing upon the true item).

I explained to my dear mama, once spoken these precious words of hers would be lost to all but my ears. If, though, committed to a very thin volume, I could peruse her tale at my leisure and no word would be lost when my fickle mind strayed to some other purpose. And better, for the excess books which would be produced from the press could be given for sale, taken around the island so others, far and wide, might delight in her careful narration.

But my mama began her life as a person for whom writing the letters ABC could have seen her put to the lash, for she was born a slave. The undertaking of committing her tale to words that might be read and set into printed form was, at first, quite alarming for her poor soul. She fretted, following me about the house and town to chatter at me of her anxiety of writing upon paper. She feared she would not have the skill to make herself understood in this form; and what if she were to make some mistake in its telling? Then surely it would be there, for ever and a day, for all to find amusement in her errors!

However, my trade is as a printer. Indeed, although it is not usually within my character to brag about my achievements, I need to explain that I am considered by many—be they black, white or coloured—to be one of the finest printers upon this island. My particular skill is an ability to find meaning in the most scribbled of texts. Give me writing that looks to have been made by some insect crawling dirty legs across the paper and I will print its sense, clear and precise. Show me blots and smudges of ink and I will see form. Let blades of grass blow together in the breeze and I will find words written in their flowing strands.

So I was able to assure my precious mama that I would be her most conscientious editor. I would raise life out of her most crabbed script to make her tale flow like some of the finest writing in the English language. And there was no shame to be felt from this assistance, for at some of the best publishing houses in Britain—let me cite Thomas Nelson and Son or Hodder and Stoughton, as my example—the gentle aiding and abetting of authors in this manner is quite commonplace.

She thankfully agreed. Then forsook the pleasures of cooking her cornmeal porridge, fish tea, and roasted breadfruit, of repairing and sowing our garments and other tasks which, in truth, were quite useful about our busy household, to put all her effort into this noble venture, this lasting legacy of a printed book.

The tale herein is all my mama's endeavour. Although shy of the task at first, after several months she soon became quite puffed up, emboldened to the point where my advice often fell on to ears that remained deaf to it. Some scenes I earnestly charged her not to write in the manner she had chosen. But, like the brightest pupil with an outworn master, she became quite insistent upon having her way. And agreeing with a resolute woman is always easier.

Now, only one further word of explanation is required from me; although this story was intended to be accommodated within the limited size and pages of a pamphlet or chapbook it, however, grew. Notwithstanding, let me now conclude this mediation so my mama's tale might finally commence.

Thomas Kinsman
Publisher-editor
Jamaica 1898

PART 1

CHAPTER 1

IT WAS FINISHED ALMOST as soon as it began. Kitty felt such little intrusion from the overseer Tam Dewar's part that she decided to believe him merely jostling her from behind like any rough, grunting, huffing white man would if they were crushed together within a crowd. Except upon this occasion, when he finally released himself from out of her, he thrust a crumpled bolt of yellow and black cloth into Kitty's hand as a gift. This was more vexing to her than that rude act—for she was left to puzzle upon whether she should be grateful to this white man for this limp offering or not . . .

Reader, my son tells me that this is too indelicate a commencement of any tale. Please pardon me, but your storyteller is a woman possessed of a forthright tongue and little ink. Waxing upon the nature of trees when all know they are green and lush upon this island, or birds which are plainly plentiful and raucous, or taking good words to whine upon the cruelly hot sun, is neither prudent nor my fancy. Let me confess this without delay so you might consider whether my tale is one in which you can find an interest. If not, then be on your way, for there are plenty books to satisfy if words flowing free as the droppings that fall from the backside of a mule is your desire.

Go to any shelf that groans under a weight of books and there, wrapped in leather and stamped in gold, will be volumes whose contents will find you meandering through the puff and twaddle of some white lady's mind. You will see trees aplenty, birds of every hue and oh, a hot, hot sun residing there. That white missus will have you acquainted with all the many tribulations of her life upon a Jamaican sugar plantation before you have barely opened the cover. Two pages upon the scarcity of beef. Five more upon the want of a new hat to wear with her splendid pink taffeta dress. No butter but only a wretched alligator pear again! is surely a hardship worth the ten pages it took to describe it. Three chapters is not an excess to lament upon a white woman of discerning mind who finds herself adrift in a society too dull for her. And as for the indolence and stupidity of her slaves (be sure you have a handkerchief to dab away your tears), only need of sleep would stop her taking several more volumes to pronounce upon that most troublesome of subjects.

And all this particular distress so there might be sugar to sweeten the tea and blacken the teeth of the people in England. But do not take my word upon it, peruse the volumes for yourself. For I have. And it was shocking to have so uplifting an act as reading invite some daft white missus to belch her foolishness into my head.

So I will not worry myself for your loss if it is those stories you require. But stay if you wish to hear a tale of my making.

As I write, I have a cup of sweetened tea resting beside me (although not quite sweet enough for my taste, but sweetness comes at a dear price here upon this sugar island); the lamp is glowing sufficient to cast a light upon the paper in front of me; the window is open and a breeze is cooling upon my neck. But wait . . . for an annoying insect has decided to throw itself repeatedly against my lamp. Shooing will not remove it, for it believes the light is where salvation lies. But its insistent buzzing is distracting me. So I have just squashed it upon an open book. As soon as I have wiped its bloody carcass from the page (for it is in a volume that my son was reading), I will continue my tale.

CHAPTER 2

J ULY WAS BORN UPON a cane piece.
  Her mother, bending over double, hacked with her cane bill into a
thick stem of cane. But it did not topple with just one blow. Weary, she
straightened to let the fierce torrent of raindrops that were falling run
their cooling relief upon her face and neck. She blinked against the rain,
wiping the palm of her hand across her forehead. When the serrated
edges of the cane leaves dropped their abrasive grit into her eyes, she
tilted her head back to permit the rain to wash them with its balm. Then
she stooped to grab the base of the cane once more to strike it with a
further blow.

  So intent was she upon seeing that the weeping cane was stripped of
its leaves—even in the dampening rain its brittle edges flew around her
like thistledown—that she did not notice she had just dropped a child
from her womb. July was born right there—slipping out to fall bloody
and quivering upon a spiky layer of trash.

  As July lay vulnerable upon the ground, she viewed the nightmare of
tall canes that loured dark, ragged and unruly around her, and felt the
hem of a rough woollen skirt drag its heavy wetness across her naked
body. Then, all at once, she beheld—wrestling a long spike of cane,
swinging it in the air and slicing at its length and leaves before hurling
the stripped pole away—the mighty black woman that was her mother.
Her mother's arms, flexing under this strenuous work, were as robust as

the legs of a horse in full gallop. Her thick neck looked to be crafted from some cleverly worked wood. Her bare breast, running with rain and sweat, glistened as if lacquered.

This colossal woman was still determined upon her work, unaware that she had mislaid anything. When July let forth a fierce, raw bellow that rustled the canes and affrighted the birds, her mother, cane bill raised, suddenly stopped to wonder upon the source of that desperate yell and saw, for the first time, her misplaced child lying there upon the trash. July's mother cleaned the blade of her cane bill and slipped it into the cloth around her waist. With one hand she then commenced to unwind a scarf that was wrapping her head, whilst with the other hand she gathered up her newborn child in the cup of her palm. Within a fleeting moment that headscarf had July swaddled secure and warm against the solid wall of her mother's back—whilst her mother, with-drawing the cane bill from the band at her waist, continued with her work.

And so ends the story of July's birth—a story that was more thrilling than anything the rascal spider Anancy could conjure. With some tellings it was not the rain that beat down upon July's tender, newborn body, but the hot sun, whose fierce heat baked the blood from her birth into a hard scabrous crust upon her naked flesh. Other times, it was a wind that was blowing with so fierce a breath that her mother had to catch July by one leg before her baby was blown out of the cane field, over the big house, and off into the clouds. While a further version had a tiger, with its long, spiky snout and six legs, sniffing at the baby July, thinking her as food. No matter what glorious heights her tall tale acquired, July always avowed that she had been born upon a cane piece.

But, reader, I cannot allow my narrative to be muddled by such an ornate invention, for upon some later page you may feel to accuse me of deception when, in point, I am speaking fact, even though the contents may seem equally preposterous. Although you may deem your story-teller humdrum for what hereinafter follows it is, with no fear of fan-tasy, the actual truth of July's delivery into this world—and you may take my word upon it.

Kitty, July's mama, gave birth to her in her dwelling hut. For eight long hours Kitty did pace about that hut—first five steps in one direction, then a further five in the other. All the while with her palms pressed to the small of her back, for she feared the protrusion at her belly had the might to pitch her pell-mell on to the ground. The coarse linen shirt she wore was so sodden with sweat as to appear to be made of gauze, and did bind about her tight as a dressing. At times she stopped in her feverish pacing to place her hands high upon the wall, lean her weight on to her arms and pant with the fury of a mad dog.

Kitty's perspiration was turning the soil underneath her feet to a slip-pery layer of mud. So Rose, the woman who was attending her, requested that Kitty stoop a little that she might be permitted to mop her face and neck with rags—for Kitty was nearly six feet tall and Rose no more than four. Rose had had two children in her childbearing days—one was delivered stiff as stale bread and the other was sold away before she had properly finished suckling him. But she was the favoured attendant for births upon the plantation, for children born by her physic thrived with the vigour of the most indulged white missus child. But Kitty would not stoop to permit Rose to wipe her. Rose was forced to jump, like some feeble house slave charged to dust a high shelf, to brush the cloth across Kitty's forehead.

Neither would Kitty smell the bunch of sticks that Rose wafted around her, 'Come, it will soothe. Smell,' Rose insisted. When, fi-nally, Rose pushed the smelly bundle against Kitty's nose, Kitty began at once to choke upon their pungency. She then wrested the sticks from out Rose's hand and threw them upon the ground. The strip of goat skin with which Rose had wanted to rub Kitty's bucking belly had Kitty crying out, 'No touch me, no touch me!' Fortuitously for Rose, she ducked just before Kitty's hand lashed out to swipe her across the room—for it was performed with such fierceness that the diminutive Rose would surely have found herself embedded within the wattle of the wall.

Then Rose pleaded that at least Kitty should eat some mouthfuls of breadfruit that had been left for her. When Kitty refused, Rose ate it herself while repeating, in tones that ranged from commanding to begging, that Kitty should squat upon the mattress to find relief from the pain of this birthing. For over an hour did Rose implore her, until Kitty, screeching louder than a cockerel before the dawn, cried, 'Hush, Miss Rose—me caan suffer yer jabber no more.'

But Kitty did at that moment fall upon her knees and, with her heavy belly brushing the dirt floor, crawl upon the mat. Soon the trash, which was the substance of her mattress, was soaked through with Kitty's sweat—it squelched underneath her as she writhed, tormented, for some position that might ease her pain. But at last Rose could reach all the parts of Kitty that she required in order to commence her fabled physic. Rose, calling from the door of the hut, commanded some children to fill a pail with water from the river. She then cursed at the tiny drip of water that the useless pickney handed her back, before shooing them from the dwelling. But Rose dipped in a rag and pressed the cool water against Kitty's dry and cracked lips.

It was after a further two hours that Kitty began to howl. Kneeling upon the mattress, her hands upon the wall, she screamed that this pain was like no other that she had endured. Oh come, driver, lash her, brand and scorch her, for Kitty was sure no trifling pain of humankind could ever injure her again. This pain was jumbie-made; its claws were digging deep inside her so this child might be born.

'Me must dead, Miss Rose,' Kitty roared. 'Me must dead!'

'Pickney soon come, soon come now,' Rose tenderly whispered.

'Pickney no come. Me must dead here,' Kitty wailed.

It was then the overseer, Tam Dewar, entered in upon the dwelling shouting, 'Why is there so much noise? Shut up, damn you. My head aches from it!'

Aroused from his supper table by the unholy row that had reached his ears, he was breathing heavy as a man sorely vexed. Until, that is, the stench from within Kitty's dwelling began to assail him. His face, that had been wrinkled with fury, began to contort into a sickened grimace—like he was chewing upon rancid meat. He placed his lamp upon the ground so he might better rummage for his handkerchief to muffle his nose and mouth, before exclaiming through the cloth, 'What is happening in here?'

Rose, curtseying to the overseer, said, 'She birthing, massa—soon come,' while Kitty quickly laid herself down flat upon the mattress, covering up as best she could with the wet cloth of her shirt. She set herself to be still and raised her eyes to look upon Tam Dewar's crooked face. In the cast of the lamplight his mouth looked all the more twisted, his hairless head all the more like it was crowned with the shell of an egg. But Kitty could not be quiet for long, for a pickney the size of the moon was pushing out from within her. She let forth a yell so fierce that it buckled Tam Dewar at his knees and caused him to wince as if it were he that had the greater affliction.

'Be quiet, be quiet, I tell you!' he squealed before commanding Rose, 'Stop up her mouth!'

Rose gazed upon this man in puzzlement. 'Stuff up her mouth with rags, come on, come on,' he insisted once more. Rose took a rag, dipping it in the water from the pail and brushed it against Kitty's lips. But Tam Dewar, exhaling with annoyance, commanded, 'Not like that!' He snatched at the rag that Rose held, then forced the damp cloth down into Kitty's mouth. 'Like this, you fool, like this.'

Rose protested, 'Massa, she birthin', she birthin'!' as Kitty choked to accommodate the bulk of cloth in her mouth. Soon Kitty bit down hard to catch the overseer's finger within her teeth, for this white man's fist was blocking her throat.

'Damn you,' he wailed. He wrenched his finger from her bite, then whipped back his hand to slap Kitty around the head.

Rose hastened to stand between Kitty and this white man saying, 'She birthin', massa, she birthin', massa . . .' for she could see this man was preparing to strike Kitty again. 'Pity, massa, pity, no lash her, she birthin', massa,' Rose pleaded.

Tam Dewar threw the tiny figure of Rose aside and was ready to strike Kitty once more, for the impertinence that still throbbed at his finger-tips. While Kitty, cowering from the coming blow, wrapped one arm around her massive belly and thrust out a splayed hand at this man to keep him far from her. And in that moment, Tam Dewar was stilled. He stared at her then dropped his raised hand. He knelt down next to Kitty, palms raised, saying, 'Shhhh, shhhh,' to calm her as he spoke softly to her. 'My sister has sent me some strawberry conserve from Scotland. It's very fine. Delicious. I was just eating it, but then the noise you were making . . . I cannot stand the noise. I have a pain in my head, you see, that I cannot remove. So you must be quiet.' He lifted up the lamp so Kitty might behold his earnest face. She saw a dollop of strawberry jam upon his cheek and smelled the sweet confection upon his breath. He turned, as if to leave, but then, leaning over again said, 'Hush, Kitty or I'll take a whip to you, so help me, God, I will, because I cannot stand the noise.'

Kitty made no reply to this man, but bit down hard upon the cloth that was still within her mouth so she would make no sound that could cause his mood to change. For Kitty had managed to live without feeling the lash from his whip for four years. But this white man had fathered the child she was birthing and if he was not gone soon, she thought to rise from the mattress, grab this ugly bakkra by the leg, swing him above her head and hurl him like a piece of cane so far-far that he would land head first in a heap of trash upon some other talked of island. But she just bit harder upon the rags, as he, pressing his handkerchief once more to his nose, stood up as if to take his leave. He made two steps before remembering a thought. Heedful to point at both his slaves in turn he said, 'And be careful with that wee baby—it will be worth a great deal of money.'

When the pickney was finally released from within Kitty she yelled with so mighty an exhalation that the trees bent as if a hurricane had just passed. Tam Dewar, startled by that immense cry, banged his fist hard upon his supper table and his precious strawberry conserve did topple down to spill upon the floor.

CHAPTER 3

S O, READER, KITTY'S ONLY child is born in upon the world at last. Kitty called her daughter July, for when she was still a callow girl, Miss Martha, who did oversee the infant workers of the third gang, had once ventured to teach Kitty to write in words the months that make up the year. Although the month of her pickney's birth was December, it was only the graceful wave of Miss Martha's arm as she scratched the flowing curls of the word July in the dirt that the older Kitty could call to mind. Kitty softly whispered the word July into her pickney's ear and July her daughter became.

And what a squealing, tempestuous, fuss-making child she was. The quivering pink tongue and toothless gums in July's shrieking mouth were more familiar to her mama than her baby's arms and feet. With such agitation coming hourly from this newly born creature, Kitty did believe that this pickney must have been ripped from some more charmed existence. That she howled for the injustice that found her now a slave in an airless hut, in a crib too small, and being mothered by an ugly-skinned black woman who did not have the faintest notion as to why her pickney did yell so.

Kitty paced her tiny hut for most of the hours in the night to try to bring peace to this cursed child's heart. Then, when the child was calmed enough for Kitty's eyelids to at last close in sleep, the driver blowing a shrill note upon the conch bade her open them once more for another day of work. Only when Kitty was ready to feed this baby, so her working day could commence, did this child decide the time was right to sleep like the dead. And only after she had wrapped the sleeping child to her back and begun her work on the second gang—clearing and carrying the bundles of spent cane from the factory to the trash house—did Kitty feel the gentle swelling of her pickney's lungs as July awakened to demand her missing food.

Oh, pity poor Kitty, for no sound so vexed the negroes that worked around her than the constant screeching of the child that was bound to her throughout the day. All in her second gang agreed that not even the shrill creaking of the carts that carried the cane from the fields to the mill—yes, even the broken-down one that Cornet Jump did drive—did pain them so much.

The call of the driver, Mason Jackson, as he summoned luckless slaves to unload that heaping cane from the carts was piercing—true—but it did not rupture the ears like that pickney. And the groaning sighs that always exhaled from Miss Anne and Miss Betsy as their sore heads were piled up high with the spiky bundles of cane, rang quite soft in comparison. As did their slip-slop shuffling as they humped the weeping poles to where they would be crushed.

The rasping of the wooden cattle mill as it laggardly turned and the weary clip-clopping of the beasts' hooves as Benjamin Brown guided them to tread their pointless progress around and around, never again seemed quite so loud to him. Even the squelching of the cloying juice being squeezed from the splitting poles or the raucous jabber of Miss Bessy and Miss Sarah as they reaped the spent cane from the floor about him, did not play so sharply upon his nerves.

And Dublin Hilton, the distiller-man (him who did know if the liquor would granulate from just gazing upon it or inhaling the vapour), will tell you that not even the crackling of the flames under his coppers, the bubbling slurp of the boiling sugar, nor the deep rumbling from the hogsheads as the filled barrels were rolled along the ground, could keep that pickney's howl from finding his ears.

Come, only the firing of the driver's cowskin whip, as he directed which to be taken where, did all within that second gang confess, was more vexing to them than the torturous din that emitted from the tiny creature tied to Miss Kitty's back.

'A likkle rum 'pon the child's tongue, Miss Kitty,' Peggy Jump, from the first gang, did yell from her door at the close of each day. While, 'Shake the pickney soft!' was Elizabeth Millar's suggestion and, 'See Obeah—she mus' haf a likkle spell,' was the thinking of Kitty's friend, Miss Fanny.

But what Kitty's neighbours did not observe was that sometimes, late into the still of night, Kitty could calm July by singing a song soft unto her. 'Mama gon' rock, mama gon' hold, little girl-child mine.' Then July would turn her black eyes on to Kitty, her lips gently mimicking the movement of her mama's mouth as she sang. That beguiled child would then hug Kitty—her little arms squeezing about her neck while she fondly dribbled tender wet kisses upon her mama.

Kitty would bounce her precious girl-child upon her knee and July would chuckle with an unbounded mirth that chirped as bright as fledglings in a nest. At those times there was no slapping, no cussing, no cursing, for July would gaze upon her mama with so deep an expression of love that Kitty felt it as heat. 'Mama gon' rock, mama gon' hold, little girl-child mine.' Sometimes, within this fond reverie, all was good. Until, that is, Kitty did venture to lay July back down upon her crib to sleep, for then that rascal child's mouth would suddenly gape wide as a hole made for cane, as she began her yelling once more.

CHAPTER 4

⟿

M Y BELOVED SON THOMAS did caution, when first I set out to flow
this tale upon the world, that although they may not be felt like a
fist or a whip, words have a power that can nevertheless cower even the
largest man to gibbering tears.

This morning my son thought to repeat that warning, whilst the first
finger of his right hand did wag upon me. Now, you may feel that it is
for a mother to wag a finger upon her child and not the other way about.
But hear this, reader, although my son was pulled with great agitation
and pain from my body, let me unfold to you that he has not always
known the blessing of a mother's affection. So you must please forgive
him this small fault of finger wagging. And, even if the face his finger
waves upon is that of his old, gracious mama, still my son might wag his
finger if he deems that a wagging finger is what is required.

But with all that now forgot, let me return to my story. For I must
change the scene for you at once, to fly this tale a few years hence. So
come, reader, worry no more upon my son's rudeness, just follow me
close.

⟿

There is a carriage upon some higher ground, see it there in a distance
that is not too far. The heat rising from the earth causes this vehicle's

form to ripple and sway as if it were a reflection caught in water. But with each step of its approach, its character becomes more clear. Several negro children gambol alongside the cart. As the vehicle's speed increases, their tiny black shapes pick up pace and purpose, as if their progress were now part of some race they were all bound to contend. But eventually the children halt in their running, realising that any race against a horse is surely lost. They commence jumping and waving around their arms instead, while this carriage moves steadily away from their play.

The single chestnut horse who pulls the gig along trips dainty as a cat on hot stones upon the rutted earth. The master of the plantation named Amity, Mr John Howarth, sits holding the reins of this vehicle. His firm legs are spread apart to brace himself as he rides, while the brim of his wide white hat flaps with the bumpy progress of the gig. His passenger is his sister, Mrs Caroline Mortimer. With one hand she struggles to hold up a parasol with which to protect her delicate English skin from the vicious morning sun, all the while pleading with her brother, 'Please go slower . . . please be careful . . . please stop showing off, John,' while her other hand grips, fearful, at the side of the gig to steady herself.

Caroline Mortimer has been residing at the great house of the plantation with her brother and his young wife, Agnes, for two weeks, yet already the heat from the Jamaican sun only makes her floppy as a kitten for the hottest part of the day. Twenty-three summers Caroline has lived upon this earth, all of them, until now, spent in the dappled shade of an apple tree by the edge of an English lawn, where the hottest part of the day brought small beads of fragrant sweat to trespass upon her forehead. The ship she travelled in to Jamaica had bucked and rolled her across the ocean so cruelly that, upon her arrival, she had complained to her brother that being strapped to a whale's back would have been no less arduous a journey. In fact, she repeated this lamentation so often that although at first it raised mirth in her brother, after its considerable tellings it merely caused him to exclaim loudly, 'Yes, well, you're here now.'

Her appetite, which she had feared she would never regain after the ravaging voyage—where no food man prepared could stay in her stomach long enough to give any of the required sustenance—was now returning. And fresh and adventurous it was too. Why, she thought the mango the loveliest of fruit—juicy and sweet. True, it did have the taste of a peach dipped in turpentine, and a texture so stringy that she was required to pull at the little threads caught in her teeth for many an hour after, but she was not a timid person, too scared to try these new experiences. And the preserves, what a delight. Everyone knows West Indian preserves are the best in the world. Guava, ginger, sorrel, even green lime. Quite the most delicious she had ever tasted.

'You'll prefer strawberry jam from England soon as we all do,' her brother said.

'Never, never, never!' Caroline laughed. 'May we have punch?' she requested, and when told, 'It's no longer drunk much here,' she stamped her pink satin slippered foot upon the ground to protest, 'Why ever not!'

'It's not the fashion,' her brother told her and regretted it almost at once when her voice, rising shrill as the squeal from the hinge on a loose shutter, said, 'What should we care for fashion. Everyone in England talks of Jamaican punch and I should like to try it. And besides, the rum and water here is milled far too weak.'

Whilst watching pomegranate, paw-paw, naseberry, and sour sop being pushed into her eager mouth by her stout, sticky fingers for most hours of the day, her brother warned, 'You are eating too much fruit, Caroline. It's not good for the constitution in this climate.' He suggested she might consider, until she was a little stronger after her journey, eating more pork instead.

'Pork! Oh, John, one can eat pork anywhere,' Caroline twittered. No, his sister said, she was ready, in perhaps a day or two, to try a little turtle. Why not? It looked delightful served in its upturned shell. For did she not eat rabbit, tripe, and pigs' heads at home? She told her brother, 'If turtle is considered fine food in this foreign place then I must taste it, even if only the once.' She wanted to try everything—oh yes, everything. Although not long out of widow's weeds, she was keen to experience the curious, no matter who counselled against it. Bring on the duck, guinea birds and jack fish, for Mrs Caroline Mortimer was eager to nibble upon their bones. Even breadfruit that was destined for the slaves' table. 'Why should I not try it too?' she asked her brother, who replied sternly that several of his slaves had been whipped for eating dirt—did she propose to try that delicacy also?

Caroline was blessed of a long, pointed nose that, while giving her silhouette a fine distinction from across a dim-lit room, was nevertheless unable to feel what was happening at its tip. Consequently there was often something stuck upon the end of it, of which she was totally unaware; the yellow stain of pollen from the hibiscus she was admiring; a white daub of cream from some milk she was drinking; even a drop of snot from a nasal chill could, like a rain drop caught upon the tip of a leaf, remain dangling and swaying for quite some time. And it was this insensible nose that, her brother began to fear, would be dipping into everything upon this plantation named Amity before too long.

But there was one curiosity which Caroline Mortimer had found herself entering upon with an uncharacteristic trepidation. The negroes. Before she embarked upon her journey, her brother had written to advise that she should be sure to bring with her a maid servant—a steady young woman, respectable, trustworthy, perhaps even of a religious character. For her brother went on to warn that negroes did not always make the kind of servants to which Caroline may have become accustomed.

This extraordinary missive caused Caroline not only to laugh, but to wish her late husband were still alive to read it. For it had always been a source of great aggravation to Edmund Mortimer that his wife's brother would boast, on his all-too-frequent visits, how many slaves he possessed in the Caribbean and, of that number, how many of those slaves toiled round and about his great house. With a flourish of the hand and the ponderous look of someone who could not quite bring it to mind, he would tell his sister and her husband, 'Oh, there are more than fifty and one hundred upon the land and well, upwards of thirty in the house.'

It would irritate Edmund Mortimer beyond torment when, upon observing their one slatternly, grubby, maid-of-all-work serving at table, Caroline's brother would eye their situation with something like pity. And there was her brother now telling her that she should bring that one miserable girl across the seas. Dress her up in her cast-offs so she might pass as a lady's maid, when he had what? Upwards of two hundred slaves at his command! Her husband would surely have turned in his grave at this suggestion, if it were not for the fact that Edmund Mortimer, when buried, was so fat that there was not the required space within the box.

So, upon arrival in this often and eagerly conjured place, Caroline was expecting to encounter several negroes about the house, for it was no more than she had been led to believe. But what she had not foreseen was that, when the door of her brother's fine property was at first opened, she would find herself quite girdled by a swarm of black faces. While her brother busied himself with an instruction to a ragged black boy upon the veranda of the house on where to take Mary—the requested maid servant who was, after the voyage, really quite sick— three negro women paused in their tasks so they might better stare upon Caroline.

One—wearing a bright-red madras kerchief upon her head and an apron at her waist that was so splattered with stains it did appear like a map—was chewing upon something with her mouth agape. Another picked at the contents of her nose, wiping it upon the filthy rag of her skirt as she angled her head awkwardly so she might better see through an eye that was bruised-bloody, swollen and half closed. The third, a tall, gangly creature, had the bodice of her dress untied, which drooped slovenly at her waist, leaving her arms, like the branches of some dead tree, quite naked. None had on shoes.

But Caroline, unperturbed by the glowering of these slaves, gazed upon them civilly, for she believed they would soon curtsey, then offer her some light refreshment perhaps. She was even unpinning her bonnet, for she was sure they would want to take it from her to set it upon some stand. But they did not. Instead their eyes, which Caroline thought appeared like shining marbles rolling in soot, commenced to peruse her slowly, from the bottom of her brown leather boots to the top of her fleshy blond head. Then, opening her arms wide, the tall gangly one said, 'Come, see how broad is she!' At which Caroline took a long step away from them—not on account of this impudent scorning, but in fear of the teeth in their heads that, as they laughed upon her, bared white and sharp as any savage beasts.

Just then a chicken had run by her, wings flapping, squawking loudly, slipping and falling upon the polished floor. It was being chased by a young negro girl, whose outstretched arms made a clumsy grab for the neck of the fowl, all the while screeching, 'Catch it up quick. Catch it up!' Soon another chicken appeared, which looked to be chasing the girl. The three negro women promptly joined in this havoc, all running around pell-mell until none could tell who was chasing who.

Caroline at once pinioned herself to the wall, for she feared she might be tripped and trussed in this commotion. Then two boys, barely clothed, appeared upon the scene from who-knows-where to jump around in this sport. All at once a piercing yell, as mighty as a tree splitting at its trunk, cried, 'Me chicken done gone. Bring back de chicken.' A negro woman, no larger than a child but with a skin wrinkled as dried fruit, appeared banging a large cleaver against a metal bucket. If it were not for her continuing to screech, 'Where me chicken don gone?' over and over, Caroline would scarce have believed that such a diminutive creature could raise so much holler.

Soon all that Caroline beheld were negroes, like solid shadows prancing before her. Oh, how many besieged her there? And where could they all have come from? Chinks in some wall, holes within the floor? Did they reside one-on-top-the-other in some chest? Or scurry like galliwasps under the house? Where? Where? Caroline cursed that the Lord only gave her two hands! For which should she do—cover her ears against the calamitous din or her nose? For the stench of their swirling bodies was malodorous as a begrimed mule in the heat.

Her brother, finally appearing, seemed to walk on through this confusion paying it no heed, 'Come on, I'll show you to your room,' he said. Then, noticing the fright which sat upon his sister's face as if sketched from a comical cartoon, he shouted, 'Will you all be silent! Be quiet. Do you hear me?' before guiding Caroline by the elbow through the fleeting breach in the bedlam.

After a few days upon the island, Caroline was moved to enquire of her brother whether all of his fabled upward of two hundred slaves did, in matter-of-fact, reside around and about them in the great house. Her brother had believed it not a serious question and therefore supplied no answer but that of a small smirk. But for Caroline, it was asked in earnest. For there seemed to be no place in that mighty house where solitude was to be found. No corner where she did not find a negro lurking. No room that was free of a negro affecting some task. No window that, when looked through, saw a view that was other than these blackies about some mischief. Even the cupboards, when opened, seemed to contain little more than black boys who, like insects caught in a trap, peered out at her from the inside.

And yet, for all these house slaves that swirled around her every day, Caroline found the summoning of any of them to do her bidding a toilsome task for which she had no skill. They just stared on her entranced, like children upon Bonfire Night before the pinwheel starts to spin.

The negro girl, Molly, the one with the bruised, swollen eye, was charged by her brother to act as Caroline's temporary lady's maid. And act she did. For this girl seemed to know nothing of the duties that were required of her. Why, every morning this dull-witted creature would attempt to incarcerate Caroline into her spotted linen spencer the wrong way round; no command in an English language Caroline knew could get this slave to place it about her shoulders in the right way. As for the tape ties at the seam of her dress, the girl merely played with them like a kitten with string, for she was unable to tie a simple knot, let alone a delicate bow.

She combed hair as if untangling some rogue threads on the fringe of a carpet and tipped a full bucket of cold water over Caroline as she sat naked in a bath believing warmed water about to be brought. When Caroline summoned her brother to protest her behaviour, this slave girl, with hair matted as carding-wool, threw herself at his feet, clutching his legs and begging, 'Me make mistake, massa. Me no do it again, massa. Me learn. Missus gon' smile pretty 'pon me soon,' to avoid her punishment.

Caroline's sister-in-law, Agnes, having been born upon the island a Creole, found no trouble in procuring the required help. Her clothing was pressed and presented to her in the mornings, a jug of water brought for washing, her night pot collected and cleared, her room swept when she was not present to choke upon the dust, and her shutters opened for her upon the daylight.

But Caroline observed that Agnes was able to command these slaves in their own strange tongue. She could bellow at those negroes with the same force that the negroes did bellow at each other. Agnes was heavy with child and although slight of frame, still she allowed no bulging protrusion at her waist to impede her when she was admonishing her slaves. Why, she jumped about as spiritedly as a mad hare—arms flailing, feet stamping, her thick red hair coming loose from its tie as she snapped, shouted, clapped and yelled to get her way.

After this exhausting work was done Agnes would lie upon her daybed with her arms dangling, too fatigued to lift them. She was then unable to answer even the simplest of Caroline's enquiries without a weariness entering her tone or a gentle snoring commencing—sometimes when Caroline was still speaking.

In her first meeting with Agnes, in the cool drawing room of the great house, her sister-in-law had, in a blast of breath that left Caroline quite giddy, proclaimed that her family was from Scotland. Excepting Agnes's flaming red hair, the profusion of freckles upon her face and neck (which she happily displayed instead of hiding with cosmetic preparations), and an abundance of tartan trimmings in and about the chairs in the room, Caroline detected nothing of the Scotch about this bouncy young woman.

'You must show them who is master and who is slave. Leave them no room to fool you. Them is tricky, Caroline,' Agnes said when instructing Caroline on the management of slaves. Using Molly as her example, Agnes called the slave girl to her and pointed her finger at the blackened eye. 'She tie me shoe so tight me have to scream. She sitting at me feet so I give her one kick. You think she ever tie me shoe so tight again? No, no, no—for she learn.' Pushing Molly forward so Caroline might better inspect the bruised wound for the imprint of Agnes's shoe, she said, 'Be firm. For these blacks be like children—all must be shown how is good and how is bad.'

And, every night since Caroline had arrived upon the island, she had been forced to listen to the panting, slapping and giggling that crept over the walls from her brother's room into her own. For this grand house, which had been lavished with so much vulgar finery—why, even the silver was gilded—nevertheless had bedroom walls that were not tall enough to reach all the way up into the wood of the eaves. The ridiculous din of the night creatures with their eternal screeching could not block the lusty sounds Agnes—oh yes, Agnes—made every night. Her brother, Caroline decided then, was quite prudent in never having brought Agnes to England, for his wife's inelegant, beastly manners and ridiculous way of speaking would surely have seen her locked away.

After two weeks in Agnes's company—where even a little light embroidery or the arranging of a vase of flowers seemed too much toil for her sister-in-law, who slept upon her daybed for so many hours of the day that Caroline began to believe that perhaps, like a bat, she was only aroused at night, Caroline was forced to admit to being bored. She even began to crave the company of Mary, her lady's maid, who had never uttered more than three words of sense in the whole time she had been in her employ; she did, however, remain awake. But Mary was still quite sick; nursed in a darkened hut no bigger than a kennel by a large negro woman who guarded Mary's feeble, sweating, panting body as

fiercely as a dog with a bone. And as for the companionship of her
brother John, he had begun to seem like a vision in the heat, for every
time Caroline approached him he would simply vanish. Until one day,
with the determination of a trapper, Caroline contrived to snare him
upon the veranda of the house.

'John, may we take a stroll around the grounds?' she implored.

'A stroll, Caroline! This is not England. In two steps the heat would
claim you. No one strolls here,' her brother replied.

'A ride then, John—I still know how.'

'The terrain is far too dangerous and, besides, I have no horse that
could possibly take your . . .' he said, prudently losing into a mumble
the words which referred to Caroline's robust dimensions.

'Oh, John, please take me around, I wish to see my new home and
understand all its workings,' she said, her voice rising shrill enough to
conjure that squeaking hinge anew.

So, reader, let me once more draw your eye to that road through the
plantation named Amity—to the gig, to the single chestnut horse and
the bumpy progress being made by John Howarth and his sister Caroline who sit within. Walking along this road in the path that the gig
would eventually take, was a large black slave woman. Upon her head
was a straw basket filled with unruly sweet cassava roots, poised so ably
she looked to be wearing an ornate hat. Her skirt, once striped yellow
and black was, from its years of being drenched in a river, pounded
against rock and baked in the sun, only whispering its former lustre. But
the child walking at her side was attired in a dress of the same fabric and,
like a draper's sample, this miniature displayed the cloth almost in its
original hues.

The little girl halted her stride so she might better peruse a scrubby
periwinkle that struggled to bloom dainty at the side of the path. She
plucked the plant and waved it gently in the air in the hope that the
woman might stop to look upon the purple petals. But the woman was

unaware that the child no longer walked at her side. 'Mama,' the girl called, and as her mama turned upon hearing the cry, the girl ran to her, holding out the flower.

The woman, bending to look upon the bloom gripped tight in her daughter's hand, tipped her head only enough so the balance of the produce would not be disturbed. She nodded a smile upon her child, then straightened once more and walked on. But the little girl began pulling ferociously at the cloth of her mother's skirt to arrest her progress—planting her bare feet firmly into the earth for a solid grip. Although only pulling with one hand, the skirt nevertheless began to strain, almost to ripping. The woman, slapping the child's hands from the feeble cloth, was forced to stop to take heed of her.

She removed the basket from her head to place it carefully upon the ground, then took the flower from the child between her finger and thumb. She lifted it to her nose before passing it under the nose of the child. Cupping her hands around her mother's broad fingers, the girl inhaled deeply upon its scent. And as the mother began to brush the dainty petals of the flower across the cheek of the little girl, they both closed their eyes in the reverie of the soft strokes. At last the woman, straightening up to place the basket of produce once more upon her head, began walking on, while the little girl, still curious, dallied to find more flowers to pick.

'Oh, how adorable,' Caroline said upon seeing a little negro girl in a yellow and black striped dress, tenderly gathering up a posy of purple flowers. Her brother, however, observing only two slaves walking in this late morning upon a road that climbs out of the valley and off his lands, had concerns of a different kind.

'Hey you, stop there,' he commanded of the slave woman as the gig drew up by her side. And it was then that Kitty turned her eyes to look upon her massa.

'Where are you going?' he asked.

'Me have pass, massa. Me and me pickney. Me have talkee-talkee, massa.'

John Howarth held out his hand so Kitty might deliver him the pass.

She took the ragged piece of yellowing paper from the folds at the band of her skirt. His snatching hand almost ripped the precious consent. 'Where are you going? It's too late for market?' he said.

'Please, massa, me go Unity Pen.'

'On what business?'

'Me mus' market me fruits.'

Caroline, alighting from the carriage, walked over to where the child stood. Standing over this little girl, Caroline watched her tiny black fingers as they plucked and gathered the pretty blooms. This girl was no more than nine years old perhaps, with wide brown eyes, fat rounded cheeks and a white kerchief upon her head. Caroline knelt down beside the child, who turned to gaze upon her. If her skin were not as dark as boot blacking, why she favoured one of Caroline's childhood dolls. 'Oh, how adorable,' drifted once more upon a sigh from Caroline's mouth. The little girl held her posy of flowers under Caroline's nose so that she might better smell their scent. And Caroline was amazed to find herself delighted by a negro. 'Oh, thank you, my dear,' she said, as she sniffed. Caroline called out to her brother asking, 'John, what's this one's name?'

'How in heaven's name would I know?' came his reply.

'But she's adorable. Do not you think so, John?' Caroline said before adding, 'What did you say she was called?'

Commanding Kitty with a nod of his head to answer his sister's question, John Howarth let go the horse's rein and got down from the gig. When Kitty said nothing, he shouted, 'Tell your mistress the name of the child.'

And Kitty spoke in a whisper, 'July.'

Not hearing Kitty's reply, Caroline asked once more, 'What's her name?' at which John Howarth snapped impatiently upon his sister, 'July, Caroline. She said July. Like the month!'

'But July is not a suitable name,' Caroline said, while her brother asked of Kitty, 'What are you called?'

Her reply, spoken softly to his feet, gave him reason to laugh. 'Kitty. I thought so. Yes . . . yes, I remember now,' he said, before calling his sister to him, 'Caroline, come here, I have something amusing for you.'

When Caroline joined John where he stood, she found herself forced to look up at the slave Kitty. For Kitty was tall and none but the stoutest ever looked upon her in the eye. Come, not even the massa had that licence. After staring upon Kitty—into the deep nostrils of her broad, flat nose, around her thick lips and past her sturdy ample shoulders—Caroline leaned toward the ear of her brother to whisper, 'Is it a woman?'

'It is indeed,' he laughed.

'And the mother of this child?'

'I believe so.'

Caroline wondered how any man under God's sky would want to lie with such a loathsome creature. And how a beast so ugly that she blocked out all sunlight before her, could mother such an adorable child?

Her brother was still speaking, waving his arm upon his slave so Caroline might best take in the full summit of Kitty. 'The amusing thing about this one is that when she was first purchased she was called Little Kitty. She was bought here as a baby from the Campbells at Nutfield. I got her cheap because she was not expected to live. Guy Campbell thought himself very sharp to have sold me such a rum deal. Little Kitty. And now look at her,' he laughed. 'Let me assure you, Caroline, that your brother is the best planter in the whole of the Caribbean.'

As Caroline stood listening to her brother blowing upon a horn that was surely his own, July, stepping to stand by her side, placed her young hand within this white woman's palm. On feeling this touch from a negro Caroline snatched her hand away. But then, looking down, she saw July's sweet face turned up to her; her eyes wide and watery. Caroline, relenting, squeezed July's little fingers. Kitty began to shift her eye from her massa's feet, where they had rested through this whole encounter, on to her child. She watched as July held up the dainty posy of flowers to the white woman as she had before held them up to her mama.

'You see,' John Howarth carried on, 'It was a gamble. It's not like with a dog—they aren't born with big paws that can give an indication as to their eventual size. So, in truth, I was not only astute, but lucky too. It's a good thing Guy Campbell is back in Perthshire because if he saw her now he'd have to chew on his own hat.'

Kitty took a step so she might wrest July's hand away from Caroline. But John Howarth shouted on her, 'Stay!' Then, flicking his hand at her, he said, 'Show your mistress your legs.'

Kitty did not move.

'Lift up your skirt and show her your legs.' When Kitty still did not take heed of his command he huffed, 'Oh, good God,' before grabbing the worn cloth of Kitty's skirt and raising it almost to her waist. Kitty turned her head to one side as John Howarth beckoned his sister. He commenced rubbing his hand up and down Kitty's leg saying, 'Come and feel the muscles.'

Caroline gaped once more, for Kitty's legs were so dark and stout, like the trunk of a tree they looked to have grown through the solid earth.

'Come on, Caroline, I have her, she won't bite. Come and feel their strength.' Caroline, with July still holding her, stepped forward to run skittering fingers along Kitty's calf. But Kitty only turned to look at the touch when she felt July's small hand do the same. 'It's the work on the cane pieces, they are absolutely made for it. This one will be in the first gang—cutting cane, holing, manuring, tasks that take a bit of strength. Although with a child ... nursing mothers usually labour with the weaklings in the second gang. It's lighter work—feeding the mill, picking up trash from the ground, that sort of thing.'

As Caroline straightened up she asked, 'And does this little girl work?'

'Weeding,' he replied, 'bringing water to the field slaves with the third gang. Nothing much. For children it's more like a game. But this one,' John said whilst slapping Kitty's thighs, 'just look at her. The overseer, Dewar, says that when negro women bend over in the field their breasts droop and dangle so much they look to be a beast with six limbs.'

John began to laugh until his sister said, 'Oh, please do not be so vulgar.'

'Can you imagine putting silk stockings over these, Caroline. Some in England would say it should be done,' he said.

Kitty drew away from his touch, but he pulled her back to stand where he had placed her. He let the fabric of her skirt drop, still smiling with the mirth of it all. As John Howarth climbed back into the gig to recommence their journey, he flicked his hand at Kitty saying, 'Go on, you can go now.' But Kitty did not move, for she could see that her child, July, was still captured in the thrall of Mrs Caroline Mortimer; her hand still grasped her, her eyes still fixed upon her.

'Go on, off with you,' John Howarth said once more.

Kitty called to July, beckoning her with an urgency that cracked in her throat. But her child paid no heed, too busy was she with her new play-mate. She skipped at Caroline's feet, sprinkling the picked flowers upon the floor before her.

'Oh, she's adorable,' Caroline said again.

Her brother, impatient to finish the journey around the estate, called out to Caroline, 'Well, bring her then.'

Kitty turned to face her master.

'Come along, Caroline. Hurry. We need to get out of the sun.'

'Can I take her?' she asked.

Kitty tried to seize air enough to breathe.

'Yes, if she'll amuse you. She would be taken soon enough anyway. It will encourage her to have another. They are dreadful mothers, these negroes.'

'She'll be my companion here,' Caroline said. 'I could train her for the house, or to be my lady's maid.'

'Well, you could try,' her brother said. 'But hurry—this heat is getting fierce.'

Kitty stepped to snatch July from Caroline's grasp. But Caroline slapped at Kitty's hands shouting, 'What's she doing?'

John Howarth raised his whip at Kitty, his face fiercely showing his intent, 'Be on your way,' he said, 'leave the child to your mistress.'

Kitty, letting go of her child, just said, 'But she go Unity Pen, massa. We have pass.'

'Be quiet,' John Howarth shouted, 'Your mistress here will take her now. She will be up at the big house. Now, go about your business.'

Caroline struggled to get into the carriage for she had July tight in her grasp and the child still carried the stench of negroes; it was hard to lift the child whilst averting her nose from her pungency. As she settled them both upon the seat of the gig, Caroline asked her brother, 'Don't you think Agnes will think she's adorable?'

And he replied, 'Little niggers no longer make my wife smile,' as the gig rode briskly away from Kitty.

CHAPTER 5

R EADER, COME WITH ME to peer through a window of the great house. But let me place you upon the inside of this fine dwelling, in a room caressed by a cooling night breeze. Rest there upon a chair cushioned in silken fabric smooth to your touch, within the shadowy gleam of several of the finest beeswax candles that perfume the air with a sweet scent.

Idle awhile. Muse, if you will, on whether to begin a game of solitaire upon the open card table. Or perhaps you may desire a refreshing drink. Yawn wide and stretch, for it is late into the evening. Do as you would. All I ask is that when this waste-wiling is done, you turn your head once more to that window.

Do not worry yourself with the openings of slatted wood which allow the breeze to carry in the raucous rattle of croaking night creatures. Nor that high-arched window on the farthest wall which, during the day, gives you a clear view over the lawn to the horizon, but at night shines so black that your reflection is caught as clear as if in a mirror. No, only concern yourself with the small window. See how the leaves of the plant life crowd out any view but that of the dense foliage that is piled and pushed up against it. With a quick glance some of the palms can appear like fingers pressing against the glass. Come, look closer still, for amongst that unruly undergrowth, if you search with a careful eye, you will see that there are indeed fleshy fingers splaying there. The fingers of

Kitty's right hand as she leans against the window in anguish to glimpse her only child, July, there within.

'No look so downcast, for your pickney will do her pee-pee 'pon a throne,' Miss Rose trilled to Kitty when she had returned to her hut without July. 'In the great house them have chair made of fine wood and them sit 'pon it—straight back and all—and them let them doings drop. And it tinkle like rain 'pon a calabash as it splash into a bowl. And when all is done them close a wooden lid 'pon the waste—so there be no odour to foul up them day. Them be so fine up in the great house. It be where Miss July belong. She knows she be overseer Dewar's pickney but never does him even look 'pon her. But in the great house she will at last feel to be a white man's child. Come sit 'pon this bowl to pee-pee, them will tell her. Is merriment you mus' be feel. Miss July at the great house! Come, she will get shoe!'

Yet every night Kitty would creep along the rutted path, sneak through the cultured garden, scale a low stone wall to crawl through that matted vegetation. At that glass she would strain to keep her leaf shape and not be revealed as an ugly negro field slave who was so out of her place that the cat-o'-nine-tails would surely be sent for if she were caught. And there she would wait—staring in upon a room so sublime that she dared not take a breath for fear the air would prove too noble for her.

PART 2

CHAPTER 6

I BELIEVED MY HAND to be improving. 'Too crabbed, Mama, you must take more care,' was the complaint from my son, Thomas. 'Look at the stains of ink upon your fingers. See then how your soiled hand prints smudges all across the paper.'

'It is the pen that drips so,' I informed him.

'It is not the fault of the pen that you place too much ink upon its nib,' said he.

'Do you resent me the ink?' I asked him.

'No, of course not.'

'Then is it the quantity of paper I might use that is vexing you?'

'Nothing is vexing me, Mama. I am just cautioning you to take a little care and tap the nib of the pen upon the inkstand to shake off the excess that might otherwise drip across the paper.'

'But this dripping and staining is not my offence—this ink be inferior,' I told him.

'There is nothing wrong with the ink,' he answered back to me.

'Then why it drip so?'

'Because you must tap the pen nib to shake off the ink before you put it to the paper.'

And so this argument went around. Reader, I am not a woman to stay within a household when all welcome is gone. I stood up from my desk and departed the room. Taking up my valise I placed within it only those few possessions that I first brought into this house those many years before—my square of lace and my blue and white plate. I would take nothing away with me that was given by my son. No feathered Sunday hat nor new Common Sense Oxford shoe, not even a spool of embroidery silk would he find about me.

Thomas, seeing me firm in my resolve to leave his house, at once began calling for Lillian. Always when he has wronged me, he calls for Lillian. All his battles his wife must fight for him, like she be his mama and he her pickney.

She entered in upon my room like a howling wind to grab the valise from my hand. How we struggled there we two! I am an old, old woman and she has not more than forty years, yet still she fought me like a fever. It was fear of cracking my plate further that made me stop.

'Miss July, please put down the bag,' said she. 'This is your son's home and you are welcome here. And you know this. Thomas meant no ill by you.'

Now, reader, although I have suffered hardships much greater than wrestling with Lillian—who would, let me assure you, have been no match for me if our ages had been equal—still I ache. All of my bones have voice to speak to me. Even the smallest of them chats the language of pain. But I bear it as best an old woman can. Yet that quarrel sent me to my bed with a head sore as an aching heart. Even my son's apology just throbbed at my ear. I believed my deliverance had come; that my maker, be him deity or devil, desired to hear my tale not written as some fool-fool book but spoken close into his ear.

But a little callaloo soup and a few mouthfuls of stewed goat, saw me much improved. Now, back at my desk, I am fitter than when I was taken.

As I write, I can see that if I tap the nib of this new pen—a fine instrument with an ebony holder which my son sent away for from Montgomery Ward in America—against the side of the inkstand that contains the new bottle of glossy-black ink, then no drip occurs across the page. Come, it makes it much easier to read.

'Marguerite, Marguerite!' That is Caroline Mortimer calling out for

July. She had resolved to call her slave Marguerite, for she liked the way the name tripped upon her tongue like a trill. Yet it was only Caroline Mortimer who did look upon July's face to see a Marguerite residing there. And so we must return to my tale.

~

Caroline Mortimer was reclining upon her daybed too limp from the midday heat to raise her hand to ring the bell. 'Marguerite,' she screeched once more, before collapsing with the effort that such bellowing demanded. Reader, many years have passed within my tale and it was now eight, maybe nine, years that Caroline has been living at the great house of the plantation named Amity. Nowadays, the heat from that Jamaican sun made Caroline floppy as a kitten from sun-up to sundown. She no longer had spirit to fight its languid thrall. A little light embroidery or the arranging of a vase of flowers were just too much toil for her.

She lay upon her daybed, wishing that the long window—with its clear view over the lawn to the horizon—was carrying into the room a cooling breeze and not, what she could always hear, the tiresome commotion of negroes. The rhythmic drone of the field slaves' work songs, a mule braying, the pounding of walking feet, the crack of a lash, the gallop of a horse, a piercing yell, the squealing of a slow moving cart. And, so close about her that it was like a nagging worry within her own head, the clatter and jabber as the indolent house slaves went about . . . well what did they go about? 'Marguerite,' she yelled once more.

~

In the kitchen, the headman, Godfrey, aroused from his nap, licked his top lip to moisten his dry mouth, before gently kicking his foot toward July and saying, 'Missus calling you.'

July, looking up from her sewing replied, 'Soon come, me busy.'

When the calling came again, sharp enough for the cook, Hannah, to say 'Cha,' from her drowsy sleep, Godfrey leaned forward upon his chair to inspect what July was doing.

'What you have there?'

'Missus's dress. She want it,' said July.

'Then go give it.' said Godfrey.

'Me can't, it not ready—it still have three button on.'

The kitchen, like in all great houses upon the island, was a large, dark hut with a wide chimney and wooden jalousies upon the open windows, that was set apart a short distance behind the main house. It took three long strides for Godfrey to go from the kitchen to the house, for he was a tall man with long legs. It was six steps for the less gangling July and the two other chamber girls, Molly and Patience. It was a long, long wearisome trudge for the cook, Hannah. Being summoned into the house to listen upon the list of foodstuffs those big-bellies wished to chew on was her torment. At the great age of sixty Hannah resented all motion but that of round and round her kitchen. But for any white missus, like Caroline Mortimer, the reverse of that journey which would see her taken from the house to the kitchen was a voyage of the most substantial distance—like the moon be from the earth.

'Miss July, you can take off that lace for me?' Molly asked. 'That will look pretty 'pon me dress.' She had turned from the window where she was staring out with her good eye, watching four chickens pecking at the dusty ground.

'Missus will see it gone from the bodice,' July said.

Molly sucked her teeth. She did not care for July. I could say that it was because July had robbed Molly of easy work; for July had gone from being a filthy nigger child—used only to working in the fields— into the missus's favoured lady's maid, who boasted her papa to be a white man even though it was Molly that had the higher colour. And, at sixteen years, July had grown into an excitable young woman with crafty black eyes, a skinny nose, and narrow lips that often bore a smile of insolence; a troublesome dusky-skinned negro girl whom Nimrod (the once-upon-a-time groom at Amity but now a freeman) was always affecting not to notice, yet talked of all the time. But, in truth, Molly just despised anyone who possessed two good eyes within their head.

'Well, me mus' have some of the button you take off then,' Molly said, before resuming her staring.

Patience stepped into the kitchen with three eggs caught up careful in the fold of her apron. 'Missus calling,' she proclaimed into the air. Patience was a woman who so resembled her papa Godfrey that you need to look upon her twice. For the first glance might have you think she was Godfrey dressed in the clothing of a woman.

Godfrey had been a fine handsome man in his youthful days, and that charm was still draped about him like the fading colours on a once glorious flower. Now his hair was white, his back stooped, his gait slower, yet still he was rakish. For his eyes ever blazed with merriment, no matter what prank or cruelty they be gazing upon. His broad back had lived forty-five years as a slave and he had ministered unto white men for thirty years as a house servant. But there was one part of Godfrey that through relentless toil had aged more hastily than any other—his male organ. Come, it was worn out. Pert, alert and ready for action from his tenth year, through demanding employ night and day for nearly thirty-four cane seasons, it now dangled limp and exhausted. No firm wide buttocks upon a bending female could arouse it to its former life. Even within its other function it remained tardy. Once his squirt could sizzle a fire out. But now Godfrey no longer had strength to stand as a man should to wait for his pee-pee to fall; he had to sit forbearing upon a pan, for his lifeless organ dribbled out water fierce as a pickney with its first tooth.

'Missus calling,' Patience said once more, this time directing her breath upon July. But she received no response for, at that moment, a little boy came in upon the kitchen yelling, 'She have the egg. Me wan' the egg. It be me egg. She have me egg. I get the egg. She tek the egg. It be me egg, me egg, me egg! Me wan' me egg . . .'

'Byron, hush up,' Godfrey shouted as Hannah, woken from her sleep, sat up fast as a living man caught in a hole for a corpse.

'Byron, get out me kitchen. I tell you once, I tell you twice . . .' Hannah yelled.

'Me wan' the egg. She have me egg. She tek me egg . . .'

Byron was one of Godfrey's house boys. He cleared the tables, he swept the yard, he fetched the water, he killed the rats. But his face was always so live in motion, that if you had asked Godfrey what Byron looked like—once Godfrey had told you that he had a high colour, lighter even than his good late wife, (God rest her soul, but please do not bring her back to him!)—then Godfrey would describe to you an indistinct blur. For Byron never stayed still long enough for Godfrey to peruse his features for recognition.

'Byron, me no wan' hear your jabber,' Godfrey said, but Byron was gone. And, in his place, there lumbered in the large brown dog named Lady, who rested its weary head in Godfrey's lap, then sat its quaggy backside down upon the missus's dress that July was working on. Come, its white muslin and gauze trailing along the dirty earth and brick of the kitchen floor was softer than a rug for the tired, dusty old beast.

'Marguerite,' came the calling again and all souls in the kitchen—including, if you listen close, the brown dog—did give a little groan.

'July, go see to her, nah,' Godfrey flashed. 'She paining me head.'

July tried to lift the missus's dress from under the flank of dog, but the hound, languid yet determined, did cling on to the moving cloth. First one paw did claw its nails into the fabric and, seeing it still stirring beneath it, a second paw then pierced it too. 'Lady, get off,' July scolded. 'Mr Godfrey, you can get the hound off the dress?' Godfrey first patted Lady's lolling head, then kicked it hard upon the rump to shoo it away.

July held up the dress to better inspect it. Come, it was one fright. For not only had the brown dog left the print of its backside upon the skirt like some filthy bull's-eye, but its mucky paws had walked a dog-foot pattern up the white muslin where none was required. But this was not the only trespass upon the garment. For Florence and Lucy, the two ever-jabbering-but-understood-by-no-one washerwomen, had returned this fancy dress from another savage laundering at their pitiless hands with all its many frills, flounces and furbelows pressed quite flat. And although made of the softest gauze, the sleeves of this dress were starched so stiff as to appear like pieces of wood. The rigid arms stuck out in front as if the dress were pleading for someone to embrace it. No pearl buttons were left upon the cuff at the wrists—for those that Florence and Lucy's frenzied pummelling did not send shooting off into the air like gunshots, July achieved their loss with a dainty snip-snip from her scissors. And the collar of lace that had wrapped like a pelerine at the neck was entirely missing. Lost either on a bubbling raft of soap, blue and starch that sailed it away, unseen by its two lathering guardians on the river's tide, or soon to be found under the mattress where Molly sleeps, while she feigns bewilderment, crying, 'How it get there?!' No need to enquire the number of securing hooks and black wire bars that were still in place upon the dress, for there were none.

As July lifted the garment higher to the light, turning the bodice to inspect the lining and tracing the frayed progress of several of its unravelling piped seams—she said, 'Mr Godfrey, me gon' get whipped for this. It mash up.'

And Godfrey, smiling, said, 'Miss July, me no frettin'.'

And here is why.

When July reached the room where her missus reclined, rigid with furious impatience, she ran in upon it with such vigour that the drinking glasses that adorned the mahogany sideboard did quiver and resonate to announce her arrival on a melody of tinkling bells. She flew to where Caroline lay and, before her missus had time to take a breath with which to start her intended lengthy, fierce and hysterical scolding, July threw herself upon the floor, held the dress aloft and yelled, 'Missus, the dress spoil! Them mash up your dress. It mess up, it mess up. Oh, beat me, missus, come beat me! The dress spoil, spoil, spoil. Come tek a whip and beat me. I beggin' you missus!'

No word had passed Caroline's lips, yet her mouth gaped as she hastily sat up upon her daybed. 'What is it, Marguerite? What is it?' July, rising on to the bed, pressed the dress close to her missus's face. The missus shrieked and thrust out her podgy hand—either to keep the howling slave from her, or to stop the stiff sleeves of the enfolding dress from bashing her about the head.

'Missus, come beat me,' July shouted as she made grab for the slipper on her missus's foot and pulled it off. Holding this pink satin shoe high in the air July brought it down with a smack against her own head. 'Come, missus, beat me,' she pleaded. She made move to hand the slipper to her missus but, as the missus reached to grab it July quickly tossed it away on to the floor, yelling, 'Oh, missus, oh, missus! No look 'pon the dress—it mash up.' July then threw herself down flat upon the floor on top of the frock and buried her face in its cloth. Her legs kicking, her arms flailing, she let out a deafening cry of, 'It ruin, missus, it ruin!' before collapsing in a heap of pure sobbing.

'Calm down, Marguerite! What has happened?' the missus screeched—her voice rising shrill enough to make Lady the dog stir in its far off slumber. 'Show me the dress, show it to me now or I will whip you . . . I will . . . I will . . . Do you hear me? Do you hear me? I will . . .'

Now, July knew that her missus would not actually whip her, for she kept no whip. If any whipping were required then it would fall to John Howarth, the massa, to perform that duty. But he of late did not flog. Since his wife Agnes's death only five weeks after Caroline's arrival in Jamaica, he had not the energy for beatings, for there was no crime, to his desolate mind, that seemed to require it.

Upon the other hand, the overseer, Tam Dewar, was ever prepared with his industrious lash. But Amity was a busy plantation with many, many, many indolent, skulking, tricky, senseless, devious slaves. On the last occasion that Caroline Mortimer had bid a stripe be laid upon July (for leaving her missus quite alone in the house for an entire night), Tam Dewar had bemoaned—whilst his chewing tobacco stained his breath a darker and darker brown for the eternity of the discourse—that he could not be everywhere at one time. In a shower of rancid spittle he had finally inferred that the mistress might do better to learn to use her own whip.

So Caroline had tried once to use the braided buckskin lash (with the terracotta-painted handle) that her brother had bequeathed to her from his wife Agnes's belongings at her death. But as she flicked it at July's departing back (on this occasion for spilling the contents of a night pot over the floor, as I recall), Caroline hit herself with the thrashing hide quite smartly in the eye. The whip then went missing. And despite a thorough search made by all the house negroes none ever managed to find where July had hid it.

The missus's favoured punishment was to strike July sharply upon the top of the head with her shoe. Although hopping and hobbling, the missus could chase July around a room for several minutes to deliver her blow. At these times July would jump, weave and spin to avoid her. For she knew that soon the tropical heat would so exhaust that demented fatty-batty missus that she would fall upon her daybed in a faint of lifelessness. But her missus was a tricky one. Any time she might creep up upon July to deliver that blow. For a punishment left unbestowed brooded within her missus like the memory of a delicious dinner left uneaten.

Sometimes, if the missus was just too weary for spirited reprimand, she might slap July about her face. Mostly one swipe with the flat of her palm. But occasionally, if July had missed the menace in her missus's eye—those two colourless, vigilant villains that squinted into tiny slits—then she might still be standing to catch the slap from the back of her hand too.

When the missus had first stuck a needle firm into the back of July's hand, the memory of that earliest smarting wound stayed with July longer than any of the other piercings that patterned her arm thereafter. For it was administered in those early days, when July was only a child of nine years and as constant to her beloved white missus as a newly hatched chick to a fowl.

July had wanted so much to learn how to sew and stitch nicely when she was still that small girl for, at that time, she loved to see her missus pleased with her. Her pink-white cheeks puffing into a grin so wide they looked to span the room as she bounced excited upon her toes. Like the time when July first bent her knee in a perfect curtsey. Come, her missus squealed louder than a trapped pig, 'Marguerite, you are a good, good, good nigger.'

Yet it was not so much the threading of the little spiky needle with a whisper of yarn thinner than her own hair. Nor that, when July had first started to sew for her missus, she began as she had seen her mama do—with broad stitches that always caused her mama's stout arm to extend in a wide arc so the long thread may be pulled tight through the rough weave of the Penistone cloth; and that her missus, seeing this lavish movement, frowned and with a wagging finger said, 'No, no, no, not like that,' before insisting upon the tiniest stitches upon her delicate fabric; stitches that did cause the needle to nip July's fingertip, sharp as the bite of a rat, if her eye should stray from its dainty path. No. It was the length of time July was required to sit in almost perfect stillness within her missus's chamber to perform the task. All day! And July had legs that just did not want to keep her there.

For they were used to spending their working day leading the pickaninny third gang of slaves—their wooden pails swinging easy in their tight fists as they walked, skipped, jumped and dilly-dallied down to the river, twittering like chicks. July, sitting with her missus, would make one stitch, two stitch, three stitch, before her legs would start to jiggle. Four stitch, five stitch, and they would jump up to walk about. 'Are you finished?' her missus would call. July, meek as a bullied dog, would sit back upon her seat to begin again. One stitch, two stitch, three stitch, as she did think of those ragged children of the third gang struggling their thirst-quenching loads out to the cane strips of Dover and Scarlett Ponds. How, with their pails full of water, their progress was slow as a line of mourners and they did grunt like crones and strain double to raise the brimming vessels far enough from the ground to carry, not drag, the slip-slopping water upon the long journey to the thirsty mouths of the slaves working the cane pieces.

Six stitch, seven stitch, eight stitch, and she would listen as familiar sounds rode in on the breeze that blew at the long window: the chant of a work song; was that Ned the mule braying? Here them all tramping up to Virgo; that be the ugly driver cracking his long lash; come, is that the massa I hear, agalloping his horse? Why they be yelling? Oh, they be running to catch the cart! And her legs would begin their jiggling once more.

Is it to anyone's wonder that July, instead of sewing the repair to the pocket of the frock (a small hole made by the missus's jagged finger-nail), took the scissors and carefully cut around the little ear of fabric until the pocket was removed from the dress entirely. Then, hiding the severed pouch away under her skirt, she brightly told her missus, 'Me done.'

Her missus, inspecting the repair, placed her hand within the pocket, up to her elbow, before she realised that all was not well. Turning the dress inside out so her eye might inspect what her hand already knew, she threw the dress upon the ground and grabbed July by her wrist. With July's hand splayed in front of her, she picked up a needle, twisted it to perform like a dagger, and stabbed July upon her hand four times with its sharp point.

'Every time you do something bad when you are stitching,' her missus said, 'then I must punish you, or you will not learn,' before pricking her hand two more times. And July cried out like a man lashed with a cat-o'-nine-tails.

'Mama, Mama, Mama!' July yelled as she jumped up and down upon the spot. And the little severed pocket of the dress then floated down from where it was hid, on to the floor. All at once her missus's face began to span the room as she leaned in close to July to yell, 'Your mama is sold away. She is sold away, you hear me? Sold away. You are mine now.' And her puffing cheeks were red as Scotch Bonnet pepper as July cried out for her mama once more.

Sitting in a corner of the kitchen, behind the stone of the fireplace under the shelf that held teetering dutch pots and jestas, curled up in as tight a ball as her knees and arms could make, you could always find July in those early days, snivelling and weeping. The longing for her mama became a pain within her fierce as hunger. When anyone came in upon the kitchen—darkening the blazing light at the door like a cloud before the sun—she would look up yearning. For she longed to see her mama standing there; vexed, sucking 'pon her teeth and rolling her big eyes; calling July that her porridge was ready upon the stone and the hut needed sweeping for the wind had blown in a mound of trash while she was in the field and cha! July must come, and come now.

With her eyes tight shut, July could feel her mama beckoning her to leave the sweltering heat of the oven in the kitchen, slapping her hand upon her thigh, 'Hurry, July, hurry before the missus comes for you.' Or holding out July's trash doll—with its stiff gingham skirt and one blue bead eye—to sweet-mouth July home to her chores with a, 'Peg be frettin' for you to come.'

But with her eyes wide open, only strangers stood yelling, 'Come, little nigger, you be sent back to the field if you not behave.' Yet, no matter whom July kick, spat, clawed and cursed upon, she was never sent home. She ran from the great house nearly every sun-up, searching for a path to the negro village—finding herself enfolded by louring trees or adrift in long grass that tickled at her chin. Yet all that followed this offence was to be chased back by Godfrey's snarling, slathering hounds before being dragged by her hair to stand before that missus.

Hoping to be lost, then forgotten, in the dews of night she hid in the stables with the horses. Stinking of their dung and rolled in so much straw she appeared like her trash dolly the next morning—yet she was not returned.

Soon the trees near the kitchen were stripped almost bare from switches pulled so Godfrey might whip July's backside—he complaining all the while of a pain at his shoulder from whacking a piece of tree so often upon her.

And July did count the time: one day, two days, three days she had not seen her mama. Four days, five days, six days, and still her mama never came. Seven days, eight days . . . she counted until all the numbers she had learned were gone. And so she began again: one day, two days, three . . . yet still she remained.

—◦

Caroline Mortimer had proved doggedly determined to make a lady's maid of July (or Marguerite as she believed her named); sure as a turkey seized for the Christmas table, July had been raised, caught and stuffed for the task. For the white girl, Mary, with whom Caroline had sailed across an ocean from England (upon her brother's instruction), had died a few weeks after she had arrived upon the plantation. It was Florence and Lucy whom the massa had charged to nurse this bag-o'-bones servant girl back from writhing with a raging fever and tortuous pain at her stomach, to full curtseying obedience.

But Mary, who had come from a place called Cork to wait upon Caroline Mortimer, was required upon the ship that sailed from England, to shit squatting with her backside dangling over the side of the deck. Now, no one but her mama had ever seen those two cheeks of hers before, and Mary believed no one but her mama ever should. Although careful to tip Caroline's full pot over the side every morning of that long journey, Mary had contrived rarely to allow her own shit to fall and held it inside her long enough for it to fell her with a mysterious ailment. She finally parted from Florence and Lucy's careful physic, and her own life, spewing forth a fetid brown waste that should have been falling all the while from that other hole.

She was buried at the same time as the missus, Agnes Howarth, and her short-lived pickney were laid in upon the ground. The missus, who had died giving birth to a son that lived only two days upon this earth, had a trailing line of mourners that so blocked the lane to the churchyard with their carriages and slaves that three of the finer women (new from England and dressed in black wool for the service) were struck down in the midday heat.

Mary, the servant girl, was laid a short walk from the back of the kitchen, near the provision ground of Florence and Lucy. For Caroline decided, on behalf of her grieving brother, that a Christian burial would not be necessary for her erstwhile maid-of-all-work. So the two negro women dressed in their finest red kerchiefs and, arguing all the while whether a white girl would need rum for her journey home, sang not only a dirge but the melody from a newly learned hymn as they laid her in a hole that delivered her into the proud arms of Godfrey's late wife. Godfrey did not attend the burial for he feared—as the earth became thin upon his wife's bones—that she might find reason to scold him from beyond.

And, oh how, Caroline Mortimer had wept in those days. Not in sorrow for the sudden loss of her sister-in-law, nephew and servant girl, for she was scarcely familiar with any of them. No. She sobbed, 'I hate this house and I hate this island, Marguerite . . . What am I doing here? . . . Did I leave England for this? . . . My brother hardly knows me . . . Oh why must I stay? . . . Because I have no choice, that is why . . .' for finding herself with not a companion, nor a friend, in the whole world, let alone the wretched island of Jamaica, except one little negro girl named Marguerite.

So menace it all she might, but Caroline Mortimer would never have commanded a militia man, nor redcoat, to take July away from her to break her upon the wheel or lock her within the stocks. July was now sixteen and never spent time in fretting that her missus might return her to the field, no matter on how many occasions that fool-fool white woman did warn it. For what would Caroline do?

Who but July could help the missus with her morning burden of sifting the skulkers from the sick amongst the negroes. With Agnes deceased, Caroline's brother in such ill humour that he rarely left his chamber or his bed, and the overseer insisting it was a task for a master or mistress to perform, it fell to Caroline to inspect those field slaves that hoped sickness might find them relieved from their work. Dusted grey, limping, their clothes all awry, straggling in a long line, that most pitiable rabble coughed, whined and limped with their assumed ailments up to the great house upon Monday mornings to stand for inspection before Caroline, who trembled and sweated at the very sight of them. Always she insisted that July remain at her side. And with each negro that presented their complaint, July would whisper into her missus's ear, 'No. Him jus' have sore head from too much rum,' or 'That black tongue not be sickness, it can be wipe off,' or 'Caution missus—yaws!' whilst holding out a violet-scented handkerchief for her missus to waft back and forth under her nose during this endurance.

And who but July would know to tip a near hogshead of sugar into her missus's morning coffee? For anything less would see her grimace with the pain of a child flayed or squeal that it was too sour. Or that she liked her sangaree, not with the juice of a lime, but embittered with the peel from a lemon. And that she required salt fish, yam and cured pork at her breakfast table, but no pickled tongue; she could not abide the look, nor taste of it. And that her back needed to be rubbed after she had drank her Epsom salts so as to release, into a belch or fart, the wind that so plagued her. Who but July could the missus call upon to pull her from the cane-bottom dining chair when, once more, it split under her ample strain? And it was only July she requested to nurse her when, with a persistent pimple upon her chin, she was forced to take to her bed.

So when July lifted her head from her sobs that day finally to obey her missus's command and show her the degree of spoiling the fine muslin dress had undergone, her face was damp with real tears, her imploring hands trembled, her breath whimpered in trepidation, yet, just like Godfrey, our July was not really fretting.

CHAPTER 7

'WE MUST HAVE BOTH turtle and vegetable soups.' This was how Caroline Mortimer began commanding Hannah, the cook, over the Christmas dinner that must be prepared. 'Mutton and pigeon pies and guinea fowl, of course,' she went on.

Perhaps, reader, you are familiar with the West Indian planters and their famed appetites. You may have had cause to entertain them at your own table and watched your house servants dash and scurry to attend upon them. If this be true, then you will also know that the flesh of many a poor creature needed to be sacrificed to satisfy their greedy-guts.

This dinner was to be a party of twelve seated at John Howarth's table to celebrate that Yuletide and perhaps, in this year of 1831, bring about the change within his spirits that his sister Caroline had so prayed for. For he was—these many years after his wife, Agnes, had howled in that final useless childbirth—still the saddest widower upon the whole island.

Godfrey, who had been standing all the while through these instructions, had his head inclined. This dutiful gesture gave the impression that he was listening to his missus's words when, in truth, he was peering out of the window at a distant tree. For, amongst its branches, he could clearly see the missus's white cotton petticoat. It had flown up there this morning after July had carelessly left it lying upon the ground. It had been picked up by a strong breeze and was now caught within that tree, flapping bold as an ensign from the mast of a ship. His eyes soon returned to his missus as she said, 'We must have the best cheese,' for he did not wish her to follow his gaze to see Byron, under July's command, feebly trying to pluck down the forlorn garment with a stick.

'A boiled ham and a turkey, or maybe two,' the missus carried on, 'and turtle served in the shell, if we must, but could we not enquire after beef in town? Stewed ducks—four if they can be got. And cheese, did I say cheese?'

These were not the only instructions the missus had delivered upon the matter of the Christmas dinner. Come, if it were, no Jamaican planter would think this a spree. Candles were to be amassed in every corner of the room. 'I have seen it done at Prosperity plantation,' the missus told Godfrey. 'Upwards of two hundred lit in a room smaller than our dining hall. And Elizabeth Wyndham's husband produces fewer hogsheads per year than my brother. There are to be as many as can be got. And has the pig been butchered?'

'Oh yes, missus.'

'Then let us have it roasted, not salted, if it will keep.' There was to be malt liquor, wine, porter, cider, brandy and rum, watermelon, mango, pawpaw, naseberry, soursop, granadilla fruit. 'And make sure the pre-serve has come from England. Strawberry or damson. Do not serve guava, ginger or that ghastly sorrel jelly. I'm so tired of Jamaican jams.'

Hannah had stopped listening, for the need to shout, 'And me to fix-up all this? You a gut-fatty, cha!' at her missus was becoming overpower-ing within her. Hannah had trudged that vast distance from the kitchen into the long room of the great house to stand, weary and miserable, just inside its door. The sunlight that floated sharp shadows across the wood floor—flashing through the crystal glasses and flaring across a silver salver—made her eyes blink and water, for she was unaccustomed to this dazzling light. She did not look upon Caroline Mortimer's face, but kept her eyes fixed firmly on her own crossed hands—for these two cal-loused and worn claws were the only things within that room that were not annoying to her. But as her missus spoke to the ceiling, as if reading a list from some celestial sheet an angel held there, Hannah lifted her eyes now and again, for she became entranced by the blond curls at each side of her missus's head that bounced like small birds pecking at her shoulder.

'We will need plum pudding,' she told Hannah before adding, 'Now, do you remember how to make it?'

Plum pudding, Hannah thought. Plum pudding . . . plum pudding. Come, let me think. How you make plum pudding? A little fruit, a little molasses, some cornmeal, eggs, plenty rum. Mash it up a bit. Put this mess in that silly round mould the missus did give her the first Christmas she arrived, and boil it until the water does run dry. And when the thing hard, then it is done.

'I do not want it to be like last year's, for that was not plum pudding,' her missus pleaded. 'It should be light, not hard as a medicine ball. I could show you if it were needed,' the missus said.

This impudence coming from the missus's mouth nearly caused Hannah to look up into her face. The last occasion that the missus did cross that breach betwixt the house and the kitchen was to show the cook how pastry could be light, edible and not as tough as a stone that edged the garden, if the fingers that lifted and raised the flour fluttered air into the mix, then folded and rolled in the fat with as gentle care as a mother tucking a baby into a cot. Hannah had sucked in her breath and held it there for the whole of the missus's instruction. For, like an ember spat sizzling from a fire on to a silken rug, until the missus was returned to her rightful place, Hannah could not exhale that wind. And she had not lungs enough for that wretched missus to sputter once more into her domain.

'Oh, Miss Hannah will make it real nice for you, missus. You see. The plum pudding will be just right,' Godfrey assured, while calming Hannah's fiery dread with a sly wink.

Whilst attending to the missus's instruction on this dinner, the sun had paused lifeless in the sky waiting on her to finish: Godfrey was sure on this. Not until all her commands were complete—including the tune the musicians should play as her guests changed from their stout travelling shoes to slippers—did the sun rouse itself to once more roam the heavens. Then, as Godfrey said, 'Please, missus, I will need plenty money for marketing,'—counting upon his fingertips to ponder the sum before telling his missus the amount that was required—the sun began to gallop. Long shadows drifted silently across the floor like a magic lantern show as he waited for Caroline's breath to return to her so she could whimper, 'How much?'

'Is what all will cost, missus. All this need plenty money. And there be a lot of rumble and fuss in town, so ship come in and people strip it like crows in Guinea corn.' Godfrey told her.

'But why so much?'

'Hear me now, missus, hear me,' Godfrey said, pressing his hands together beseeching. 'The fine candles, the beeswax that missus do prefer, be six shillings and eight pennies for the box. Me must fill the room so plenty box must be brought. Now the tallow candle is one shilling and one penny for the same number . . .'

'Tallow! Is my room to smell like an abattoir? This is to be a fine party, not a crop-over feast for niggers.'

'Then is six shillings and eight pennies for the box.'

The missus stared upon Godfrey's face, once more wordless. Yet he knew what was causing her worry; she would have to beg her brother for more money for this feast. Trip up the steps of the counting house. Tap lightly upon the door. Wait with negroes peering at her from the garden, from the kitchen. When finally allowed permission to enter, she would be bellowed at to close the door behind her. A moment would pass before all around would hear the massa's voice blowing through the stone walls of the counting house as he found passion enough to thunder, 'That is too much, Caroline, too much!' No pitiable pleading about Prosperity plantation or beeswax candles would quell him. When the door of the counting house once more opened, the missus—red-faced and sobbing into a handkerchief—would slowly descend the steps.

'My brother says you cheat me. How can everything be so expensive?' the missus asked.

And Godfrey, holding her gaze, unflinching, answered softly, 'It is not that things be expensive, it is just that you can not afford them.'

The missus suddenly swung her fist around and struck Godfrey hard upon his ear. Godfrey stumbled. The blow had caused him no hurt. Come, he had known worse than that. Nor was he weak—he could have snapped her wrist if he had needed. It was his surprise that his missus would strike that had him cringe like a fool. For it was done with a movement of such swift zeal, that even Caroline appeared stunned at its force. Yet it was what he glimpsed in the expression of Hannah's eyes that caused him to feel its agony. That old woman—his companion of many years, whom he often shared a well-sucked tobacco pipe with at the end of each day—was looking upon him with pity.

'How dare you question me,' Caroline Mortimer said. 'I know you cheat me. Now, just get me a good price or I'll have you whipped.' Godfrey straightened himself and, once more, inclined his head dutifully to his missus.

From a small linen purse she counted out money into her hand. Then, passing the coins to Godfrey, she said firmly, 'And be sure to lay the best linen cloth upon the table. The Irish linen should raise Elizabeth Wyndham's envy quite nicely.'

From the moment that July had opened her eyes upon that day, she had found herself put to work. She had had to wake Molly! Usually, Molly did wake her by slapping her flat palm against July's ear until it rang like a bell. But this day, July stood above the sleeping Molly's open mouth— her snoring releasing all manner of foul odour into July's face—and carefully dropped a small stone into Molly's gaping maw. Molly woke into that dark morning choking—too busy coughing to realise she had not breathed in the tiny object for herself.

July went to the kitchen where Patience placed within her busy-busy hands a tray of sour oranges. She required July and Molly to clean the hall floor. And July is a lady's maid! There was no protest to make to Godfrey that was not met with his shaking head, for this was an extraordinary day. So, on her knees July had had to go. The cut upon her thumb filled with smarting as she rubbed the juice from the halved oranges into the wooden floor—it pained her bad as a lash-stroke rubbed with salt pickle, yet still she had to polish until the shine rose bright as sunlight upon water. And, all the while they polished, Molly insisted upon beating her coconut brush against the floor and singing loud in her no-tune voice, 'Mosquito one, mosquito two, mosquito jump inna hot callalu.' It made the nasty toil harder for July, not easier as the fool-fool Molly declared it would.

Twelve people for a fancy feast was enough to intrude upon the slow routine of the kitchen in the sad-to-hell massa's house. But to snatch the two washerwomen, Lucy and Florence, from the province of their stream—to stand them shifting upon their bare feet in the corner of the sweltering kitchen, their wide-eyes staring perplexed upon the pile of massacred fowl, rabbits and turtles to be cooked—was a cruelty.

For these two women, trying to obey the peculiar orders that were barked upon them, ducked with each command as if the words were striking them. And, no matter how Hannah yelled upon them to raise the flour for the pastry from fluttering fingers and roll it soft with light intent, Lucy and Florence treated that dough like a soiled undergarment that must be cleaned. They banged it, they beat it, they swung it around their head and dashed it against a stone.

Hannah had little time for pastry, for all the hucksters came in upon the kitchen that day in an eager, yet lazy, line to sell their wares.

The negro woman with skin so black it was blue called 'mango gwine pass' as she strode to the kitchen door in her gaudy striped skirt with a basket upon her head. Showing Hannah the plumpest of the mangos from her provision ground, she bent slyly to the old cook to murmur what she had heard from the preacher-man about them all soon to be free. Whispered close, yet spoken fast, Hannah did not hear every word—something was lost about the king and the massa—but she nodded with feigned understanding.

The mulatto woman who had bought her own freedom and a cart upon the same day and sold cedar boxes full of sugar cakes frosted in pink, white and yellow—the one who was saving for a donkey so it was no longer she that had to push-pull the produce—she had heard that it was the King who said there were to be no more slaves.

The fisherman with his barrels full of blue-grey shrimp that slopped puddles of water over Hannah's feet as he lifted up the squirming crustaceans for inspection, had heard nothing. Come, this skinny man with one leg shorter than the other, did not even attend the chapel in town. But that free coloured woman with brown skin scoured to light, who informed any who would listen, 'Me never been no slave,' the one who rode in a cart, pulled by a ready-to-dead mule, and twirled upon her parasol as her jars of guava and lime pickle, ginger jelly and pepper sherry were lifted to the light to be inspected, said all this chat-chat was nonsense—that the white massas were correct, the King-man had said nothing about them being free.

Many came to the kitchen that morning with their yam, plantain, artichokes, pineapples, sweet orange, green banana, cheese, and coffee beans. They came to grind the knives, mend pots and bring the dozens of boxes of beeswax candles. Yet Hannah had no time this day to chat gossip about what was heard at the Sunday chapel—the one held outside the blacksmith's in town where everyone gathered to hear preacher-man talk about free. Come, with all these hucksters arriving, she barely had time enough to puff her pipe through several bowls of stringy tobacco with them.

Godfrey, sitting upon his chair by the kitchen, carefully attended to the parade of hucksters for he had to pay for their produce and service from his purse. His cupped hand cautiously guarded the leather pouch which he held close within his lap. After each transaction he counted the money that remained—his lips wordlessly miming the sum without looking upon the coins. It was fortunate that his hair was already white, for this day was a trying one for Godfrey. Where was Byron? It was a long time ago that Godfrey had sent him to fetch water and the boy had not yet returned. And there was still the table to be laid, the candles to be placed, the yard to be swept, the dogs to be tethered.

When July appeared saying, 'Mr Godfrey, this cloth you give me be a sheet for the bed, not for the table,' he, with a careless flick of his hand, told her, 'Go lay it 'pon the table.'

'But it be a bed sheet, Mr Godfrey.'

'How you know that?'

July inhaled the breath. She intended to respond to this very simple question—for the difference between a fine quality linen for a table and a simple cotton sheeting for the bed was within a field nigger's grasp to understand—but instead she began to smile, for she scented Godfrey's mischief.

'Miss July, is that a bed sheet you be holding?' he asked once more.

'No, Mr Godfrey, it be a fine tablecloth,' July replied.

'Then go put it 'pon the table,' Godfrey told her as a hog ran past him, chased by the dog. 'Wait, the hog not dead yet?' he suddenly cried. 'Catch up the hog, where is Miss Patience? Catch up the hog.' All at once, Patience was there, bending low, her apron outstretched as she sought to corner the squealing pig against the walls of the kitchen. While Miss Hannah, at the kitchen door with a pan in her hand said, 'What, the hog not dead yet, Mr Godfrey?' And Godfrey, kicking the dog away from the confusion called, 'Byron, where is that boy? Why the hog not dead yet? Byron!'

CHAPTER 8

C AROLINE MORTIMER WAS RESOLUTE; nothing would be allowed to mar this Christmas dinner for her. Mrs Pemberton of Somerset Penn and her two cousins from England had sent word that they were unable to grace her table. Why? Caroline was never to know, for the small negro boy who had been despatched had tucked the note containing the precious explanation into the waistband at his trouser. This urchin had then run so far, so fast, that his soppy sweat had rendered the note into nothing more than a spreading grey stain upon Mrs Pemberton's fine laid paper.

'What did it say, boy?' Caroline had asked.

And in front of the Anglican clergyman, Reverend Pritchard, John had replied, too tersely indeed, 'Oh, for pity's sake, Caroline, look at the shabby wretch, do you believe he can read?'

Yet Caroline had merely laughed off this reproach, and the clergyman's look of discomfort. Then, as the sun had set, the startling pink hues of that dusk had so reddened the sky that Henry Barrett, the tiresome old attorney from Unity, had left off slurping upon the malt liquor (his third glass), to comment that it appeared that they were all caught beneath a sheet soaked in thinning blood. 'Fine aspect you have here, though,' he added, finally heeding the appalling image he had left upon his listeners' mood. John, remembering a similar sunset that occurred the night his wife Agnes had died, whispered noisily into Caroline's ear, 'Bloody fool.'

And oh, oh, oh! Caroline Mortimer had been assured by Godfrey—not once but twice, perhaps even three times in the asking—that the group of negro fiddlers engaged to play pretty tunes such as 'Whither My Love' or 'The Red, Red Rose' could also play 'Silent Night' tolerably well. An extra shilling Godfrey had asked, to bribe them from a Joncanoe masquerade in town. Yet the clatter they made as her guests changed their shoes, was unrecognisable as a tune. Come, throughout the whole melody an ugly buck-toothed negro at the front thrashed his tambourine as if to fright crows from a field. Yet it was a silent enough night for some, for the old negro poised upon the triangle looked to be asleep.

'My dear, everyone knows these slave musicians play better asleep than awake,' Elizabeth Wyndham from Prosperity had said before rolling her eyes to her husband, with no qualm that Caroline might witness the rebuke. Charles Wyndham added that, next time she needed music, to let him know and he would see to it that one of the brigade's bands came from the nearby barrack or enquire if there were a ship in dock that could supply some excellent naval or merchant players. 'Niggers cannot render civilised music,' he told her.

'Some play a wee bit by ear,' Tam Dewar said. All spruced up, with the small amount of hair he had slicked against his head as if drawn on with a quill, the overseer had intended the comment as a comfort. However his smile, although meaning to be gracious, reminded Caroline of her grey mare when she bared her gummy, brown teeth.

'But they do not know of sharps and flats. They are like small children in that respect,' was Evelyn Sadler, the skinny mistress of Windsor Hall's, pennyworth of wisdom upon the subject.

'I've suffered worse,' her husband George added. Upon which note this exchange but not the negroes' rumpus was brought to a close. And, once the sunset had stopped eclipsing Caroline's elaborate room decoration, all the guests agreed, as they took their seats for dinner, that the profusion of candles rendered the room quite magical . . . if not a little hot.

Godfrey clapped his hands as a signal for the food to be brought in upon the table. When none of his wretched boys appeared from the kitchen he stood within the doorway to yell like a market caller, 'Byron, come bring the food, nah. You no hear me clap?' Elizabeth Wyndham found this cause once more to roll her eyes. But soon all the dishes—a delicious-looking boiled turkey, a ham, a platter of plump guinea fowl, several turtles and stewed ducks, pigeon and mutton pies with pastry that appeared passable, and a vivid abundance of fruit—were laid along the table.

Henry Barrett may have leaned back upon his chair, tucked his napkin under his chin and commenced with what he considered conversation, but to all other ears was dreary sermon, 'I suppose all of you have heard that the negroes have got it into their heads that the King has given them their freedom. Some say it spells trouble.' Caroline's brother John may have suggested to him that he save that thorny subject for after the ladies have left the room. And he, slurping down a whole glass of red wine, might have agreed, 'Quite so, quite so,' before carrying on, until only the pushing of thick slices of ham into his busy mouth gave any pause in his oration. 'They believe it is only we planters standing in the way of them and some heaven on earth, once they are free. What do you think on this, Howarth? Those preachers have put it in their head that they are as worthy as white man. Baptists. They're just a bunch of . . . Better not say with ladies present, eh, Howarth? I'm ready for them if there's trouble. Good chance to put all those niggers back in their place . . .'

Molly may have slopped most of the vegetable soup over the floor as she searched the table for somewhere to rest the tureen. And Evelyn Sadler may have whispered into her husband's ear, 'Oh no, not turkey again.' Yet nothing, no, nothing, nothing was going to blight that coveted evening for Caroline Mortimer. Not even George Sadler quipping to general amusement that, 'The boy on the triangle has just woken up,' when the old negro musician tripped over a chair as the players were commanded to leave the room.

But, reader, let us follow the fiddlers' example and run from this place. For I fear you will never forgive your storyteller for resigning you to listen upon the puff and twaddle of such dull company. If you were to stay supping at that table you would soon feel yourself as wearisome as Caroline Mortimer's dinner guests. Nothing was going to mar that dinner for her but, before she breaks a bite from Florence and Lucy's crust upon that pigeon pie, come let us remove to the kitchen to see what arises there.

On the stretch of ground behind the kitchen—out of the sight for any view from either the house or counting house, behind a row of sweet orange trees but boarded by the lemon and tamarind, in the area where the chickens roamed but the pigs and goats were tethered, was a noisy gathering of slaves. Let me make an amend. For some of those negroes gathered can now read. And should they perchance find themselves referred to in this publication as slaves, then trouble will chase me. No. The noisy gathering was composed of house servants. For none in that lordly flock ever enjoyed to be reminded that they were, in fact, white men's chattel.

Clothed in their fine livery of white muslin for the woman, white jean for the men and waistcoats in a fancy green and red chintz for both, the most pretty-pretty of the house servants were, doubt me not, those from Prosperity plantation.

When that crowd of neighbouring negroes first stepped in upon the land by the kitchen, those that were present from Amity turned their view from the setting sun that blushed overhead to marvel instead upon those dress-up guests. July's mouth did water, for they appeared to her like a sweet confection. Of course, Molly's mouth did sneer, but Hannah's mouth did gape at the one, two, three, four . . . Oh Lord, why so many servants is come?

But the massa of Prosperity and his huffish wife could not travel that short distance to Amity—along the town road that rose over the hill—without their groom to drive the barouche. Their groom, James, was a short, stout fellow who was prized for miles about for his ability to bleed all malady from the most suffering horse. Although befitting of the owner's vanity, that puff-up barouche was unsuited to the terrain as it had a faulty wheel that must be watched. So James could not manage this carriage without his boys to accompany him. He needed Cecil and Sam to climb down to remove obstructions from the road and, now and then, whack the bolts upon the roguish wheel with a hammer.

Their massa having heard rumours that the road they were to travel may not be safe after daylight had commanded Giles—his slave who could shoot a bolting steer between the eyes from seemingly any distance—to travel behind the barouche in the old pony cart, carrying both a fowling piece and a big stick. Throughout the whole of the journey to Amity, Giles complained loud to the one-armed driver of the cart, Bailey, to keep the 'raas-t'ing' from bumping. Giles had an aching head. He had spent the days before at a masquerade with his face chalked white with clay, strutting about upon tip-toe, pointing over here and there whilst barking, 'Is it ready to strike? Is it ready to strike?' in mimic of his white massa inspecting the teaches in the boiling house.

Now, despite each servant Elizabeth Wyndham asked, replying to her, 'Me no know, missus. Me long way from there too,' that missus kept enquiring of her slaves as to the condition of the ground at Amity. Would it be puddled with rain water, squelching with mud, or firm as a level of logs? In the end, Clara had to accompany her missus to carry not only her kid, satin, and leather shoes, but also her missus's silk stockings, her shawl and her wooden box containing all the dressing for her hair lest her curls droop in the damp breeze.

Clara was not only a lady's maid, she was a quadroon. Clara's mama was a handsome mullatto housekeeper to her papa, a naval man from Scotch Land. Her papa died just before he was to manumit her and her mama. The papers were drawn; she has them in a box, if you care to see them. So, although still a slave, on some days, in some lights, her skin did appear whiter than her missus. And haughty! When commanded to travel in the pony cart between the rum-soaked Giles and the one-armed sambo, Bailey, alone, she screamed, fainted away, and had to be brought around with salts. Clara insisted to bring her own girl Mercy (who was a stupid negro, still sucking upon her thumb when there was no one to see it, but what could Clara do for that was who she had been given), to help her carry all those missus's things and, lest she faint away again, to yell upon Giles to watch his mouth.

Of all the servants that had come from around and about—including the two from Windsor Hall, Frederick from Unity, the housekeeper of Tam Dewar from just down the path—it was Clara that July could not take her eyes from.

'Is me dress you like or me pretty fair face that make you stare so?' Clara asked July.

July shrugged nonchalant at Clara's words, yet persisted to gawp upon her like Clara were a blue flower blossoming upon a bush with only yellow blooms. For the tip of Clara's nose pointed upwards like a white woman's—no matter that she were peering down that slender feature to sneer upon July, the black pips of her nostrils could still be seen. Her lips were so thin they looked to have been embroidered upon her face in padded satin stitch. And when she lowered herself upon a chair, it was with the gentility of a missus perching side-saddle upon a delicate horse. July was wearing her best—a new blue kerchief upon her head, her pale-blue cotton blouse stitched with lace and two pearl buttons, recently fallen from her missus's garment—yet within the shade of Clara's distinction, she felt as ragged as a half-plucked turkey.

It was a thought escaping when July exclaimed, 'Me missus give me cloth to make a new dress,' into Clara's proud face.

'Cast-off?' replied Clara wearily. 'I cannot abide to be dressed in cast-off.'

The cloth July had been allowed was indeed her missus's discards; a worn-out cotton dress drained away from bottle-green to an exhausted grey. And, because it had once wrapped all of her missus, unpicked and pulled out, the ugly fabric stretched for yards!

'No,' July snapped, 'it be the finest white muslin from a ship that just come in from England.'

The sound of Clara sucking upon her teeth was as delicate as the chirp from a tiny bird. 'You no tell me true,' she said, 'Your massa have no money for white muslin for you.'

'Me massa have plenty money,' July replied.

'Me hear that not be so,' Clara said.

'Is so true,' July said. 'Him make plenty hogshead. And they do come from town and buy them. And him does take all the money in a big chest. Him can hardly lift it. Him must call Mr Godfrey to help. But not even them two can carry this chest, it be so full up with coin.' July stopped to look upon Clara's face and saw two scoffing green eyes staring back at her.

'You no be telling me true, for what your missus be wearing is bad. No worthy white missus be wearing cotton printed with stripes,' Clara said, flicking her hand to shake July from her.

'But your missus does have an ugly face,' July retorted.

'How dare you impudence me missus,' Clara said. Her umbrage rose her from out of her chair, so July quickly sat down upon it. Folding her arms, July then planted her feet down firm as a tap root so she could not be moved. Clara, even more piqued, shouted rough as a washerwoman, 'Well, your missus has a big-big batty.' And oh, how July desired those gold buttons upon Clara's waistcoat as they shimmered in the skirmish. She may have made grab for one or bit it off with her teeth, if it were not for Byron running to her to say, 'Them finish with first course. Mr Godfrey say come.'

Despite all the candles that lit up the group of servants as they entered the room, none of the guests at that table, not even Caroline Mortimer, paid any heed to that parade of gentle scavengers as they began lifting the plates from around them. Godfrey, standing by the table, ordered with a silent sweep of his hand what was to be lifted and taken where. Leaving only fruit in the centre of the table and laying down two platters of cheese, he bowed and left the room, walking backwards. (He may have somersaulted or jumped high, clicking upon his heels, reader, but there would be none to report it, for no one did see him.)

The feast of food was then carried from that high table within the dining room and laid out upon a low table that rested upon four large stones in the yard by the kitchen, until the makeshift table—wilting with the weight of food—had to be propped with a fifth stone before it snapped in the middle. And Molly again did slop the soup over the floor—the turtle soup this time—while looking for somewhere to place the tureen.

Godfrey, looking to finally fill his glass with a big slop of forget-all brew, sucked his teeth as Giles, James and two of the musicians—numb with rum and slurring words about them soon to be free men—passed his now empty bottles between them. Godfrey called July to him, 'You can take Byron and get us some rum?' July, her cheeks swollen with pigeon pie, nodded and ran off as Godfrey called after her, 'Or anything that you can get. No come back with nothing. You hear me, nah?'

July usually performed her pilfering within the dining room when, with only the brass candelabra upon the table, the two candlesticks upon the sideboard, and her massa and missus chewing their food in silence, the room was quite gloomy. With the massa's stock of drink unlocked for this big-big dinner, July thought to slide herself invisible as a duppy towards the cabinet that held it. But all those candles saw her dark corners chased away. She had to step cautious—pressed flat as the pattern upon the wall. At one step she stood still when she thought her missus did spy her and the tip of her kerchief was singed within the flicker of a candle flame. But her missus's head was merely resting upon one hand, her eyelids drooping with the effort of staying attentive to the talk from that wearisome old man from Unity. Her massa, although nodding to this man's chatter, idly banged a spoon against an empty decanter in front of him. While the other guests, paying this man no heed at all, continued to nibble and drink at what they could. Except for one, for if July's eye was seeing true, the massa from Windsor Hall was sound asleep.

The fiddlers, now playing in the yard for the servants' gathering, began to strike up a song. No more clatter or unrecognisable tune—the sound of a sweet melody came whispering through the open window. For, like most slave fiddlers, it only amused them to play bad for white ears.

July had been promised by Patience that, when the fiddlers struck up a good quadrille, then she would teach July all the steps to the Lancers. And it was a quadrille July could hear. It was just the confusing question of which was her left hand and which was her right, that stopped July from skipping this dance very well. Once she had that matter learned, then she would dance it better than Molly—for with only one eye Molly did lose her partner on every spin; it did mess up the set for everyone. July yearned to return to the kitchen before the dance was done for Cupid, the old fiddler, had promised her that she might get a bang of his tambourine, and she was hungry for more pie.

Byron hissed at the window, 'Miss July, you there?' so loud that July feared Tam Dewar had heard. For suddenly the overseer declared, 'Not so. We won't have trouble with negroes here. There are good negroes and there are bad . . .' Although Byron was hidden deep as a shadow upon black velvet, still July held in her breath, then waved her hand out of the window as signal for him to hush up and wait.

Hordes of night creatures lured to the candles' open flames dropped upon the wooden top beside her—scorched and smoking, they whiffed of baking food. As the talk-plenty old man from Unity said, 'Well, I hope you're right, Mr Dewar . . .' July whipped a bottle from the cupboard top and passed it quickly out of the window. Another bottle she picked up was already empty. She shook it, then placed it back. But two more that were full, soon sailed over the window's ledge into Byron's tiny grasp.

Not too many, and all must be open, Godfrey had instructed July when first teaching her this little deception. That way the massa never knew what had been drunk by his guests; so any accusation of thieving was made with a hesitation from the massa which allowed Godfrey to perform his well-used, big-eyed display of affront.

July was waving another bottle—was it heavy glass or was it full? Hearing the slop of liquid, she was about to pass it through the window when the man who was sleeping suddenly awoke. He stared upon her with a look so keen that July felt it like a finger poking within her forehead.

'What are you doing there?' he shouted. July stood as still as her quickening breath would allow, in the hope he would think her just a likeness from a portrait upon the wall.

'What are you doing?' he said again. And the whole table turned to see where July was standing. July, stepping out of the meagre shadow, held the bottle as if she were about to pour it for these guests.

'Oh, Marguerite, thank goodness,' her missus said. 'Are you bringing the second course, we've been waiting an age?'

'Yes, where is the second course?' her massa said, 'Tell Godfrey the ladies have been waiting quite long enough for their sweet.'

But the man from Windsor Hall said, 'Can't you see that she's stealing from you?'

There was a quarrel begun at the table. July knew that she was its cause, but she could not follow what the white people were saying of her, for a noise like the rush of a wave over stones filled her ears. Her missus was blushing and flushed. Her massa's eyes were rolling and peevish. Tam Dewar, looking to the window, began rising from his seat.

'Come here, girl,' someone said. But who? July was not sure. Was it her missus? Should she fall to her knees and beg her not to have her whipped?

'I said, come here.' It was the man from Windsor Hall. Him who had just woken to expose her crime. He beckoned her to him with an angry gesture, while her missus nodded for her to obey him. July wanted to run from this place and hide in the stables with the grey mare. Mr Godfrey, a scream within her head yelled, Mr Godfrey, come get me from here.

'Come here now, nigger!' The command came, once more, upon a vexed breath. July's eyes were blind with tears and she took the smallest steps her feet would allow. Eventually she arrived by the side of this man. His drunken breath, blasting upon her face, rocked her giddy as he said, 'What were you doing there?' Then, as his ill-tempered spittle dried upon her cheek, she felt his hand, discreetly, out of all view of the other guests, searching across the back of her skirt. Fiddling at a seam, pulling upon the fabric, groping like a tiny rodent looking for a dark corner. His sweaty fingers soon found the opening to the garment and quickly burrowed in. Placing his full palm over her bare buttocks he squeezed her flesh and said quietly, 'Well, what were you doing? Stealing, weren't you?'

'Me no steal, massa, me no steal.' July said. His finger had a jagged nail that scraped across her skin as it probed to find other holes to fill.

'You're a little thieving nigger, aren't you,' he almost whispered into July's ear.

'Oh, come on, let her go so the ladies can get the second course,' the Reverend Pritchard said from across the table.

'Not until she admits she's a thief,' the Windsor Hall massa told him.

July kept as still as she could within this white man's grasp, for the fingers upon his rude hand began to nip and pinch at her buttocks. But then, suddenly, there came a great commotion of running feet from outside.

The doors to the room suddenly swung open with a fierceness that extinguished most of the dying candles. Two men dressed in militia blue bounded in upon the room, bringing in the wood-smoke and dung stink of the night air. July was sure these men had come to take her away—to the stocks, or the wheel at Rodney Hall. She twisted herself from the man's grasp and his fingernail tore the flimsy seam of her skirt as he snatched his hand from out of it.

July dashed under the sideboard and clung her arms around the wood of its leg. She gripped it tight as the snake that was carved there, lest someone made bid to grab her.

But no one came. They did not even glance her way.

'There is trouble.' A deep, hoarse voice began addressing all at the table. 'A great deal of trouble. The negroes are burning plantations in the west. We need every man here to report for militia duty now.'

At once, many feet began passing by July in her hiding place—clattering around upon the wooden boards before her. Tam Dewar's sturdy brown boots were out the door with the militia men's muddy black shoes following. The massa from Unity's slippered feet skipped a dance as he said, 'The day is upon us. The day is upon us.' Byron's little bare feet slapped in upon the room, chased by the four paws of the dog, who barked and slid into furniture. The music stopped. Names—Clara, Giles, James, Bailey—were yelled upon fretting breaths. Beyond the window, horses' trotting hooves shook the ground and cart wheels creaked.

Only July's missus, Caroline, remained seated at the table. The massa, leaning down close to his sister's face, whispered with urgent command that she should not worry; that all this would be in hand soon enough; that he would return to her as soon as he could; and that, until such time, he wished her to stay within the house. Did she understand him? he asked her. Yes, perfectly, came her resolute reply. 'The negroes will see you come to no harm,' John Howarth told her before pressing a small pistol into her hand and kissing her upon the forehead. 'Now, where is Marguerite?' he said. And, before July knew, her massa's troubled face had breached her hiding place, 'Marguerite, get up from there,' he said, pulling at the cloth of July's flimsy skirt. 'Come and look to your mistress. She needs you with her.' His feet then strode to the door in five long strides.

As July crawled out from around and under the sideboard she heard her missus sighing. July, moving to stand at her side said, 'No be feared, missus, no be feared. Me here, missus.'

But her missus began quietly to weep. Then, through a halting pause, as she wiped her snivelling nose upon the back of her hand—which still gripped the pistol—she said, 'Marguerite, that is a bed sheet on the table, not the Irish linen. My God, Elizabeth Wyndham will soon testify to everyone that a soiled bed sheet was on my table through this whole beastly dinner.'

CHAPTER 9

$\sim$

S OMETIMES MY SON DOES confuse me with all his education and
learning until I do not know if I be in the right or in the wrong.

'But this is the time of the Baptist War, Mama,' he tell me. 'The night
of Caroline Mortimer's unfinished dinner in your story is the time of
the Christmas rebellion, when all the trouble began.' He then commenced to blast me with fierce commands.

I should tell, he said, whether the firing of plantations started in Salt
Spring when the negro driver refused to flog his own wife. Or, whether
it began at Kensington Pen, up near Maroon Town. I must write all I
know of Sam Sharpe, the leader of this rebellion—of his character and
looks. I should make it clear how every negro believed themselves to
have been freed by the King of England; how they had promised to do
no more work until that freedom was felt; and how the negroes swore
to wrest their freedom from the planters' thieving grasp if it was not
given willingly. And I must be sure to add how the noise of the shells
and horns being blown at Old Montpelier and Shettlewood Pen did
manage to frighten off the militia.

Plenty, plenty commands did trip lightly from my son's mouth—too
many to lavish my black ink upon here—until I told him, 'Hush up,' for
my head did ache with his requirements.

Now, reader, it is not that your storyteller is indolent and idles about
when there is work that must be done. No. The reason I have little to

advise upon these truths is within the nature of those olden times; for news did not travel as it does today. Most was carried upon the breath of ragged little boys who once having run far with the tale then struggled to recall it while you fed them some yam. Or it was passed upon the gossips-breeze—the chat-chat that blew from ear to ear across the island.

Yet in these more modern times, I may write a letter at my table and someone too-far-to-run-to will read its contents within the week. And, imagine this, an instrument called a telephone can carry talk to ears within some other household in the time it takes to whisper it from your own lips. My son says that this telephone can even allow you to chat with someone in another district—that you may be in Falmouth, yet your talk may be raising the eyebrows of someone in Kingston. But this is obviously fanciful, and no calling for Lillian to tell me that it is indeed so does make it true. But, if there were such an invention at the time of this Baptist War (as my son does name it), then I am sure I would have known what was going on everywhere at one time. But there was not.

So, should you desire a fuller account of what happened during this time, then perhaps you could peruse the pamphlet that my son of late brought to me. It is written by a Baptist minister named George Dovaston with the title, *Facts and documents connected with the Great Slave Rebellion of Jamaica (1832).*

Although nothing that appears within this minister's pages was witnessed by my eye, and what my eye did see at the time does not appear in this man's report, my son assures me that this account is very good. Try that if you so desire. Do not, however, read the pamphlet written by the planter John Hoskin. For the man is a fool who does blame only the sons of Ham and men of God for what occurred. None of my readers should look upon that time through his view. I know this sort of man's character, and his eyes would clearly be shut to all but his own consequence. *Conflict and change. A view from the great house of slaves, slavery and the British Empire* is the pamphlet you must run from. If you do read it and find your head nodding in agreement at this man's bluster, then away with you—for I no longer wish you as my reader.

What I do know is that when those fires raged like beacons from plantation and pen; when regiments marched and militias mustered; when slaves took oaths upon the Holy Bible to fight against white people with machete, stick and gun; when the bullets sparked like deadly fireflies; and bare black feet ran nimble through grass, wood and field—at Amity, the loudest thing your storyteller could hear was Miss Hannah gnawing upon the missus's discarded ham bone.

CHAPTER 10

⁓

'NO BIG BLACK NIGGER gonna get past me, missus,' July said, holding up her fists so her missus might see those two fearful weapons— that were, alas, no bigger than ripe plums.

Three days, Caroline Mortimer had been alone in the great house, with only her company of house servants. At first, the missus had been more concerned with raving at Godfrey over the dirty bed sheet upon the dining table, and wagging her finger upon July to note that if she had been stealing, as the massa from Windsor Hall had accused her, then she was lucky to have escaped punishment by his hand, than considering her uneasy plight.

But as the sweaty, humid hours lumbered past her and no white face appeared to give her a civilised view upon the situation; as the horizon to the west became lit with a faint dash of quivering pink light; as the horn of a conch blew unwonted first from far, then from near; as dogs howled over there, over here; as the moon began once more to light her familiar view with a peculiar gloom and still no word from her brother, Caroline at last realised that perhaps she should fret.

'Is there any word yet?' she asked July.

'No be frettin', missus,' July replied, 'for you is alone with no white people near to calm you—no massa, no friend, no bakkra—for no nigger gon' come near, missus, when me two fists is raised so.' Caroline's face now carried such fright within its features that July was reminded of a pig just before a keen blade slit its throat; for her blue eyes protruded with the same soon-meet-thy-maker dread. But her missus had not yet squealed with an equal passion.

So, suddenly cupping her hand to her ear, July said in a loud whisper, 'But listen, missus, listen. Me can hear a horse riding close.' July then ran to the window and pressed her face and hands upon the panes of glass. 'Me can't see who comes, missus. But no fret,' she shouted. 'No fret for, look see, me two fists is raised. Them no take you from me, missus.'

'Is it my brother?' the missus asked.

As July peered out into the night light, the hazy form of the horse and rider came into her view. After disappearing behind the solid bricks of the counting house, the tiny form reappeared nearer the kitchen and the rider of the horse was caught in a flash of moonlight—for he was dressed all in white.

Nimrod. July knew the rider could only be Nimrod. And oh, what breath of joy she found. Nimrod had come from town!

Like a shadow show upon a wall, July watched Byron's black shape run to hold Nimrod's horse as he, bright as a star in this play, dismounted, patting Byron's head and shooing away Lady the dog as she jumped up upon him. Godfrey's lanky outline then drifted in—his hand outstretched. Nimrod patted Godfrey upon the back and leaned in to whisper in his ear, but then straightened when Molly arrived skipping around as frisky as the dog.

'No, it be no white massa. It be a nigger,' July taunted her missus. But Caroline Mortimer did not squeal with fright as was July's intention, instead she ran to July and clung her arms about her waist. It was such a tight embrace that July was as choked for a good lung of air as her fearful missus.

'Let me go,' July said. The sodden silk of her missus's dress, her pungent spicy scent, the hot moist flesh of her ample arms did all enfold July in a sweet, sticky softness. July made move to wriggle herself from under this squelching grasp, but her missus clung on tighter. And July did regret having made her fret so. For Molly was seeking to charm Nimrod while July was captured like a moth upon jam.

'Missus, let me go so me can see who this nigger be,' she said. But her missus just squeezed her tighter. 'No fret, missus, for me will turn the lock in the door.' Caroline let forth a slight whimper, to assent or protest, July could not tell.

'Just till the nigger be gone, missus,' she said softly. 'Then me soon come back and set you free.'

Even within murky moonlight, July knew that Nimrod would be hungry to gaze upon her. It did not matter that she wore only her ragged grey workaday clothes that were renk with the cow she had milked for her missus's warm cinnamon milk punch. Or that her hair, itching stiff with dirt, poked out of the ugly green kerchief upon her head through several holes within the shabby fabric. As she walked, swinging on her hips, towards Nimrod, she knew he would tilt his head to feign an ordinary greeting—like he might give Molly or Patience—but that his breath would rise to hold the message within his throat until he had to cough it out, 'Ah, Miss July,' cough, cough, 'greetings,' for he admired her so.

Now, Nimrod was not tall—no taller than July—for his legs were bowed as if waiting for the horse he had just dismounted to return and slip back under him. Yet still he walked proud, for Nimrod was a freeman. Although once the groom at Amity, he had purchased his freedom many seasons ago, laying down two hundred pounds in coins and notes while the massa's mouth gaped.

July thought Nimrod's skin black as coke and his nose too flat and broad. But he was not a slave. He now commanded white people to look upon him within the eye. Although one of his eyes was apt to wander, which made knowing which eye to fix upon as he spoke a little confusing. But still, as a freeman he did hold that respect.

The hair upon his head was lush at the front but at the back there was a sovereign-sized hole in the covering that did glisten in sunlight. And the scar upon his lip that Tam Dewar had left him with after a punishment, looked like a disfigurement to July when he was still white man's chattel. But now Nimrod was a man with his own name—not given, but chosen—that jagged mark made him look brave. Nimrod Freeman or Mr Freeman was the name that all white people had to address him by, or he would give them nothing of what they required. For, like the wind, the sun, or the flowing river, like a soaring man-of-war or a beetle under a stone, like a spider at a web or a crab scuttling sideways across a shore, Nimrod was free. And, 'Miss July,' cough, cough, 'greetings,' Nimrod did indeed say as July approached.

' 'Devening, Mr Freeman.'

'Miss July, you know to call me Mr Nimrod,' he said, standing from his seat, yet stooping his head toward July, as if there were some need for him to bend himself shorter to deliver those words. He did not wink on her, for all at Amity were there to see, but he did raise his eyebrows to July two times to imply some fellowship between them as he offered her to sit. He then cleared his throat with a further cough, cough as he sat to continue the tale he had been telling to all who were gathered; Godfrey and Hannah, sucking upon their pipes; Molly loudly devouring a red love apple; the washerwomen, Florence and Lucy, straining to hear from a little way off; Byron, of course, sitting almost still while inspecting a scab upon his knee; even Patience had come.

'So, me continue,' Nimrod said and July felt him looking straight upon her with a keen glare . . . but then so did Molly. 'Three white men come looking for the negro them call the Colonel—him the leader of this band that torched the trash house up at Providence plantation—the flames licking till all that remained was the jagged, scorched stones that did appear like a black-tooth grin within this breach. In upon the carpenter's shop they come—looking here, looking there. But them no see five negroes hiding from them.'

'Five, you say?' Godfrey interrupted.

'Five,' Nimrod replied.

'And where they hiding?'

'In a cupboard,' Nimrod said.

'Five men in a cupboard. That be a big cupboard,' Godfrey said.

Hannah, sucking upon her teeth, snapped, 'Hush up, Mr Godfrey,' before nodding for Nimrod to carry on.

'Suddenly them flew from their concealment to jump upon these white men. Them seized their cutlass. Bound their hands. Blindfolded them and marched them to the works. And there . . .' Nimrod looked from one person to the next, as best he could, whilst saying, 'them threw those white men into the boiling sugar like them was three pieces of temper lime.'

July gasped. As Nimrod leaned in closer to July, the little tuft of beard upon his chin waggled like a goat chewing upon grass as he whispered loud, 'Only their hats floated upon the liquor.'

July wished to pull at the bouncing strands of hair upon his chin to beg him to tell her the beginning of this tale, for it was lost to her while everyone else sat silent within the thrill of this fright.

Except, that is, Godfrey, who after sniffing loudly said, 'And where was the boiler man when them throw three men in his good sugar teache?'

Nimrod leaned back, folded his arms, and lifted his eyes to the sky to answer, with a heavy sigh, 'Him was drunk.'

'The head man was drunk, you say?' Godfrey said. Everyone, even Patience, sucked their teeth upon Godfrey, for he was clouding up this tall-tall telling.

'Mr Godfrey, the boiler man was drunk 'pon rum him had stolen from the stores,' Nimrod answered. And all gasped except . . .

'And you say all this be going on as we sit,' Godfrey said.

'Let God be my witness. Let the Lord strike me down now if what I say is not true.' Nimrod lifted his arms to let God declare him a liar by frying him in a fire bolt before this gathering. When no lightning struck, he carried on with, 'Hear me now, the island is ablaze. They be fighting everywhere and white men be running for their lives. Them say militia so feared for the situation that they will pay Maroons good money for a pair of rebel negro ears.' Nimrod leaned forward upon his seat to grab Byron, 'And them no worried if there be no head in between. Who'll give me a penny for these?' he said, tugging the boy's lobes. And oh, how everyone screamed . . . except Godfrey.

As Nimrod sat back upon his seat, folded his arms and grinned, July noticed that he had lost more teeth since last she saw him, leaving his smile as mangled and forlorn as one of the missus's broken-down hair combs. But at least those ugly chops were upon a freeman.

'And so is we now all free?' Molly asked.

'Ah, well,' Nimrod pondered.

'Is we or is we not, Mr Nimrod?' Godfrey questioned, with deep annoyance in his tone.

Before answering, Nimrod carefully raised one cheek of his backside from the chair and, with a grimace of intense concentration, let forth a loud fart. Then giggling, he waved his hand in this emission to waft its pungent smell from him. Distaste clouded everyone's face. Except Nimrod, who found it very amusing. Once the stink had passed, he composed himself enough to say, 'Well, as you know, Mr Godfrey, I am a free man.'

And no sooner had those words left his crooked mouth than Patience shouted, 'Hold them!'

July jumped to her feet to throw herself betwixt Godfrey and Nimrod. This movement was well practised by all the house servants at Amity; it was just that, on this occasion, July was the nearest to perform it. She held her arms wide between them, looking from one man to the other. Molly, poised keenly, was ready to catch Nimrod should he lunge, and Patience, marking Godfrey, was willing to do the same.

For these two men could never be in each other's company for long before some quarrel would erupt between them. Let the one over a hand of playing cards be my first example. Godfrey waved a fowling piece in Nimrod's face and threatened to blast his head into meat for a hog if he did not admit to cheating. Then there was the weeks of sulking, protestations and dispute that went on when Nimrod, still the groom at Amity, was granted a boy from the massa to hold his mule— which made three within the stables—while Godfrey was left with just his one within the kitchen. And oh, reader, I have just remembered, but will you believe me? The flight of fancy which found these two men squabbling upon which one of them the coloured Miss Clara from Unity did find more agreeable. All but those two quarrelling buffoons knew that Clara would rather roll herself in horse dung, then walk naked down the main street than be friendly to either one of them. Yet in trying to settle this row, they delivered bloody noses and bruised eyes to each other's faces.

Nimrod thought Godfrey a fool. For here was a light-skinned man with opportunity as abundant as pods on a tamarind tree to relieve his situation. Yet when did the man ever heed Nimrod's wisdom? A slave cannot steal from his master. The breath Nimrod wasted upon explanation could have been better used to blow a cooling breeze across the island. 'Mr Godfrey, whatever is your massa's, belong to you. When you take property from your massa, for your own use, him loses nothing. For you be his property too. All is just transferring. Everything you now hold is still your massa's property. You just get a little use of it. What harm there be?' Yet, instead of thanking Nimrod for this holy reasoning, Godfrey just talked of theft, magistrates, treadmills and floggings. Cha! Where did his virtue find him? Still a slave to white men who had grabbed, stolen and shackled his liberty. And now look, the fool has worked so slowly for his freedom that some nigger with fire and machete does have to complete his task.

Godfrey, on the other hand, could not endure that Nimrod—black as sin, ugly, sly, rough, rude and no taller than a girl—was free. For Nimrod's manumission was purchased with cunning. He poached from the massa—from behind his back and before his eyes—to raise that precious cash. Nimrod was noted in town for the dances he held. Come, Nimrod was known as the first steward of these occasions. Godfrey had told the massa this. He also made the massa aware that the knives, forks, plates and candles used at Nimrod's parties were all supplied from the stores at Amity, as was the wine, spirits and often a bottle or two of champagne. Godfrey showed the massa the cards that Nimrod had printed to use as invitation (and costly ticket) to his regular guests—a promiscuous crowd of all colours—to come once more to his 'club' (on some back street in town) for an evening of 'quadrille and merriment.' Godfrey even enquired of the massa if he had ever noticed that, on the days that his horse seemed to require a lot of resting, his fine damask waistcoat and linen jacket were often missing, only to appear later in need of a wash. Yet the massa paid no heed to Godfrey's enlightenment—come, he rolled his eyes at the preposterous nature of it. For John Howarth was wholly convinced that his trusted groom, Nimrod—with his bow legs, crossed eyes and silly, toothless grin—was far too stupid to concoct such devious arrangements. And nothing Godfrey could say did change his massa's belief.

Godfrey was loyal and yes, he had begun of late cheating the missus a little by telling her that produce was dearer than he knew to be true. But what did it matter? He was still a slave and Nimrod was free to fart in his face.

And yet these two warring men sought out each other's company for they believed themselves to be like brothers. As few at Amity had any notion of how brothers behaved to each other, in that kitchen being a brother had come to mean two men in constant, bloody fight.

But on this occasion Godfrey just gestured to Patience and July to once more sit, for there would be no blows or cussing today. He then stared upon Nimrod and smiled. In the silence that followed this curious truce, the missus's voice was heard calling out for Marguerite. Nimrod, hearing this hoarse but plaintive mewl frowned, 'What, your missus still here?' he said.

'Why not?' answered Godfrey.

'The massa gone to militia, but the missus still be here? She is not safe,' said Nimrod.

'Oh come, there been plenty-plenty trouble like this before,' said Godfrey.

'No, Mr Godfrey, there never been trouble like this.'

Godfrey sighed. 'What fuss-fuss.'

'Mr Godfrey, come, let me tell you—I have not seen a white person in town for many days.'

'No say.'

'Me speak true. Some say they all gone.'

'Gone!' Godfrey said, 'Where they all go to?'

'Some say them all sailed away when all this trouble start. Them pack up them belongings and leave the island, for they be frighted by the negroes that live all about them.' Godfrey sucked his teeth while Nimrod looked upon his face as if staring upon a firm friend.

'Is true, Mr Godfrey. The island is ablaze.' Godfrey, seeing Nimrod's concern leaned back and yawned.

'You no feared?' Nimrod asked him.

'What I must be feared of?'

'That them negroes fighting for them freedom come here with gun and wan' you join them. Them no say, "Oh, please," all nice-nice. "Oh, please, come help us burn and bust up this place till we is all free." Them say, "You come or we burn the house, you come or we kill your missus."'

Godfrey, staring silent upon Nimrod, heeded his words with no feeling, 'If they come for the missus, they can have her,' he said.

July gasped, 'Mr Godfrey, no say that!' and was surprised by her own self. For the idea of her missus actually being seized by a rabble of black men did suddenly alarm July. All at once, there was Caroline Mortimer in her mind's eye, her breath quick and gasping, her round cheeks red, puffy and wet with tears, her blue eyes swelling with pleading, her arms outstretched with podgy fingers splayed like a baby needing comfort, her fearful voice squeaking, 'Marguerite, Marguerite, help me, please,' while her blond curls quivered. Within that vision of her missus's ravishment, July became soft with worry for her. For if anyone was going push her missus into a sugar teache until only her petticoat floated upon the brew, then it must be she and not some vengeful nigger. 'But them will boil me missus in sugar,' she cried.

'Miss July, she must go to town,' Nimrod said, 'There be a ship in the bay. She must aboard that ship. She will be safe there.'

'Marguerite! Let me out,' the missus's voice interrupted once more, shrill as the pipe of a bat.

'Go tell her she must get to town, Miss July, to the ship,' Nimrod repeated while looking to Godfrey to see if he agreed with this command. But Godfrey, yawning once more, just lifted himself from his seat to let out a deep and resonant fart.

CHAPTER 11

⁓

'FORGOT!' CAROLINE MORTIMER CRIED. 'I am forgot!' She paced the room before July, so furious that the breeze she created blew out two of the candles.

'All have left me to my fate, Marguerite. They care nothing of what becomes of me.' July made rush to re-light the candles as her missus yelled, 'How am I to see what must be packed, Marguerite, if you cannot keep the room lit? Will there be dining aboard the ship?' She looked into July's face with earnest, wide-eyed inquiry. July stood motionless—too feared to shrug in case her missus once more broke down into time-wasting sobs. 'Oh, why am I asking you?' her missus said, before answering her own question with an impassioned cry of, 'Because I am forgot that is why, completely forgot and am in need of advice.'

Her hands shook as she bit on her fingernail. 'Will I need formal attire, Marguerite? Or will my smart day-wear, with a little ornament, do? Well, Marguerite, you are all that I have, what do you think?' Having little knowledge of those social manners, July was left with no option but to shrug. Her missus then began ranting. She was in front of July scolding, behind her yelling, rushing past her sobbing, and then suddenly, she was before her, pointing a pistol at July's head.

'What good is this to me?' she said. July swiftly ducked as the missus, swinging the weapon about her, shouted, 'My brother has abandoned me! I am forgot. And I do not even know how to fire this piece,' before dropping the gun to the floor.

July, taking a step closer to her, had intended to once more reassure her missus that she would be safe and among other white people upon the ship in the bay. But before her breath was gathered for this assertion, her missus shouted, 'And how do I know you are not lying to me and wish me from this house so you may steal everything we have. Who told you of this ship? Who came?'

As July uttered the words, 'Mr Nimrod,' her missus stopped dead as if suddenly stiffened by salt.

'Nimrod is here?' she said with a gentle frown.

Thinking the missus now calmed at the thought of Nimrod being near, July nodded. But her missus, almost quietly, began, 'He made start on my garden, Marguerite. Took all the money for the work, of course, yet I have not seen him now for weeks. All manner of weeds are growing upon that ground now. My brother says Nimrod must have more pressing work than my garden of vines. But I had paid Nimrod to complete it and now my brother won't hear a word from me upon the subject. Is Nimrod come to finish my garden?'

'No, missus,' July said, 'him never mention your garden.'

The fierce sigh the missus let forth blew out two more candles. 'I am forgot,' she wailed, 'I am forgot and left with only negroes.'

⁓

Caroline Mortimer bounced upon her toes, muttering over and over to herself, 'Oh, I am forgot! Must I go? Should I go,' as she waited with her packed belongings by the door for Godfrey to bring the carriage. 'Where is Godfrey?' she asked July, then yelled, 'Come on, Godfrey, let us be gone.'

Godfrey, slowly ascending the steps at the side of the house, was carrying a lamp which he set down so he might have both hands free to scratch the back of his head.

'Hurry along, Godfrey. Pick up these things,' Caroline said. Godfrey stared at the sack, the small trunk and the cloth valise that stood between him and the missus. His missus, with an exasperated sigh, indicated again at the items she wished Godfrey to transport.

But Godfrey, still scratching upon his head said, 'You wan' me put these on the cart and take you into town?'

'Of course, into the gig. And I am in a hurry to be gone.'

'So you wan' me lift them into the gig and then drive you to town?'

'Godfrey, do not play the fool with me. You know I must go to town for my own safety until all this trouble is past. Now, let us be gone.'

And Godfrey, looking down on the missus, sucked loudly upon his teeth before saying, 'Then you must pay me, missus.'

July cupped her hands over her mouth so her gasp and giggle would not escape. While all Caroline managed to utter was, 'What did you say?'

'Me said,' Godfrey began, 'that me will need payment if me is to take you into town.'

'Payment?' the missus repeated. She frowned upon Godfrey, then looked quizzically to July for some explanation of his behaviour. But July was silent—her mouth fixed with a grimace of a child in the thrill of a game.

'Don't be ridiculous, Godfrey,' Caroline said, 'Now, pick up the things or I will see you punished for this.'

Godfrey sighed. He then walked past the missus into the hall and sat himself down upon one of the massa's wooden chairs. 'Then punish me, missus,' he said as he lifted first one leg, and then the other, over the arms of the planter's seat and sat as if waiting for someone to remove his boots.

Caroline Mortimer stamped her foot hard upon the ground. 'When my brother hears of this, you will be whipped in the yard.' Godfrey picked at one of his fingernails. 'I will tell him to spare you nothing. The cat-o'-nine. I will say, use the cat-o'-nine-tails. He'll whip you like a nigger. You'll see.'

Godfrey leisurely rested his head upon the chair back. He took a deep breath and spoke to the ceiling saying, 'Missus, if them fighting for free niggers find me 'pon the road with you, then me throat will be cut, sure as yours. So me wan' payment for taking you.'

Caroline suddenly pulled July roughly to stand her in front of Godfrey. 'Tell him, Marguerite, tell him I am quite forgot here and need to
get to town.'

She shook July so briskly that Godfrey said, 'Leave her, missus. Let
her go.'

'Then are you ready to lift my belongings on to the gig and take me
into town?' she demanded.

And Godfrey said, 'Of course.'

Caroline pulled upon her skirt to compose herself and said, 'Good,' as
Godfrey carried on with, 'Soon as you pay me, you may be on your way.'

'Get up, get up!' Caroline jumped twice in her fury. 'Do as you are
bid,' then made to strike Godfrey with her closed fist. But Godfrey
seized both her wrists with so tight a grip that the missus's face con-
torted into a wince. Her mouth fell open in wordless agony as Godfrey
raised himself from the chair. As he stood higher, he bore down upon
the missus's wrists until the pressure of the pain impelled her to kneel in
front of him. As the missus, overwhelmed by him, went limp upon the
ground, Godfrey let go her wrists.

July made move toward the missus, but Godfrey shouted, 'Stop!'

He sat once more, and began playing with his fingernail, while Caroline Mortimer, quivering at his feet like a fish newly landed from the
water, slowly lifted her head, wiped her snivelling nose upon the back of
her hand, and quietly asked him, 'How much?'

No, Godfrey decreed, her house girl Marguerite could not accompany
Caroline Mortimer upon this journey into town. Why? Because Godfrey said so. And, oh yes, a point the missus must remember, her house
girl was not named Marguerite—her name was July. Three times, Godfrey made Caroline speak that name. July giggled the first time of hearing the missus commanded to say it, but then bit her lip and looked to
her feet when Godfrey insisted the missus repeat it into July's face,
louder, and then louder still.

And the gig with the chestnut horse that Caroline requested for her carriage was waved away by Godfrey, who decided that the mule and cart would do better and called Byron to bring that contraption around instead. When ordering the missus to lie herself down in the back of the cart, the missus had asked Godfrey, 'Is this necessary?' He did not reply, but the vicious eye he turned upon her, gagged her as sure as if he had clamped his hand across her mouth.

'Bring a blanket to cover the missus,' Godfrey requested of July. No, not the one from her closet, but the old one which was used in the kitchen and . . . well, get the dog off it then. The missus and her belongings were lying, hid under the stinking cloth in the cart when, in a muffled squeak of sneezing and snivelling, Caroline complained of extreme discomfort to Godfrey. But mounting the cart with a youthful bound, he merely bellowed on the whining white woman to hush up and remain as still and silent as death.

'Move along,' Godfrey commanded the mule. But the sleepy beast did not obey until it felt the crack of a whip upon its back. 'Move on,' Godfrey called, as the mule began to clop a slow progress away from Amity.

And if July had known then—as Godfrey, straight-backed atop the cart, slid that lumbering buggy along the path into the pink-purple mist of the morning—that she would never see Mr Godfrey again, then perhaps—oh, reader, perhaps—July may have raised her hand to wave him goodbye.

CHAPTER 12

O H, WHAT A HUSH did settle upon that house. With no missus nor
massa within it the wooden planks of the floor did stretch and
yawn, as no heavy foot was about to pound them. The chairs did breathe
a sigh, for no fat-batty was about to crush them. The moats of grime that
swirled within the gleams of sunlight floated softly down to rest. And,
no longer required to look their best, the drapes at the windows
drooped.

July slid the length of the polished floor within the hall upon her
dirty apron. She had never before reached so far in one glide. She
thought to call Molly to witness this daring . . . but stopped. For with
Godfrey away, looking upon mischief other than hers, if she kept far
from the kitchen and the gaze of Molly's good eye then, at that moment,
she was free.

So. Peering upon the lid of the silver salver within the dining room,
July's nose appeared to her as big-big as a boiled ham, her pursed lips
plump as rolls of Miss Hannah's chocolate. And in the large serving
spoon she, and the whole world, was reflected upside down, then back
upon the ground in the spoon's other side. On her head, on her feet, on
her head, on her feet. And the spoon made the glasses upon the sideboard tinkle with tune when she tapped the metal upon them. The big
ones went bong and little ones sang ting. Bong, ting, ting, bong.

Those funny pictures upon the wall that the massa called maps were just like the marks that patterned the missus's white blouse after she had dribbled her tea. They were not pictures really, for there were no scolding eyes within them to follow where she walked. Unlike that portrait of the dead missus in the drawing room; she watched July all the while and did tut when July threw the missus's chair cushions upon the floor to jump from one to the other so she might feel the soft silk yield between her toes. July had to leave the room under that dead missus's scorning.

And the mirror within the bedchamber gasped when July's dark face appeared within it. Only white skin with pitiless blue eyes usually preened there. July, flouring her face with a puff of the missus's face powder, sneezed away the stink from up her nose before she ran from that peeping mirror's gaze.

If this were her house, July decided, she would not have a cupboard so tall-tall that it did not allow her to look with ease upon all the pretty plates displayed there. She had to carry a chair from across the dining room, and stand upon her tip-toe to reach the first shelf alone. She would have those pretty blue and white plates resting near at hand so that at any time she might tangle herself within the story that lay upon them—fly with those birds that soared above the tree that shaded the house, that sat near the bridge, that spanned the river, that carried the boat. July, sipping the air from one of the cups, stuck out her little finger, just as white people did when they tipped that heavenly porcelain to their skinny lips.

But oh, July was exhausted—all this freedom did tire her out. Landing herself upon her missus's daybed she cried, 'Marguerite, come fetch me some tea.' Her voice, running around the room, found no one to obey the order. 'Marguerite, where is my tea?' Still no one came. She sighed. Oh huff, oh puff—what a difficult life it is to be a white lady upon this island.

Then, as she rested, quite forlorn, she heard, 'Ah, Miss July,' cough, cough, 'greetings.'

She nearly bit the birds off the fancy cup for Nimrod startled her so. Her little finger was still raised as Nimrod, grinning, carried on saying, 'What you doing there, Miss July?'

Nimrod's white waistcoat was smeared with something green, while his trousers carried sooty prints from his hands. And this man's legs were bowed so July could still see the closed door behind him as he stood before her. His few-few-tooth-grin tried to muster some sort of charm, but was hindered—for while his one eye looked firm upon her face, the other roamed up and down her body and everywhere it pleased. But still, it was a freeman who stood over her, seeming ready to gobble her up. July put down the cup and, looking firmly upon the eye that needed to be taught to stare, said, 'Bring me some tea and be quick.' Nimrod, scratching his head, frowned for the briefest second before those lonely teeth once more set out to enchant. Then he bowed low.

The knife, fork, spoon and blue and white plate that Nimrod laid at the end of the dining table for July were placed well enough, but still she had to punish him. For he was too slow. He was a dull and indolent nigger. She took the spoon and hit it upon his head. He yelped—oh—at the sharp pain, then promised her he would do better. Yet he did not pull out the chair far enough for her to sit, nor push it in close enough for her to eat.

'You are a very stupid nigger and I will see you whipped,' July cried.

And Nimrod cringed, 'Sorry, missus,' before her.

The orange upon the plate was not peeled. 'How am I to eat this?' July asked him. As Nimrod leant forward to splice the fruit with a knife, July hit him once more upon the head with her spoon. 'You are too close to me, nigger,' she told him. And, as he jumped back from her, she yelled, 'What about this fruit? Am I to peel it myself?' When he leaned over to attempt a second splice, she slapped him about the ear. 'Are you disobeying me?' she asked him.

'No missus,' he said, breathless.

'How dare you speak to me while I am at my table,' she said, before striking him again with her spoon.

The glass Nimrod filled with red wine overflowed, the dark-plum contents dribbling upon the table. 'Be careful, nigger, that is our finest wine,' July was forced to yell.

Nimrod fell to his knees before her pleading, 'No beat me, missus, no beat me.'

'But I must,' July said, slapping his head, 'or you will never learn.' Her fingers, still sticky from the orange, wrapped the stem of the glass, then lifted it to her thirsty mouth. She gulped two mouthfuls before the pungency made her splutter and cough. It was disgusting. She had never tasted anything so renk. 'Are you poisoning me, nigger?' July said.

Nimrod's fearful face was all July could see through her watering eyes. She coughed again and again and again. But then the wine gradually soothed to a warmth at her throat. She licked the sticky drops from her lips. Then took another sip that tasted a little sweeter. And then another. Until Nimrod, inclining his head, asked her if she would like him to pour her some more.

And soon July had the urge to tickle Nimrod under his chin. She leaned to grab his little beard so she might feel those spiky hairs, but her elbow slipped from the table—her hand clutching nothing. This was very, very, very, funny to her. So funny that her wriggling and giggling slipped her from the chair to land her upon the ground. And suddenly all was dark, for her head kerchief had fallen across her eyes.

Under the table was as gloomy as a stormy sky. 'Come, put me back,' July cried out, for she did not have the strength to lift herself from the floor. She was stuck to it. As Nimrod caught her around the chest to raise her, she said, 'Bring me more wine, nigger.' And as he sat her back upon the chair, she made grab again for his chin. But missed. He handed her the wine glass, which swayed until the sweet and precious wine did spill wet upon her skirt.

'Is me pretty, Mr Nimrod?' she asked as he took the glass to fill it again. He did not answer which was so, so, so vexing to her. This man was fussing—he was around her this way, he was around her that way. He was making her dizzy. 'Sit, sit, Mr Nimrod. Sit still so me can know your answer,' she said. And Nimrod, not sitting as she commanded but fretting still with something, called out that she was prettier than any white woman he knew.

'Prettier than Miss Clara?'

'Miss Clara. Cha. You is prettier than Miss Clara,' came a reply from across the room. Which was very, very, very pleasing to July because Miss Clara was not dark like she and so she was pretty. Oh yes, Miss Clara was fine.

And Nimrod had plenty women in town, for Miss Hannah did talk of them, but only when Nimrod was nowhere near. One, a sour-faced woman, owned a house that had little bow-legged pickney everywhere, Miss Hannah said.

'Mr Nimrod, how many pickney you have?' July called out to him.

He was in the room but she could not see him. But she felt the breath he blew out on the back of her neck for he was behind her, holding up more wine. 'Tell me,' she said. But he just sucked long upon his teeth and began speaking about . . . he was speaking about a pony. A pony. A Shettlewood pony. His Shettlewood pony. Nimrod was speaking of his Shettlewood pony. Not even white people can own such a fine beast, he said. And he looked so serious, staring his obedient eye upon July while the other gazing upon her chest looked so comical. July could not help but giggle. And her nose did run with snot. So she wiped it upon her skirt. And July wanted to ask if she might get a ride off him—the pony. She opened her mouth to ask, but forgot what she was to say, for Nimrod said that if she was his woman she could come and visit him in town. Which was very, very, very funny, yet July could not remember why.

And Nimrod said that he would talk to her massa about making her free because he was an important black man in town, a freeman. And again he mentioned the pony. Which reminded July of a song she sang that Miss Rose had taught her about a pony. It went la, la, la, de dum, de dum. No. It went de dum, de dum, la, la. Was he holding her hand? Did Nimrod have her hand in his? They were running through the house and she could not keep up, for the walls were moving in and out.

But the bed was cold and soft. She did fall upon it and wish to sleep. But. But. It was the massa's room. The massa's big-big bed. No, no, no, the massa would not like her in his bed. He hated the smell of niggers.

The massa would have her flogged. 'Massa no like us in his bed,' July told Nimrod.

And Nimrod said, 'There be no white bakkra here—we don' chase them from this island. Black man gon' rule now.' And the way he looked upon her with a sly eye was so, so, so funny.

The pillows were soft, but when July closed her eyes she began to fly. Up to the ceiling she went, then soaring down, swerving swiftly, then swooping around. 'Me flyin' in the room, Mr Nimrod. Me a bird.' Only when she opened her eyes was she back upon the bed.

And there was Nimrod, resting upon one elbow saying, 'But you is very handsome, Miss July.'

This did make her chest jump with a hiccup before she said, 'You wan' marry me, Mr Nimrod?' And his look was so serious that she could do nothing but laugh, especially when Nimrod leaned over her to press his lips upon hers.

July was not woken by Nimrod snoring his foul breath into her face. Nor by the constant bucking of the cloven-hoofed donkey that was surely trapped within her head and butted and butted and butted her skull for release. No. It was the massa, John Howarth's, voice shouting, 'Oh, Caroline, leave me alone, for pity's sake. You're back now. What more is there to it?' that startled July awake.

A feather pillow under her head, morning sunlight through shutters, a blue bowl upon a nightstand, a clock, a rug, a chest with drawers—she was still lying, trespassing, within the massa's bed! She parted her lips to call Nimrod awake, but her mouth was as dry as a flour barrel. 'Mr Nimrod,' she croaked, for her voice had a devil's gruffness. She had to shake him.

Rudely roused, his two eyes fixed her with an ill-tempered glare before he listened and heard all at one time. Then, moving fleet as a winged being, those two trespassers leaped from the bed and scurried beneath it, just as the massa flung open the door to the room yelling,

'Caroline, please, please, have you any idea of the seriousness of what is happening here. Have you? Oh ... oh ... oh ... Shut up,' then slammed the door behind him.

Two corpses could not have lain as still as Nimrod and July beneath that bed. While the massa paced the room from this side to that—his boots shedding mud across the floor, then pounding it to dust as he went back and forth, back and forth—they lay lifeless, yet keen as hunted runaways.

All the while, the massa was mumbling a lamentation of garbled words. This droning, sometimes punctured by howls of, 'It's intolerable,' or 'How could they?' went on and on and on. July was too feared to gaze upon Nimrod when the massa suddenly stopped with his pacing, lest she detect some fright within Nimrod's eyes at this tricky situation. The massa scraped the legs of a chair along the floor, then sat down heavily upon it, just in front of them. And Nimrod, with an almost imperceptible movement of his shoulder, managed to convey that he did not understand what the massa was doing.

Trapped within this stifling quiet, July began to fret—how long would they have to stay hid? She needed to piss water. But the massa remained still. The blazing, striped shadow from the sunlit shutters inched its way across the floor toward them. And still the massa sat—his breath sometimes heavy and weighted with sighs, sometimes shallow and quick, as if he were being chased.

A gecko scrambled over both Nimrod and July's head. And still the massa sat. He moved his left foot a little, then he crossed one leg over the other before parting them to sit astride again. The gecko, returning, scrambled back the other way across them. And still the massa sat. And he sat.

July began to wriggle. She needed to stretch her limbs, to find air that was not heavy with the stench of Nimrod's breath. She needed a little moisture for her parched mouth. But Nimrod, laying a hand upon her shoulder, held her firm. And their eyes, finally meeting in the anxious gloom of that cave below the bed asked each other silently, What is he doing? When can we go?

Then the massa's mumbling began again. He was fiddling with something. There was the sound of a click and the scrape of a fingernail upon
wood. Suddenly there was a flash-bang! so loud, so bright that Nimrod
and July, jolted by the burst of it, both struck their heads upon the bed's
underside.

A shot! It was a shot! And the massa, felled like a pole-axed steer, clat-
tered on to the floor. His head struck the ground an arm's length from
where July and Nimrod hid. Dirty smoke billowed from his open
mouth. His eyes were wide and staring upon them with grim shock, as
if he had just discovered them concealed there. But he had not. For a
thick spout of blood that sprang from the back of his head spilled down
his blackened face and across the floor.

CHAPTER 13

⁓

RUN! RUN! GET FAR from here. Trouble! White man's trouble! Flee! But there was no time. For Caroline Mortimer was already within the doorway—her face pallid, her mouth slack, her breath stopped. Trapped lying beneath the bed, Nimrod's limbs twitched with phantom running, and a fretful July still needed to piss water.

Seeing her brother lying upon the floor, Caroline decided to believe him drunk; after all it would not have been the first time. The overturned chair, the unmistakable clap of a pistol firing (for she now knew that sound well) would, she thought, have some simple explanation; as would that grey drift of gun-smoke that dimmed the room. 'John,' she said, almost gaily, 'what has happened?'

But then Tam Dewar entered in upon the scene. He pushed roughly past her, then dropped to his knees next to her brother and turned his prone body over. He leaned his ear to her brother's chest before prising the spent pistol from between his fingers. It was only when the overseer, taking her brother's head within his hands, stared aghast at the grievous lesion—the gory blood-black crater that was once the back of his head—that Caroline Mortimer's innocent fancy vanished. Her legs went limp beneath her. She staggered across the room to land with a hefty fall upon the bed. She did not hear the overseer declare her brother dead for she was too busy screaming, 'Bring the doctor! Someone, someone run for the physic! Marguerite, quickly! Marguerite! Where is Marguerite? She must bring the doctor. Marguerite!'

Molly, arriving, took in the circumstance faster than the missus did with her two good eyes. 'The massa be shot,' Molly shouted. While Byron, eyeballs gawping like a whistling frog's, ran in-and-out, in-and-out the room, proclaiming, 'Massa dead, massa dead.' Which brought Florence and Lucy to the doorway. 'Dead, dead, him is no more,' they relayed over their shoulder for who knows who to carry it upon the next breath. It was Patience who caught the blare of that fierce chat-chat. She rushed in upon the room, demanding loudly, 'Massa John? Is Massa John dead? Dead you say, Massa John?'

'Stop your gawking,' Caroline exclaimed, 'and bring the doctor.'

The dog growled wild at the overseer bent fiddling over the massa's body. And, Molly, smirking unmistakably with the excitement of it all said, 'Lord, how him head mash up, missus. It mash up.'

'Shut up! Just hold your tongue, the lot of you,' Tam Dewar blasted upon the air. He stamped his foot, lunging at the dog until the hound turned tail. He grabbed Molly by the scruff and threw her at the doorway. She landed, stunned, against the frame. Patience, he pushed, punched, and poked, toward the door. She stumbled over Molly and both scrabbled from the room on all fours. He landed his boot upon our little Byron's backside with so hard a kick that the boy was lifted from the floor by it and cried for several hours after. He showed his fist to Florence and Lucy, for they stood too far for him to reach with a blow. With the room now purged of negroes, he shut the door behind them with an almighty slam.

July, firmly pinned by the droop of her missus's backside as it squashed the bed down finally had to allow her piss to soak her. While Nimrod, with no sound, nor movement, without taking breath nor making gesture, resolutely commanded July not to reveal herself but to stay . . . stay still . . . stay-oh-so-still.

'He is dead, Mrs Mortimer.' Even as the overseer lifted his two thick palms to Caroline, which were marbled with her brother's blood, she still asked feebly, 'Are you sure?'

'Aye. He has shot himself.'

'He has what?'

'He has taken his own life, Mrs Mortimer.'

'His own life, you say?'

'Aye.'

'Are you saying he inflicted this upon himself?'

'Exactly.'

'Nonsense. My brother would never do such an unchristian thing, Mr Dewar,' Caroline informed him. The room reeked like a butcher's shop—there was just not enough air within it. Was it the overseer that stank so? Caroline got up to move toward the window. She had to, or she would faint, she knew it. But his noxiousness trailed her.

'Look, look, see for yourself,' the overseer said. It was with his boot that he flipped over the head of her brother so she might have a clearer view of that dreadful wound. 'The shot went in here,' he carried on, as if her brother were some freshly slaughtered cattle, 'and came out here.'

'Don't touch him. How dare you touch him? Leave him alone.' Caroline rushed to stand guard over her brother's body.

'He put the pistol to his mouth,' the overseer said.

'He would never do such a thing, he would never. It is against God.'

'It's the best way to do it, and he'd know it,' the overseer told her.

Caroline was determined to think carefully upon this situation. Her brother was dead. Shot. Perhaps by his own hand. By his own hand! Oh God! She needed to deliver to that ghastly overseer the action that she required him to take. For it was he that was in her brother's employ and not the other way about. But first, as his tender, loving, bereaved sister, she would clasp her brother tightly to her sorrowful breast, wipe his pitiful brow, and deliver a kiss of sweet parting upon his cheek. She would prepare his melancholy soul for that everlasting hereafter by washing his face with her grieving tears. But, oh Lord, he was a bloody sight. Caroline Mortimer could not bring herself to gaze upon his gruesome corpse, let alone embrace it.

'He's left you with a pretty mess,' the overseer said. And the bald truth of that assertion buckled her knees until Caroline fell back upon the bed sobbing.

Perhaps if Tam Dewar had been a gentleman—her and her brother's equal, and not just the son of some lowborn Scots fisherman who, in England, she would not even deign to look upon, let alone solicit an opinion from—Caroline Mortimer may have wished to ask of the overseer why he believed her brother was driven to perform such a profane act as taking his own life. And, perhaps, if Tam Dewar were a person for whom despair and the sorrow of death were still disquieting intruders upon his soul, and not the stuff of his daily bread, then he may have thought it an act of Christian solace to disclose to Caroline Mortimer what he and her brother had witnessed after they had left her table to join their militia.

He may have started by recalling for her the uneasy ride through town that he and John Howarth took as they rode to join their regiment, that was barracked up near Hope Hill. There were no higglers upon the road. No black faces calling boisterous for these white massas to buy their Guinea and Indian corn, their nuts, their sweet cakes, their bundles of firewood, piles of cane, their colourful ribbons or coarse pots, their jack fruits, sweet potatoes, their yams, berries and beans. Not even that curious old woman, who sat with a turkey atop her head upon the corner of Main Street, was to be seen that day, and she was always found wilting beneath her prize bird, no matter what the season.

The negro blacksmith upon the parade near the coopers—him who kept three slaves himself—he was all shut up with 'gone to visit me sister' chalked upon his door. That expensive preserve shop, the dry goods store, and every single laundry hut in town were deserted. No food was steaming upon fires along the wharf; no groups of raucous negroes chatting and chewing over those victuals there.

The courthouse saw no restless crowds jostling, anxious, around its doors, nor heard the sharp calls from the buying and selling of the luckless human harvest that was usually being exchanged. There were no ragged children tormenting dogs and chickens about the square. No white people, in their straw hats and bonnets, walked along the road, stepping their fine shoes carefully out of the harm of a puddle of water or dung, while holding their noses away from niggers. Their house slaves were not to be found haggling for them, or being scolded for the dear price as they tripped at their owners' heels.

Even those three coloured girls who worked in the boarding house along King Street, were not at their open window laughing at the ugly hats that went by them.

All this absence muffled this usually bustling town with a disquieting gloom that the overseer—and perhaps even John Howarth—thought draped around those elegant streets heavy as a black velvet cloak.

———

They gathered in from all about the district, from plantations, estates, pens, churches and town, the regulars of the Trelawny Interior Militia under the practised command of Captain Shearer. These white men's pistols were cocked, and their powder was plentiful and dry. Rebel slaves were firing the trash houses up upon Castle Estate. Be warned, they were told, there are a lot of them—forty, fifty, reports were unclear. One or two hundred, someone said, armed with stolen muskets, fowling pieces, carbines, pistols, and shouting, 'War! War! War!' Some say these nigger rebels had come from Montego Bay, where they had taken a whole barracks—seized the arms. Nonsense, what piffle, Captain Shearer said, for negroes were never so shrewd.

The militia's orders were to punish the guilty—all principals and chiefs in these burnings—without mercy. For those who surrender—if they yield themselves up and beg, beg, beg, then, perhaps, they will receive a gracious pardon from his majesty for their crimes. But certain death to all those blacks who foolishly hold out.

The forty white men of the Trelawny Interior Militia rode on to the level land of the Castle Estate in one phalanx. Among them were planters whose families hailed from Canterbury, Bloomsbury and Camden Town; attorneys who talked of home in Bristol, Whitstable and Fife; overseers from Galway, Great Yarmouth, Cardiff and Bow; ministers and curates whose families fretted for them in Exeter and Norwich, St Austell and Sheffield; bookkeepers who had just run from the mills of Lancashire, the mines of Glamorgan and an asylum in Glasgow. All advanced to the vicinity of the plantation works with their jaws jutting with resolve.

Soon they came upon intense flames—a trash house was being devoured with the swiftness of a dragon licking tinder. The bitter smoke from the crackling dry cane leaves blew dense about them, choking at their throats and smarting their eyes blind. Suddenly, from their left and from behind, came bursts of discharging musket fire. Ping, ping. This was not forty negroes, ping, not fifty. Ping, ping, ping. This was a thousand. Maybe ten thousand!

The Trelawny Interior Militia were surrounded—caught stumbling and trapped. These white men, charged to protect property, women, children and loved ones, were men of the land—oh, how the truth of this rumbled through the guts of every man there—they were not soldiers, they were not redcoats. Hold your nerve, Captain Shearer had to order of them. Hold your nerve!

But then the light from that fire spread a golden daylight across that black night, as if the sun had just risen. And there, revealed in their pitiful hiding places, were the few old negroes who had set the fire. Those slaves were suddenly exposed, clear as players in limelight, as they crouched to aim their old cutlasses and fowling pieces.

The noise of the thousand muskets firing was the bamboo burning—the air inside the grass all around them popping with the heat. By gad, it sounded to them like gunfire. But now those revolting niggers were shown to be clutching rusting, squeaking, wood-rotten, useless weapons—last-century stuff that needed an hour to re-arm—that those sneak-thieves had hidden in their roofs or under their huts for years. Oh, what a relief. It was not these ragged rebels that were terrifying the gallant Trelawny Interior Militia—it was popping bamboo!

Bang, bang, bang—and those few old slaves fell dead upon the ground.

Bang, bang, bang, silhouetted against the light, they were as easy to shoot as pots off a fence. Some slaves ran from their hiding places to lose themselves in long grasses, but were chased and felled like squealing wild boars. Others came grovelling to kiss the feet of any militia man who would spare them. Shivering, their eyes wide with fright, stinking of shit, and protesting that they were forced at the point of a nigger's bayonet to enjoin this fight, they were put to work dousing their fire with pails of dirt.

But then they were shot anyway, those gutless black Moses, Cupids and Ebo Jims, for who would want them back after this? When slaves turn wild, they are useless to all but worms. And there would be compensation for the owners for the loss of their property.

The bamboo still smouldered lively, but those rebel slaves upon Castle Estate were quelled. And how they strutted—those gallant white men of Trelawny Interior Militia—not soldiers, not redcoats, but, oh, a force to be feared upon this island.

It was later, as John Howarth and Tam Dewar made their way back to the barracks for regrouping, that they found themselves split from the main body of their militia, riding the town road with two other men who were gossiping this Castle Estate episode into quite a heroic tale to tell. At the bend in the road, where it narrows to barely a path, they heard a woman screaming. A white woman. Most white men upon this island believe the sound to be quite different from that of a negress; the cry is softer, higher, and has a more melodious cadence, even when pitched with the same terror. Now the holler of a negress could go unmarked, but a white woman screaming must be investigated by the militia. So they turned off the road with some haste.

Soon, there before them, in front of a small house with a neat garden, was the white woman. A red-headed woman, whom Howarth often saw about the parish—indeed, a woman who so reminded him of his late wife Agnes, that on two occasions he was forced to acknowledge her when she caught him staring upon her.

Now she was raging, hollering, and jumping. This woman at once clutched at her loose and tangled hair, then fell to her knees, banging upon the ground with her fists, before she was back upon her feet, arms outstretched with imploring. In front of her, sitting tied to a chair, motionless, limp and slumping to one side, was her husband—the Baptist missionary of this parish—Mr Bushell. Usually quite blond and pink of face, now this man's skinny naked body was black, for he was daubed with slimy tar. And the blood-dirty feathers that quivered over him, from his head to his toe, made him appear, at swift glance, like a freshly flayed negro.

The missionary's two small sons, dressed in their stripey bed-shirts, clung together in the open doorway of their house, too astonished at the sight before them to cry. For encircling this scene upon horse-back were, it appeared, nine badly dressed, burly white women. And one of these women was attempting, with breathless panting, to lasso the seated man. The boys gasped every time the looping rope soared down to strike their father like a lash, before being pulled back for another clumsy attempt to capture him. When, at last, the rope finally caught, it tightened to topple the missionary, who thumped to the ground in a cloud of grit and dirt.

Howarth dismounted his horse. He ran to the missionary and pulled off the binding rope before he was dragged along the ground by it. 'What's happening here?' Howarth yelled at the female riders.

Yet it was the bass tones of a male voice that answered him saying, 'Leave alone, Howarth. He deserves this. All this slave trouble about us is his doing. We're teaching him a lesson. This is our affair.'

The missionary's wife fell to her knees in a faint. Suddenly Howarth, peering from one assailant to the other, realised that they were not women atop those horses, but white men bundled into skirts, bodices and bonnets for tricky disguise.

Now, by the entrance to Belvedere Pen, John Howarth and his companions had earlier that day passed by the putrefying bodies of sixteen dead slaves. 'The stench was discernible from quite a distance—near the actual spot it was almost overpowering,' one of his compatriots would later report.

These slaughtered slaves, shot by another militia for good reason, as would also be established, had been rotting in the sun for a few days. The carrion crows, in a squabbling tempest of black wings, were wrenching at sinews, pecking at crusty drying entrails, and cleaning a leg bone to bright white as John Howarth came upon the corpses. He shooed the birds. Bucked his horse into the affray until the crows soared like a thunder into the air; which just left a filthy shroud of flies and maggots feasting. But the discussion among this militia group of who should bury these dead negroes ended with John Howarth shrugging away the task as unnecessary. They rode on, leaving the crows to return, greedy, to the carnage.

Half-way between the town and Shepperton Pen, they had come upon a naked slave woman, tied to a coconut tree by her arms. As her feet could not reach the floor, she was slowly spinning in the sun's heat. Dangling juicy as roasting meat upon a spit, crows kept pecking at her to test her as food. As she spat and kicked to shoo them, she would start to spin faster. She had been beaten before being tied up—with a stick or a short riding whip—for her skin, dusty and black, was in places torn off, creating a speckled pattern that appeared like dappled sunlight upon her. John Howarth frowned to himself, briefly, as he pondered upon the crime this negro must have committed for her to be given such a public disciplining. And then he rode on.

John Howarth did shake his head in mild reproach at the punishment of a negro boy they came across. The small boy had been running with messages to rebel slaves—a crime—there was no doubt in Howarth's mind upon that. But the boy was then sealed into a barrel which was roughly pierced with over twenty-five long nails hammered into the shell. The boy, still trapped within that spiky cask, was then rolled down a hill. Howarth believed this reprimand to be a little . . . wanton.

But, upon that day, the act that made John Howarth question his God for allowing such barbarity within a world he knew, and gasp at the cruelty of his fellows, while a righteous anger fermented within his belly until he felt sickened, ashamed and disgusted, was the sight before him now: nine white men dressed as women.

To John Howarth's mind, those ugly-beauties atop their horses were what sullied the good name of Jamaican planters. Using the frippery of the fairer sex as diabolic disguise branded them all merciless, callous and depraved. Nine gentlemen dressed in a clutter of bonnets and petticoats urged to humiliate, torment and torture a fellow white man before his children, before his wife. Tarring and feathering a man of God. A missionary. A Christian soul! To John Howarth this was cruelty beyond all reason. This was shame.

'Stop this at once,' he bellowed at that ludicrous group, 'this is savagery.'

'Leave alone, Howarth. Go about your business,' came in petulant reply. And although John Howarth was staring upon a fat strumpet crowned in a blue turban with a feather that dangled like a dilberry from it, he at once identified the voice; it was that boring old attorney from Unity; he who had been supping at his table not a few days before.

'Mr Barrett. I know you and this is not the act of gentlemen. No matter what this man has started, he does not deserve this,' Howarth yelled at him.

Suddenly there was great commotion 'Whose side are you on, Howarth? . . . Don't give names away . . . On your way, on your way,' was shouted from that bevy of jack-whores.

And in those angry faces Howarth saw George Sadler—that idiot from Windsor Hall—wearing a red stole and a gypsy bonnet. Had all left his table to raid their wives' closets for this odious masquerade? 'Have you no pity? Have you no shame? This is a man of God,' Howarth pleaded with them.

Someone spat upon the ground to his left before saying, 'This man is no better than a nigger.' And Howarth leaped up to grab that man from his horse. Pulling fierce upon the rider's leg, the man in a jumble of skirts and ripping cloth, tumbled to the ground.

In the scuffle that ensued, Howarth grasped a matted scrap of a wig from this man's head, and the bookkeeper from a neighbouring plantation was revealed, staring quite sheepish upon him. Until, that is, he lunged to punch the most painful blow upon Howarth's face. Howarth reeled back, holding his nose to catch the spout of blood that gushed from it as if tipped from a jug. Another man who had dismounted, held up his skirts, dainty as a madam, before kicking Howarth. 'Leave us, we're taking care of this. It is all deserved,' was yelled, while a pistol was waved in Howarth's face.

It was Tam Dewar who had to pull John Howarth out of this affray. Like a small boy snatched from some tomfoolery by a nursemaid, he felt his overseer lift him from the ground and carry him to his horse. Still cursing and swearing those nine gentlemen as whore-sons, John Howarth was led away.

And the dazed wife of Mr Bushell, seeing them leaving while her husband still lay in a pose of death wailed, 'Come back. Mr Howarth, come back. Help him. Help us, please.' But Howarth, forced to sit awkward upon his horse so his bloody nose could be held high, had to just ride on.

~~~

But of course, Tam Dewar said nothing of these incidents to Caroline Mortimer. So, quite blind to what John Howarth had encountered during those few bloody days in that Baptist War, Caroline could find no good reason why her brother should be in any fatal distress. Indeed, he had seemed perfectly at ease to her when he had found her.

She had been abandoned—like a stray dog!—upon the wharf in town by Godfrey, who, having pointed out the ship she must board, ran off to who knows where. Her brother, discovering her left quite alone during this difficult time, was a little agitated perhaps. For when she commenced recalling for him, in some detail, what had befallen her when left at the mercy of the house slaves, he had placed his hands over his ears and begged her to be quiet. But he had been doing that to her since she was a girl.

No. Caroline had seen her brother so downcast that he would not get from his bed for weeks. But of late, he had begun to bless each sunrise— she was sure of it. So when Tam Dewar, with some temerity, began to say, 'If your brother has taken his own life . . .' she replied, 'But he has not, Mr Dewar.' When he persisted with, 'But if he has . . .' she quite sternly and finally, she believed, ended the exchange by declaring, 'But he has not!'

For Caroline Mortimer surely knew that as it was a crime as well as a sin for her brother to take his own life, she could stand to lose everything they held upon this island. Why, her neighbour when she still lived in London, Jane Glover, had lost her home, her prospects, and every penny that she ever had to squander upon those showy silk caps of hers, when her father was found dangling from a beam in their house. Jane Glover had everything seized! It was the talk of Islington for several months. Her father's body was even refused a burial next to his wife's at St Mary's churchyard. Caroline could still recall the look of anguish upon Jane Glover's face as she was driven away in a cart to be taken in by a cousin and used as a common housemaid!

⁓

Now, reader, no matter what you may have heard Caroline Mortimer declare as the next act in this story, for she gave her own fulsome account of that day to the militia, several magistrates, lawyers, and indeed anyone who ever graced her dinner table, this that I am about to tell you, is the truth of what occurred next within that bed chamber. Do not doubt me, for remember my witness still lies beneath the bed.

When, after demanding—for what was the fifth time—that Tam Dewar bring the doctor to administer to her brother, the overseer yelled upon Caroline, 'Dear God, woman, look at the man, he has no head!' Upon saying that, he knelt down in an agitated state to demonstrate, once more, the lack of skull upon her brother's person.

Now, was it July gulping to swallow or inhaling a fearful breath? Did Nimrod twitch his shoulder or waggle his stiff foot? Perhaps, with this hateful overseer, it was just the scent of niggers. Who is now to know? But something drew Tam Dewar's eye away from the massa's corpse to glimpse into the gloom under the bed. And there he saw two wide eyes—one staring back on him and one not.

He had the back of Nimrod's neck grasped within his hand before Nimrod had even realised he had been discovered. 'Out,' Dewar cried, as he wrenched Nimrod roughly from the hide-hole.

Caroline Mortimer, seeing this negro pulled from under the bed like a wriggling whelk from out a shell, at first inhaled so startled a breath that she sounded to be gasping her last. But then, with more art than any player upon a stage, she amended her mood to cry, 'Ah, it was he who shot him. I saw him. I saw him.' And here her story was made.

July, still lying unseen beneath the bed, watched as the overseer struggled with Nimrod, who squirmed and writhed within his grasp. Suddenly, in an effort to still him, Dewar punched Nimrod hard within the face with the resonance of a mallet striking wood. Nimrod's eyes rolled like a drunkard's, as a slobber of saliva and blood spewed from his mouth. Then he wilted limp as a doll. And July listened as the missus firmed her story.

'I saw him he . . . he . . . walked up to John who was sitting . . .' July saw the missus right the chair, seat herself upon it, and bounce her slippered feet, excited as she carried on, 'He crept up behind my brother and he shot him, here.' The missus patted the back of her head several times, until the overseer said, 'No. You'll need to get your story straight.' And the missus replied, 'It is not a story, Mr Dewar, it is the truth.'

'The truth, madam,' the overseer began, 'is that he shot himself. I know it and so do you.'

'I will not have you speak to me in this way . . .' the missus said as the overseer, not heeding her words, carried on.

'But you can have a culprit. You can save your skin and your plantation, but only if you tell the story as I say it.'

July heard the missus gasp as the overseer insisted, 'Now, listen here, woman. Your brother was shot from the front. This nigger shot your brother from the front. Any man who has ever held a pistol will see that in the wound.'

And she heard her missus say quietly, 'Of course, from the front. I meant from the front.'

'In the mouth. The nigger shot him in the mouth.'

'Yes, in the mouth, Mr Dewar.'

And July heard the overseer say, 'And you shot the culprit as he tried to escape.'

'Me!'

'Yes, you. With your silly, wee, pearly handled pistol. You, you shot him! I was nay here until after you killed this nigger.'

And the missus gasped, 'Killed!'

July was sure that soon Nimrod would press his feet firmly to the floor to stand proud in front of these white people. He would look them both within the eye while declaring—with a cough, cough—that he had heard enough of this fanciful tale, before firmly informing them that he was not a nigger to be used with as they pleased. No. He was freeman. Nimrod Freeman. Or Mr Freeman to them.

But instead, Nimrod stood shamefully silent upon the spot, trembling, shaky-shaky, as a cock-eyed buffoon. When the overseer arming his pistol shouted, 'Run for the door, nigger,' Nimrod let out a weeping howl and clasped himself, craven, to the overseer's knees. Struggling to kick off this clinging negro, the overseer, with swelling temper, hit Nimrod hard about the head with the butt of his pistol. Nimrod collapsed to the floor, gashed and bloody. The overseer then placed his pistol at the back of Nimrod's neck. But before he squeezed his finger to trip the hammer and fire the ball, he said to the missus, 'Remember, you shot this nigger as he was making his escape.'

It was with cold panic that the missus pleaded, 'But, but, but don't kill him.'

'Why not?' asked the overseer.

And, looking about herself as if the answer floated somewhere around this island if only she could see it, the missus replied, 'He hasn't finished my garden yet.'

The overseer, at first staring upon the missus as if there might be some wisdom lying hidden within her statement, soon gave a scornful laugh as his eyes rolled to the heavens. He then aimed his pistol once more.

And, before thought or reason could cower July, she had bolted from under the bed, over the body of the dead massa, to charge headlong at the overseer—crashing into him with her whole being, pitching him to the floor with a fearsome force. There was a dazzling flash-bang as the shot he had prepared for Nimrod's head blasted off into the ceiling. The missus screamed when, suddenly, the debris of wood, slate, stones and bits of living things dislodged by the pistol fire, came pelting down upon her from on-high. Cringing away from this onslaught, the missus tripped over the overseer to land heavily on top of him. Under her ample crushing, all breath belched from out the overseer like wind from sturdy bellows.

July had expected her punishment to begin without delay. But then, gaping upon this confusion, she realised that the tangle of missus and overseer she had just tied, would take a little longer to loosen. So July grabbed Nimrod about his chest, dragged him to the door, opened it and lifted the weakling through. And after she slammed that bedroom door behind her, she crafty turned the key within the lock.

⌒⌒

Nimrod was a weight to carry. Oh how July struggled with him upon that day, to get him as far from the great house as she could. She dragged him, she pulled him, she tugged at him, to stand upon his feet. With panting breath she pleaded, 'Oh, Mr Nimrod, please walk. Step, Mr Nimrod, step.' And once, maybe twice, this man placed one foot before the other in an effort to stumble. But mostly he clung about her neck, heavy as a sack of logs. Yet July hauled him across the garden, on to the path, and through a field of long grasses, until she smelt the wood-smoke of the fires from the negro village and heard pickneys calling loud in a game.

Soon she was staring upon two woman field negroes who were pounding at corn within a mortar. They stopped in their work to gape upon her. July let Nimrod finally collapse to the floor as one of the women said, 'She be from the big house,' while the other with a wary eye, called over her shoulder, 'Come quick-quick! Come quick!' A small crowd soon gathered, all staring upon July—that lordly house slave come to trick them by trespassing-in on their place with this bleeding and bust-up man.

Then an old woman small enough to peer eye-to-eye at a dog, stepped forward to ask, 'You be Miss Kitty's pickney?' July's legs buckled beneath her at the sound of her mama's name. This woman still knew her mama, yet her mama was sold away by the missus. July landed hard upon her knees.

'Me be Miss Rose—you know me?' the woman asked, before turning to the crowd to tell them, 'This be Miss Kitty's pickney, Miss July. Me did pull her with me own hand 'pon this world. Miss Kitty's pickney—Miss Kitty's pickney has come home.'

Chapter 14

~

R EADER, WHAT POINT IN wasting toil on the pressing of petticoats? For a petticoat be a garment for none to see. A little crease upon the lace or ties will never speak of idleness in the wearer, for none will know except the wearer themselves. However, my son's wife, Lillian, is very particular upon the matter of petticoats.

While my son and I were sitting peacefully this very morning—he eagerly perusing the story within the pages you have just read—Lillian started to make one fuss over her three daughters' ruckled-up and wrin-kled undergarments. Unless all petticoats within our household are pressed warm and flat, Lillian tosses at night within her bed unable to sleep; for judgement upon her character resides in that work for Lillian. But not for me.

I am sure, reader, that there be tasks round and about your own household which you likewise find tiresome: the dusting of china orna-ments upon an open shelf, the plumping of cushions, fancy needlework upon a stocking, may be your example. But before you slap this book shut in frustration at your storyteller having strayed so far from her tale, let me bring you back so you can find reason within this old woman's diversion. For it is at this point within my story, reader, that we must once more seek out Kitty. It is at this time that we must walk again within the company of that field slave that is our July's mama.

Kitty had, many years before, been persuaded by Miss Rose's tireless pestering that risking the massa's wrath by every night taking that rutted path to climb the low stone wall and hide like a jumbie in the window of the great house was not wise. 'Your pickney not sold away, Miss Kitty,' Miss Rose had said. 'She here seeing sun-up and sun-down in same sky as you and me. You wan' be lock-up in the stock for seeing that? T'ink on it, Miss Kitty, and save your pity. You might chance you pickney any season.'

And it was true. Kitty had seen July on a few occasions during the eight or so years that had passed. Whilst pressing at the window of the great house, Kitty had first spied July tethered to a table leg by a long yellow ribbon about her wrist. Then once, from a distance, she thought she had seen July struggling a basket of wet washing into the house. More recently, upon her way to Sunday market, Kitty believed she saw July waving a long stick to chase some chickens home. But Kitty had never, since that day when she last stroked her daughter's cheek with the soft purple petal of a flower, been close enough to touch, speak or trade a look with July.

Now, like your storyteller and the pressing of her petticoats, there were many jobs upon the sugar plantation named Amity that Kitty found grievous to perform. Come, the listing of tasks that she found agreeable would be a much, much, much shorter undertaking. But no work provoked such dread within Kitty's heart as the pitiful task of manuring.

Canes, once planted in the regimented holes dug for their purpose, become one of the most indulged plants in the whole of the Caribbean. They must be fed like suckling babes if they are to grow tall with their cherished sweetness. For this purpose, the droppings that splutter and fall from the backside of any stock—be it cattle or mule— are hoarded and prized as steaming treasure. For months in any year, Kitty and the whole of the first gang are required to convey this dung from backside to cane piece. And there they must spread it about at the base of the growing canes, so the plants might sup upon the fetid goodness.

Some of this mess is taken from the pen to be shovelled into baskets and slung either side of a mule. The mule then, unaware of the load it carries, trots off as happy with this weight as with any other. But the wicker dung-baskets—overflowing and spilling—that Kitty carried to the cane pieces of Dover, Virgo, or even as far as Scarlett Ponds, were borne in the way of most slave burdens, upon her head. The weight was no sufferance, for Kitty could carry much heavier, much further. Come, it is true, the smell would see our white missus faint clean away with just one sniff. But the Lord, in making the nose, fashioned a shrewd organ; although so renk that upon Kitty's first breaths the solid odour did choke her at the throat, after mighty coughing and a few strong inhalations, all the air about Kitty, be it sweet or bitter, came to smell like shit, so the offence was lost.

But for her poor tongue, there was no such accommodation. When, unwittingly, a piece would fall into her open mouth—which it did when she turned her head or a breeze blew or she struggled to catch her breath as she climbed the hill that led to Virgo—it would burn so fierce upon her tongue that she feared a hole was being bored right through it. For it was sharp as rancid lemon and did make her retch. Everything she nyam, be it food at the cane piece, or her porridge after her day's work was done, come to taste not like a repast but like . . . well, the putrid splutterings that fall from the backside of a mule.

And if this dung did find its way into her eyes—for the brown juice from this waste matter did ooze through the weave of the basket to slip-slide all down Kitty's face—then, oh! its sting did well up such tears as to leave her blind.

At the day's end, Kitty would squat in the river—the water rippling over her shoulders, around her neck—and she would scrub with leaves of Bald-bush to rid this muck from her skin. But, reader, you see the dung did cling, so the stream would glide over her as if it be running across the pelt of some water rat. And so was true of the few garments she possessed; no pounding in the river seemed to rid them of their stink. At Sunday market none would come close enough to study Kitty's sweet cassava roots or limes, excepting the flies. For they encircled her as a mist—tickling to explore up her nose, in her mouth, upon the moisture in her eyes and down her ears. Come, at manuring, Kitty did think on herself as shit walking tall.

And so it was upon this day. Kitty and her gang were returning to the village from the cane piece called Virgo in a ragged line that moved slow as lame donkeys—for Kitty had trod that two-mile route from the stock-pen to the field six times that day. As was usual, the flies did mass around her, even as she swotted the pests away with fancy flapping. The sun baking upon her back had her so drowsy that she heedless kept resting her hand upon the shoulder of Peggy, the woman who walked at her side. 'Miss Kitty, me finish with me load this day. Me caan carry you now,' her companion said many times before Kitty heard her plea.

On the lane that follows the boundary stones—just before Kitty entered in upon her village—a breeze of gossip reached her ears. Some negroes from the second gang, squatting within the yard of the bad houses, called out to Kitty that they had heard that Pitchy-Patchy had come from town. That this raggedy masquerade man—adrift from the Christmas Joncanoe—was in the mill yard, growling so as to fright all the pickney in the hope of mango being thrown.

Then, under the thatch roof of the head-man's kitchen, there was a huddle of men—two coopers were there, but the head-man was not. All were chatting upon the situation. These men told Kitty that, no, it was not Pitchy-Patchy that had fallen from the long grasses, but two persons that had escaped from this fight-for-free war-war that was raging upon this island—a very little man, who was bust-up and limping, and a young girl who stood, fiercely pleading for all about to help them. The argument among this gathering of men, so Kitty understood, was whether to chase these bad-wind strangers upon their way, or take pity upon them. However, 'Trouble, trouble, gon' come,' was all the men within this noisy quarrel could agree upon.

On the lane that leads to Kitty's home, the fires out front of the huts had been left unattended; for all who lived there were at the mill yard. They had gone to gawp their big-eye upon the ghoulish sight of those blow-in visitors. Kitty had to shoo three hogs that had their snouts deep within their deserted pots.

Ezra, calling Kitty to chat, kept her long-long. All his talk was of the fires and the bloodshed, 'But we is good niggers,' he told Kitty over and over. 'We no strike blow for free like them did tell us we mus' do. We no sit down, Miss Kitty, we no sit down.'

By the time Kitty did reach her hut, she was too weary to worry upon all the fuss-fuss that blew about her. To squat in the river and scrub with leaves of Bald-bush was her only prayer.

But, shuffling up the lane toward her, came Miss Rose. Limping, yet still kicking nimble at the chickens within her path, Miss Rose eventually landed heavy upon the stone in front of Kitty's fire. She then caught her breath enough to whisper loud, 'Miss Kitty, your pickney is come. Miss July is come. The bad-news stranger girl with hurt man 'pon her shoulder be Miss July, all grow up. And she say massa be dead. Massa John be dead!'

Now, all knew that lavish words were as scarce to Kitty as beef in her dutchy pot, but upon hearing that her daughter, whom she had missed for so many years, had just fallen out from the long grasses—her hair picky-picky and nasty with thistle, skin clawed raw, dress slashed to a scrap and covered with mud and bush, eyes wild as a hounded beast, bearing up a lame man with a head cracked to crooked, who trembled within her grasp while she raved upon all who came too close, that the massa was dead—Kitty stood without breath or blink for so long that Miss Rose believed she had turned to stone. Miss Rose swore it—upon the good book if anyone doubted the witness she bore.

But Ezra said Kitty was felled, like someone chopped the back of her knees. That she landed her backside upon the ground so hard that every chicken around them took to flight. While Tilly—whose furious running from hut to hut saw that the words 'massa dead' were spread so far and away that slaves in London Town were soon chatting it—said Kitty started to fret, 'Me pickney, me pickney,' as soon as she heard that a quarrel was raging within the mill yard over whether to hide these 'bad-wind' strangers or tell bakkra of them.

But upon one thing these three did agree; when Kitty—smelling renk as a dung hill in the sun—left them to find July that day, she walked out with such singular purpose and so little care that she trod her bare foot upon the fire, yet was insensible to the burn of it.

Cornet Jump's house was along the route Kitty strode that evening and he was convinced that it was Kitty's passing footfall that had shaken his house to trembling. But his wife, Peggy, swore that the rumbling of the earth that had so rocked their feeble dwelling that night was started as the militia began advancing upon them. It was those white men upon horseback charging upon the negro village—ten, twenty, thirty—how many, she did not know. But the throb of those galloping horses tipped her jug of milk from off the table to shatter the pot upon the dirt floor.

It was then that Bessy burst in upon them screaming, 'Run, run, Miss Peggy. White man come. Bakkra gon' mash us!'

Peggy insisted that Bessy flew through the door of their hut with such force that it broke it back to sticks. She said the useless door was under her foot when Bessy had told her that the militia were seeking those two blow-in strangers, for they had killed the massa. Peggy remembers then rushing over the ruins of that door to grab Kitty from going to the mill yard—to turn her and get her to flee to the cane pieces with her. But Miss Kitty did shake her off so she might carry on her march to the mill.

Yet Cornet declared that his hut door was ruined when the driver, Mason Jackson, kicked it down while blowing the conch for everyone to gather in the yard; for that driver had wanted to bust down his door from first Cornet had dared to put a lock upon it.

Like a boy swirling a birch within a red ant's nest, the negro village soon erupted into furious motion. According to Giles Millar, the militia rode in amongst them with great speed. That tempest of white men galloping in upon horses besieged the dirt lanes. Flailing with whips, branches, cutlasses, they slashed from side to side, striking at anyone— man, woman, child or beast—caught fleeing within their sweep. The hooves of their rampaging horses collapsed the mud-and-stick walls of homes easy as a bite taken from a dry biscuit.

After a rattle and a crash, Mary Ellis found herself no longer hiding under the corner shelf in her hut, but helplessly choking upon debris and staring upon the moon. Everyone, Mary said, caught with no shelter to shield them, streamed on to the lanes for escape. They all ran frantic alongside the squealing hogs, flapping chickens and crazed dogs.

A fire with a large pot of scalding water was overturned by a bucking goat on to two naked children. Crying out for their mama, they slipped within the boiling liquid and were danced upon by the harried goat. And an old woman, cowering with her arms over her head, was slashed with a sword; her severed hand flew off to land, open palmed, before her.

The fires were started, so said James Richards, by a young, hatless, white man, who rode in holding a blazing, tar-tipped torch high-high. He hurled this firestick on to the thatch of James's kitchen. Whoosh! The kitchen and house were gone. Those flames then jumped to raze all the huts that lay within their greedy lick.

Dublin Hilton agreed that the rider was white and hatless, but he insisted that this bakkra used the flame from the torch to burn several houses in one galloping sweep—like this white man was lighting a row of stubble upon a cane piece.

Miss Kitty? Dublin Hilton could not remember seeing Kitty, but James Richards could. He recalls her pulling a white man from his horse; the bakkra had raised his whip to strike her, but she grabbed the thrashing hide, wheeled him in by it, then toppled him on to the ground. Not so, said Elizabeth Millar, for all was heat and smoke and black as the houses burned. Who could know Miss Kitty in that confusion? And a white man flung from his horse by a nigger? What a tall-tall telling—all would have been hanged for it.

Wilfred Park said he found Miss Kitty walking at the edge of the village, toward the mill yard, within a river of creatures; lizards, bull-frogs, beetles, spiders, cicadas, cockroaches, scorpions, snakes, snails, all seethed around her feet. Wilfred, seeing this exodus of bug-a-bugs free to creep from their hide-holes to scurry, run, hop, slide and slither away with her, asked Kitty if they were all free now—like Mr Bushell the missionary had told? But then a big stick hit him so hard upon his head that everything went black before Miss Kitty did answer him.

But Wilfred was of simple mind. According to Wilfred's neighbour, Fanny, it was not a stick that hit him, he was struck by a galloping horse. Fanny had to drag the stunned Wilfred into the shit hole to hide there while two other horses did trample over the top of them. The itch-itching of the wriggly life within the stinking pit soon had Wilfred awake. But Fanny had seen Kitty running to the mill yard in amongst the bug-a-bugs that were fleeing from the singe of flames and the burn of smoke, just as Wilfred had said. Kitty was running with her damp-ened skirt held up about her mouth, coughing and choking and spitting and gulping at the air, but determined upon her course.

Who sighted Kitty next? Samuel Lewis. He saw Kitty creeping amongst the legs of the white men's horses that were tethered in the works yard. Samuel had been seized while carrying a lighted torch (which he swore he was using to catch crayfish upon the river), and accused of setting light to the trash house. The young militia man who had tied him up, had warned him not to move or his head would be cut off. So Samuel was sitting with his back against the works wall very still indeed when he saw Kitty.

At that time not many negroes were penned there (unlike the confu-sion that was to follow within that yard), according to Anne Roberts and Betsy, who were roped together for throwing stones. The stocks were not even open, for the doctor had the key. And the militia men, afraid at being alone with flimsy-tied niggers, were yelling, 'Someone find the fucking doctor. Where is the fucking doctor?' when the blast of gunshot went off.

And that is when they first saw Kitty—for suddenly she stood up from within the legs of the horses, bold as Nanny Maroon. Those two jumpy militia pointed their shaking pistols at her fleeing back, but so intent was Kitty to get to the mill yard that she was not feared.

'Miss Kitty? She fly, oh she fly. Her feet no longer upon God's earth; me see her soar t'rough the air. Give me the book so me can place me hand upon it. Me tell you, she fly!' so said Miss Sarah.

Sarah was creeping from the mill to the works with the purpose of untying Anne and Betsy. But then she saw Tam Dewar, the overseer, riding in upon the mill yard. The strangers, 'deh nasty girl and deh fenky-fenky man,' were being held there by the driver, who ran off as soon as he saw Dewar approach.

The driver, Mason Jackson, later swore that he did not run away. He knew Dewar's horse, he declared, for it had a white patch upon its nose that glowed within moonlight. He watched as Tam Dewar, using his horse to coop them, backed those two strangers up against the stone wall of the mill. The girl, still holding up the limp man, could not move beyond the beast's tramping hooves. She was caught. Then, the driver declared, he saw no more as he walked away.

But Miss Nancy, who was secreted within a nearby bush, said the girl was pleading, pleading, pleading with Tam Dewar, 'Him no kill massa, him no kill massa!' over and over she said it. At once imploring, then crying, then shouting, then jumping this way, then skipping that way, before falling once more to begging.

Benjamin Brown—a cattle-man watching this torment from within the mill—knew that the young girl's pleas would be no more troubling to that dog-driver overseer than the screech of a bat. Once Tam Dewar had them ensnared, he dismounted, and seized the man from her in one move. And then the overseer, holding the negro-man up before him like some stinking rag, started to shake him fierce, as if all the dirt of the world resided within this black-man's bones. And he shouted upon him, 'Don't look at me, nigger. Don't look at me!'

The stranger-man put up no fight, according to Sarah, except to continue to fix his eyes upon Dewar. But the girl—oh, she did spit and claw and thump her fists upon the overseer. Until, with one blow from a hammer fist, Dewar whacked her so hard within the face that she fell to the ground. Then the overseer pointed his pistol at the man's head and . . . boom! Sarah said that the negro's face simply exploded—that it burst in fragments on to the air and soon, like a bloody rain, started to gently pitter-patter down.

Benjamin was sick. Nancy just ran and ran and ran.

The overseer tossed the limp remains of this negro aside, like he was a piece of spent cane just stripped through the mill. The girl, blood-stained as a butchered hog, grabbed Dewar around his ankles to plead for her salvation. He seized her by a fistful of her hair to hold her steady as he rearmed his pistol. 'No, massa, no, massa, mercy, massa, mercy,' she struggled savagely. Some defiant spirit within her fought to keep her life. The overseer could hardly hold her. 'Shut up, you dead fucking nig-ger, shut up.' It was as the overseer raised his hand to strike her with his pistol that Kitty flew.

'She was 'pon deh overseer like breath of wind!' Sarah said. But Sarah was ignorant as to why Kitty did imperil herself for this young girl. For she believed this girl to be just some lordly house slave who had never once felt the sun brand her back or the earth callous her hands hard as pig's foot. She did not know that she was Kitty's taken daughter.

But Benjamin did. And what he also knew was . . . 'July was overseer Dewar's pickney. Many times him bent Miss Kitty over—many, many times when him first come upon Amity.' Benjamin had worked with Kitty when the baby July was strapped to her. On the second gang he had cleared the spent canes with Kitty, and sucked his teeth at the pickney-howl that came ceaseless from Kitty's back. He knew July from her scream—he swore it. 'If me know it, then her mama, Miss Kitty, mus' hear it in her pickney too. So her did run to her—her did run!'

⁓

What happened next has been told in so many ways by so many peo-ple—some who were not even in the parish at the time, some who were not even born into the world yet—that it is hard for your storyteller to know which version to recount. That Kitty grabbed Tam Dewar before he could strike July once more, is one thing that is certain. That she was upon him with such force that he, startled, dropped July from his grasp, is also true. That Kitty, with anxious urgency, commanded July to run— to the cane piece, to the woods, anywhere—but run! And that July, upon seeing her lost mama again, stood so aghast that, apart from her mouth slowly gaping, all her movement ceased. Kitty had to stamp her foot to wake her daughter to start her flight, she had to shoo her—once, twice and yell out, 'Run, July, run now!' All this is certain truth.

But did Kitty, in the fierce struggle that commenced with Tam Dewar, hack her machete upon his ankles like he was a piece of cane to be cut? Did she grab his neck, swing him in the air, then land him back down upon the ground with a thump? Did she bash his head upon a stone until it split like a ripe coconut? Did she twist his arms up his back until she felt them snap? Did she kick him? Did she jump upon him? Reader, we will never know, for none saw. Where once all could see, despite the confusion of the moonlight and the smoke, suddenly no one did have recall. Not one soul saw Kitty assail Tam Dewar. Not one.

All that is known is that Tam Dewar was found, not yet dead, but spread upon the ground of the mill yard with a broken collarbone, a fracture in his skull, two broken ankles, two broken arms and his ribs mash up. Wounds he would die from two days later—fitting, spewing and boiling hotter than bubbling cane liquor.

And the militia man who captured Kitty—bound, gagged and secured her that day—said the slave was sitting motionless within the yard, a little way from the lifeless corpse of a freeman negro, but next to the mangled body of the overseer of Amity. And that when she was seized, that devil nigger had a grin upon her face.

CHAPTER 15

KITTY WAS BEARING A broad halter of blackest iron about her neck the next time July saw her mama. The chains that ran down from that collar bound her mama's wrists so strained that her hands were forced into a devout pose. Her mama's wounded face was bulged to the size of breadfruit—her blackened eyes swollen and closed, her cheeks puffed up with bruising, her bottom lip split and her tongue so bloated that her mouth could not close about it. The leg irons that chained her ankles hobbled her to limp and shuffle as she was compelled toward the gibbet erected within the market square.

Although favouring more beast than woman, Kitty's beaten face still managed to carry a look of puzzlement. For she did not realise that the trial for her crime against Tam Dewar had already been heard and judged. She believed that she had merely walked through the court-room. That the brief glimpse of white people she saw—sitting in rows, fanning themselves in the courthouse heat and yelling, 'Devil, devil!' upon her—was just the beginning of the ordeal. Yet her chains were tugged to leave the room before any solemn pronouncements demanded that she struggle to lift her head.

So when she was once more outside the courthouse building she asked of the jailer who was driving her along, 'What you do with me?'

The white man pulled on her hair to wrench up her head so she could see the three stiffened corpses swinging upon the gibbet before her. 'You want freedom, don't you?' he said. 'This is the sort of freedom we'll give you, every last devil of you. Sabbie dat, murdering nigger?'

Bacchaus, the dull-eyed negro hangman, leaned a ladder up against the gallows, then wearily climbed its wooden struts to cut down those who had finished their turn. The three dangling human fruits of that gibbet fell on to the heap of rotting bodies left below. So many had been hanged that day that the pile was interfering with the drop. But it would be evening before the workhouse negroes were shuffled in to remove the corpses of those once hopeful 'fight-for-free' negroes that now festered in a pile of bared teeth and broken limbs beneath those fatal beams.

The hangman tested the flap upon the scaffold—opening the lumbering gate to knock aside any lying below that hindered its workings—before beckoning the jailor to bring Kitty along. As the iron collar about Kitty's neck was removed she swung her head around in a blessed freedom, before the rope noose that replaced it once more pinned her firm. And then she stood waiting. For this gibbet would accommodate three and could not be dropped until its full complement was trussed there.

Once all in town had gathered with eagerness to witness the punishments of the slaves who had troubled not only white people with their fire and fuss, but also the King of England in that Baptist War. Now those house slaves and those field negroes and those mongers that laboured within the market, could not be bothered to cease their haggling to worry for the souls of those that were led from the courtroom. Nor could white people be persuaded to stand in the heat to watch niggers being lashed five hundred times or hung by the neck from the gallows. For these punishments had gone on for so long—day upon day, one after the other, after the other—that all in the town, black, coloured and white, had grown weary of them.

'You have been found guilty of the worst crimes that can be perpetrated, and must be hanged by the neck until dead.' The two men who had just heard those words spoken to them in the courtroom were placed on either side of Kitty upon the gibbet. One was being hanged for burning down his overseer's house to a pail-full of ashes. While the other was, alas, losing his life for merely staring open-mouthed, upon the flames.

When the flap finally dropped on that straining scaffold July, hidden within a corner of the square, watched as Kitty, kicking and convulsing at the end of her rope, elbowed and banged into the two men that dangled lifeless as butchered meat beside her. Her mama struggled. Her mama choked. Until, at last stilled, her mama hung small and black as a ripened pod upon a tree.

PART 3

CHAPTER 16

THE COFFIN WAS BORNE through Falmouth, high upon the shoulders of six men. July and Molly walked within this procession in the company of black negroes and fair-faced coloureds—the ragged, the coarsened, the garish, the dressy, the gaudy, the haggard, the tattered and the careworn of the parish. This motley crowd were led in muffled solemnity by a white Baptist minister and his family. At the chapel yard all came to a stop as the minister raised his pointed finger to the moon, then let out a grave and strident cry of, 'The hour is at hand. The monster is dying.'

Some in this congregation fell upon their knees, others mumbled prayers on halting breath, or rocked within the rhythm of a softly sung hymn. Until suddenly, the minister raising both arms heavenward shouted, 'The monster is dead. The negro is free!'

Although the hour was midnight, the elation that rose from all glowed like a sunrise to light this splendid occasion. As the coffin with the words, 'Colonial slavery died July 31, 1838, aged 276 years,' was lowered into the ground, a joyous breeze blew. It was whipped up from the gasps of cheering that erupted unbounded. When the handcuffs, chains and iron collars were thrown into that long-awaited grave to clatter on top of slavery's ruin, the earth did tremor. For at that moment every slave upon this island did shake off the burden of their bondage as one.

As the minister bid that the thanks to almighty God for this deliverance be raised louder than the trumpets of Jericho, and that the 'hoorah' for the new Queen of England who had freed them, should shake the buildings in London Town, Molly did do the strangest thing; she threw her arms about July and hugged her fiercely. And then . . .

CHAPTER 17

I CAN GO NO further! Reader, my story is at an end. Close up this book and go about your day. You have heard all that I have to tell of a life lived upon this sugar island. This wretched pen will blot and splutter with ink no more in pursuance of our character July. I now lay it down in its final rest.

Within this hot-hot and dusty day your storyteller has suffered an anguish and an indignity that she just cannot endure. My son, Thomas, has come to me in a state of great agitation—the pulsing vein upon his head throbbing and wriggling as if about to be born from within him. (But his face remaining as composed as a man wishing to enquire my favourite colour—be it red or blue? For that is my son's character; he will not breathe words upon you to speak what he intends—he must give you some other sign.)

I did not worry, for I believed this vexation had its cause in the noise and fuss that has recently blared within our household. Lillian and her daughters, Louise, Corinne and May, have of late taken to quarrelling over any and every little thing that does occur. You never will have heard the like, reader.

This morning, those three mischievous girls greeted me at the table, each with their big lip pushed out so far in sulk that it turned me from my porridge. And the cause? Their mama requires them to wear pink ribbon within their hair, when yellow is the fashion. So wear yellow, I tell them. They have not yellow, they weep, before them bang, slam, crash every door within the house. Come, it is not only the floors that do shake when there is such commotion. So I believed my son to have had rough words with Lillian and his pickney about the carry-on.

Upon entering my room, my son produced the pages that you have just read and commenced to wave them in front of my face. The realisation that the person who was rousing my son to feeling was me—his old and frailing mama—was my first surprise. The second, was the question he required me to answer: 'What of the son that July gave life to?' he asked.

It was so rudely spoken that I believed my ears to be hearing a little devil's prank. So I replied, 'Wha' ya say?'

He blow out his breath in a sigh; for my son is such a gentleman that he prefers his mama not to speak in this rough way but to say pardon, like I am some lordly white missus. 'Oh, pardon me, son, but did I hear your words correctly?'

'Mama,' he go on, 'July gave birth to a son whom she then abandoned at the door at the Baptist minister's manse. Why is there no telling of this within your story?'

Reader, those words slapped my face as fierce as any hand my son could have raised. What was he now demanding? Does he require to direct what I write within these pages? I am sure that within those publishing houses in England, the ones my son does speak of with such licky-licky praise, those white people do listen with a greedy ear upon what the storyteller has to tell. Them do not say, 'Oh, let us know the devilment of this person here, or the nasty-nasty deed of that character there.' No. Them is grateful for any story told. But not so my son.

This tale is of my making. This story is told for my amusement. What befalls July is for me to devise. Better that my son save his wrath for those parts of his household which deserve to see the anger he can raise, was my reply.

'Mama,' he say to me, 'do not take me for a fool. This is the story of your own life, not of your creating, I can see this.'

'No, it is not,' I tell him.

'It is,' him say.

'It is of my making,' I tell him.

'It is not—it is of your life lived,' him tell me.

'Oh no, it is not.'

'Oh yes, it is.'

We did step this fancy argument too long for my delicate stomach. And my son's finger did wave upon me for the whole time. It is not for a son to wag his finger upon his mama, but the other way about! And he huffed and puffed to me that I needs tell why he was abandoned and that I must speak true.

Sometimes his demands upon me are as constricting as the corset they bind me in to keep me as a lady.

But I must do as my son bids. Else I may wake to find my valise— with my piece of lace and my cracked plate—placed outside the gates of this house, and my aging nagging bones cast out to join them. My son may shake his head upon this circumstance, but his old mama has now witnessed that possibility within his eye.

So I must upon this page affirm that a son was indeed born to July. After the grievous pain of birthing—for July was still a young girl who did not possess the width within her body to push out this child's enormous head with any ease—Nimrod's son was born in upon this world.

His legs did not bow (unlike those of the man who sired him), and up to now, that son has a good head of hair. But still, July, at that time, did look upon this tiny newborn and think him the ugliest black-skinned child she had ever seen. There, these words are true—so does my son find joy within them? He has a mama whose lip curled with disgust when first she saw that a child of hers was as black as a nigger. And even if my son now wishes to beg his storyteller to change this faithful detail, alas, it cannot be done.

July had no intention to suckle this misbegotten black pickaninny. But neither did she wish to leave him mewling upon a mound of trash, nor whimpering within the wood. She found no strength to smother him, nor will to hold him under the river's swell. After two days of hiding her son from all that was this world, July fixed upon the notion of leaving him to the minister-man. For July had heard tell that minister-men did say that even ugly-ugly slaves with thick lips and noses flat as milling stones were the children of God. So she wrapped her pickney in a rough cloth, tied her red kerchief at his head and within a moonless night walked the stony trail to the Baptist minister's house. There was no hesitation shivering her breast as July placed her baby upon a stone by the gate. Preacher-man would shelter him—she knew. And that, reader, is what preacher-man did do.

So come, ask my son to tell you of those days. Will he drum his chest with maddening rage or wipe tears of lament from his clouded eye at the loss of his mama? No, he will not. Rather, he will sing you a joyous melody of the sweet life lived with the English preacher, James Kinsman, and his saintly, good-goodly wife Jane. Do you think that you will be able to go about your day before my son has told you all? Then think that no more.

My son will begin with how Mr Kinsman and his wife procured a wet nurse to suckle him. He will then state how this princely nourishment grew him strong (and doubtless add to this, the feature tall—but even to this day, my son is not tall). He was baptised Thomas—after one of Jesus Christ's twelve apostles—in the chapel just outside the town. Although he was required to lay his bed within the servants' hut of the Kinsman household, my son will assure you that he was considered as much a member of that family as their own two sons, James and Henry. Of course he was required to work for his board, but his chores—sweeping the yard, feeding the chickens—were no more burdensome than that of any house boy. And on Sundays he was allowed to sup at the same table with the family. My son was not a slave, but a freeman from his second year.

'The salvation of the savage' was Mr Kinsman's mission. He believed that even the blackest negro could be turned from sable heathen into a learned man, under his and God's tutelage. My son was given a Christian education within his school and Mr Kinsman was pledged to write a paper upon the progress of his learning for the *Baptist Magazine* in London. On the first day of his schooling, my son received a pair of the finest leather shoes. Even today he has those shoes hung from a hook upon the wall in his study. Shoes upon a wall! He will not discard them, for those two tiny cracked-leather boots contain all the dear memories he has of the Kinsmans and his scholarship.

Oh, see my son's eyes light with merriment as he recalls for you the time betwixt sunrise and sunset of each day that he did spend at that Baptist mission school. He read the scriptures with distinction and accuracy, and could write with considerable knowledge upon both civil and sacred geography. Every Wednesday he was tested upon his understanding of the biblical antiquities, followed by an interrogation—for his general examination—of the emblems, figures, parables and most remarkable passages of the Bible. My son could recite every word of 238 hymns—indeed the whole number that were contained within the *Sunday Scholar's Companion*. And his arithmetic was advanced as far as vulgar fractions.

A school feast was held every year in the chapel yard beneath the shade of the orange trees, where a gathering of people from about the parish came to observe the miracle of the little learned negroes of the Baptist mission school. Even July came once to stare. And my son— standing in white breeches with his shoes upon his feet, hands clasped at his front, head erect, mouth open wide as a toad and lungs swelling with tune—led the little black-faced choir in the joyful singing of the hymn, 'Eternal God we look to Thee.'

When Mr Kinsman's paper for the *Baptist Magazine* was complete, he published it under the title, 'Tree of the Lord's Right-Hand Planting: The Remarkable Effect of the Good Christian Education upon a Negro Foundling on the Caribbean Island of Jamaica.'

My son was that Baptist minister's boast. Go ask him. With humble hesitancy (that will not linger long), my son will report how often times it seemed that Mr Kinsman and his good-goodly wife, Jane, found more delight in him than they did in their own sons. When it came time for

James Kinsman and his family to leave Jamaica for London, after the completion of their mission work, none within that household could conceive of sailing from this island without my son amongst them. And when he journeyed to England with the family aboard a ship called the *Apolline*, it was not as a servant, oh no, it was as, 'the remarkable negro boy, Thomas Kinsman.'

Not a snivel nor a moan, will my son send forth while singing the tale of his young life. Yet still, you may think to judge July harshly. But, reader, if your storyteller were to tell of life with July through those times, you would hear no sweet melody but forbidding discord. You would turn your head away. You would cry, lies! You would pass over those pages and beg me lead you to better days.

Shall I oblige you to read how many times Caroline Mortimer ordered that July be pinioned within the stocks as punishment for her wrongdoings after those riots? Should I paint a scene so you may conceive of how often the sizzle of the sun's heat fried July's skin to blisters and scorched her mouth so dry that she did not have spittle nor breath to shoo away any creature or beings that came to plague her within those long nights?

Or maybe I should find pretty words that could explain to you what befell Patience in those days? How, after the massa had been laid to rest in the churchyard, she walked from Amity in the hope of finding Godfrey in town, and returning him to his proper place; calming the fretful and arranging the duties within the kitchen. She was caught upon the road by the militia, who charged that she was a runaway rebel. She received fifty lashes for her crime. Would you like me to describe the lesions upon her back and let you hear the woebegone howl she emitted when the stinking cloth that had wrapped the wound was pulled off? Perhaps you would care to watch her die. Or see the anguish that so clouded Miss Hannah's soul that she crawled into her grave two days after Patience. Shall we walk in the procession of these two burials? Perhaps to accompany Florence and Lucy as they hold up Molly—ragged and raging and screaming fearful that she will be sold away. Reader, would you like to hear Byron weeping?

In those dark days our July—that mischievous girl that you have come to know, that could twist her missus to any bidding and tease Molly to tears, that grinning girl who did slide the whole length of the hall upon her dirty apron, and gaily put a bed sheet upon a table and wine out of window—that July was forsaken by her ravaged spirit and soon departed. And a withered and mournful girl stumbled in, unsteady, to take her part. With eyes dulled as filthy water, this July was so fearful a young woman that the barking of a dog, the slamming of a door, the clatter of a dropped spoon, would see her tremble as if the earth did wobble beneath her. Every fresh morning she puzzled over whether she had woken, for, as in her sleeping dreams, each tree she did gaze upon saw her lost-found-lost mama dangling there within the rustling leaves and sagging fruit. Every mouthful she ate tasted only of Nimrod's blood. And always beneath her feet, a low rumbling of galloping horses menaced her.

That miserable July had no misgivings. She devised a story that told how the black-skinned baby she gave life to died rigid and grey with the very first lungful of air it breathed.

And this is why I can go no further. This is why my story is at an end. For I know that my reader does not wish to be told tales as ugly as these. And please believe your storyteller when she declares that she has no wish to pen them. It is only my son that desires it. For he believes his mama should suffer every little thing again. Him wan' me suffer every likkle t'ing again!

CHAPTER 18

⁓

R EADER, MY SON IS quelled! Kindness has once more returned to his
eye. Despite what you may have learned within my last pages, I beg
you do not think ill of Thomas Kinsman. He is a good son and has come
to his mama with his head bowed in abashed apology.

Within his hand he carried some papers which, he explained to me
with childish passion, was an edition of the magazine of the Baptist mission in England. It seems that this publication has been in my son's pos-
session for nearly as long as his little leather boots; and it is evident that
as much care has been lavished upon this document's sadly browning
and brittle pages. He desired his mama to peruse it, he said. So I did as I
was bid.

Oh, reader, imagine my surprise when I alighted upon an essay
printed within this august volume which was penned by none other
than the wife of the Baptist minister-man—the saintly, good-goodly
Jane Kinsman! Within it, she wrote of the time when she—living in
Jamaica with her husband and her two sons—found a negro slave child
abandoned outside the door of their manse. After taking in the child and
baptising him Thomas, she then ventured to find out who had mothered this slave. A person within the nearby town (she did not within this
essay say whom) believed the baby to have been the pickney of a house
slave called July. Imagine, July's name was printed there for all in
England to read!

The story then carries on that this house slave, July, was approached secretly within the gardens at Amity by Jane Kinsman. When this slave realised that the woman who had her pickney was now standing before her, she did begin to shake with fear. She then begged Jane Kinsman to keep her son or else her missus (this paper did not say Caroline Mortimer, but all would know, for there was no other missus at Amity) was determined upon selling her slave baby away. Our author then goes on (at great length and in a very ponderous style that could have done with some lightness within its tone) to say that this is what she did—she promised this slave girl that she would rear her baby so the baby would not be sold.

Oh, reader, how this article did make me laugh when this missionary's wife went on to say that when she assured the slave that she would take good care of her baby, the slave was so pitifully grateful that she did drop to her knees, snivelling and crying and kissing this woman's hands. And you know what? It is true, reader! For it was exactly how July behaved upon that day; come, how else was she to get this white woman to raise her black baby?

But then Jane Kinsman did add (in this too sentimental essay, full-full of self-regard that was so beloved of white women at this time) that she did ask the little slave girl (that is our July), 'Was your son born in wedlock?' Jane Kinsman then states that this guileless, naïve and simple negro (these are her words, reader, and not my own) did then reply, 'No, missus, him was born in de wood—where be wedlock?'

Reader, let me assure you now and make as plain as I might—July said no such fool-fool thing to that white missus, at that time or any other! Cha.

My son agrees, I must now return to my story with some haste, before another foolish white woman might think to seize it with the purpose of belching out some nonsensical tale on my behalf. But before my son does accuse me once more of falsehood, allow me to make a minor amend.

Do you recall, reader, that midnight hour when slavery ended? The pages within my tale which told of how the coffin that fancifully contained that oppression was buried within the earth? That remarkable night where Molly did fondly hug July? Well, here is where my correction must come. As far as your storyteller is aware, Molly did never once embrace anyone in the whole of her days. And July was not within the town to bear witness to the portentous revelry of that night. Your storyteller did find the chronicle of that occasion written within the pages of some other book—the title of which is no longer within my recall.

For I feared you would think my tale very dull indeed if, when the chains of bondage were finally ripped from the negro, and slavery declared no more, our July was not skipping joyous within the celebrations. But, alas, upon that glorious night of deliverance, July was, as you shall now read, confined within the tedious company of her missus.

⟵⟶

CHAPTER 19

TICK-TOCK, TICK-TOCK, tick-tock. Through one ear July could hear the long clock within the drawing room as it counted down for her the appointed hour when the false-free of apprenticeship was ended, and she could truly no longer be held as a slave. Tick-tock, tick-tock, tick-tock. Her other ear, however, was forcibly required to heed the babble of her missus.

Caroline Mortimer was engaged in belatedly answering the points of an argument she had recently had with her overseer John Lord—just before that overseer, in a bluster of contempt, had run down the piazza steps, mounted his horse and galloped away out of her employ.

'I should have said, what I should have said, oh how I wish I said it. What I should have said was, "Why must I have the expense of an overseer when I am then required to do the work myself? Must I keep a dog and also bark?" Oh, if only I had said that, Marguerite, he would have held his tongue about making us visit the negro village. But it is so hard to think of a clever riposte within the time. And that worthless man just assailed me with his instructions. He would never have had the courage to speak to my brother in that manner. If my brother were alive (God rest his soul), he would have insisted that the overseer sort out the negroes' worries for himself—as was his employment. My brother would have told him to go to blazes. But he believes he can make any request of me because I am a mere woman. Well, I will not do it—I will not. There is no need of it. I have another overseer who will perform his tasks properly and good riddance to John Lord with his ugly whiskers and shockingly bushy eyebrows. Oh, Marguerite, I should have said, "Shall I bark myself?" If only I'd thought to be so sharp . . .' And with that her missus fell upon her daybed, still twittering like a bird sorely distressed.

John Lord was the tenth—no wait, perhaps the eleventh—overseer that had been employed at Amity since Caroline Mortimer had taken over the running of her deceased brother's plantation. He had stayed a little longer than most—past a year.

It was six years since Caroline Mortimer had laid her brother's body to rest within the hallowed ground of the churchyard, to the left of his wife Agnes, and on top of his short-lived pickney. After that sombre burying, a long parade of white people from about the parish— dressed from their top to their tip in the black of crows—had come to pay their respects to our missus. And every one of those guests that solemnly entered in upon that great house at Amity was treated to the ghastly story of what befell John Howarth upon that wicked night, when he was brutally and savagely slain. Come, there was even a guided tour included within the tale, directed by the missus, through the pertinent rooms.

At first her account was soberly enough conveyed; a nigger was waiting beneath the bed and shot her brother within the face; the murdering nigger was then pursued to the slave village where the nigger was captured by the overseer; but during the dreadful riot that had erupted, the overseer was attacked by a fearsome slave and died later of his wounds.

But the panting anticipation of her listeners, the clutched breasts and hastily sat upon chairs, the gaping mouths, the astonished wide eyes and the compassion—the, 'Oh my dear . . . Oh, you poor, poor woman . . . Oh, good God in heaven, what you have suffered . . . Oh, you brave, brave woman, your brother (God rest his soul) would have been so proud of your fortitude . . . You, my dear, are a credit to the name of Jamaican planters . . .'—that caressed Caroline Mortimer's esteem, gradually grew the story that exhaled from her into a tale worthy of the most flamboyant writer.

Soon, Caroline Mortimer, seeing the nigger shoot her brother, picked up her pearl handled pistol and gave chase. Mad with grief, though she was, she determined to bring that nigger to the gallows herself. And Tam Dewar, who at the start of her storytelling was just the overseer, who everyone knew as a rather vulgar, disagreeable and boorish Scotsman, gradually turned into her gallant knight. He took her into his arms to swear that he would move all within heaven and earth to bring the culprit of this heinous crime to justice. The nigger, Nimrod, needless to say became barbarous and bloodthirsty, cunning as a wild dog and base as a lowly worm. July made no appearance in any of the tellings, except once to spill a jug of water, like a buffoon, in fright. And as for the slave that attacked our gallant, brave and forthright Tam Dewar (that is Miss Kitty), she was a black devil woman, who with pitiless savagery, brutish fists and sharp teeth, hunted down white people upon this island to burn.

With little worry that anyone who could be believed (like July) would step forward to recount the events from some other view, Caroline Mortimer became, by the fifth delivery of her narration, the story's resolute heroine.

Caroline then grew so convinced of her own audacity, so enamoured by her oft-conjured boldness, and persuaded by her imaginary competence, that when it came time for those planters and busybodies about the parish to give guidance to the missus upon what should be done with her brother's plantation, the missus was so puffed with self-regard that she declared, 'So help me, God, I will see the plantation of Amity prosper and grow that it may serve in absolute memorial for my dearly departed brother!'

Not even two surprisingly generous offers by her neighbours to the west and to the south—for the land, slaves, works, great house, and even to include the costs that should surely arise with the reinstating of the slave village and burnt-out hospital—did persuade Caroline Mortimer that withdrawing from Jamaica to England for quiet retirement in Islington, might be the better claim upon her resoluteness.

Nor did she approve the notion of an attorney handling her brother's affairs. No. The fiction within her memory seduced her to declare that no one understood Caroline Mortimer if they believed these misfortunes and tribulations would see her broken. She alone would make Amity the most prosperous estate in the whole of Jamaica. Her brother would have expected no less from her.

However, it was not long before the firm nip of plain truth began to deflate the missus. Once she entered in upon the fetid dank room within the counting house to begin in earnest to peruse her late brother's records of business, she soon realised that the fortunes of Amity were not as bounteous as she had always imagined them when dozing upon her daybed.

Within her first year as proprietor, she had to let the cane pieces of Virgo and Scarlett Ponds fall into ruinate, for she did not have the slaves to work them. Some had perished in the riots, others made feeble or limbless at the behest of justice and the law. Even after the seven slaves, carpenters mostly, who were loaned to Unity Pen by her late brother were begged return, she could not raise labour enough to keep the mill constantly turning and the teaches forever bubbling. And able black bodies could not be bought to replenish her stock with neither smiling friendship nor charmingly negotiated cash. For every planter within her circle pleaded that they were suffering from the same fate. Within that year of passing the ownership of Amity from deceased brother to deluded sister, the amount of hogsheads rolling out from the plantation works had dropped tenfold.

So the missus agreed with her then overseer (the third I believe, the second having fallen insensible to the pox), that he should decree to all those slaves who were idle, indolent and not working well, that their houses would be the last to be restored if their performance did not improve. She approved that her slaves should for a period, until the plantation named Amity was in the pride of health again, work without the break of their 'off time.' In her second year she permitted a new dungeon to be created near the burnt-out hospital for the correction of those negroes who proved to be incorrigibly feckless. 'What harm could it do?' she said of these arrangements.

Then apprenticeship was finally forced upon our missus and all the planters of the Caribbean. Hopeful as the Hebrews leaving Egypt, the many slaves that toiled at Amity walked from their plantation to the town to listen to the white man, 'de massa from a H'england,' as he explained to them, from the balcony of the courthouse, the details of the preparations for freedom.

Though they were still bound to the missus to work for six years without pay, after hearing their Moses-in-beige-breeches declare slavery at an end, the slaves believed themselves to be actually free. They refused to work no more than the forty hours a week now required of them by King William and the law of England. No call to orderly conduct and 'obedience to all persons in authority' had any effect upon Caroline Mortimer's negroes. And forty hours a week was just not enough time to take off a sugar crop. No inducement, nor overseer (certainly not the two drunken Welsh ruffians who managed the fields through that time), could get her negroes to task any longer.

Yet Caroline Mortimer was required to care for those negroes in the same way—with lodging and food and clothing. The missus bemoaned that compensation from the government may soon start to tinkle within her pocketbook, yet still her crops would remain within the field. Sweet teeth in England just did not know the trouble she bore for them.

Then upon one rainy, blustery morning, a sodden and bedraggled pack of some of the most forlorn, woebegone and wretched-looking negroes shuffled up in weary deputation on to the grounds of the great house. They had complaint about the dungeon, they called out, and had come to parley with the missus.

Caroline would not permit this nasty group to enter further than the end of her garden. Barely managing to stand against the gusting wind, these feeble apprentices had to shout. And they called out a tale of such merciless torture and despicable conditions within that house of correction, that the missus was forced to conclude that it must be the whip of the wind rendering the tale fanciful to her ear.

So with a look of pity, but a roll of her eye she sweetly said, 'What nonsense.'

Come, see for yourself, was begged—not once, not twice, but over and over as the missus shook her head, waved them away and asserted that she had not the time.

With desperation, one of the scrawniest and ill-fed of this troupe (James Richards, a carpenter) summoned breath enough to blast, 'Massa would have come if him been livin'.'

And Caroline's attention was summarily seized. She mounted her horse that very afternoon.

The overseer, Henry Reed, could not be found, so it was his callow, pungently perspiring bookkeeper who reluctantly obeyed the command to lead the missus down into the dungeon.

The narrow passage and two arched cells of this prison were perfectly dark when the missus entered. The stench—like a dead rat decaying—was thick as gruel, yet still she believed those tiny stone-built chambers to be empty. But like bats first sensed within a cave, she began to detect the black walls moving as her eyes slowly adjusted to the gloom. The wriggling of the murk, however, was not caused by flying rodents, but by the many negro inmates of these cells writhing upon their chains. Sensing visitors, they began to move with more urgency. The scraping of metal, the clatter of shackles, the complaint of hoarse voices, all assailed her with one dissonance, as both languid and frantic eyes fought to find her within the black gloom. A man (Richard Young from the first gang) was pinned to the wall by his upheld arms. A naked woman (Catherine Wiggan, also from the first gang) was chained to the floor by her neck. A child (Catherine's youngest daughter, Liddy, I believe) was encased within a stock by her ankles. And more this way. And yet more that. The dungeon was crowded.

The missus fled.

Arriving back at the great house, Caroline Mortimer directly took to her bed before plunging herself into the solace of a bottle of her sweetest Madeira. July found her missus vomiting upon her bed sheets and slurring the command that a trunk be packed for her as she was intending to take the next ship back to England. 'I had no idea of it, I had no idea . . . I believed a prison cell with water and bread and rough furnishings . . . I am a Christian woman . . . Believe me, when I say I had no idea of it.'

How the missus did not know the pitiless conditions within that dungeon at Amity, July just could not comprehend. For every negro upon that plantation, even those within the kitchen, feared its viciousness. Come, negro children had even devised a rhyme for it, which they recited during the playing of passing stones:

Me mama beg de bakkra na t'row mi in de dungeon,
Me sista beg de bakkra na t'row her in de dungeon,
De missus tell de bakkra go t'row dem in di dungeon.
So down de dread dungeon dem did go.

As her missus whimpered her useless innocence July, with a shrug of her shoulder said, 'Then close up the dungeon, missus.' When Caroline lifted her head to gaze upon July, her expression was quizzical as a guileless child. Her missus's tipsy eyes were rimmed with deep red, her cheeks were of the dullest grey pallor, her lips were crusted with drying vomit, and her hair was as awry as a fallen cockatoo's. A brief beat of pity pulsed within July for this forlorn white woman—her fat-batty missus—but then was gone.

'Tell overseer-man,' July began again, with cautious authority, 'tell that man him must close up that dungeon and use it no more.'

And that is exactly what Caroline did. 'Close it up. Close it up,' she commanded the overseer, 'and hope the magistrate never heard tell of it.' She made Henry Reed not only empty its chambers of all the captives but also, at July's suggestion, fire the dungeon to smoke out its callousness. Henry Reed may soon have left her employ bewailing that he now had no inducement that could extract more effort from the idle, the indolent, and the not working well, but that dread dungeon was no more.

And so puffed did our missus become after that splendid resolution that she proclaimed that, from that day onward, her housemaid July (or Marguerite as she still insisted upon calling her) should serve her also in the administering of the plantation. For when her brother was alive, was it not July who stood at Caroline Mortimer's side to sift the skulkers from the sick upon Monday mornings? 'No. Him jus' have sore head from too much rum,' July would tell her or, 'That black tongue not be sickness, it can be wipe off,' or, 'Caution, missus—yaws!' If July could assist her then, when she was no more than a child, what better help could she be now? There was the register of slaves to be taken, compensation to be claimed, always overseers and bookkeepers to be found . . .

'Me can't, missus,' July told her.

'Nonsense. I say you will, then you will,' the missus twittered. 'We will bring the negroes in a line and they will tell their name and you will put it in the ledger. I will need it for inspection for the compensation.'

'But me can't, missus,' July repeated, 'Me can neither read, nor write.'

Her missus was nearly felled by the force of that sudden understanding.

'Oh, Marguerite,' she said with exasperation, 'why ever not!?'

⌒⌐

Name, sex, age. These were the earliest words that July could draw—although her tongue poked from her lips to follow every stroke. When, with faltering breath, she at first enjoined the sounds of the letters into the word, her missus jumped upon her feet and clapped, 'Yes, yes, oh yes, Marguerite.'

Caroline Mortimer proved a very able teacher—come, she had a blackboard, chalk and pointer brought from town. She took July's hand within her own to trace out all the letters of the alphabet. She wrote simple words upon the board, commanding July to make her own, rather clumsy, copies. She even read loudly and deliberate from books while moving July's finger along the words, before demanding her pupil, 'Repeat . . . repeat . . . repeat.'

But long after the missus had tired of these lessons—the dusty blackboard taken away to be used as table top within the kitchen—July was still eager to continue that learning. There were many papers and books that lay about the great house—papers covered with a grey print of letters dense as stains—that July commenced, out of cussedness, to study, one slow word at a time, until their jumble danced with meaning. Head, tradesman, inferior, field, domestic—soon July began to read those words fast as conversing, and to write them without the aid of her tongue.

July was now a young woman, tall but not with the colossal bearing of her mama, Kitty. Her hair was no longer that picky-picky-head tangle of her youth but braided neat and always wrapped within a clean, coloured kerchief. Her full mouth still had that mischievous turn upon its corners, where a wry tale or tall-tall truth looked about to escape it. But within her spirited black eyes a keen observer might sense the anguish that stalked her. For her dreams were so tyrannical, so pestering with tormenting episodes, that July contrived to rest no more than four hours within any night. In unguarded moments, a droop within her eyelids, a sag at her jaw, could dull her features to morose, swift as a doll with two faces.

But so important was July to Caroline, that her missus had received thirty-one pounds in compensation for the loss of July as her property. Florence and Lucy were worth much less—nineteen pounds and ten shillings—being inferior slaves that could only wash, launder and thump the missus's dresses to rags. Byron—now the fervent young groom at Amity—raised only thirteen pounds and four shillings for his gangly frame.

July had been pleased with her price. Thirty-one pounds! She used to boast of it. Then, one day, whilst perusing some papers, she discovered that the missus had also received thirty-one pounds in compensation for the useless, one-eyed Molly as well.

Now, July was a servant who did read and write—better than many white people upon the island; she did have wit enough to negotiate the best prices from even the most craven of negro traders, and consequently kept the stores full upon a meagre purse; she quelled house servants' quarrels, and kept house boys tasking; she rode a horse at her missus's side and could steer her in a gig; she brushed her missus's hair and laced her missus's clothes; and at her missus's bidding she would visit the boiling house—her feet being chalked upon entering that Hades—to examine the liquor within the teaches and convey her missus's commands to the head man. And so much more—too much to list with my miserable supply of paper.

And Molly, reader? What did she do? Well, Molly was now the cook. She could kill you with her custard and make you sigh with wistful longing for the deceased cook, Hannah, with every mouthful of her disgusting fare. Thirty-one pounds for Molly! Cha! But there is slavery's spite, reader. That pitiless document left our July so downhearted that in that moment she wished she had never learned to read; so shocking was it to know that high-high, bewhiskered white men in England believed her and Molly to be of the same value.

⁓

Tick-tock, tick-tock, tick-tock. When the clock finally chimed the midnight hour upon that night that slavery ceased, July counted along with soft breath the one, two, three, four . . . until that last, fateful chime of twelve shuddered, sonorous, through the room.

Yet, her missus was still twittering, 'If I had told him of the overseer arriving swift on his heels to take his place, that would have struck at John Lord's throat. Oh, I should have told him that. I should have said that, Marguerite.'

Through the long window, past the hissing of the cicadas and the chirruping of night creatures, July could discern yells and hallooing whistling upon the air. Drum beats pulsed from afar. Conches peeped and squeaked to awake the free. And her missus carried on, 'I should have told him about the correspondence I have had from Mr Goodwin from Somerset Pen. Several letters of recommendation that overseer carries with him. He is coming as soon as tomorrow. Even Mrs Pemberton has talked very highly of him. She says he will understand this business better than John Lord ever could. I should have told him about this new overseer. Oh, why can I never think of clever things to say in time . . .'

In an effort to interrupt her missus's ceaseless babbling, July considered raising herself from her seat and treading her bare black feet within the footsteps of all those white overseers' boots—to walk down the veranda steps and out of her missus's employ. But instead, while still seated at the window, she commenced to yawn out loud and stretch herself long. Caroline Mortimer soon stared at her.

'Are you no longer listening to me, Marguerite?' she said.

'Surely, missus,' July replied, 'but me just be t'inking that me is now free.'

Her missus was suddenly quieted. How long did she gaze upon July in that muzzled silence? Long enough for the distant sound of a fiddle and a cymbal, that tripped-in softly through that open window, to gradually arrange its tangled notes into clear verse and chorus within both their ears. Then Caroline Mortimer's reddened cheeks and troubled eyes began to strain with a smile that she had wished would look gracious. And, all at once, the missus, with quiet breathlessness said, 'But you would not leave me, would you, Marguerite?'

CHAPTER 20

⁓

IT WAS AT 11 A.M. the next day, that a horse was heard approaching
the great house at Amity. The rider dismounted his steed to bound
up the steps at his own gallop. Robert Goodwin did not enter in upon
the veranda growling at Byron to hold his horse steady or he'd see him
whipped, as so many other overseers had done before him. He did not
call out, 'Oi, anyone there?' while banging with his fist upon the pillar
of the eaves, causing the whole house to shudder. He did not arrive slurring his words, as the Irish overseer did, whilst burping the foul odour
of porter and rum upon the air. And he did not slap July hard upon her
backside, feign the movement of fornication to her, then shout, 'Tell
yer missus it is 'er lucky day.' No. Robert Goodwin stepped on to
the veranda with his arms held high, like a preacher engaged in the glo-
rification of the almighty.

'A new day is come, Mrs Mortimer,' he said. Then, with a broad,
blithe smile that even shed its gleam upon July, Robert Goodwin raptur-
ously declared, 'Behold, a new morning has broken. Slavery—that
dreadful evil—is at an end.'

⁓

This new overseer was neither a ruffian nor a drunkard; he was a gentleman, the son of a clergyman with a parish near Sheffield. A man of six

and twenty with soft hands, clean fingernails, and hair thick and dark as river silt. Although only standing to the same height as the missus, his upright and steadfast bearing made him appear two feet taller, at the very least. And no ugly whiskers nor shockingly bushy eyebrows befouled the youthful roses that still flushed at his cheeks. Robert Goodwin was someone who, in England, the missus could, with all propriety, have shaken by the hand. Come, his mother's family even had a baronet residing somewhere within its ranks.

After a long and lengthy visit to survey the field negroes at Amity, Robert Goodwin delivered his findings to the missus thus: 'Such a number of poor, miserable black people I have never seen before, Mrs Mortimer. Their houses and gardens have been neglected—some are in perfect ruin.'

Now, these words were precisely the same ones employed by the last overseer (just before that bluster of contempt for our missus had run him away, out of her employ), yet Caroline Mortimer gasped with such astonished ignorance at Robert Goodwin's words that any would believe that this was her first time of hearing this charge. 'Oh, whatever can be done?' she exclaimed. 'Just tell me, Mr Goodwin, and it shall be my wish, too.'

When he continued with, 'Firstly, madam, we must endeavour to restore their best feelings to you by telling them how fairly you intend to treat them now that they are free,' and informed the missus that, 'I will address all the negroes shortly within the mill yard. And Mrs Mortimer, you must accompany me on that mission—we must leave them with no question on whose authority I now speak,' he was unaware that words similar to these, requesting actions that were identical, had once caused the missus such offence that she nearly—if only she'd thought of it in time—told the last man who uttered them to go to blazes. Although Robert Goodwin was wise enough for his brow to furrow in the fear that so forthright a command might cause his employer some displeasure, he need not have fretted, for the missus responded to him with unbounded enthusiasm.

'Of course! Whatever you say,' she said. 'But do you think the negroes will heed us, Mr Goodwin?'

'Oh yes, madam,' he replied and when his frown moved from worry to pensive contemplation all in the raise of one eyebrow, the missus leaned forward upon her chair so she might listen with deeper fellow feeling.

'Negroes are simple, good fellows,' he went on, 'They need kindness—that is all. When it is shown to them then they will respond well and obediently.'

She tilted her head and a sympathetic smile appeared.

'They are not so far from dogs in that respect,' he said, which allowed our missus the chance to emit an attractive titter. 'Please do not misunderstand my meaning, Mrs Mortimer.'

Oh, no, no, no—our missus shook her head.

'The African stands firmly within the family of man. They are living souls. God's children as sure as you or I.'

Of course, she mouthed soundlessly.

It was only when he continued with, 'But I know within my heart that now that they are free to work under their own volition, they will, if treated with solicitude, work harder for their masters,' that the missus let a little doubt widen her eyes.

She asked, 'Are you sure of this, Mr Goodwin?'

His reply, 'I know it as surely as I know anything, madam,' made her once more relax and adjust the lock of hair that continued to flop on to her forehead, despite the use of a pin. 'It is for this reason that I have come to Jamaica. It was my father's wish, of course. My father believed wholeheartedly that slavery was an abomination. "Take kindness to the negro, Robert," he told me. "Show them compassion. Pledge yourself by all that is solemn and sacred to never be satisfied until the negro stands within society as men."'

'Really?' escaped our missus, but she lifted her fingers to her lips to smother the rogue quip.

'England,' he carried on, 'that great, noble, Christian land of ours, must be cleansed of the abominable stain that slavery placed upon it, do not you think, Mrs Mortimer?'

And said she wholeheartedly, 'Oh yes, Mr Goodwin.'

'Oh how that gladdens me, madam,' the overseer carried on. 'If only all planters upon this island felt as you do. The attorney at Unity, my first position, simply laughed in my face. And Mrs Pemberton at Somerset Pen, although a good Christian woman, just could not reconcile labour with kindness. Both were unwilling to hear my father's simple message.'

'But not I,' the missus said quietly and demurely. This simple compliment that the new overseer had paid her—that he, on such short acquaintance, could discern that she was indeed more compassionate than Mrs Pemberton and more reasonable than that dullard at Unity—caressed Caroline Mortimer as surely as the light fingertip strokes she began to lay upon her own neck. And although the overseer was about to carry on with more of his papa's musings, he did not yet realise how capable our missus could be with her own windy-words when roused.

'I inherited this plantation,' she continued while staring earnestly into his face, 'from my own dearly departed brother. And even though he was brutally and savagely slain at the hands of a fearsome, bloodthirsty negro—but let us leave that distressing story for another day—I have, since becoming mistress of this plantation, always endeavoured to be kind. I have, in the past, been thwarted in my mission by the sometimes thoughtless actions of my agents and overseers. I hope that now that you are with us, Mr Goodwin, the improvement we both seek will be upon us soon.' Then she smiled broad upon him.

When Robert Goodwin took his leave of the missus that day, he bowed low with elegant grace. And following him out on to the veranda, she waved good-day to him as he departed, as if he were her valued guest and not her employee. Then, once he was out of her sight, the missus suddenly grasped July tight by the arm. She leaned toward her with a playful giggle, as if July was a great friend with whom the missus simply must confide her secret and said, 'Oh, hasn't he the bluest eyes, Marguerite.'

Not all negroes were present to hear Robert Goodwin's address as he stood atop the empty barrels in the mill yard. Many were still laid upon their beds with heads too sore to listen to no bakkra man. Some were now too free to follow commands, while others, packed up already, had fled from that benighted negro village. But nearly one hundred negroes did linger before him—fanning themselves with banana leaf, eating yam, calling pickney to them, shooing a dog, scratching their head, picking their teeth, yawning, chatting upon the show of his brown leather boots.

They had come to see this new overseer who did ride in from Somerset Pen 'pon his tall-tall horse with him head filled with big ideas. There was Peggy Jump, fresh from the river, still with her washing piled upon her head, soggy and dripping through the wicker basket. She and her husband, Cornet, the mule-man who rode the cart to and from the fields, long ago did think that when free did come, them might leave Amity to seek their daughter, who was sold by the dead massa to a far, far away plantation in Westmoreland.

Peggy did chat upon Mary Ellis that the last overseer, John Lord, was a good bakkra and how all the pickney did follow him to stare up his nose hole, for so much hair did sprout from it. Mary, straining her neck to get a little look at this new overseer said, 'But him not a tall man. With no hat 'pon him head or barrel under him, he be lost in crab-grass.'

Mary, who worked the first gang with Peggy, had for too long shared a house with Peggy and Cornet; for her own home perished under hoof and flame upon that dreadful riot night. And up to now, never repaired! Just two sticks of it remain—worthless but for cruel remembering and tethering the goat. Mary's Sunday prayer was never to hole, never to strip, never to manure, wretched cane no more. But, if she could get a little use off Peggy and Cornet's house once them had lif' up for Westmoreland, then without Cornet to snore her out of every bit of slumber, she would sleep blessed under that stout roof.

And there was James Richards. Any word this new overseer man would utter was going to vex him, and the white man had not opened his mouth yet. 'Me never be a slave no more. Me a freeman,' this carpenter did complain to any who could hear. 'Me no have to listen up no bakkra no more.'

'True, true,' the boiler-man, Dublin Hilton, said. Dublin did think of going nowhere. Come, him was too old and now them seal up dungeon, all was not so bad. Plenty-plenty place worse. And Elizabeth Millar, who did come from her provision ground still carrying her hoe over her shoulder, told James loudly that the Queen did command that negroes must stay in their houses and work their lands.

Samuel Lewis hissed on her to hush so him could hear. Him made plenty money from his fishing and grounds. Him was a man of trade now and must come to some likkle arrangement with the bakkra so him may stay near the river.

While seated upon the ground in the line of some shade were Bessy and Tilly. Bessy was on the light-work people, since two of her fingers were crushed off in the mill. She did think to stay but had heard that bakkra must fetch a jobbing gang from Unity, and she would not work with no niggers from Unity. Oh no. For them be filthy, tricky, and idle. And Tilly was just staring on the scarlet bow upon the missus's straw bonnet and wishing she were a white woman too . . .

But all who saw Robert Goodwin—dressed in his brown cutaway jacket with a striking panama hat upon his head—had no doubt that this new overseer was a preacher's son; for his oration possessed the ardour of the most divine sermon. He began resonant and clear, 'Good morning to you all. Your mistress, Mrs Mortimer, who is seated here beside me has, by the grace of God, and the law of England, granted you your freedom. No one can now oblige you to continue to work for her.'

One roaring hurrah ran out from that crowd before him. The overseer had to raise his palms for quiet once more. 'But there is something that each one of you must remember. So listen to me well. The houses that you live in and the grounds that you work, do not belong to you. They are the property of your mistress. No matter how long you have lived within a house, how much effort you have extended to fix up that dwelling, or labour you have put in upon your garden and provision ground, these still belong entirely to your mistress. Now, be sure to heed me well, every one of you. If you will not labour for your mistress as you have done before, then you cannot expect to remain within your house. If you do not work hard for her then you cannot expect to continue to harvest your provision grounds. Those good souls who are willing to work for fair and reasonable wages, you may remain within your houses for a small rent and you may work your grounds as you have always done. The industrious and well disposed of you, will do well. The idle, disorderly, indolent and dissolute, will neither thrive nor remain. I hope that you will all choose to work hard—within the cane fields, the works, the pen or wherever your superiors decide that your industry is needed—so that the plantation of Amity may thrive and prosper for your esteemed mistress.'

Here the overseer lifted his arms to the heavens as he said, 'And now you must all show yourselves grateful to your masters for having made you free. You must humbly thank God for this blessing of freedom. And you must prove to the Queen, the people of England, and your mistress, that you are worthy of the kindness that has been shown you.'

James Richards nearly swallowed his last tooth, so long and hard did he suck upon it. And he was not alone in his cussing. Come, suddenly there was so much sucking of teeth that it did hiss like the draining of a well. This commotion soon caught the overseer's ear and Robert Goodwin knew the insolence of that sound very well. He raised his palms to implore them to quell it. But angry muttering and chattering did begin to swell from that crowd. Some even walked away. Robert Goodwin had to yell raucous as a street caller to be heard when he lastly cried, 'But know this. When a man pays money for labour he will only employ those who will work diligently and cheerfully. Heed me well. Diligently and cheerfully.'

Caroline Mortimer, seated composed upon a chair throughout this whole announcement, had been gazing up upon this new overseer with the rapture of a lonely boy before a shooting star. She began to clap when he had finally finished, but soon stopped when she felt a hundred pairs of black eyes look upon her. Oh, what a storm negroes did conjure for the missus. So many savage eyes. She nearly passed out at the sight. She commenced to waft her sweet-scented handkerchief back and forth under her nose with some vigour, as she asked her overseer, 'Do you think we have now restored their best feelings to me, Mr Goodwin? Do you think all will be well now?'

And her new overseer, smiling broadly while dabbing sweat from his forehead with a white handkerchief, said confidently, 'Oh yes, madam. Absolutely. I have not one doubt upon the matter.'

CHAPTER 21

'MARGUERITE.' JULY HEARD HER missus call as fearsome black clouds reached across Amity to encase its lands, firm as a lid being sealed upon a box. The wind whipped the bamboos until they bowed within it. It stripped the cotton tree of all but clinging vines and compelled those leaves to dance. Lightning—those devils' sunbeams—cracked with startling, jagged veins before rain began spilling fierce as if overturned clumsy from a colossal pail. And her missus cried out again, 'Marguerite, come here at once. I am calling.' Streams ran everywhere July looked—snaking around bush, stone and tree to find the quickest path. Four-, six-, eight- and one-hundred-legged creeping things crawled to mass within the wet; lizards, excited, jumped from hidey-holes to feast, and mosquitoes waking from puddles launched as vicious mist. 'Marguerite, where are you? Marguerite . . .' After sultry heat, it was now chill enough for July to give a little shiver. She raised herself slowly from the stool upon the veranda with her skilful timing. Her missus found July dashing in from . . . somewhere; eyes wide with concern to do her missus's bidding . . . of course.

'There you are, Marguerite, did you hear me call?'

'Oh me run so, missus, me be out of breath,' July puffed.

'Go to Mr Goodwin's house and ask if he would care to dine with me this evening. A heifer was killed in the pen so Molly has some beef that must be eaten. I know he will be interested in beef.'

Caroline Mortimer had begun to find such interest in her plantation that her daybed became quite neglected—come, its horse-hair was at last beginning to recover its shape. For, standing upon the veranda straining to look over the fields, peering through the windows or pacing the long room to find reasons why July must get a message to Robert Goodwin at his house—'At once, Marguerite, at once!'—was how her missus now filled her day. 'Perhaps I should enquire if everything is to Mr Goodwin's liking at his house? Yes, tell him to pay me a visit . . . I must know of the new bookkeeper the overseer has hired. Tell him to ride over to me on his way to the fields . . . A fine mistress I would be if I did not insist my overseer come to tell me how many hogsheads are going to the port today . . . Byron said that the negroes' pigs have got into the fields again. Run and tell Mr Goodwin to deliver me a full account of any losses to the crop . . .' And so on and so on.

July knew every stone, bush, hole and curve on the winding path that led to the overseer's dwelling. In dry weather it was eight hundred steps from the spreading tamarind tree at the great house to the sweet orange tree that shaded the wooden steps that led into his door. But when she was forced to walk it in a storm—when the wind gusted so that she had to fasten herself to a trunk of a tree and crawl to hide within the refuge of a rock lest she be blown away to England; when she did slip and slide in filthy mud, then wade through rain water that did gush from the hill to eddy around her knees like the tide of a swelling river, then July lost all count of her stride.

July looked from her missus to the window, where the deluge of rain was obscuring the view sure as muslin curtaining. 'Me can go to the overseer when the rain stops,' July said.

But her missus replied, 'Oh, it's only little rain, go now.'

Free. Cha! What change had free brought that July might seize?

⁓

By the time July reached Robert Goodwin's house that day, she was bedraggled and sodden as a mound of rotten trash. Her white cotton blouse, the one with the lace trim at the neck, clung to her tight as skin. She had to wring out her blue skirt as she ascended the steps, for the heavy rain water hobbled her tread. And even when under the shelter of the eaves, her red head kerchief continued to trickle a tide of water down her face as if a sly cloud had pursued her into the house so it might continue its drizzling.

Upon entering the long room of the overseer's quarters, a turmoil assailed July. In the centre of the room, Robert Goodwin, his shirt dangling loose and untied over his breeches, was prancing lightly upon his toes, while first waving his arms, then pointing here, then pointing there, before clapping his hands at four negro boys who were upon their knees about the room. These boys, in an attempt to obey the overseer's tangled directions, were fussing in corners, peering at the base of the wainscot, pouncing at cracks in the boards of the floor, throwing chairs aside, scuttling under the table, and generally rushing from this side to that, as the overseer bellowed upon them, 'Look, look over there. There were some in that corner! Here is one, here is one, Elias! Horatio, look to here boy!'

The overseer had never before been within his house when July had had to call—she usually left her missus's messages with his house boy, Elias. And always she had to repeat those missives several times, for that rude boy just stared entranced upon the rise of her two breasts as she spoke. At other times, when even his house boy could not be chanced, she was obliged to seek an audience with his man servant, Joseph, a skinny man of five and thirty who always giggled like a being of thirty years younger, before anything and everything he said.

July, observing this new overseer, was struggling to understand the task he was engaged upon. For this young white man so gracefully stepping lightly, skipping, turning, stepping lightly, skipping, turning, could have been dancing a quadrille, not tasking scruffy boys. And his exertion was producing such perspiration upon him, that his hair clung damp to his neck in black curly lines, and his white shirt was blemished with dark stains about the armpits.

When the overseer did at last behold July within the doorway, he held up his finger in quick acknowledgment for her to wait, before turning away again. But then, just as hastily, he turned back to her. And the overseer began to gaze upon July with the same captivity as Elias staring upon her breasts. From the soaking wet kerchief upon her head to the mud dragging at the bottom of her skirt, his eyes attentively perused her. It was only a boy calling, 'Come, massa, look here,' that drew his attention away. He held his hand up to July once more saying, 'One moment. I will be there in one moment,' before turning to pay heed to the crouching boy.

'Me have some, massa!' the boy cried as he held up something within his two hands for the overseer to look upon.

The overseer saying, 'Good, good, excellent . . .' began retreating. But the boy just followed, as if obeying this partner in a dance. The man almost tripped over an upturned chair in his prancing to avoid the boy's proffer. 'Good, yes, yes, just carry on,' the overseer commanded. 'I must just . . . I must just see to . . .'

July was what he 'must just see to' and, 'You're very wet,' was what he presently said to her. July opened her mouth to begin her message, but was stopped when the overseer said, 'I think I can see steam rising from you,' and smiled. But then a dark frown swiftly replaced that grin. 'Did your mistress send you out with a message for me in this storm?' he asked. There was such agitation in his tone that July, well practised to deny anything pronounced with passion, nearly yelled 'no.'

'I cannot believe,' he carried on, 'that even she would require you to step out into this weather.'

This overseer then commenced to blast aspersions at her missus's character with eagerness. What could possibly be so important? he wondered. He had never known anyone make so many demands, he said. Why did she have so many messages to give? He had only seen her early this morning, what could be so urgent now?

Soon the air grew so thick with these reproaches that July began to feel a curious concern for her missus. Come, July feared that soon she might defend her fat-batty missus and announce that Mrs Caroline

Mortimer was not so villainous. Luckily he left her mouth no opening, for he spoke rapid as hail upon a roof.

'My father,' he went on, 'always taught me that even servants should be treated with respect and not ordered here and there at a whim. But I fear Jamaican planters have learned over the years to behave another way.'

And then he stopped to sit down hard upon his chair. With his arms folded and his lips pressed firmly together, he glowered at the desk in front of him—searching it with intent, as if some mislaid fortitude were scattered there.

July was now finally free to deliver her message and would have, if it were not for two large brown dogs that chose that moment to rush in upon the room. Ungainly bounding, slipping and scraping on the wooden floor, they knocked into July and stumbled her against the overseer's desk. These barking, playful dogs immediately brought the negro boys to their feet as they ran to shoo them. The overseer cried, 'Wait, wait,' as the boys ran gleefully out of the room after the hounds. He then sighed forlornly and slumped lower within his chair. Only Elias remained.

July was about to deliver her message again when Elias arrived at the overseer's desk and set down before him a box. This wooden box, which was no bigger than a serving plate, held within it an ugly squabble of floundering black cockroaches. Some dead, some crushed, some crawling for release, some being crawled over, some upon their back with their legs flailing the air, some with their armoured shells and fidgeting feelers scratching their distress upon the wood of the box as they writhed within it. Elias had run off as soon as he had laid down the item. He took little notice of the overseer, who at once sat up within his chair, and called out after him, 'Elias, don't leave this here!' His house boy's voice was small and very far away when it came back saying, 'Soon come, massa.'

And at once July knew the nature of this fuss—the overseer was trying to rid his house of the hundreds and thousands of cockroaches that lived with him there.

Casting a hasty glance to July, who still stared down upon him, the overseer coughed into his hand, then purposefully moved an ink stand, a pen, and a blue and white patterned side plate—with the drying pips of an orange upon it—a little way away from the bug-a-bug box. He then swallowed hard, sat back upon his chair, folded his arms, took a breath of composure, and said to July, 'You have a message for me?'

At last.

'Me missus,' July began, 'wan' to know . . .' But this overseer's eyes would not stay upon her. Gradually they returned their gaze to the restless creatures within the box. 'She has beef,' July said, hoping a greedy stomach might wrest back his attention.

'Beef . . .' he repeated, heedless.

'Me missus say—you wan' come to eat beef for dinner? Heifer be killed in the pen and me missus . . .'

'Heifer . . .' he said.

July thought to yell, 'A tiger be gnawing the missus and a monkey be wearing her petticoat!' Tiger . . . monkey . . . softly spoken would surely be this man's careless reply, for his focus rested so fast upon that box. When one brave cockroach hooked its scabrous legs over the rim while calling on all who were still alive below to follow in this escape, the overseer slowly began to push his chair away from the desk.

'So what shall me tell me missus?' July carried on.

But the overseer just yelled out, 'Elias, come and take this wretched box away!'

Raising himself swiftly from his seat he rushed to the door to shout, 'I pay you to catch them and take them away. Come back here now! I demand you come back here now, boy.'

Elias soon appeared before him, grinning as only mischievous negro boys do. 'Me find plenty more, massa. You wan' come see?' he said.

'Just take that box away. Get rid of them. And do not leave them on the veranda, like last time. Take them far away. Do you understand? Kill them and take them far away.'

Elias, grabbing the box, soon noticed July's two breasts and, for a moment, stopped to stare upon them before saying, 'Me find plenty more roach-bug, you wan' see? Me can show you, Miss July.' July did not actually slap Elias's head, nor command him with harsh words to, 'Take it now or me bash your ears till them ring all day.' She just gave him one look, then stamped her foot down hard—and this did say and do it all for her. Elias carried out the odious box as if walking with a tray of precious jewels across a swamp, for none must spill to scurry home, past his fuss-fuss massa.

The overseer sat down at his desk, then looking to July said, 'I am so very sorry. Could you please repeat your mistress's message?'

As July opened her mouth—to talk again of the heifer and the beef and the dinner—the biggest, blackest, monstrous beetle you ever did see, fell from a beam in the ceiling on to the desk, right in front of the overseer. This miscreated creature was surely the colossus of the cock-roach dominion; for so immense was it that the blue and white plate that it landed upon seemed to crack under the bug's hard shell and the little pips of orange that were scattered upon the dish bounced into the air like jumping beans.

Now. That the overseer jolted upon his seat, then stood up in fright upon seeing the creature land, is certain. That he leaped from his chair, somersaulted three times backwards away from the desk to arrive at the other side of the room with his legs wobbling beneath him like a new-born calf's while pulling upon his hair and shrieking wild as missus gone mad, may be hard for my readers to believe, but that is how July remembers it. The white man was terrified—tears of fear soaked his face as he flapped before July, frenzied as a moth caught within a net.

July was quick to snatch this ugly bug from the plate and dash it hard on to the floor. But this well-defended creature hit the ground clattering like a propelled stone, then merely flipped itself over and commenced to walk away. July had to stamp upon it with her heel. Its shell then shat-tered with the snap and splatter of a rotten coconut bursting.

The overseer fixed a gaze of wonderment upon July—he was speech-less. Until slowly, upon an exhaled breath, he stuttered, 'Thank you.' Then he began to awaken back into this life, 'There are just so many cockroaches in this house,' he sighed. 'They are simply everywhere.

There was one on my pillow yesterday. As I was going to bed, I pulled back my sheet to find it sitting there.'

'But them just be bug-a-bugs,' July replied. 'Plenty 'pon this island, massa, them have no harm in them. Me is no feared of them.'

'No? Well, you now know that your master is very feared of them,' he said. 'And you may laugh at me now all you wish. Who could blame you? You may tell everyone you meet how ridiculous the new overseer is when there are cockroaches anywhere near him. I cannot hide it now, can I?'

Then, as he sat back down upon the chair at his desk, he said, 'Look at this! It's made a crack in this plate.' He handed the blue and white plate to July. Now, July knew that the cockroach did not make the crack in the plate, but as she took it from him she stared upon the pattern, for it was one she recognised. And he asked her, 'Do you like it?'

'Oh yes,' she said. And, before she knew, she was telling him, 'See upon this plate there be a tale. There be birds flying and the river has a likkle bridge that . . .' But feeling him staring upon her intently, listening to her fool-fool reverie, July suddenly forgot all she was thinking and stopped. She held out the plate for him to take it back.

'Keep it,' he said.

July, sure she had not heard correctly, held the plate a little closer to him. But he shook his head. 'Take the plate, if you like it. Keep it as payment for saving my life.'

Never before had July been given something so precious by a white man. It was now her turn for words to leave her. But then when he asked, 'Tell me something, what is your name? Your mistress calls you Marguerite, but Elias called you . . .' July interrupted to say clearly, 'Miss July.'

'Miss July? Then why does your mistress call you Marguerite?'

'Her t'ink that pretty name to call a slave. Now her can say no other.'

'Well,' the overseer said, 'May I call you Miss July?'

'Surely, massa, for that be me true name.'

'Then, Miss July, what is your message?'

July had almost forgotten the reason why she was standing before this man. 'Oh yes,' she began, 'Me missus wan' you come to dinner, for her has beef that must be eat up.'

'Beef! I haven't had beef in a while. Beef. Now that leaves me with a dilemma.' Suddenly this man leaned back upon his chair to call out over his shoulder, 'Joseph, what is it you are preparing for my dinner tonight?'

There came a little giggle from the kitchen before his man servant yelled, 'Godammies, massa.'

'What on earth did he say?' the overseer asked July.

'Him say, godammies.'

'And what is that?'

'That be fish, massa.'

'Fish! Oh, fish again. I think beef sounds much better—do not you think, Miss July? Please tell your mistress that I gratefully accept her invitation. I would like very much to eat beef . . . in her company, of course.'

And, as a broad smile lit upon his face, July realised then that, for once, her missus was right—he surely did have the bluest eyes.

CHAPTER 22

A T THE EDGE OF the town, upon a quiet street that is arid and dusty as a flour barrel, walks our July. Her task within the town upon this hot-hot and parched day is the purchase of some bright-yellow kid gloves for her missus—'With a Bolton thumb, Marguerite, if they can be found.' For now Caroline Mortimer has often to entertain a guest at her table, all her many pairs of gloves are just too mucky to wear.

Walking along the street, July passes a group of negro men wilting within the shade of a veranda and smoking upon pipes. One drowsily calls her name. And she, straining to recognise the caller under the shadow of the eaves, soon raises her hand to wave; it is Ebo Cornwall, that rascal African who often supplies her candles and earthenware. A ragged old negro woman, fussing with a weary donkey that refuses to move, sits down upon the road fanning herself with a banana leaf before turning to stare with hungry eyes upon July. Two pigs start a little squabble at the corner that disturbs the crows into squawking and flapping upon the roofs above her. A dog raises itself in anticipation of a chasing but then, upon a second thought, merely stretches its legs in turn before curling back to sleep. A young negro man sitting at an open window wipes a wet cloth around his neck as he calls out, 'Hey, miss, miss, pretty miss,' but July certainly does not notice him. For a cart being pushed recklessly by a running boy passes her and its wobbling wheels churn up the dust to such a fog that it catches at her throat.

As July wiped the stinging grit from her eyes that day, there came from out of the dirty haze a startling apparition. From the other end of the street appeared a tall woman. A tall, graceful woman. A tall, graceful, coloured woman dressed entirely in white. She walked . . . no . . . she glided—for no heel nor toe of this golden beauty did seem to touch the solid earth—towards July. Atop her head she wore a white turban adorned with a long feather that pointed so high-high it did tickle the chin of God. The sleeves upon her muslin dress billowed like soft sunny day clouds. The cloth of the lavish skirt gushed from the band at her tiny waist to cascade like foaming water to the ground. And the hem of this glorious garment was so festooned with embroidered flowers that this lovely surely had walked through the garden of Eden and all that was pretty had attached itself there. Even the fringed parasol this fair-skinned maiden twirled could rival the sun for brightness.

No adjusting of July's red kerchief upon her head made her feel worthy to linger within the wake of this fair-skinned beauty. In her ugly grey skirt, with the rip at the knee that was stitched so badly in black, her yellowing blouse with no button left upon the fraying cuffs, and her skin, of course, so nasty dark, July was shameful as a field nigger. But then as July, with her head bowed, stepped to pass that elegant miss upon that shabby street, she heard, 'Ah, Miss July, you walking to town this day?'

It was with revulsion that July at once realised this coloured woman she was glorifying was Miss Clara. Come, if July had recognised her haughty figure before, there would have been no meeting. For our July would have dived into the cover of near bush, or stood skinny behind the pillar of a house, so Miss Clara could not find her.

⸺

Reader, you must remember Miss Clara? I have written of her before. Miss Clara, who was once the house slave at Prosperity? Who did feign to faint away at any rough word? 'Is it me dress you like or me pretty fair face that make you stare so,' Miss Clara. The quadroon whose papa was

a naval man from Scotch land. Yes, that one! The dreadful Miss Clara. Come, let me tell you of her.

Miss Clara did grab her freedom before many others. Not because she continued to brandish those aging manumit papers that her papa did bequeath her within her missus's face. No. Miss Clara's missus was pleased to watch her haughty backside sashay out of her employ for, 'But me be a quadroon, missus,' was all she would say to each and every task required of her. Soon the choosing of her missus's attire for the day—or for the evening—was all Miss Clara would deign to do. The thirty-one pounds compensation money for the loss of Miss Clara as her slave was of much more value to her missus.

Then, once free, Miss Clara proceeded to flounce into town to begin a little business. Like so many other women with tinted complexions varying from honey to milk and oft-talked of papas—from England, Ireland, Scotland or Wales, fine, upstanding, white gentleman all—the cooking and selling of jams and pickles became her employ.

Her ginger preserve and lime pickle were popular, but her guava jelly . . . 'Miss Clara's guava jelly—oh, have you tried it?' soon became the call of so many white people within the parish. Caroline Mortimer sent July often to Miss Clara's little shack upon Trelawny Street. (Oh, I must call it a shop, for Miss Clara may read this volume.) And every time July entered that shop, Miss Clara's green eyes and delicate mouth would conspire to sneer pitifully upon her. 'Oh, Miss July,' she would say, 'your missus send you all this way on this hot-hot day for me guava jelly? But you must be tired out,' before inflicting one big-big jar upon July that could hardly be lifted as she said, 'Me know your missus love it so. Me make this just for her.'

Her make it? Cha! You think you would ever see Miss Clara's pretty fair face leaning over a steaming pot? 'No, me is a quadroon. But me supervise the cook-up in every way,' was her answer. And hear this, Miss Clara's recipe for guava jelly was *her* secret, she proclaimed—she would allow no one to have it. It was to be her companion within her grave.

But why should my readers have to tarry so long? Here is that unsaid

recipe for you to cook up if you so wish: Take the basket of guava and cut and boil them in the usual way until they are soft; put the mush-mush in muslin to hang till morning so the liquor will drain; add as much sugar and the juice of a lime to the liquor; then (and here is Miss Clara's big-big secret) fish out the flies and spice up with cinnamon and rum; and boil it, boil it, boil it, until the jelly forms.

There—Miss Clara's grave need now only carry her pretty fair bones.

With the plenty profits Miss Clara made from her preserving, and a little money she did receive from the selling of simples for the relieving of indigestion and bilious complaints, she took upon herself the arrang-ing of a series of social dances and gatherings at the assembly rooms within the town. This society was sorely needed. For an unfortunate acquaintance of Miss Clara's (let me not use her name, but just say that she was a mulatto woman whose papa was a lawyer-man from County Wexford in Ireland) had been pressed by a coloured man into keeping house for him. This coloured man said that his mama was a mulatto housekeeper from Westmoreland. He then swore that his papa was a bookkeeper from London Town. This would make him a quadroon, and a quadroon was what this honey-coloured man avowed himself to be.

But the subsequent child that was born to this mulatto and supposed quadroon came forth dark as cocoa nut! How could this be, Miss Clara's friend wailed? Far from raising that mulatto woman's colour nearer to white, her offspring had taken her backwards. Yet, despite the shame of this rogue pickney, the woman refused to give up either the deceiving man or the sable child. Miss Clara could no longer be a friend to her.

But Miss Clara determined that she would lose no more from within her circle after her mulatto seamstress, believing her union to be with a mulatto man (which Miss Clara had cautioned her against, for only another worthless mulatto could result), found the smooth-tongued man to be nothing more than red negro. A sambo was brought forth into this world, and a broad-nosed one at that. Come, Miss Clara was left with no one to stitch her fine needlework.

The tar brush, reader, is quick to lick. For a mulatto with a negro, or a

quadroon with a sambo, will produce the misfortune of a retrograde child. And that dusky offspring will be sent nowhere but spinning back down to sup with the niggers in the fields. A mulatto with a mulatto, or a quadroon with a quadroon, will find you suckling a 'Tente-en-el-aire'— a suspended child. They will neither lift forward to white, nor drop back to negro.

Only with a white man, can there be guarantee that the colour of your pickney will be raised. For a mulatto who breeds with a white man will bring forth a quadroon; and the quadroon that enjoys white relations will give to this world a mustee; the mustee will beget a mustiphino; and the mustiphino . . . oh, the mustiphino's child with a white man for a papa will find each day greets them no longer with a frown, but welcomes them with a smile, as they at last stride within this world as a cherished white person.

Forward only to white skin became Miss Clara's mission.

So only white men were allowed introduction to the coloured women at Miss Clara's Friday dances. Be he a red-haired attorney from Galashiels who talked of nothing but home; a drunken Bristol naval man with a fearsome crimson face; a handsome Irish overseer who never learned to dance; a lecherous planter from Liverpool who had many more than two hands, or a foppish merchant from Surrey with plenty missing teeth, as long as their money tinkled with the correct sound, any of these white men would be welcome to partner her coloured women for a quadrille or a Scottish reel. Or fetch them some Madeira and punch. Or perhaps take their arms for a stroll in the evening air. But only white men.

It was a great relief to all. Soon, 'Have you been to Miss Clara's dances? Oh, you must come to Miss Clara's' became the call of all coloured women within the parish. And Miss Clara did puff up and puff up higher than any guava jelly did ever take her.

But do you believe Miss Clara would let someone like our July walk happily into that exalted company? For the coloured women who desired association with these white men, Miss Clara prepared a list of features that they simply must possess to be approved admittance. July advanced no more than to the door of one of these gatherings before Miss Clara descended upon her.

'Now, Miss July,' she said, 'you know me dances be just for coloured women.'

'But me is a mulatto, Miss Clara,' July informed her. For a mulatto July had to be, at the very least. Her papa was a white man.

'You is just hoping to lift your colour, Miss July. You is not a mulatto. Be on your way,' Miss Clara told her.

'Me is a mulatto!' cried our July.

'Your papa be a white man?' Miss Clara scoffed. 'You is too dark for your papa to be white.' For July's skin had to be light. Honey to milk hues only, could Miss Clara approve. No bitter chocolate nor ebony skin ever stepped a country dance in her presence.

'Me tell you true, Miss Clara. Me papa be a white man.'

'No him was not.'

'Him was.'

'Him was not—him was some nigger.'

'Him was the overseer 'pon Amity.'

'Him was not.'

'Him was a Scotch man.'

'A Scotch man! You no speak true.'

This argument between the two continued for so long awhile—too long for me to give detail of it here—that Tam Dewar did enter in upon this squabbling. Yes, reader, Tam Dewar! For you and I know that he was indeed July's papa. And within July's telling he rose again. In the face of Miss Clara's scorning he dallied within July's story; no longer the pitiless and brutal overseer she knew him to be, who did imperil her reason, pursuing her once in life and now through every cursed dream. No. As he was a white man, he now became July's much cherished papa who had made promise to one day take her to Scotch Land before he was struck down by a fearsome nigger.

'Me is a mulatto, a mulatto, a mulatto, you hear, Miss Clara!' July did state until Miss Clara wearily and reluctantly offered to inspect her.

Within a little room, before the dimming light in the window, Miss

Clara proceeded. First she measured the width of July's nose with her finger, before turning July to see how far that nose lifted from her face. For no broad, flat nose was tolerated. Miss Clara then stared into July's eyes. Were they much admired green, vastly coveted grey, prayed for blue or simply dull brown? Removing July's head kerchief, Miss Clara felt her hair. She lifted it to see if it fell back or stayed up like fright. Hair must be good. Straight with a little curl is best, be it fair, brown, red, or black. For no picky-picky head would ever tangle and frizz around her white men. She required July to open her mouth while pouting her lips forward. Miss Clara then pinched them to feel their bulk before demanding July close her mouth and turn to profile. No fat lips ever sipped porter or punch at her gatherings. And then, with a slow, searching, measured glare that travelled up and down July two, three, four times, Miss Clara perused the whole of her. For without the whiff of English white somewhere about her, July would just never do.

'Your lips not too bad,' Miss Clara finally pronounced, 'Nor be your nose too broad. But your hair not be good. And your skin—your skin be just too dark. Oh no, no, no, you will not do. You is too full of negro. Me men only like a fair skin and pretty face. And your dress, Miss July, why you no wear one of your missus's dress? Oh, me remember now, she be too broad. But your dress be a house-nigger's dress. You is not fine, Miss July. No, no, no.'

Miss Clara did not kick July to see her gone, for she would never countenance such an indelicate gesture. And even though July folded her arms under this scorning and raised her not-too-broad nose into the air and told Miss Clara that she did not want to wiggle at this fool-fool dance, and would one day come to jig upon Miss Clara's grave, and that she knew her mystery guava jelly had in rum and cinnamon, and that she did cook it up whenever she pleased—yet still our July came to feel the forceful impress of Miss Clara's pretty, pale, slippered foot upon her backside as she was spurned for being too ugly to market.

July had not seen Miss Clara since that day. But no, let me make an amend; Miss Clara had never chanced upon July since that time.

But now upon that hot-hot day within the shabby dusty street, Miss Clara was once more peering down her slender upturned nose and pinning her disdain upon the top of July's head. July felt it land heavy as a firm hand. Soon those green eyes and that delicate mouth would conspire to sneer pitifully upon her, until July would feel the ugliest thing that coloured woman would encounter that parched morning.

'Good day to you, Miss Clara,' July said with the hope of moving quickly on.

But Miss Clara caught July's arm to bind her in conversation. July did not notice the four gold rings upon Miss Clara's fingers. Four! Two with green stones that clicked together—big as swollen knuckles, yet July did not see them. Nor did she regard the delicate ruby beads mounted like pin pricks of blood within a striking gold chain which laced about her throat.

'You have no parasol this day, Miss July? You be get very dark,' Miss Clara said.

July did have a parasol—a hand-down from her missus—but Molly did recently sit upon it and bust two spokes, so it hung like a broken bird wing. When she returned to Amity she must remember to once more punch Molly for the nuisance of that misdeed.

'So, Miss July, you still working 'pon Amity for that broad missus?' Miss Clara asked from upon high.

'It be so, Miss Clara, although me missus be no longer so broad,' July responded.

'Not what I have heard,' Miss Clara said before carrying on, 'I could not abide to still be upon a plantation. Me upon a plantation!' And how Miss Clara did laugh. She raised her hand to cover her mouth as little puffs of mirth were discharged within it. Then, composing herself, she gravely shook her head to say, 'The wife of a white man upon a plantation,' before a sweet titter again escaped her at such a ludicrous affront. 'Me husband would never allow it.'

Husband! Oh yes, July had heard the chat-chat of Miss Clara's husband. Come, the whole parish knew how Mr William Walker the attorney at Friendship plantation had paid for her dance and bought her hand. Her husband! That fat-bellied, peel-headed, ugly old white man had a wife and five children in England. There was never any marriage ceremony—at least none that a crowd could stand within a church to witness. Miss Clara just clasped this rich Englishman's shrivelled private parts and now led him around by them.

'He buy me a lodging house, me husband,' Miss Clara carried on. 'You know it? It be the big white house 'pon the corner of Trelawny Street, near to me shop.' She airily waved her hand around in the general direction of that nearby corner before turning her devilish green eyes full upon July to glory delightedly within her envy.

But July would let not a muscle, nor a hair, stir to admit jealousy of Miss Clara. Come, a gutted fish upon a slab did speak its thoughts more tellingly.

'You did not know of me lodging house?' Miss Clara went on, 'I believed everyone did hear of it. But wait.' She felt within a small, white satin pouch that dangled from her wrist and produced a calling card. She held out the card to July. But just as July inclined to take it, Miss Clara withdrew it saying, 'Oh, but me forget plantation slaves cannot read.'

July soon snatched it from her saying, 'We be slaves no more, Miss Clara. Me nor you.' And holding up the card to her eye, July began loud and clear to read, 'Miss Clara's boarding house, for the con . . . the con . . .' July stumbled over the word convenience for she had never before seen it. So many letters, but none made the sound of sense within her head.

'Oh, your missus let you read a little now,' Miss Clara said.

There was something upon this card written about military men and families, gentlemen and ladies' finest, clean lodging house, etc., which July could read at a glance—but, to her vexation, she was still struggling with that word convenience, when a cart rode into the street. Both women stepped away to let pony and cart pass at a distance, for they required no more dust to churn up and choke them. But then a man's voice, shouting, 'Hello there, hello there,' made them both turn their heads to find the caller.

And there, sitting alone atop the cart, dressed in a brown cutaway jacket with a panama hat upon his head was Robert Goodwin. The spirited smile that excited the overseer's eyes as he said, 'Good day to you,' had the gladness of someone addressing a dear old friend. July turned to observe Miss Clara's response, for she felt sure this white man must be greeting her. But then he said, 'Are you on an errand for your mistress today, Miss July?' And even though Miss Clara twirled upon her parasol so its brightness could entice even a blind creature to her, Robert Goodwin kept his eyes firmly upon July.

'Surely be, massa,' July said.

'Then may I drive with you back to Amity? I've finished my business here and I am returning,' he asked her.

Now July was, as matter-of-fact, walking in upon the town and had not yet searched for those yellow kid gloves that her missus so required. But only she knew this. And what did her missus need with another pair of gloves? Bolton thumbs, cha—how was she to find Bolton thumbs? There were no yellow kid gloves with Bolton thumbs within this town—July became sure of it. For travelling off alone within a pony cart with a white man, while Miss Clara stood looking on, had now become July's only purpose that day.

'Yes. Thanking you,' July said to Mr Goodwin. Then, handing Miss Clara back her calling card, July said, 'Good day to you, Miss Clara.'

Miss Clara told her that she may keep it to give it to this white man. And July replied that he had no need of it and that she should take it back. All this was spoken without a word sounding between them. That mute message was conveyed with the slight motions and tiny tics of a silent language learned from dread of white people's intrusion—and even the fair Miss Clara still knew how to speak it.

As Robert Goodwin jumped down from the cart to help July board it—like she was some dainty white miss—Miss Clara stepped forward to hand the card to Mr Goodwin herself. But he, with a curt rudeness that no white woman would ever witness from a gentleman, waved it away without even a glance to her.

Then, as the cart proceeded along the street, July, sitting atop it thought, what a shame Miss Clara did not consider that gutted fish upon a slab; for July was able to read every one of Miss Clara's feelings within the gaping expression upon her face.

CHAPTER 23

⁓

THE CART WAS STILL within that parched street, not yet out of Miss Clara's gaze. Come, it had not even reached to pass by Ebo Cornwall, yet July—while telling this young overseer for the third time that, 'Yes, yes, she be quite comfortable,'—began to wonder what style of dress she would desire to wear if she, like Miss Clara, could catch a white man for a 'husband.'

So when Robert Goodwin, with a slight frown of hesitation, flicked his head toward where Miss Clara stood and asked, 'Miss July, is that woman a friend of yours?' our July, quite tingling with the notion that this tender young man might be caught, was keen to impress him.

'Oh, yes. Miss Clara be me good-good friend, good-good friend, since long time. We always do chat upon the road when we does meet, for we be so friendly. Oh yes, Miss Clara be me good friend,' July answered. For she was sure that this white man would be beguiled to see that such a lowly, dark-skinned mulatto house servant as she, did enjoy the close society of a quadroon as fine, beautiful and fair-skinned as Miss Clara.

But when she turned to him to bask within his approval, she found his cheeks slightly reddening, his chest rising with a heavy breath and his lips pinching into a tight line. Now, English people can be hard to read, for they do believe that a firm face with no sentiment upon it is a virtue. But July was an expert in all their guiles and knew without hesitation that she had delivered this man the wrong answer. But for what reason, our July had yet to grasp.

When he at once said, 'Really? You are friends,' July was quick to respond, 'Me not be that friendly since she has been within the town, for me does hardly see her. No, we not be such friends . . .' but was sorely troubled when he interrupted to ask, 'Do you attend her dances at the assembly rooms?'

Would a 'yes' or a 'no' secure this man's favour? July was now confused. A 'yes' might hear him gladly say, 'Then it would be my honour to accompany you next time, Miss July.' For maybe he enjoyed to trip and spin within this company; white men from all across the parish did delight in attending those dances and he was a white man. And the truth within a 'no' would prove her an outcast—too dark and ugly for those fair occasions. Yet although July always feared telling the truth to a white person (for her fictions were often better understood), something within his manner—a furrow in his brow? his hand too tight upon the reins? his foot tapping upon the board? (she could not tell you what)— implored her to say, 'No.'

What a breath July did exhale when he said, 'I am so glad to hear it, Miss July.' And when, with peevish disdain, he went on saying, 'Those dances are not a place that a Christian person should attend,' July all at once supposed she was beginning to understand this particular white man.

'No,' she said, 'me prefer to rest at home.' And then, in a moment of sweet inspiration added, 'Me does like to stay home to read me Bible.'

His face lit with such clear delight that some in England might have thought him disloyal for letting such obvious pleasure glow upon it. 'Your Bible. You enjoy to read the Bible, Miss July?' he asked.

'Oh yes,' she carried on.

'Do you have a favourite story from that good book?'

'Yes,' July said without hesitation. 'Me like the story of how the whole world did be made best of all.'

In truth, there was no indecision within July for this was the *only* story she knew from that holy book. When Caroline Mortimer was teaching July her letters she at first used that big, heavy, dusty tome for

July's instruction. But the little print was so hard for July to read or construe, that the missus began to drift into dozing long before God rested from his labours upon the seventh day. Her missus then swapped the book from which July was to recite, for one where two silly sisters—white women who were required to do no work—did spend their days fretting and crying over the finding of husbands. The missus's Bible was now used only for the wayward to place their hand upon it to swear they speak in truth (come, Molly did have to slap it so often she thought it a drum), but rarely did it open for stories to escape it.

'Are there any other passages you enjoy?' Robert Goodwin continued. July raised up her eyes, as if to ponder upon his question. 'The story of the Good Samaritan, perhaps?' he asked.

'Oh yes, me like it very much,' said July.

'And what about Moses parting the Red Sea?'

'That is a very good tale.'

'Or perhaps the story of the three little pigs?' he wondered.

'Me does like them all,' July told him. 'But the resting 'pon the seventh day tale be me favoured.' And he, glancing at her sideways, did grin so wide a smile upon her that she feared she may have amused him in some way.

So July decided she would speak no more unless he continued to press her. The beat of the pony's hooves clopping upon the road and the rhythm within the squeaking and creaking wooden cart made a queer sort of music as they travelled. And although July was wishing to appear as demure as a white lady touring within a carriage as she sat with her hands resting together upon her lap, she was mightily aware that the overseer's leg was pressing hard against her own. She could feel it tensing stiff as he held himself steady with the effort of guiding the cart and pony. Once a tricky movement was complete she felt the strong muscle of his thigh ease and relax. His jacket sleeves were rolled up about his elbows and exposed the tiny black hairs upon his bare forearms to quiver with the breeze of his motion; while his hands, gripping the reins, were held dainty as if leading a woman to dance. And July did sniff a sweet scent of wood-smoke drifting from him.

But as she craftily glanced upon his face and beheld his eyelashes—

which were so dark and lush as to appear like a silk fringe upon his lids—she was at once aware that if she was noticing all about him, then would not he be slyly assessing her; the badly stitched tear in her ugly grey skirt, the tatty red kerchief upon her head hiding her picky-picky hair, her still-too-broad nose, her dull-brown eyes and, of course, her black skin? July became rigid with unease as the cart bumped upon the road and gently threw them together—sometimes her against him and sometimes him against her.

When the watchman's stone hut at the gate of Amity appeared in the near distance, July longed to assure this white man, before they parted, that she was not a rough negro. No. She was a mulatto. Even though he may see her skin to be a shade too dusky, she wished him the comfort of knowing that she was not a nigger's pickney, but a white man's child. So she breached that silence she had so hard determined to keep by saying, 'Massa, you ever been Scotch Land?'

'Scotland?' Robert Goodwin enquired with some puzzlement. 'No, but I've heard it is very beautiful. But why do you ask?'

'Me papa be from Scotch Land,' July was pleased to be able to inform him.

'Your father was a Scotch man?'

'Oh yes, he be from Scotch Land.'

'Your father was a white man?'

'Oh yes. Me be a mulatto, not a negro.'

'A mulatto?'

'Yes, a mulatto. You must not think me a nigger, for me is a mulatto.' July then waited to witness his esteem. She was sure it would be forthcoming. But the overseer's expression did not exclaim joy at her salvation. Come, there were those reddening cheeks, that swelling chest and pinching lips once more. But why? July was truly bewildered.

'Did your father know you, Miss July?'

And Tam Dewar was once more called upon to step up and take his part within July's narration. 'Oh yes.' July said.

'Was he good to you?'

'Good to me, massa?' July faltered, for she did not want to construct a tale of that devilish man's goodness only for Robert Goodwin to frown it away.

'Did he give you his name?' the white man went on, 'Did he see you were baptised? Were you schooled?'

July nearly threw up her arms to the heavens—she felt to scream, for this man was vexing her so. What fanciful fiction she would have to weave to please him—for surely no truth could help her win this young man's favour. So she said, 'Him say him would one day take me to Scotch Land. Him did say him would take me . . . one day,' while all the while examining the young overseer's face for distress. When he continued to merely listen and nod, she carried on, 'Him did put me 'pon him knee and him did pinch me cheeks just so.' And she demonstrated this pinching upon her own cheeks, pulling them wide to show her papa's playfulness. 'And me papa did say, "One day, me little cherish,"—for him did call me "me little cherish"—"me gon' bring you to Scotch Land."'

And the overseer's face did soften a little . . . perhaps.

'What was your father's name?'

'Me papa name be Mr Tam Dewar.'

'Tam Dewar,' the overseer repeated, 'I know that name. Was he not the overseer at Amity once upon a time?'

'Yes,' July said. 'Him was a fine overseer. Him be a kind-kind massa to all.'

'Was Tam Dewar married to your mother, Miss July?'

What sort of fool-fool question was this? Tell me, reader, did you ever, up to now, hear of an overseer upon a sugar plantation thinking to marry a slave he has befouled? A senseless liar would July be proved if she answered him, 'Yes.' And a 'No' would surely see this man turn from her.

July all at once gave up the whole notion of charming this white man, for there was too much work to do within it. And what a foolish endeavour it was. She needed no glass to tell her that she was too dark and lowly a house servant for a man so fine English as Robert Goodwin to find beauty within her. So although July did not, with honesty, answer that her papa just bent her mama over several times to do his business, but that her mama did later kill him for it, there was some nimble truth-tripping within what she actually said. 'Him pass on, massa. Jus' as me papa was to take me mama, them both dead in the riots.' Then, as the words left July's mouth, she lifted her hands to her eyes. To stop her tears from flowing? No. This was just fancy feigning.

Now believing her to be crying, Robert Goodwin was suddenly concerned. 'I am sorry,' he said. 'Have I upset you?' he asked. 'Forgive me,' he demanded. Then, within a brief moment, he placed his hand tenderly upon July's arm. And that touch did tingle upon her skin so.

Of course July fell against him as he helped her down from the cart, for she tripped her foot upon the board—it is easily done from a pony cart. And in his embrace to steady her, he held her solid and firm within his arms for a long moment. Their faces were so close that July took breath from the same air as he, while his clear blue eyes never strayed from hers.

'Miss July,' he said while releasing her, 'I have a book on Scotland.' He took a breath with which to continue, but faltered. His tongue licked to moisten his lips as he went on, 'It was given to me as a gift.' He glanced quickly about himself before saying with a hushed tone, 'Perhaps you will allow me to show it to you one day?' Then he stepped back away from July so quickly that some might consider that he jumped. And his face blushed pink as a boiled shrimp as he raised his hat to her in parting.

'T'ank you, massa,' July responded with a broad smile, 'Me will.'

White muslin, July decided as he, calling for Byron to attend the pony, walked away. A white muslin dress would be her desire.

⟨⎯⎯⎯⎯⎯⟩

Robert Goodwin was resting within his hammock so peacefully that as July tip-toed up the steps of his veranda she motioned to two mockingbirds to hush their trilling song. They would not be stilled by her waving hand, nor by the small stone she aimed upon them within the bough of the orange tree. But their persistent carry-on was not troubling the overseer within his midday slumber. It was a week since July had last gazed on him and she stood over him a long while.

She had never before seen anyone, except perhaps a newborn, lying so tranquil upon this island. His dangling legs were splayed over each side of the hammock. His feet were bare; his tall leather boots standing patient and purposeful at the side. The white shirt he wore was untied at the neck to reveal the shy black hair upon his chest curling out from beneath the cloth. One arm was crooked under his sleeping head, while the other was thrown across his forehead with dramatic gesture. Long and straight was his nose. Thin and wide was his mouth. And so still was he in repose that, excepting for the faintest drone of a snore that hummed from him, he could have been dead.

His greedy-eyed house boy, Elias, had pushed out his bottom lip in a sulk when disclosing to July that Robert Goodwin always slept upon his veranda in the heat of midday. For the overseer had requested the house boy to keep his quiet ritual a secret, lest any negroes knowing him confined thought to hound him with more dispute over their rent or wages. But by turning Elias's ear until it felt to be tearing from his head, July had eased this secret from the house boy—for she required the overseer to be alone when she came to view his book.

Was it those clamorous mockingbirds or the intensity of the gaze with which July beheld Robert Goodwin that roused one of his eyes to open slowly to peruse the sensed intrusion upon his rest? Finding July standing over him, he nearly spilled from the hammock in his effort to be upright. Of course he was surprised—for not only was July peering upon him with a comely smile, but she was looking so fine. Her kerchief was not ugly, but her best blue. And her dress—a missus cast-off— was tucked and stitched and trimmed until the pink, blue, green, and mauve flowers upon the cotton cloth of the skirt, the puffing of the sleeves and the white of the cape collar arranged themselves so pleasingly about her, as to present to him a vision of a rare exotic beauty.

He stood up, hurriedly tucking his shirt into his breeches. 'Miss July, have you a message for me?' He ran his hands through his untidy hair, clearly worried that sleep had left it not looking at its best—which was true, for several tufts sprung like bristle from it.

'No, massa,' July said, 'me come to see the book.'

Still dazed as a small boy roused before sunrise, he asked, 'The book?'

'With picture of Scotch Land?' July reminded him.

'Of course, of course,' he said. 'Forgive me. The mockingbirds— there are two in that tree—they were singing so beautifully I just fell asleep for a moment.'

'Yes—them does surely like to sing,' July said. While he, as if perceiving her for the first time, passed one long gaze over her—from the tip of her unclothed toes to the top of her well-dressed head. Then he managed to repeat the words, 'The book,' before all his breath and most of his sense left him.

At once he began looking around himself as if searching for someone to rescue him. So awkward did he become that he could no longer regard July's face, and speak. As his mouth opened to say, 'Are you . . . are you . . . ?' he examined his bare feet. As he attempted to begin once more, with a little more clarity, 'Miss July, are you . . . ?' he sought to catch sight of the mockingbirds within the tree. And as he gulped to say finally, 'Are you alone?' it was his wringing hands that held his attention. When July answered with a gay, 'Yes,' come, the man nearly swooned.

Suddenly he turned to walk into the house saying, 'I have it somewhere in here. It may take me a little while to . . .' before turning to gaze once more upon July. His barefoot stride continued only after he bit his lip to summon his fortitude.

July followed him through that door, very close behind.

'You have plenty book on Scotch Land, massa?' she asked as she strolled around his small withdrawing room. She stopped to look upon a side cupboard on which rested a draggletailed posy of pink periwinkles within a blue vase. And by its side was a miniature portrait within a metal frame, no bigger than a missus locket that was worn about the neck. The picture showed a severe-looking white man with bushy whiskers staring back upon her. July leaned in close to view the fine details—there was a cross at his neck and a ring upon his hand, but she saw no more for she straightened again when the overseer said, 'No, I just have this one. It was given to me by my last employer. I do not now recall why. But it has pictures of that country. Scotland. Ahh, here it is.'

He took the book from the bookcase with very slow care—inching it out only a little piece at a time. July soon realised that he was fretting that a suddenly awakened cockroach might fall from it. She held her hand to her mouth so he did not witness her amusement. 'Yes, this is the one,' he said. And he took the book over to his desk to lay it out upon it.

'Do you know where your father was from?' he enquired.

'Me father?' July asked as she walked across the room to stand so very close behind him.

'Yes, you said your father was a Scotch man.'

'Oh, me papa,' July said. She could see her breath fluttering the curling black hair at the back of his neck as she spoke those puffing words.

'Yes, your papa.'

'Yes, me papa be a Scotch man.'

'Well, let us see what we have in here,' he said.

He flicked quickly through the book and as July leaned in closer to look over his shoulder her breast, by chance, pressed against his arm. For a brief moment he stalled in his browsing but then carried on. He stopped at a drawing of a castle.

July, moving closer, squeezed her body up against his as she pointed at the picture saying, 'Be that where me papa live?'

His voice stammered as he responded, 'I . . . I . . . I doubt it as that is a castle.'

The little laugh he gave to follow these words rubbed her further against him. 'There are many castles in Scotland, but I doubt that any are home to overseers from the West Indies.' And as he turned to look at her, his lips nearly stroked her cheek.

He immediately began to rifle through the pages again in a businesslike manner. Most of this book was not pictures but dense black printed words. But there came a sketch of a small house with some sheep about it. 'This is probably more the thing,' Robert said, lifting the book a little so July might see it more clearly. July ran a finger along the roof and up over the chimney saying, 'This be me papa house?'

'Well, not actually this house . . . but . . . but,' Robert was now staring intently upon July as she perused the picture.

'And what be these?' she asked, pointing at the sheep.

'They are sheep,' he said.

And July, who did not know these woolly creatures, turned her face full on to his to ask, 'What be sheep?'

The book dropped back on to the table with a thump. The overseer's hands could no longer hold it, for they were shaking and limp. Like a rushing wind July felt his breath coming faster and quicker as he clasped her with a ferocity like anger. He was kissing her upon the mouth before she realised. His wet and loose tongue licked her like he was gorging upon greasy chicken.

July was overjoyed. Miss Clara, Miss Clara, boil up some water, for Miss July Goodwin is coming to take tea! The swelling of his private part began pressing hard upon July, and she knew that what she must do now was lead this tender young white man around by it.

But at once the overseer pulled sharply away from July. 'I am sorry, I am sorry. Forgive me. I am sorry,' he said, as he moved quickly across the room. Some might consider that he ran. Certainly, July thought herself to be chasing him when she followed behind him urging, 'No, no, it be right, massa.' But every time she approached upon him, the man would take a stride backwards away from her. What sort of dance was this? She stepping forward and he jumping back? Around and around that room they went in this manner. Come, it was quite comical.

But July, skilled in the catching of rats, soon trapped this man within a corner. He held out his arm to keep her from him, as he kept repeating upon a panting breath, 'My father, my father, my father,' before finally completing the plea with, 'My father would not approve.'

'But your papa not here,' July said softly.

'My father,' he carried on, 'has the highest contempt for white men who abuse their position with negroes.'

'Me is a mulatto, not a negro. It not be wrong, massa.'

'My father sent me here to do good. He is a righteous man.'

'Him will never know,' July said, almost gaily. But when he glanced full upon her, July recognised the anguish stricken within this white man's face.

'I can see my father before me and I must not.' He lifted up his head to plead heavenward saying, 'I will not give in to this temptation, Father, I will not.'

And July, looking up to that same spot where he could see his papa said, 'But there be no one there.'

'Please go, Miss July.'

'Your papa want you to be kind to negroes, massa,' July said as she moved a long step closer toward him.

'No, Miss July. Please leave now. Please, please, please, I beg you. You are too beautiful, you are too good . . .' The rest of his words were muffled and lost as he covered his face with his hands.

It was now July's turn to feel all her breath leave her. For this white man thought her beautiful. This white man thought her good. She lunged at him to catch him about the shoulders, for this prize was just too close for July to give up upon it now. But he pushed her off so fiercely that she nearly fell.

'Please, Miss July, please just go now.' Then clenching fistfuls of his own hair as if to wrench it from his head, he howled, 'Help me, Father, help me, Father,' before sliding down to sit in his corner and sob like a child.

CHAPTER 24

R EADER, I MUST WHISPER you a truth. Come, put your ear close to this page. Lean in a little closer still. For I am moved to speak honestly regarding the last chapter you have just read. Are you listening, reader? Then let me softly impart to you this fact. That is not the way white men usually behaved upon this Caribbean island.

CHAPTER 25

AFTER THAT DAY ROBERT Goodwin was forever watching July. She would find him at the garden's edge, astride his grey mare—enthralled, motionless—as she, seated upon the veranda steps ate an orange and licked her sticky fingers. Never did he come close when the sun was high and never did he greet her by name. But she caught him in open-mouthed reverie gawping upon her swaying hips as she walked the long path through the stony provision lands to do her business there, secretly, instead of using the pit near the kitchen. And wherever he did chance her—within the garden, upon the veranda, crossing to the kitchen, walking a path—anywhere, anywhere, he did spy her alone, July would sense the overseer's watchful pining. And, oh, how his blue eyes did gaze. Only the imagined commands from his tormenting papa did slap, shake, and rouse him to stop this foolish yearning and go about his day.

The overseer even surrendered his book to her—the one with the pictures of Scotch Land. July found it abandoned outside the door of her dwelling. And upon the pages where he had pointed so delightedly at her papa's house lay three pink periwinkles, compressed thin as gauze, within its leaves.

Then, one evening after sundown when all the shadows were gone, July was walking back from the garden after collecting up the windblown pods from the tamarind tree when she heard a palm bush panting. 'Miss July,' was called with urgency. She turned to find her eye bedazzled by a candle lantern held high and swinging. She knew it was him, but strained to see his face as it danced in and out of shadow. He held out his hand in front of him, his fingers splayed with insisting, 'Please stay quite still, Miss July, quite still.' July parted her lips to speak but he commanded, 'Please, do not speak.'

As she slowly lowered her arms to her sides, the handful of tamarinds she had collected scattered on to the floor. She planted her feet to stand as still as she might. Lifting her chin she stared into the lantern light. His hand upon the lantern held it so tight that the knuckles upon his fingers shone white as hens' eggs. And although his face was lost to shadow, his gaze was so keen upon her that she felt it like a fingertip stroking.

It traced a line that brushed over her forehead, caressed her nose, touched the bulge of her lips and stroked her throat, before resting its phantom pressure upon her breasts. Then Robert Goodwin whispered, 'This is wrong, I know this is wrong but I cannot help myself.'

Throwing the lantern to one side, he suddenly stepped forward to seize July about the waist. He was hot as the bread oven. July was puzzling whether to push him from her or close his embrace, when he threw her away. She stumbled. As she righted herself to stand before him she thought to shout, 'Careful, me nearly did fall,' but the sound of him weeping stilled her. She lifted her hand to find his face in the dark. His cheek beneath her touch was damp. At the feel of her fingertips upon him, the overseer placed his hand over hers. 'It is against everything,' he said. 'But, Miss July, you must know that I have come to love you. I love you.' And he softly kissed her palm before pulling away from her to vanish within the dark.

Yet it was to be a few weeks before July encountered Robert Goodwin again. Seated at the far corner of the veranda where a breeze occasionally blew the sultry still air with a little cooling, July was mending her missus's undergarments—the ones where the rats had eaten out all the sweaty parts—when the overseer came from out the house and saw her.

July, thinking that the overseer would only stare upon her, for it was daylight and morning, lifted her eyes to gaze up at him, but continued to stitch the nasty garments. It was when his quizzical expression changed into a broad smile of recognition and he commenced to walk towards where she sat, that she, in astonishment at his approach, dropped the needlework over the rail of the veranda. He was soon upon her. He pulled her to her feet, then looked quickly around himself for somewhere to hide her, like she were some stolen booty, before steering her down the veranda steps and around the corner to shelter within the secrecy of a large clump of bamboo.

As they stood concealed together he lifted her face to meet his by placing both his hands upon her cheeks. 'Look at me, Miss July. Look at me,' he said. At once July began to pull away from his grip for the urgency within his tone startled her. But he held her face firm. 'Listen to me, listen to me,' he carried on, until the shock within her expression began to reach him. He let her go.

Blinking to look softer, smiling to look calmer, he stepped back and raised his hands to show he meant no harm to her. But his boyish excitement soon overcame him again when he said, 'I have made a plan which I have just this minute set into action,' and he squeezed her face once more. 'Oh, Miss July, I have a plan that means we can be together. A plan,' he went on, 'so I might have you. A scheme that my father will have no quarrel with. Indeed, he will rejoice in it. He will thank God. I believe . . . I truly believe that my father will thank the Almighty for delivering his son from this temptation.'

Robert's blue eyes were large as moons. For a long moment they stared down upon July—until, that is, he leaned forward to kiss her. His lips brushed so gently against July's mouth that she became entranced by his sudden tenderness. She could think of no response to him. But the missus calling, 'Marguerite, Marguerite,' very close, soon ended July's quandary. For she and the overseer sprang apart like beans upon a fire. And he, dropping to crouch low as a sneak-thief, began whispering, 'Soon, Miss July, soon.'

He slipped away and out of all sight just as the missus rounded the corner to find July alone. 'Oh, there you are, Marguerite,' said the missus. July, now searching for the needlework she had thrown into the bush, began to babble to her missus about the breeze snatching the undergarments away from her, and how they flapped like some monstrous bird as they flew across the garden.

But Caroline Mortimer hushed her by waving her arms in front of July's face. 'Not now, not now, not now. No, no, no, no, no, there is too much to do,' her missus squealed. 'Oh, Marguerite, there is just so much to do.' Then, with the aid of her fleshy fingers, each of those splayed digits struck in turn, the missus commenced to list the tasks that must be done. There was pink satin silk that must be found, blond needle lace that must be sent for, slippers that must be trimmed with ribbon, a gown with fashionable bishop sleeves that must be made. 'And where are those yellow kid gloves?' The pig must be slaughtered, all the chickens too, a cake must be baked, 'But not by Molly,' cards must be printed, candles must be bought . . .

It was only July's quizzical look that made her missus stop between breaths to ask, 'What, have you not understood?' Then, sighing hard, for the missus was quite winded with all this activity on such a hot day, she carried on, 'Oh, I have not said.' She giggled. 'I have not told you.' She laid her hand upon July's arm. 'I have such news, Marguerite. I accepted him just a minute ago.' And she smiled broad, as she said, 'I am to be married. I am to be married to Robert Goodwin.'

PART 4

CHAPTER 26

S OMEWHERE, READER, THERE IS a painting, a portrait rendered in oils upon an oblong canvas (perhaps an arm's span in width) entitled, *Mr and Mrs Goodwin*. This likeness was commissioned by the newly married Caroline Goodwin from a renowned artist who did reside within the town of Falmouth. The painter—a Mr Francis Bear—produced, in his evidently short life, many portraits of Jamaican planters and their families; indeed, at one time, it was quite fashionable to have a Bear in your great house.

The sitters in this portrait sat for several weeks within the long room at Amity making no movement nor sound, as requested by the artist, whilst steadily perspiring their finest clothes several shades darker. But what became of this portrait I do not know. It was lost or stolen or perhaps even nibbled to tatting by some of the many ravenous creatures that live here upon this Caribbean island. However, if you should perchance alight upon this portrait, *Mr and Mrs Goodwin*, please be sure to make a careful study of it—for hidden close within its artifice lies the next piece of my tale.

Standing tall in the foreground of this splendid picture you will find Robert Goodwin. His manner is casual, one leg crossed in front of the other, while he leans his elbow upon the chair back in front of him. He wears a light linen jacket with a waistcoat of cream silk embellished with a tracery of green floral stitching. There is no hat upon his head, and although his curling hair and bristling whiskers confer the distinction of a gentleman upon him, they also cause him to look a good deal older than his years.

Not yet married a full year, his countenance appears serene enough. But, come, look closer still, for the beam within his blue eyes is pure relief, the spirit within that meek smile is satisfaction; for Robert Goodwin had finally been released from the long-preserved state that, in deference to his good father, he had kept achingly intact until his wedding night—his virginity!

However, it was not Caroline that plucked him. For while Robert Goodwin's new bride lay reclining upon her bed—the ribbons at the neck of her nightgown untied and the garment teased down low to reveal the ample mounds of her primped and scented breasts, as she eagerly waited for her new husband to finish his business within the negro village—he was in the room under the house, frenziedly dropping the clothes from off our July's back.

He had turned July around within the feeble light of a tallow candle like an anticipated birthday gift finally unwrapped. And, as if to confirm that each inch of her was indeed as delightful as his possessed mind's eye had conjured, he studied her close. Laying her down, his hands stroked all over her. And where his hands roamed, his tongue and lips soon followed. When he entered her his breath came so fast and he yelled so loud that July slapped her hand across his mouth to stifle the sound lest her missus hear this obscene intimacy seeping up through the boards of her floor. Afterwards he hugged July close to him—her back against his front. He had married 'that woman,' he told July softly into the dark, just so he could be with her like this—just like this. And then he whispered to July over and over that he loved her, oh how he loved her.

By the time Robert Goodwin finally arrived at his new wife's chamber, he was exhausted. He promised Caroline that their coupling would take place soon and not to bother him now, for he was very tired as the negroes had quite worn him out with their demands . . . and, oh please could she cease mentioning it . . . and certainly she was his love, but would she stop incessantly whining, for it was making his head ache . . . and, of course, of course, he desired her, but had she not heard him? . . . soon, he promised, soon. Then he slept sweet as a suckled and belched babe.

Whose suggestion it was that the backdrop for this portrait—*Mr and Mrs Goodwin*—be the open landscape of the plantation and not the long room at Amity, is arguable. The artist—who took several months to carefully figure the grounds into a tropical idyll—claimed it was his. However, Robert Goodwin maintained that he saw a similar background used in a painting of some English gentry and so declared the idea his own. But whoever fathered the notion, Robert Goodwin stands before the trunk of what appears to be a rather puny baobab tree. No longer a lowly overseer, he looks every part the master of the beautiful view that the artist has constructed. Come, his chin is held high. And why would it not be?

⁓

Eight letters Robert Goodwin had received from his father which had urged him with increasing passion, to think of marrying soon. His father wrote of his age—how he was no longer a boy; of his circumstance, which would be greatly eased with a wife to share his burdens; of temptations that were easily overcome within marriage; and of Lucinda Partridge, a young girl within his father's village in England who always talked of Robert with affection and had ambition to travel.

Robert Goodwin had longed to oblige his father with this seemingly commonplace request. But he loved a negro girl. He loved July. And to marry a negro . . . to marry a negro! Oh, who could countenance such an indecent proposal? Certainly not his father. To bring kindness to the negro, to minister to the negro, to pity the negro, was his father's dearest wish for him. But for his son to marry the negro—that would surely kill him.

However, within the next letter that he received, his father had written: 'Remember, Robert, that a married man might do as he pleases.'

Now, although Robert Goodwin had never dared to even hint to his father of the troubling attraction he felt for the negro house servant, he somehow came to believe that those instructive words were meant as suggestion. A married man might do as he pleases.

If, Robert Goodwin had pondered, he were a married man, then might he not be able to keep July outside his marriage but within his firm affection? Could he not fulfil the promises he made before God to a wife and still treat tenderly the woman who had his heart? And who would know? Who would suspect? And if they did, might not they turn a blind eye upon a married man? Of course they would—he had known his father do it many times before. And there was such blindness upon this Caribbean island.

Besides, to marry Caroline Mortimer would be to help her further. Robert Goodwin's firm conclusion had been that she would benefit greatly from the arrangement. His standing with the negroes upon the plantation would rise once he was no longer merely the overseer, but master of Amity. The simple negroes would surely do anything that was required of them if they were bid by him—their new, beloved massa.

Robert Goodwin had soon come to believe that it was not only his father, but God the Almighty, that compelled him to conceive this plan—for it was to the injury of no one, and the advantage of all. So his chest is puffed proud within the portrait—for his marriage now kept two women quite content with him and his father above pleased with his son's turn of fortune. Indeed, the letter of congratulations he received from his father read:

My dearest son, Robert,

How proud you have made me by your marriage. Your new wife, Caroline, is welcomed into our family with arms both open and embracing. We pray that one day we shall have the honour of receiving her into our home here in England as willingly as we have taken her into our affections. It spoke a great deal of your wife's wisdom and contrition when you wrote how earnestly she desired that the negroes—whom she once considered as her property—were now treated as well as can be under her employ. I am sure that as the new master of the plantation called Amity, the injustice of that abominable state of slavery will become just a distant memory for the negroes in your charge. Once burdened like beasts, they will now be able to go happily and joyfully about their tasks under your compassionate guidance. My dear son, Robert, you are a credit to your family and the pride of my heart.

Your ever loving father.

Within the painting you will find the missus, Caroline Goodwin, seated upon a chair—the one that her second husband leans upon so casually. She is arranged at a decorous angle within the frame, one that shows off the slope of her shoulders and the intricate array of twisted braids and curls within her hair very well. Her hands, resting demurely on her lap emphasise the billowing folds of the full skirts of the wedding gown she wears, and also succeed in flaunting the fashionable tight cuffs of her bishop sleeves. Indeed, so attentive was the artist to render truthfully the detail of this gown, that the pink silk of the garment shimmers as if the actual cloth were pasted upon it.

However, not wishing to offend the woman who was paying him well to execute this portrait, Mr Francis Bear has allowed Caroline Goodwin to seem a little more slender than perhaps any who knew her would recall. For example, what appears to be a rat escaping from under her skirts in the picture is, in truth, the artist's notion of the missus's foot within her cream slipper, if the missus's foot had been dainty.

The intention was that Caroline Goodwin would gaze from out this canvas upon the viewer with so attractive a smile, that all who saw it would contemplate with envy this perfect scene. But no teaching the artist had ever received made him skilled enough to make Caroline's smile alight not only at her lips, but also within her eyes. No matter what pains Mr Bear took (and he took plenty—reworking her features for a full three days), her smile stayed resolutely only at her mouth. And, in consequence, all who ever viewed the picture were left puzzling as to how a woman that appears to be smiling so heartily can look so downcast.

Caroline Goodwin had been married for nearly a year and yet her new husband had only come to her once—no, twice—in all that time. Upon that second occasion he was so full of Madeira that his organ was limp as the tongue of a thirsty dog. And Caroline had a secret wish (perhaps it was not too late for her with such a youthful husband a dozen years younger than herself). She wished for children. She would be a very good mother—none who knew her did doubt it. Yet the nearest she had ever come to having a child was with . . . But she could hardly bring herself to think upon it—that little thing she had given birth to all those years ago in London. It had been taken away by the midwife, wrapped like a pennyworth of fish in a copy of the *Evening Mail*. Her first husband, Edmund, had complained that he had not yet read the contents of that newspaper's pages. After that, he never again came to her in a husband's way. And even though his morning decision was always whether it was wiser to fasten his breeches pulled above or pushed under his enormous belly, he told Caroline that she was too fat for him to find much that was desirable in her.

But her new husband, Robert, was not of that mind—he thought her handsome, he said so all the time. Only, sometimes, when he looked upon her she thought . . . but no, she must be wrong . . . she thought . . . no, no, she was his love . . . but she thought sometimes she could see a little disdain sitting coyly at the corners of his mouth.

It was those wretched negroes that kept him from her so long. So determined were they to enjoy the first fruits of their freedom that they were more indolent, gloomy and demanding than ever before. Every night her husband returned home to her at such a late hour and in such a state of exhaustion that all he wished to do was sleep. He was too sentimental with that bothersome race of people. Why, he treated Marguerite almost as if she were one of his own kind.

He demanded Caroline call her Miss July. Quite insistent he became about it. He once yelled upon her, 'Desist, desist!' when she forgot. She wished to oblige him, of course she wished to oblige him—he was her husband. But it was very troublesome for her to remember the change. And Marguerite was such a pleasing name to call about the house.

She was only idly chattering—sitting upon her husband's knee, curling his hair fondly around her finger, and idling chattering—when she asked, very sweetly indeed, if instead of her having to remember the tiresome change to her negro's name, might he not consider knowing her nigger as Marguerite too. His mood need not have changed quite so quickly. He need not have tipped her on to the floor, nor banged his fist down as he said, 'But that is *not* her name, Caroline. Her name is Miss July.' It was only her thought!

And did her husband now require her to have polite society with 'Miss July'? Did he wish her to enquire after 'Miss July's' family whenever she were in her presence? Was she to invite 'Miss July' to sip port and Madeira with them? Did he desire her to engage 'Miss July' in chatter on whether she hoped for a Christmas breeze this year or invite her to join her other guests from the parish for an evening's entertainment at whist? Was his instruction to her that she must shake her nigger's hand? He need not have grimaced so, as if the mere sound of her voice were causing him pain, nor shouted, 'Oh for pity's sake, Caroline, shut up.' What did he expect her to say after he had bid Marguerite to sit at the table with them!

Having enquired of Marguerite one dinner time upon the availability of pickle to have with his meat, her husband proceeded to enter into something not unlike a conversation with her negro. Firstly he laughed—for a reason Caroline could not comprehend—when Marguerite informed him that she would be happy to go into town to purchase some pickle for him. And even though Caroline still required the ham to be laid down and her napkin to be picked up from the floor where it had fallen, she was obliged to wait while her husband, having told Marguerite that he preferred his pickles hot, smiled gladly upon the negro as she replied to him that she thought sweet would be more his fancy. The prattle on who in town made the best pickles went back and forth between them like gossip, until her husband, quite glowing with merriment said, 'Oh, come and sit down, Miss July.'

Caroline's breath was entirely ripped out of her. Yet her husband was merely surprised by her shock. What would be the harm, he wished to know, for Miss July to sit at table with them on occasion? What could possibly be the harm? At first Caroline thought him to be making a joke, or perhaps teasing her for her outdated West Indian planter sensibility— after all, it would not have been the first time. So, not wishing to appear insensible to his humour, she laughed. For a negro servant sitting at table as if a guest, would have been enough to have her friends upon the island scoffing openly that she had lost her morals along with all her senses; why Mrs Pemberton would have quite foamed with apoplexy. But Robert just repeated the wicked nonsense—what would be the harm? While Marguerite looked between her master and mistress with a smile so impertinent that it would once have seen her whipped.

And it was not Caroline's protest that changed her husband's mind upon the social suicide he required of her. Her yelling no! no! no! no! no! no! no! in a manner hysterical by anyone's reckoning, seemed to have little effect upon him beyond his screeching, 'Oh, Caroline, please, please, speak in a lower key.' No. It was Marguerite quietly thanking him for the invitation, but informing him that she had to return to the kitchen, that released Caroline from the promise of such shame. And Marguerite now looked upon her with pity—Caroline was sure of it.

⁓

Appraisers of the artist Francis Bear often commented that his use of the negro within his portraits added a reliable touch of the exotic to what might otherwise be a dull work. So, even before the artist and Caroline Goodwin had agreed upon the fee for the portrait, they had decided between them that a negro boy should appear within the picture carrying a parasol and a fan.

However, within the room under the house another plan was devised. For upon hearing that a likeness was to be painted of the owners of Amity, July, jumping excitedly within Robert Goodwin's lap, asked, 'Me can be in it? Oh, tell me me can be in it. Me long to have a likeness made. Oh, can me be in it?'

Having promised July that, 'Of course, of course, of course my little Miss July can be in it,' (addressing her in the baby tones he had, at that time, been so fond of), Robert Goodwin then proceeded to counsel first his wife and then the artist against their idea of a boy, with the obvious reasoning that there was not a negro boy upon Amity, or indeed upon the whole island, who was capable of staying still the required amount of time.

So there within the painting, wearing a white muslin dress with a red silk turban upon her head, you will find July. Quite inspired by the way the robust scarlet of July's headdress created a pleasing counterpoint to the fair hair of the seated woman and the dark head of the upright man, the artist was content to pose July standing full sideways next to Robert Goodwin.

Caroline, however, insisted very loudly indeed that, 'She can't stand there!'

'Why ever not?' her husband had asked.

Caroline, who could find no reasoned words to present as argument—for it was just a feeling of unease within her stomach that made her protest—looked upon the artist to plead for help. He then decided that the composition and balance of the painting would be better enhanced if the negro were kneeling before Caroline, offering her up a tray that contained an array of sweetmeats. And oh, how Caroline Goodwin had clapped at this suggestion. 'Yes, yes, yes!' she said to that.

So within the picture July, now sideways to her missus, leans toward her with one knee bent, proffering the contents of the tray she carries. And although the artist requested that July look towards her mistress with obedient esteem upon her face, July's countenance craftily contrives to catch the eye of the viewer with an expression that says quite clearly, 'So, what you think of this? Am I not the loveliest negro you ever did see?'

However, this posture did cause a deal of trouble, for July could not hold its slavish attitude for long. Firstly, her stooping knee would begin to tingle. Then, not awhile after, she would lose all feeling from within both her legs. A few minutes of this blessed numbness and a pain sharp as a dog sinking its teeth deep into the flesh of her thighs, would seize her. Only rising from out the pose and stamping hard upon the ground did relieve it. Yet each time July was forced to perform this curative dance the artist, looking out from behind his canvas, would let forth a deep moaning sigh. And Caroline would scold, 'Stay still! Stay still! Stop moving!'

Now, although July was quite able to cut down her missus with a look that exclaimed, 'You wan' try bending your fat white batty down like this for hour and hour and hour, cha!' she was no longer required to. For a troubled glance—or even just the hint of one—in the direction of her Mr Goodwin . . . her Mr Big-big blue-eye . . . her Mr Sweet-sweet massa, was all that was needed to have him, with full masterful bluster, defend her with the reply, 'Can you not see how her pose is painful to maintain, Caroline?'

'But she is prolonging the difficulty by continually fidgeting. I manage to stay quite still.'

'You are comfortably seated. If Miss July were comfortably sitting then I am in no doubt that she too could remain as immovable as you.'

'Do you propose the negro to sit within this picture now?'

'All I am saying, Caroline, is that if Miss July had been left to stand next to me instead of being forced into this ridiculous pose, then she would have been able to hold that position for longer without it becoming stiff and painful to her.'

'But Robert, it is Mr Bear's idea to have her model in that way—not my own . . .'

And so on and so on. These arguments did not erupt every time that

July moved, but they occurred enough for the artist to roll his eyes and wearily rest his head upon his hands for the duration of the ill-tempered scene; and for our July to throw her arms about Mr Goodwin's neck the next time they were alone, and peck a hundred kisses upon his cheek for not permitting the missus to 'insolence' her.

~~⌒~~

Husband was July's favoured name for Robert Goodwin—for every time she said it, 'Come sit, husband . . . please start nyam, husband . . . oh, hush now, husband,' he responded obediently by calling her wife. 'You are my real wife,' he told her. 'This is my real home,' he said of their damp little room under the house. What would happen if he did not find her waiting for him every afternoon after conch blow? July had wanted to know. Would he search for her? He surely would, he told her. Would he cry? Boo hoo-hoo, he had said.

So July once hid herself. She lit no candle and squatted within the farthest dark corner, behind a chair. In he came to search for her, keen as a miner in quest of a seam of gold. He called her name but she did not move. 'Wife?' he said as he lit a candle to breach the gloom. 'Miss July, where are you?' he asked at the open door. So fretful did he become that he looked grave as a pickney lost from home. July could not endure this teasing, for she longed to have her arms about him, to feel her face against his warm neck. She wished to scratch her nails down that ribbon of dark hair that ran from his chest to his navel, and watch his white skin streak pink. She wanted to hear his moans as his hands upon her pinched and slapped.

She abandoned the foolish hiding game and pushed over the chair in her eagerness to have him. And as she captured him firm from behind, he squealed with surprise. He pushed her down on to the mattress. His weight on top of her was how she liked it. Unable to move under the bulk of him was what she loved. Him lying so heavy upon her that she could not even inhale breath, while his manhood rose up thick and strong between them, was what she required.

But her husband protested at the prickle of her bed. 'My wife will not sleep upon something so coarse?' he said, and bid his boy Elias carry down a plump horse-hair mattress from the rooms above. It was soon followed by a wooden bed frame with a headboard elegantly carved with two birds.

Although Molly did begin to look with one green-eye upon July— whispering jealous chat-chat of the arrangement beneath the house in hushed tones—July paid that silly woman no mind. For as the beloved, true wife of a white English man, July did now dazzle even a haughty quadroon like Miss Clara into a dark drab.

Come, Robert did not want July's little feet to walk upon the filthy dirt floor—they should walk upon silk, he said. The red and blue patterned rug he gave July he brought from the floor of his own study. And he kissed first the toes upon her left foot and then upon her right, as she stood pressing her bare feet into the soft pile of the mat. And oh, how Elias cussed, as he struggled down to their little room with a dining table and two ill-matching chairs upon his back. But her husband wished her to sit at table with him so they might chat upon England, his papa, the wretched negroes, and the problems of his day. Her husband at the head of this table, and she with her chair pulled up close to his, so she might peel a mango and feed him the segments of sticky fruit, one piece at a time, from her own lips to his.

For in only a few hours the missus would expect her husband up in the house. And July would be commanded to ready the table for dinner. 'Before he comes, before he comes, everything must be ready, hurry up, Marguerite, he will be here soon,' her missus would fret upon her. July would then have to direct the house boys to set the table (and slap their heads to get them to do it again, properly), while she unlocked the wine from the cupboard. She would then need to attend the kitchen to inspect the food. After enquiring of Molly what the nasty dish was meant to be, and insisting that the sulking cook add a little more salt, she would have to charge the house boys to carry in the dinner to their massa's table. And July would have to enter in upon the dining room. And while still tender and damp from love-making, she would have to prance about the table serving her husband and the keen-to-please-him missus their food.

⌒

As I earlier disclosed, the artist Francis Bear was obliged to employ some invention within this portrait, *Mr and Mrs Goodwin*. My example upon that occasion was the not-quite-as-fat-as-she-should-be missus and her unduly slim foot. But the tray that displays the sweetmeats hides another trespass. That July is offering a tray to the mistress is correct, but the colourful and abundant sweets upon it were, in truth, added later. For every time July became weary in her pose the tray would tip and the sweets would slide and scatter on to the floor. After this spilling occurred for the fifth time, the artist suddenly yelled, 'Enough!' He then posed July with an empty tray and set up a still-life of confection in his studio so he might paint them later, at his leisure. However, this resolution was to be the artist's excuse when a quarrel arose after the picture's completion.

So pleased was Caroline Goodwin with the finished picture, *Mr and Mrs Goodwin*, that not only did she have it replace Agnes's portrait within the long room, but she also sent the artist two bottles of Amity's finest rum. She then invited all her neighbours within the parish to view it. Her intention was to bathe herself within their envy.

However, after commenting how Caroline looked strangely sad in the portrait, the next observation from anyone who viewed it, was that her husband, Robert, appears to be gazing firmly upon the nigger. Now although Caroline insisted, 'No, no, it is the sweetmeats that have his eye' (and the viewers tipped their heads upon the picture, first to the left, then the right, eager to agree), finally, everyone of them had to declare, 'No, no, he stares upon the nigger.'

Robert Goodwin was indeed gazing upon July through the whole of the portrait's execution. For July was carrying his child and he wished to stare nowhere else. Indeed, a few months after the completion of this portrait, July gave birth to a daughter for him. A fair-skinned, grey-eyed girl who was named Emily.

So furious was Caroline that the artist had caught her husband's folly, that she insisted he take back the portrait to his studio to rectify this error. Now, although Francis Bear retouched the likeness for several more weeks, still his daubings could not raise Robert Goodwin's eyes from off our July. Caroline then placed all her wrath at the situation with Francis Bear. She was enraged—for was it not he who so cleverly managed to capture that scene for her friends to view? Come, Caroline was forced to hang the picture within a room that was rarely used. And obliged to demand that the artist return to her the gifted rum!

CHAPTER 27

⟋

Reader, I believed after all the fuss-fuss my son Thomas did make over the last pickney born to July, that I would soon have to endure his reproaches anew. Once he learned within my tale that July gave life to another child then the pulsing vein upon my son's head would throb and wriggle once more. And with a face untouched by the fury that he felt, he would ask his mama, 'Is this baby soon to be left upon a stone outside a preacher's house, like the ugly black pickaninny July gave birth to? Or because the child Emily is coloured, a quadroon with fair skin and a white man for a father, did July look to cherish her instead?'

But an old-old woman should not be scolded by her own son! So I hid myself from him within the hut in our garden, for several hours while he perused those pages. Miss May, my son's daughter, soon joined me. Seeing her old grandmama sitting small upon the tiny seat in that little wooden place, amongst all the broken-down things that were forgotten there, amused her. We two played old maid to pass the time and I beat her at every go. Oh how she wailed! I should let her win, she tell me. Why? I ask her. Because she is young was her only reasoning. Then she has time to learn to beat me, was my reply to that.

But my knees did ache from being folded so long within that wretched place—I was soon forced to hobble back to the house. And there my son greeted me without ever having missed me. As he handed back those pages he said with a thoughtful tone, 'One thing, Mama . . .' And how my heart began to race—come, it beat nearly through the cloth of my dress. Until he continued, 'I believe I may have seen some of Mr Bear's work,' and commenced to describe for me, in weary detail, another of the silly artist's pictures.

Reader, my son's moods must now be as much of a puzzle to you, as they are to his own mama.

As I write, Miss May stands before me, shuffling her pack of cards. She commands me to stop scratching my pen upon this paper and play another hand of old maid with her. Come, I fear I will first have to allow this child to beat me if I am ever to get peace enough to continue my tale. Cha!

CHAPTER 28

THE OLD DISTILLER-MAN who toiled within the boiling house,
Dublin Hilton, was one day wandering up near the great house
when he did spy a white man with a fancy feathered hat upon his head.
This man, standing still and erect as a doorpost, was wiping a small
brush upon a large board that was resting stout upon an easel. Dublin
Hilton, approaching upon this man from behind, did strain his neck to
see what this man was doing. Painting a picture, Dublin soon said to
himself. For there upon that board was a good likeness of Miss July
(serving up something), a not-too-bad copy of the new massa, and a
white woman resting upon a seat who looked like the missus—but nah,
for she was too narrow.

After watching this man for a long while, Dublin Hilton soon came to
think that this must be the artist he had heard so much chat-chat of.
Leaning upon a stick Dublin dallied awhile longer, observing the artist
painting the view of the lands of Amity into the background of this picture. One strange picture, Dublin was to tell everyone later. For the
artist-man was looking down the hill and over the scruffy thatched tops
of the houses within the negro village.

Now Dublin Hilton stood only a few feet behind the artist and yet
this white man, gazing out with frowning absorption upon the view
before him, time after time painted another bush where Dublin could
clearly see the higgledy-piggledy of the negro village.

Soon Dublin approached this man with the question, 'Pardon me, massa, but you can no see the negro dwellings?'

'All too clearly. Now, be off with you, nigger,' was the reply Dublin Hilton received.

However, Dublin being no longer a slave (and a man who had no need to dabble a skimmer to see if liquor would granulate) decided that now he was a free man he was able to enquire anything of this white man he desired. So he posed his question once more. The artist-man, with a heavy sigh, then told the old boiler-man that he admired the view of the lands from that position, but had no intention of including the disgusting negro hovels.

'But they are there before you,' said Dublin Hilton to he. At which the artist barked upon him, that no one wished to find squalid negroes within a rendering of a tropical idyll, before promising Dublin that he would set his dog upon him if he did not leave him alone.

'But you paint an untruth,' said Dublin Hilton.

And the artist-man did stamp his foot and scream upon the old man, 'What business is it of yours? Away with you, nigger, away!'

Now, according to Dublin Hilton, it was just after this encounter with the artist-man that the trouble with the new massa, Robert Goodwin, did begin. However, Peggy Jump did not agree. She recalled that the massa Goodwin had already rode in upon the village to pull Ezra from out his house by his hair before she had heard the story of the artist-man. But Cornet, Peggy's husband, agreed with Dublin. He remembered that day well. The day when the massa, caught in a devilish rage, shook Ezra like a dog with a rat for neither labouring, nor paying his rent. Come, how could Cornet forget, for he had raised a stick to the massa, yelling upon him to let Ezra go or else he would thrash him with it. And even though the massa soon calmed himself and pulled Ezra to his feet, that white man's clear blue eyes, staring anger upon him, still haunted Cornet's mind's eye when he slept.

But Cornet remembered chatting with Dublin Hilton long before that day, upon the change in the overseer since he became the massa by marriage, and he was sure it was then Dublin had told him of the picture, the artist and the missing negro village. For Cornet thought the artist a cunning man to turn his eye blind to those run-down negro places.

No, the trouble had started at Christmas tide, when Robert Goodwin had sent the driver, Mason Jackson, to round up all the negroes still residing upon Amity and gather them into the mill yard. Cornet recalled that to press this gathering to move faster the driver had fired his whip. And one commotion did break out as Giles Millar and Betsy wrested that slaving cow-skin from out that dog-driver's hand. They were slaves no more, they yelled upon him, and would dance to no lash! They threw his whip into the river and would have drowned the driver too, but the massa Goodwin had already begun to speak.

There were three fields of cane that must be taken off, the massa told everyone from atop his barrels. Those that worked to bring in this crop would be paid a full day's wage for a full day's toil. Come, he smiled, as he urged all to work hard over the coming days so the cane might be brought in.

But it was Christmas. Most before him were dressed in their fine holiday clothes. For example, Miss Sarah, from the first gang, had been making her costume for the Joncanoe festival in town for the whole year. She was a blue girl. As Britannia, she was to be paraded along King Street with a trident in her hand and a helmet made in blue silk and silver upon her head. Long time had she waited for the honour of raising the banner that said, 'Blue girls for ever.' So no, she would not work the two off-days of Christmas.

And Peggy and Cornet had their daughter (the one who was sold away) upon a visit with them. They had not seen her pretty face for many years. She had walked with her little pickney from far, far away, and had arrived just as Peggy and Cornet were finally packed up to leave, to seek out her. So they would not work at Christmas, for they had already killed and plucked three chickens for this joyful holiday. And Mary Ellis, who still did live with Peggy and Cornet, had no intention of missing that feast. Nor did Ezra wish to lose those two off-days from his provision ground as his cow was about to calf.

Soon the massa Goodwin was staring upon nothing but shaking negro heads. And the words, 'No, massa . . . no, massa . . . not me, massa . . . no, sah . . . no, sah,' were called out to him. Several times, massa Goodwin looked to be about to plead or say something. But no words came to him—he just stood with his mouth agape.

After most had moved out of the mill yard to go about their business, the massa approached Benjamin Brown, who was untying his mule from the fence. The massa Goodwin smiling upon Benjamin said, 'Oh, my old faithful Benjamin. I knew you would be willing to work. I knew you would not let me down.'

Benjamin, however, then began to tell the massa that no, he could not work over Christmas as he was to assist the minister at his chapel . . . But the massa did not let him finish. According to Benjamin, the massa turned suddenly away from him, ill-tempered and muttering, 'Ungrateful, indolent wretches!' or some such bluster, before mounting his horse and riding away.

Fanny, who worked the second gang, claimed that Robert Goodwin, returning to them after Christmas, had his face once more set kindly. When he appeared at her door she enquired of his new pickney. She remembers it well for, as soon as she asked after his daughter Emily, his face reddened. Fanny then realised that perhaps this white man wished no one to know that Miss July's girl-child was his own. However, this friendly mood was spoiled when the massa then commanded her to work for him, and be paid by the task.

Once all the cane from Virgo had been stripped, she would receive her wage, the massa told her. Now, Fanny had heard too many negroes complain that they had stripped cane for a week, to receive only a day's pay. What negro upon Friendship plantation or at Unity, or Montpelier, or Windsor Hall, or any of the planted lands upon the island did agree to work by the task? None! She would not work by the task for, like a dog who will be fed once he has caught his own tail, the task might go on forever. And this she told the massa. And so did Anne and Elizabeth, Betsy and Nancy. Soon everyone upon Amity that the massa commanded to work at this task told him 'no.' No! They will work by the day, and by the day alone as they had done before.

'Then I require all negroes to work six days. The cane on those pieces can be taken off, stripped, the liquor struck and cooled ready for the hogsheads if everyone works six days,' was the massa Goodwin's proposal.

Six days a week! James Richards was sent to the massa to speak for all.

'Me tell you what, massa,' was how James began while looking firmly into the massa's eye, 'four days we work for you and we work hard.'

'Four days? Four days a week would not be enough time. With four days working, most of the cane would spoil. It must be six.'

At this point in the talk James could see sparks of anger flickering in the massa's eye. 'Cannot you see it must be six?' the massa went on, 'Like it always was when the crop was ready to be taken off.'

James, fearing to vex the massa Goodwin further, stopped looking at him within his face.

'You know that boy,' the massa went on, 'you've always been a good negro. Six days were worked for the last crop, when I was still your overseer. It must be six days with this. You would all still have a rest day upon Sunday for church or market. But you must work six days. Go and tell them, boy—all of you must work six days.'

James, not wishing to let the irritation he began to feel at the massa talking to him—a skilled carpenter and freeman!—like he was a slave to still be commanded, busied himself by tapping out the spent tobacco from his pipe upon a stone.

'Are you listening to me?' the massa suddenly shouted upon him.

'Yes massa, me does hear you,' James replied softly, 'but me did say four days. This crop, it be four days we work.'

'Six, damn you, six! Do you understand me? Every last one of you will work six days!'

It was then that James determined that he must speak sharp, for was he not free to be as vexed as any white bakkra? 'We no longer slaves and we work what suits,' said he. 'We work what suits.'

Grumbling with a huff and puff while walking around and around like a beast at a mill, was the massa's reply to those blessed, long-time-coming words, 'we work what suits.' One hour, James Richards claimed the massa paced within this troubled state. Until, as James's story told, the massa Goodwin stopped before him, took a sigh so deep the trees did bend within it and said, 'Then tell me, how will any of you make your obligation for rent or food if you only work four days a week for me?'

Now, James had near three acres of provision land bursting with plantain, cocos, yam and corn. In a little corner section he had some pigeon peas and sweet potato. Two horned cattle he had grazing, and he had recently sold his young steer to the overseer at Somerset Pen for the market price of eighteen pounds.

Elizabeth Millar had five acres under shaddocks, callalloo, peppers and calabash. Mary Ellis made plenty profit from her half acre land of tobacco. While Fanny and Anne Roberts sold the meat from one of their heifers only last week to Molly in the great house kitchen, so she might serve it to the massa boiled with peppers and peas.

Betsy tended the best arrowroot upon the island within her garden. While Giles had money to waste upon gambling marbles, thanks to his three acres of limes, pawpaw, star apples and melon. And Samuel, with his fresh water turtles and salt fish business, was made a big man in town.

All worked their old provision grounds and gardens; for those lands that once they had been forced to tend as slaves so there might be food enough to eat, within the liberty of their freedom now flourished, with produce and profit. Even Wilfred Park made a living from hawking his eggs. While Peggy and Cornet turned a nice penny into plenty of pounds with their mule and cart, wobbling slow and piled high with goods to be carried to market.

James could not recall whether he spoke those words aloud into the massa's ear about the negroes' efforts upon their provision grounds, or whether the speech rested voiceless within his mouth. However, he did remember that when the massa said, 'What a bunch of idle niggers you are,' the foreboding James felt gripped around his throat to make him choke.

'I expect you think your masters will just keep providing for you,' the massa went on, 'even when you refuse to do any work when it is required. Well, I will not. And if any of you do not make your rent, then you must leave your houses and your lands. So think upon it. Think very carefully upon it. Six days a week I require you all to work. Six days.'

When James, recovering his voice said, 'No. Four days we work. Me say four days,' the massa turned sharply upon him, raised his arm and swiped the pipe from out of James's hand. He then stamped a jig upon the broken pieces of the bowl until it was nothing but dust.

                                            ⌒

Tilly cried when first she heard that the nice Robert Goodwin was troubled. She had never known this massa to raise his hand, nor even his voice, to her. Whenever he smiled a greeting upon her, he always asked if her old mama was still living. And once he presented her with a green kerchief for no reason other than she was happy to work for him.

Tilly wished to offer herself for six days working, as he wished, but Miss Nancy caught her wrist and twisted it, saying that the massa had struck the carpenter James Richards and so now everyone, including Miss Tilly, will work only four days.

So when a whole cane piece got spoiled after some cattle from the pen trampled in, there was no one about to drive them out, for nearly all were away working upon their grounds. Only Wilfred and Fanny were present. They flapped their arms, hollered, and chased the beasts through the cane to get them gone, but the mischief was done.

Tilly cried once more when she saw the menace in the massa's eye when he came to the village to scold. He took the hat from his head and dashed it to the floor. Then he roared, 'Where were the pen-keepers, why were they not with the cattle? Where were the watchmen? Why were the watch-fires all out? And why were no conches blown to summon help? One of my best cane fields was ruined, trampled to pieces, while you were all about your own business. Is that your gratitude to your masters? You care nothing for my interests—you think of no one but yourselves!'

And Tilly would have called out that she will work longer, just to cheer him, but Miss Nancy smothered her mouth, hurled her into her hut, and locked her in there.

Ezra was so surprised when, a few weeks later, he found a grinning massa Goodwin standing within his doorway, that he dropped the calabash he carried, which spilled the dirty water it held over the massa's boot.

'Ezra, Ezra, do not worry yourself about that, for I have something important I wish to ask you,' the massa began before saying, 'Are you happy, boy?'

Trick—this be a trick, Ezra thought, as the massa waited for his reply. Happy? Come, he had never heard that asked of him in the whole of his days and had no notion of what he should reply.

But the massa carried on, 'Ezra, listen carefully to me,' while leaning in close, like he had some secret for Ezra to learn. 'Why do you not leave your provision lands and work just for me? I will pay you a good wage, better than anyone in this parish. Enough for your rent, your food, and fine clothes for any wife you may wish to keep. You would want for nothing. And think, with that money upon your person, you would have no need to walk all the way to your lands, for you would have pennies enough. Imagine, you would not need to attend market every week—you could sleep in a hammock or go to church on a Sunday. And in the evenings you could have leisure to do whatever it is that you enjoy to do within the evenings. What do you think on that, Ezra?'

Ezra recalled that he had replied only, 'But me ground done feed me dis long time,' before the massa Goodwin held up his hand to halt Ezra's speech. He then stepped a pace back to call for Miss July.

And there was Ezra's proof! For Ezra always believed that the massa Goodwin did not understand negro talk. In walked Miss July, her face set with a house servant's sneer, like some bad smell was distressing her nose. And the massa said, 'Please say what you were saying again.'

So Ezra spoke that he did prefer to work upon his own grounds, for labour in the cane fields was hard and long, and yet he got to keep no profit from the crop he planted, fed and cut. But the toil upon his grounds rewarded him with produce that was his to keep. The massa then turned to Miss July who repeated all that Ezra had just spoken, but with a bakkra's exactness. And the massa's eyes dimmed as he listened.

Then the massa began to say again what he had already said—about the hammock, the church, the pennies, and the fine clothes for a wife—but with his voice raised. Come, he ended with a cry of, 'Savvy dat, boy?' that was so loud it did wake his pickney that was bound across to Miss July's breast. And as the pickney did holler, the massa did begin to cajole, 'Well, boy, will you not do as I suggest? Will you? Say you will, and there will be an end to it. Come on, Ezra, say you will work for me alone.'

And Ezra, trapped within his own hut by one 'gwan high-high' house servant, her bewailing pickney, and the massa's persistence, soon realised that, no, he was not happy, he was not happy at all!

Nancy, Benjamin, Anne, Peggy, Cornet and Mary were then visited by the massa who approached upon them with his smiling sweet-talk. 'If you worked for me alone,' said he, 'you would receive a good wage. There would be no need for you to spend so much effort upon your lands as I would provide money enough for you to buy food from the market and more besides.'

But Samuel remembered no smile upon the massa's face by the time he reached him. Come, his arms were folded, his mouth pinched as a dose of pepper and his brow cut deep with frown. Samuel was poised to reply to the massa's request—he would, like the others, work a little for a wage but could never give up his fishing—but was silenced when the massa bid him wait. He then beckoned to Miss July to repeat for Samuel everything that he had just told him. And even though Miss July hesitated to carry on when Samuel said, 'Yes, me savvy, massa, but . . . yes, me catch, but . . . Miss July, me does savvy, but . . .' the massa Goodwin kept commanding her to continue.

Only after Miss July had repeated every blessed word, was Samuel permitted to speak. Yet he had only drawn breath to say, 'You see . . .' before the massa screamed, 'Why will you not do as I say?! It will be for the good of us all. Just do as I say, damn you!'

While Fanny recalled that the massa at her house was quite bedevilled. But not with her—even after she informed him that the work upon her lands allowed her to know free. No. His vexation was with Miss July. For when Miss July began to speak Fanny's words for him, he growled upon her, 'I know what she said! I'm not a fool,' and then blasted out of the hut. That haughty house servant, Miss July, had to run to follow him out. But the massa was already atop his cart and riding away. Miss July had to call after him to wait. It was only after her pickney began to howl—one screech that did crumble the wattle of Fanny's wall—that he stopped the cart to allow Miss July to catch him and climb aboard.

Following these visitations, the massa Goodwin then let it be known that he had spent many days in prayer and deliberation. He summoned all to the mill yard so they might hear the consequence of his careful thought. Standing atop his barrels, he proclaimed to his audience of leery negroes that, henceforth, the rents for their houses would be separated out from the rents for their provision grounds.

And, what is more, he said, he now believed it right and Christian to allow those negroes who did not wish to work upon the sugar plantation named Amity, to remain both within their homes and grounds, providing that all obligations to pay their rent, upon time, and with good grace, were met.

Come, those negroes who had of late called him 'massa ground-itch,' for being more pestering than that accursed foot ailment, hung their heads. No. Massa Goodwin was a good man, a kind man, a handsome man, a clever man, a fair man, a tall man, and a credit to his papa. Only Benjamin Brown did not join in this cringe for, he always avowed, from the first they were uttered, he sensed a trick within those fine words. A white man is a white man, no matter how friendly he believed himself to be with God, was Benjamin's judgement.

But Fanny recalled Benjamin's mouth gaping as much as anyone's when James Richards read aloud the tariffs of rents for houses and provision lands that were nailed upon the mill door.

A month's rent upon the cottage was a day's wage, as it had been from the first. And a day's work could see it discharged. But the rents for the provision grounds! Read it again, was called out to James Richards—so sure were they that he had read in error. Bring Dublin Hilton to see it, he can read numbers better, was yelled when James Richards repeated the amounts. But when Dublin Hilton stepped forward to squint upon the paper and pronounce exactly the same rents, the gasp that flowed through that crowd disturbed the air so that it was felt in the town as a chill.

For the massa was to charge a full week's wage in rent for every acre of land worked! Who could ever earn sufficient to pay it? None. While scrawled by a hurried hand within a corner of this grievous note were the words, 'To fish the river is no longer permitted.'

Elizabeth Millar said later that the deputation that marched to the great house to request a parley with the massa Goodwin about these rents, were surprised to find him waiting for them. He stood with his arms folded and his legs astride upon his veranda, as if he had been lingering a good while. He greeted them with the words, 'I know why you have come, and I intend to give you a good explanation for my actions.'

Now, although James Richards had been rehearsing a speech—

muttering the lines to himself that pleaded for fairness and mercy—he only managed to draw a breath before the massa silenced him by raising his hand to say, 'Listen carefully to me, all of you. I have taken this measure of increasing the rents upon your provision grounds for your own good. All of you lived too long as slaves. All of you were too long in shackles to really understand what is now in your best interest.

'I do not blame you for wishing to feed upon the first fruits of your freedom, but as your master and as the master of this plantation, I am the one who understands how you will best be served. Some of you believe that the Queen of England has granted you your lands to do with as you will, but this is not the case. Your provision grounds belong to me, and I can rent them to whomsoever I choose. The Queen, and indeed all the people of England, agree with my actions. Working for the common good is what will prove to be right for every one of you over the course of time.

'I know you hold your lands dear, and I know that you have laboured upon them long and hard for the time you have been living at Amity. But you must now relinquish those lands so that your labour will be confined to the tasks required to be performed upon a sugar plantation. You will now all agree to work upon Amity for good wages.

'I understand that it is the same work that you formerly performed under the dreadful tyranny of slavery. But you are no longer slaves, you are freemen, and all freemen in England—yes, white men—work for wages. It is the way of the world. And, thanks to the grace of God, you are now free to take your part within that world. You must labour for wages upon Amity with the same enthusiasm as you have worked upon your lands.

'I have been driven to this action by your refusal to listen to my reasoning and by your defiance to work as I require. But let that all now be at an end. Let us work together to make the plantation named Amity once more the pride of Jamaica, of England, and of her Empire.'

Not one word did James Richards manage to utter of his practised argument before the massa strode in upon the house and closed the door. And all who had marched to parley, then stood in dumbfounded silence before the massa's sealed home.

Only Dublin, sucking upon his teeth, then saying, 'Slavery. Slavery has just returned to Amity,' destroyed their mute reverie. Come, Cornet ran to find the shackle that had once secured him to the wall of the dreaded dungeon. His intention, he said, was to bind his wrists before this white man, whose demands had seized his freedom once more. But Dublin and Giles held him back. There was another way, they told him, a better way.

So upon a heavy, dismal night, a palaver was called within the negro village. It gathered before Peggy and Cornet's hut, but so many did arrive that the crowd soon pressed into Betsy's garden. James Richards began by repeating massa's speech as best he could remember it. But disbelief at Robert Goodwin's words soon had his congregation chanting, 'Wha' him say? . . . No! . . . Him lie . . . no, sah . . . me will not . . . cha . . . me is slave no more . . . it be changy-fe-changy . . . me work what suits.'

While Benjamin, standing upon Peggy Jump's three-legged stool, begged all to listen to his talk. The minister at his Baptist chapel intended to purchase lands that negroes might work, he told them. Fanny, sucking upon her teeth, said that the minister-man was a white man too. But a man of God, said Benjamin, before the stool did topple him.

Giles then spoke very long about some lands just outside the borders of Amity that could be squatted—lands that were there for anyone to take. And as Giles detailed the trees, the grasses, and the slopes and dips of this soil, Elizabeth Millar repeated over this droning sermon, 'Massa not speaking true. Massa tell lie and story.' For, she explained, she still believed the good Queen in England had granted them the gift of their provision grounds.

Dublin then called for hush, but got none. Only when James Richards pressed Ezra to blow the conch was this gathering brought to order. And once the squabbling did wane, this aroused assembly soon began to speak with one voice.

All agreed that those who remained living within the negro village would continue to reside as before. They would work their lands, they would work their gardens, and they would hawk their produce at market. But none would raise even a forged penny to the massa for the renting of their provision grounds, none. No one would pay the rent upon their houses. And, within a solemn oath that was taken by all with joined hands, they agreed that not one person amongst them would work even a day for Robert Goodwin.

CHAPTER 29

'THIS DAY IS TO serve as a warning to all the negroes of the village,' was how Robert Goodwin began. 'You will not be required to evict every negro from their house and provision lands, but just enough to act as example that I, the master of this plantation, mean to deliver upon my word; that those who have not paid their rent must now work for me, or be removed from their dwellings and grounds.'

July had once cautioned Robert Goodwin to be mindful that negroes were not as biddable as perhaps he and his papa believed. She had whispered it upon him within the closeness of their bed. He had laughed and teased that her own naughtiness towards him made him very aware of that. But as he stood there, resolute upon the veranda before the mishmash gang of white men he had summoned from around the parish to assist him with the evicting of negroes from Amity, July wished she had given him that lesson with more urgency. For his right hand, that he held hidden behind his back, was uncontrollably trembling as he spoke.

'Are we to burn them out?' was shouted by a rude white man who was picking his front teeth with a sharpened stick.

Robert Goodwin's fist landed upon the veranda's rail heavy as a fallen stone. 'No,' he said, 'do not burn down the houses for they will be needed again once the negroes have agreed to return to working.'

The bafflement at this soft command appeared on every face that heard it, while the panic of seeming weak before this assembly suddenly lit within Robert Goodwin's eyes. July, seeing his distress, thought to run down amongst that impudent mob, grab a few by the throat and rage upon them to listen up—for him, Robert Goodwin, her husband, was a better man than all who now looked upon him—so them must heed him and do as him say.

But there was no need of her meddling, for he did not betray his worry to that audience, but wiped his arm across the perspiration upon his forehead to shield them from it. He then held his trembling hand within the other, behind his back, and rocked upon his toes to proclaim, 'But you can throw any of their belongings out into the lanes. And kick over the fires. Scatter any animals. And keep as many chickens as you can find.'

His gaze briefly met July's before he carried on with greater confidence, 'Make sure any pigs or goats are shot. I do not want them screeching their way into the fields. You can trample any crops that might be in a garden, but do not burn them.' Most within this rabble did begin to grin at the promise of such sport. But when Robert Goodwin added, 'Use your weapons with care—I want no one accidentally maimed or killed,' the eyes that were heeding him did suddenly begin to roll. 'Many of you have done this before and do not need my instruction. Make as much noise as you can,' he said. 'They will be mostly women, the superannuated, children, lame males, for I intend for the able-bodied to be putting out the fires upon their grounds.' And the shouts of approval that rose from the pack steadied Robert Goodwin's hand enough for him to raise it to appeal for hush so his plan might be better heard.

'Because that is how this will all start,' he said. 'I have here a map which I have drawn myself,' and he beckoned to July to perform the task he had asked of her before the crowd assembled. July grabbed Elias to shove him forward with the map that he had requested her to hold up. As Robert Goodwin began to point at this chart, his hand once more began to shake until, again, it was hidden.

'Well, you may all step up and look at it when I have finished addressing you. First you must ride out to these provision lands—I will allocate who is to go where—and once you arrive upon them, see that they are burned to the ground. If the crop is wet and won't burn, then just destroy it any way you can. You may shoot any cattle or livestock, or drive them out. But do not run them into any cane fields. While those negroes are busy saving their crops and cattle, it is then we will go in and evict enough from the village to bring those obstinate ingrates back to obedience.'

Having finished his instruction, Robert Goodwin then pressed this restless group to bow their heads to join him in prayer. 'Almighty God,' he began, 'who desireth not the death of a sinner, but rather that he may turn from his wickedness and live—grant us this day the blessing to turn the negroes of Amity back from sin, to the path of righteousness, so that they will labour once more upon this plantation, as is your divine will. Amen.'

Not long out from England . . . still a bit green . . . his dad's a parson back home . . . believes we should be nice to niggers . . . married well— was the meagre reputation that Robert Goodwin had enjoyed with the men that stood before him. But, after finishing the devotion he lifted his head to say, 'Be in no doubt all of you, I mean you to frighten every last one of those negroes and remove their livelihoods until they beg to work once more for me,' respect soon puckered the mouth and brow of all who stared upon him.

CHAPTER 30

W HEN JULY HEARD, 'MARGUERITE,' whispered softly at her door,
she at first believed it to be the wind breathing through a crevice.
'Marguerite.' Or perhaps the call of a night bat. 'Marguerite, are you
there?' Or maybe even a duppy prowling the garden. She did not think
it was the missus. For, since the missus had taken Robert Goodwin for
her husband, she would have rather walked through the whole house
than come by way of July's dwelling. The missus would have sooner
circled the entire garden than ascend the stairs over July's home. Come,
if the missus were ever forced by circumstance to pass by July's abode,
she would have neared the lime-washed wooden door of that intimate
room under the house with her eyes closed tight shut and her ears
blocked by her fists.

So when July opened her door, she was vexed to find her missus
standing before her. The moonlight had dulled all colour, yet July knew
that the grey pallor of her missus was her cheeks flushed with pink, her
eyes rimmed with red. But that unwelcome plump face in the gap of her
doorway—so anxious and fretful that even her blond curls shivered—
soon had July saying, 'Cha, wha' you want? Me no have to serve you
now.'

'Come and sit with me,' was what the missus said to her.

July sucked upon her teeth for a long while; being called Marguerite
by this woman was what began the cuss, but its vent was lengthened for

having this missus bid her, as if she were still her slave, to sit with her. Sit with her! Cha. The last time the missus had required July's company she was still giggling upon the blueness of her overseer's eyes.

Come, she had not looked upon July's face since . . . well, since July's pregnant belly became a bulge that none could miss. So aghast was the missus to realise July was carrying a child that she stared upon July's face with the distress of a big-eyed puppy dog seized to be drowned. July had nearly felt pity for her as the missus staggered back away from that protrusion, desperate to escape its bitter meaning. Since that day, the missus had ceased even addressing July—she clapped, flapped, tush-tushed, banged the table, flicked her fingers, waved her arms, but all in mute command.

'Please, Marguerite, please come and sit with me.' The missus was, without any doubt, pleading, and a bedevilling sound it was to July's ear. To get this white woman gone from her door, was all July had wish of. So July, gazing carefully upon the missus said, 'But me must look after me pickney,' before adding, 'Emily, me baby girl, must be fed.'

For according to the missus, July had no child. According to the missus, she had never ever, ever, seen July with a child. She had never heard a cart draw up carrying the midwife from the village. No sets of rushing feet ever ran across the veranda, down the stairs, and under the house. Caroline Goodwin did not see her husband pacing about the garden for hours and hours, biting hard upon his fingertips. Nor hear mewling break upon the air and feel the sigh of blessed relief that emitted from her husband's chest. Never had she heard a baby crying, nor whimpering around the house. No cooing ever seeped up from under her floor. To the missus's recollection, she had not once even heard mention of a child. Her husband had never spoken the child's name at the dinner table, nor requested to have her brought to him after the meal. She had not chanced upon Robert rocking the child on his knee as he sat on the veranda. Nor had she ever found white christening clothes and a sweet wooden-faced doll amongst his belongings. Not one person in town that the missus could recall, had ever whispered of the shame of Caroline Goodwin's husband keeping a negro woman with a bastard child . . . and in the same house, in the same house! No one ever spread that gossip behind their hand as the missus approached them. Why, the very idea! No, there was no child.

So when, with a quivering lip, the missus replied, 'You may bring your baby with you, Marguerite,' it was July, once more compelled to yield to this woman's wishes, who did then pale grey within that moonlight.

~

Entering in upon the drawing room, July at once understood why her missus was driven to breach her own deceptions to seek out some companionship. Cries, yelling, shouts, banging, and screams were escaping the negro village in a furious squall that jolted through the thin glass of her window. That commotion did haunt the room. The sideboard bounced and rattled within it, the candle flames spluttered, and the daybed, where the missus bid July to lay down her baby, appeared to wobble. Having settled upon the seat before the window, July was forced to heed her missus as she pranced about the room ceaselessly chattering.

'The negroes have driven him to this action—I mean, what choice was left to him? . . . No one does more for the negroes' welfare than he. He cares too much . . .'

All at once, July's awareness was snatched from her missus's fretting when a murky pink glow framed the horizon, as if the sun were about to rise upon it. So pungent did the smell of burning become that it irritated July's nostrils, while a gloom of smoke misted the room.

'But niggers cannot be reasoned with. If those abolitionists in England had ever actually lived amongst negroes then they would have known it was folly to free them . . .'

A black stain of startled birds flew from the tree tops when a clear strike of repeated rifle shot caught in the air. Was it the birds that squealed so as they rounded in the sky?

'His father is quite wrong. Negroes will never be civilised, nor will they ever do as they are bid.'

Flames, clear as the candle beside July, glimmered in the distance.

'But now it is too late. They have been made free. Free not to work. Why, those niggers will not rest until every planter is in the work-house . . .'

And the missus's pacing began vibrating under July's feet like the low rumbling of galloping horses.

The negroes were running down the lanes now, July knew it. For in her mind's eye she was once more amongst them. All was crazed motion. Into the fields, into the trees. Seizing belongings, kicking chickens, struggling with goats. Standing flailing sticks and machetes. Cussing curses upon the white men who would dare to enter their homes. Screaming to find lost pickney. Where you be? Where you be? Confusion, smoke, fire. Run, July, run. Pull that white man from his horse and stamp upon his hand. And that one, quick, fright him with that fire stick. Mash him. Bash him. But then run. Run!

Suddenly, without warning, July had to slap her hand across her mouth to catch the vomit that began to spew from her.

'Marguerite, where are you going?' her missus yelled as July fled from that room.

July's sick splattered over the veranda. She retched. Her throat was scoured hoarse by it. And she retched. Her stomach ached with it.

But the terror of the din that rose from the negro village was now louder with no glass to curb it. It hurled July back inside. She wiped snot from her nose, tears from her eyes, and breathed as deeply as her foreboding would allow.

When she re-entered the drawing room she found her missus stooping low over Emily—tenderly tickling her baby's throat as she lay upon the daybed. Her missus's face, at first rigid with frown, soon pursed about the mouth. And she whispered upon her child, 'What a little one you are.' Staring fixedly at the baby, the missus widened her eyes, then slowly opened and shut her lips. Then she smiled and patted her hands together in a soft clap. As she offered her little finger into the baby's mouth she sensed July staring upon her. Without turning to July, nor taking her gaze from the baby, the missus said, 'She looks just like him.

She's so fair. Not like a nigger's child at all.' Then, looking up to find July's eyes upon her, she added, 'But she is adorable,' before returning to her cooing. 'What did you say she was called?' the missus then asked.

July bounded that room in a leap to wrest her child from out of her missus's affections. 'Marguerite, I was doing no harm,' her missus said as July snatched her baby from the daybed. But the sound of a heavy footfall stomping briskly up the veranda steps had both July and her missus turning, startled, towards the door.

Robert Goodwin rushed in upon the room.

His hat was off his head. His hair wet. His face blackened with soot and striped by slides of dripping sweat that ran down. His shirt hanging out his breeches—dirty as rag—had a slash of blood at the collar. His brown jacket was ripped—at the sleeve, at the shoulder. His boots were enclosed in putrid mud. A ragamuffin, not an English gentleman. Yet he bestowed an air of wholehearted jubilation as he said, 'It has been a great success!'

Who he was addressing, July could not tell, for he looked at neither she, nor the missus, as they both gaped upon him.

'The negroes finally understand where their duty lies. And it is to their masters and to God.'

He hesitated, as he stepped further into the room, on where he should rest his gaze. 'I have returned them to their rightful work,' he addressed first to the missus, who glowed quite crimson before him. 'The negroes are to commence taking off four of the cane pieces at conch blow tomorrow morning, they have assured me of that,' he continued to July. 'All is well,' he laughed before lifting his head heavenward to declare, 'If my father were here, I believe he would shake my hand upon this day. Yes. Yes. I believe my father would be very proud of his son.'

But then Robert Goodwin clasped at his arm—the one where the jacket sleeve was ripped—and staggered as he took a further step. The missus squealed like a poked pig—as if it were she that felt some pain—and pitched her fat white batty across the room to steady him. July had never seen it move so fast, nor wobble so wide.

'Oh, Robert, Robert,' the white-woman twittered, 'What is it? Robert, Robert,' as if he could not recall his own name.

As he placed his arm about the missus's shoulder, the feeble woman nearly folded to the floor. For nothing heavier than Nottingham lace had ever bore hard upon that limp neck before. Come—she teetered graceless as a bakkra drunk on rum under his burden. Yet as the missus bumped and jolted him to a seat she boldly impudenced July by commanding her, 'Get some water quickly, Marguerite.'

Cha. July was not there to serve her. July had been required only to sit with her. For was it not July who nursed the pickney of the master of this house? Was it not July who wore his gold cross and chain about her neck? Was it not July who, curled tight within Robert Goodwin's heart, unfurled only at his will?

July lingered, waiting for Robert Goodwin to throw off the missus's succour and reach out his hand to her. July dallied, expecting soon that he would request she help him out of his boots. He would wish to gaze upon his child soon—to caress a gentle finger across her cheek or coo-coo upon her sweetness. So July waited for him to grumble, 'Oh for heaven's sake, Caroline, leave me alone,' so July might send a sneer across the room to spitefully slap her missus's face. But when Robert Goodwin, with so little care, snapped upon her, 'You heard your mistress, Marguerite. Bring some water,' it was July who was abruptly struck.

<hr />

The next morning, July did not find her Mr Big-big blue-eye, her Mr Sweet-sweet Massa, sleeping close against her in their bed, his renk morning breath warming her ear, his rogue knee pressing at the small of her back. No. July found Robert Goodwin sleeping within his hammock upon the veranda.

And where once, when she watched him, he lay sprawled and tranquil in sleep like a newborn, now he twitched. His lips, caught in a silent discourse, chattered together. His eyes, trapped beneath darkened lids, fluttered restlessly. His arms, embracing a pistol, gripped it tight. As she drew near upon him, he suddenly awakened with the jolt of a fearful quarry.

'Did you hear the conch blow?' was what he asked her.

And July, at once aware that indeed this bright blue morning was more tranquil than any she had ever known, replied, 'No.'

CHAPTER 31

OH, HOW THE FLOOR did quake as the missus bustled through the long room at a galloping pace. 'Marguerite!' July was nearly flattened to the ground so fast did the missus fly at her. 'Marguerite, we must send Byron quickly,' was all she managed to utter before her panting breath choked her. July rolled her eyes waiting for this convulsion to pass. When, finally, the missus had breath enough to continue she said, 'We must send Byron or Elias to the cane piece at Virgo.'

When July sucked quietly upon her teeth—that such fuss-fuss could be made from so little a request—the missus fixed her pale eyes close upon her to say, 'No, you don't understand. I have just been told by an odious little man who rode out to the fields with Robert this morning, that he has begun acting strangely. When I asked him if Robert was unwell, the man just said, "Well, you could say that." Then he picked his teeth with a stick right before me. When I enquired why my husband did not return with him, he said that Robert refused to be moved from the cane piece. But whatever could he mean, Marguerite?'

July rushed to the stables to command Byron to harness up the pony and cart. She would go to the cane piece herself. She would send no foolish house boy who would think only to shine the massa's shoes if he found him wretched or bleeding. If Robert Goodwin was struck down with a fever from the sun then he would wish only her to gather him up to nurse and cool his brow. If he was broken then no one else must raise his fractured bones, for only she could perform that ministration with enough tenderness. If he was bitten by a snake then who else but she could suck out that sting?

But the missus ran to follow after July screeching, 'I must come too.' July was unable to stop that fool-fool woman from gathering up her fancy skirts, tying on her bonnet, and fussing with her parasol before struggling her batty into the cart.

July was careful to ride carelessly over the stony paths so the missus would be bounced about that cart like a leather ball. 'Must we go so fast?' the missus kept pleading with July as they travelled. Only as they approached the negro village did July rein in the pony to slow.

July recalled that, at that point in the lane, she should have been look-ing upon Miss Peggy's dwelling place. But that boarded hut with the string of calabash hung over the door was no longer there. In its place only the crooked arch of a door frame was left standing, while a pig lay dead under a pall of black flies before a disordered heap of splintered wood. Further down that lane, Miss Fanny's hut—where July had chased out after Robert Goodwin, not so very long ago—still possessed its stone walls, but had no thatch upon the roof. Outside its open door, a broken-down chair lay upturned beside a dutchy pot that was crushed almost flat.

As the cart moved along, July saw that all was devastation within the village. The blackened ground was strewn with a debris of tables, stools, mattresses, cooking pots, fragments of cups and plates, branches of trees, smashed and rotting fruit. Wisps of smoke rose here and there, releasing a woeful stench of scorching. While many of the huts that were still where July knew them to have always been, now stood forlornly crip-pled by missing walls, windows, roofs. And apart from a brown dog—whimpering and lame, dragging its useless bloody back legs along behind it, and some chickens pecking heedless about, there was no one to be found there.

Where were the women cooking outside their homes or steadfast pounding at their grain within a pestle? Come, where were the pickney chasing their goats? The men? Why were no tired-eyed men sitting smoking their pipes in the shade? Always eager faces came to stare when the massa's cart rode by. Where were they, those busybodies keen to get some chat-chat of what the missus be wearing today? As July and her missus rode on to pass through the peculiar silence of a deserted mill works, her missus's face began to shrivel with frown. For the missus finally deemed something amiss enough to ask, 'But . . . But . . . But where are all the negroes?'

When the cart reached the edge of the cane piece the missus, suddenly sitting up straight, remarked, 'But look, Marguerite, there is a negro. Go and enquire of the whereabouts of his master.' July rode the cart in closer.

He looked like a negro, this figure standing small before a louring barbed wall of yellow-parched cane. Ragged, filthy, black. He was stripped to the waist and clasped a machete, holding it high above his shoulder. But only when he struck it down and slashed the cane in the middle of the pole did July realise she was staring not upon a negro— who would have felled that cane skilfully at the base and be casting it away by now—but upon the frame of Robert Goodwin.

Grunting loud, he began slashing the cane from side to side like he were scything guinea-grass, cursing with the effort of every swipe. July jumped from the cart, ignoring her missus's plea for assistance. And she caught Robert's arm as he raised it once more to cut pitiable at the cane. He twisted to look upon her. Snorting fierce as an overworked beast, his mouth gaped as he gasped for breath. His eyes, at first wild with anguish, soon filled with spite. Until he stared such hate upon July that she shrank from him.

'What you be doing?' July asked, with a voice more tremulous than she had ever believed herself to be.

He snatched himself from out her grasp. 'Do not touch me. Get away from me,' he said. Then he seemed to soften before her. He sighed and wiped his arm across his forehead while quietly saying, 'The negroes are all gone.' His blue eyes were red. 'All of them have taken their belongings and gone. There is not one left upon Amity. Not one. There is no one left to take off the cane. Nor to turn the mill. No one is at the coppers in the boiling house. No one filling hogsheads, nor delivering to the dock. They have all deserted me. So . . . So . . . I have decided that I will bring in the cane myself.'

'Come, you cannot cut cane!' July said.

But he shouted loud over her, 'I've no need of niggers, I will do everything myself.' He turned to slash at the poles of cane once more—feeble as a small boy at play with a stick. The disturbed barbs upon the leaves flew to sting in July's eyes. She seized his arm again, but he shouted, 'Get away from me, nigger, get away.'

She would not let him go. She struggled to hold him—grasping tight at his arm while he twisted and turned in an effort to shake her away. She would not leave him. But then he caught her throat so tight within his hand that her tongue protruded under the grasp. July wrestled to free herself from his hold as he raised his machete high above her. And, all at once, July heard herself crying, 'Mercy, massa, mercy,' as she cringed away from him.

It was the missus seizing the machete from out of his hand that spared July from that fearsome blow. 'Robert, what are you doing?' the missus yelled.

His arm was still poised to strike, his eyes still vicious, when Robert Goodwin heartlessly threw July away. He glared upon the missus—perusing her—from the top of her blond head to the tip of her slippered toes. Until his gaze rested calm upon the captured machete that she held clasped to her. Soon he dropped to kneel upon the trash, first one knee, then two. Then he bowed his head, held his face within his palms, and wept.

CHAPTER 32

COME, LET US FIRST find the field negroes who once resided and worked upon the plantation named Amity. We must ride a good way to follow the path they journeyed when they abandoned that place. The trail they travelled—carrying their salvaged mattresses, chairs, clay pots, tin pans—has been worn down over many years by hundreds of bare black feet just like their own. It was walked by negroes who wished to be undisturbed by white men. It was run down by excited slaves chasing wild boar. It was fled down by runaways and hid along by the needful.

But the negroes of Amity escaped by it with flapping chickens hung over their shoulders; with bleating goats tethered together in a line; with the pickney shoved along; and the old, leaning upon sticks or thrown together atop the lumbering carts whose wheels creaked and stuck in the mud; with obstinate donkeys who were coaxed with whips to slip-slow under the load they carried; and vexed cattle struggling under their yokes.

The path they took twists and turns through a thick fern wood, where a dark canopy of furry fronds blocks most the light. But then it rises out of this soft dank dell to become steep and covered with bamboo and log-wood. Those are cotton trees that now line our route—bare of their own leaves, but with their spreading branches draped lush with wild fig and creeping plants.

As the land begins to level out, stones appear, and the way is hindered by boulders pushing their jagged way up through the earth. On past those fallen trees and that scraggly sprawl of yellowing banana plants, and there we find our first glimpse of the clearing where our negroes came to rest—the ramshackle camp that was raised upon these back-lands just outside the tumbling borders of Amity.

Peggy and Cornet took one look at this woebegone place, packed up their cart, said their farewells, and rode off to Westmoreland. Benjamin left to join his minister-man to work his own piece of land in a place called Sligoville. Samuel could not stay, for he needed the river to be deeper for his shrimp pots and the tributary that trickled through this place could be crossed in a stride. Tilly wept and begged for them to return to the plantation until Miss Nancy slapped her. While Mary Ellis stood silently, looking about, doubting that there was enough land to feed them all.

But Giles spread his arms wide to show the glory of this place with no white men to haunt them. He showed them the sprawl of the over-grown flatlands just beyond the wood. Come, trees over there already abundant with fruit. Soon those lands would be cleared and planted with plantain, cocoas, yam and corn. And they had goats, chickens, plenty-plenty boar, and did not Ezra manage to steal five of the massa's cows?

James Richards held the plan for the felling of trees, the cutting of wood, the making of huts. While the clearing of the land, where even the old and pickney had a part to play, was driven by Elizabeth Millar, soon known, when she was too far to hear, as the black bakkra.

And, reader, you may only see before you a forlorn clearing in a wilderness where scruffy, hungry, tired and pitiful negro men, women and children laboured long, yet where not even one wall of a hut can be observed. But upon this rough, squatted land, 'This is free,' was cried hearty every morning by Dublin Hilton. After the conch was blown for work to commence, that old once-a-distiller-man did raise his voice to yell upon all who now lived there, 'Wake now, all, for this be free.'

And now we must return to the place they left and ride through the lands of Amity. Through the acres of cane pieces where the poles of cane are already being bound and choked by weeds. Some of the crop lies trampled and flat as discarded trash. Without the negroes, already much of the land has fallen to ruinate, useless ticky-ticky.

See the trash-house door is open, while the flimsy spent cane, being blown by the wind, spills like jumble weed. The wheel is fixed by a creeping vine already, and unable to turn, even if there were still workers or beasts willing to drive its spindles. And there is a breach in the cane juice gutter. If that precious liquor ran from the mill down to the receivers in the boiling house now, it would never reach, but spill halfway into the river and feed the fish its sweetness. And the works—where once the enormous coppers steamed, foamed and bubbled loud with molten liquor turning to granulate as sugar—is quiet except for the scratching and squealing of creatures who now have their home within the bowl of those vacant teaches. And so many rats! With no small boys to trap them, see how boldly they befoul the once clean floor of that boiling house.

Look upon the grey stone of the temper-lime kiln as we pass—it is cracked and half obscured by plants. But shield your nose from the stench, flap your hands to scatter the flies, and be sure to avert your eye as we travel alongside that petrified negro village.

The gate that guards the path up to the great house is hanging broken from its hinge. The watch hut is empty. But as we near the stables there is the sound of laughing. Byron sits playing marbles with Joseph at the door. Both squatting upon tiny three-legged stools, those two long men have their knees up by their ears as they watch the marbles run.

But let us quickly pass by to find Molly snoozing upon her chair in the doorway of the kitchen, her arms folded across her belly, her grey kerchief slipping to one side. There is no need of tip-toeing, for nothing would wake her as we now take those six small steps that cross that vast breach from the kitchen into the great house.

There, in the dining room, Robert Goodwin idly examines the tarnish upon his silver knife as he sits, leaning an elbow casually upon the dining table. While at the other end of that long piece of furniture, his wife Caroline is seated as upright as her chair back demands. He is reciting to her the instructions that he found in the last letter he received from his papa concerning their arrival in England. How his father advises that they should hire a carriage and pair to take them to Chesterfield rather than taking a post or stage coach. While at the other end of the table Caroline recounts for him, with complex hand gestures and very shrill giggling, the details of the last sea voyage she undertook those many years before.

And your storyteller must report—for it cannot be rendered upon paper in any other way—that Robert and Caroline Goodwin are both speaking to each other at one and the same time.

Robert Goodwin is now quite recovered from his malady. After he was brought home from the cane piece, a sickness confined him to his bed. Curled up tight as a fern frond he lay there for many weeks. He would speak to no one, nor open his eyes to look about him. He took no food, nor sipped any proffered water. There was no mortal illness the doctor could find—no yellow, nor denghie fever, no malaria, nor snake bite. But the doctor warned Caroline that, if he continued to refuse water, his grave would claim him just the same.

Yet no matter how Caroline cajoled, wagging her finger upon him to 'drink or die,' stamping down her foot, squealing, shaking her fist at his unreasonableness, or stroking his brow to beg him, 'Whisper, Robert, whisper to me what is wrong so it might be put right,' he remained insensible to her. She sat vigil beside him—day and night—poking and squeezing a dampened sponge against his lips. Yet still his blue eyes sank into the shadow of their sockets as the bones of his face gradually outlined the skull beneath. She wailed upon him, she dropped to her knees to persuade him to live, she even shook him—although the flimsiness of his gaunt torso nearly had her faint.

Then, one afternoon, a baby's cry broke outside the window and Robert Goodwin was suddenly roused to swivel his eye towards the sound. Within the hour, Caroline had brought his baby Emily to him. She placed the naked baby upon his pillow. At first he made no movement but when that little child leaned over towards him to grab a handful of his hair within her tiny fist, he almost smiled. He raised his hand to gingerly catch the baby's fingers in his. But she would not let go his hair. Caroline had to pick her from off the pillow. And the baby kicked and fretted so as she was raised away from him that he lifted his hand to his lips to hush her, then waved weakly to her as she was taken from the room.

After that, he would sip water. After that, he would suck upon a mango. When he chewed the tiniest morsel of guinea fowl, Caroline became quite determined that now she could return him to health. He reminded her of the kitten she had once found in London many years before. 'It was skinny as a pipe cleaner after being near drowned by some brute,' she told him as she carefully spooned beef tea into his mouth. 'Edmund had said that it would surely die. But it grew and grew under my nursing.' However, what she did not disclose to him was that she fed the kitten so much that it died a few months later, a big round ball of fur in front of an untouched saucer of rancid cream.

Come, Caroline would let no one go near her patient except she! Only she must feed him, only she must wash him, only she must take his weight upon her shoulder to walk him about the room. As he regained some strength, visitors came to call and Caroline waylaid them at the sickroom door to jabber her instructions upon them. One visitor may enter at a time only; do not approach him closer than the foot of the bed; resist asking too many questions of him, but do comment heartily upon how much improved he seems. And never, ever, under any circumstances, talk of negroes—for nothing must agitate him in any way.

And fine progress he made under this mighty care—stronger and more contented every day. Until that is, George Sadler from Windsor Hall paid him a visit. Within a second of Caroline having left the room, George Sadler, flouting all instruction, pulled up a chair to sit close beside Robert Goodwin. He wished to speak within his ear, the better to apprise him of the new idea that the planters of the parish were planning—an idea which would end all of their problems with those indolent, feckless, troublesome negroes and return their plantations once more to profit. By the time George Sadler had left that room, Robert Goodwin was sitting up in bed, excitedly talking of coolies.

'Of course. What a perfect idea. It's the only answer to our problems. Immigration. We must bring in labourers to work the lands from some other country. And where better to find them than India. Indian workers have proved themselves already upon the island of Mauritius. Yes, coolies must be brought here. George Sadler has ordered one hundred to be sent from India on a seven-year indentureship. I intend to do the same,' Robert Goodwin told Caroline, before insisting that he should soon leave his bed and go into town to arrange it all. 'Every planter upon the island is of one mind, Caroline. Boatloads of these men are already upon their way. And George Sadler assures me that those that have already arrived work far better than any negro. They have never been slaves, you see, and have not that antipathy to white men. They come just under obligation to work. Coolies! Coolies are the answer I have been looking for. Coolies will soon have this plantation working again.'

Caroline sent once more for the doctor. She wished to ask him whether, in view of the seriousness of her husband's malady, his need to rest, his need for quiet so his problem did not return, that perhaps, for his own good, he should be tied down to the bed?

The doctor told her, 'Madam, your husband is a gentleman, not a lunatic!' But what he did prescribe was a long visit back home to England, so he might better convalesce away from the source of his unease.

And oh, how Caroline squealed with delight, 'Of course, why did not I think of that? I must take him to England. I must get him far away from here. Robert, Robert, the doctor has decided that you must go to Youlgreave at once to visit with your family.'

So there sits Caroline Goodwin, quite flush with high spirits, that this was their last evening upon the island for well . . . for well . . . for well, we will see. She longed to behold England again now her Robert was well—now he was so very much improved. And she had not yet had a chance to speak with Robert about it, but there was a man in London—

an agent for a titled gentleman who lived in Bristol—that wished to talk to them about the possibility of purchasing the lands and the great house of the plantation named Amity.

But she does not mention that as they sit at the dining table one last time before sailing to England. For she is too busy telling the tale of her last sea voyage. 'Robert, did I ever tell you that the ship I travelled in to Jamaica bucked and rolled me across that ocean so cruelly that being strapped to a whale's back would have been no less arduous a journey?'

But we must, for a moment, leave Mr and Mrs Goodwin at the table—come, we have heard that tale before and wait . . . wait . . . I believe she is about to repeat it again! Let us move on quickly through the doorway of the dining room, out into the hallway. For there, stationed behind the door, clasping an oval, silver, dome-lidded serving dish is our July. As she instructs Elias—who stands before her, wiping his nose with one hand while fidgeting to adjust his itchy breeches with the other—she leans forward to speak as close into his ear as the awkward salver within her hands will allow. Her command to him is to place this dish, 'Before the massa, you hear me, nah? What me just say?'

When Elias shrugged, she kicked him awkwardly. 'Before the massa, not the missus. What me say?' As Elias repeated, 'The massa, the massa, the massa . . .' she handed the salver into his outstretched arms with the command, 'And be careful you no drop it.'

Elias walked the twenty paces from the door to the table, quick as a lizard escaping a snake. July, peering upon him through the crack of the door, inhaled a fearful breath, which she did not release until the fool-fool boy had placed the dish upon the table in front of Robert Goodwin. As his massa turned his head to find Elias asking, 'What is this, boy?' Elias ran from the room without reply.

As Robert Goodwin was saying, 'Yes, yes, Caroline, I did hear you the last time you told me of that voyage,' he placed his hand upon the handle of the salver's lid. He then lifted it. A thousand black cockroaches, suddenly freed into the light, scurried from out that dish. They swarmed across the table top like a spill of dirty water to drop pitter-patter from the table on to the wooden floor. Some fell into his lap. Robert Goodwin was too stunned to feel the crawl of them. He sat entranced, staring at a hideous mound of dead and crushed roaches that were piled high upon the salver. He took a while to start yelling. But then he jolted to his feet—hopping and swiping at his lap, his chest, slapping his arms and face, as the pitiful roar of a donkey painfully dying emitted from his mouth. Caroline stood upon her chair to shriek.

While July, silently watching this frenzied scene through the crack in the dining-room door, did hope it would make her smile, did believe it would make her laugh, and was quite vexed to find that it did not.

CHAPTER 33

READER, MUST I NOW show the fuss-fuss that went on as the massa and missus of the plantation named Amity finally took their leave from this Caribbean island? Do you desire to hear the squealing of Caroline Goodwin one last time within this tale, as she directs their belongings loaded up on to the carriage? 'Byron, be careful, be very careful, boy, that is very valuable . . . Slower, Elias, do not run . . . Robert, where are you? Elias, where is your master? . . .'

Or shall we pass on by to a quieter place? To find our July sitting a little distance from the garden, within the cooling shade of a tree, regarding all this commotion with a glad eye. For come, it was not 'Marguerite! Marguerite!' that was being called.

July had at first asked kindly to be allowed to attend Robert Goodwin upon his sickbed. She meekly appealed to the missus. Following that, she pleaded with her. Finally, she was obliged to drop to her knees to kiss the missus's slippered toes and beg her. Seven times in all, did July make her requests (or every minute of the night and day for weeks and weeks, if you care to take Caroline Goodwin's version of July's remonstrations).

'He must not see negroes,' the missus had told her.

And July informed her, 'But me is not a negro, me is a mulatto.' Her missus—frowning with deep puzzlement—just replied, 'Oh, who upon this earth cares about that silliness? You are still a negro, and it is negroes who have brought him to this. You will come nowhere near him, Marguerite. He does not wish to see you. He wants you to stay away from him. Do you hear me?'

The missus had then tasked Joseph to guard the only unbolted door into the great house. His sole command was to shoo July—to get her gone, to shout and curse upon her that the massa no want to see her.

Only when resting quiet in that little room under the house could July be anywhere near Robert Goodwin. For she did hear him in his room above her. If her breath was held she did feel him turning fretful within his bed. If she stood upon her tip-toe she would catch his sigh as he stared, bored, through the window. His muffled voice did often drift down to her, but too indistinct to be worth straining for his meaning. But sometimes at night his resonant snore did rattle in to rest beside her.

When, one evening, she sat nursing Emily, softly singing, 'Mama gon' rock, mama gon' hold, little girl-child mine,' his laughter came tripping through her ceiling. 'Papa,' July said to Emily, who was suckling with her one hard tooth. The missus's footsteps skipping heavy across the room above her were not unusual. Nor was her giggling. July thought nothing of the silence that followed.

She laid Emily into her box, sat upon her bed, and snuffed out her candle to preserve it. It was in that gloom that her ceiling began to creak. And soft moans and breathy sighs and panting began drizzling down upon July's head. The bed began to bounce above her, rhythmic and strong. Thump, thump. Come, July had felt a tickle of dust gently falling. Then, slap! He enjoyed to spank bare flesh. Ouch! He loved to pinch. Oh! And to bite. Faster and faster, the bed had bumped upon her ceiling. And although July blocked up her ears with her fists, the missus did not think to stifle Robert Goodwin's mouth when he at last discharged his final cry.

July spent many days gathering up those cockroaches for Robert Goodwin's leaving dish. It was not, however, a thousand roaches that menaced Robert Goodwin, for they became quite hard to find. But more than one hundred, July managed to capture. Most were crushed, for they were the devil to keep in one place. And not all were cockroaches, but beetles and centipedes and tumble-bugs and strange black slithery things that squirmed within the shitty pit-holes. But all were diligently hoarded by July, for far too easily had she just been discarded.

July heard Robert Goodwin command not only Joseph, but Byron and Elias that, 'Miss July must be allowed nowhere near the house, or the garden. Do not let her return to her room until we are quite departed. And she must stay far from the kitchen. Do not, under any circumstances, permit her to approach the missus or myself. She must be warned that if I glimpse her anywhere within my sight then, so help me God, I will have the policeman brought from town to incarcerate her in the lock-up. Anywhere! Savvy that? Anywhere! And neither your missus, nor myself, wishes to bid her any sort of goodbye.'

Their departing carriage disappeared that day, rippling and swaying in a heat haze. July watched it go until the last black dot of it appeared to simply vanish.

July turned her gaze to watch Emily, who sat at her feet. Her pickney was singing a song to herself—a nonsense song, for she knew no words. And as she sang she played with a piece of lace, turning it over and over in her fingers until she began sucking it keenly within her mouth.

The lace had been gifted to Emily by Robert Goodwin. He had hoped July to stitch it into a christening dress for his daughter. The christening would now never take place, but July leaned forward to her pickney to promise, 'But me still gone make the dress for you,' as she wrested the soggy lace from Emily's sticky hands.

It was then that Molly arrived. She stood before July saying nothing, just staring her one good eye down upon her. So long did Miss Molly remain silent, that July thought to ask her where she would go now there were no white people within the great house who required her nasty food.

Molly lifted her gaze to the clouds to at last speak. She began by saying that she had milk. It was warm and fresh and straight from the cow and should she take Miss Emily to feed her some? Then she smiled upon July.

July thought nothing of it as she handed her pickney to her, for Molly often fed her. But perhaps if she had noticed that Molly was wearing a hat—a missus cast-off with a blue satin bow that hung down comically in need of a stitch—she would have waved her away. Oh, reader, if July had remembered that Molly, in the whole of her days, had only ever smiled in spite, perhaps she would have just clutched her pickney tight to her.

But she did not.

July walked the path up to the great house, where every window and every door of that big place was barred and sealed to her. Only the veranda remained open to welcome. July lifted herself into Robert Goodwin's hammock. As she rocked there she watched a column of red ants determinedly climb the veranda steps. They marched in their thin red line straight under the bolted door of the house. Where once July would have chased them back with a broom or threatened them with a fire stick, now she let them go. And there was no missus to squeal, 'Marguerite, Marguerite! Come quickly, there are ants!' Come, so quiet did it remain that July could hear the pitter-patter of the ants' legs as they walked that wooden floor. And she fell asleep there, rocking within a hammock that smelt faintly of an Englishman.

When she awoke, it was nearly dark. The commotion that roused her was made by Byron and Elias returning from town. They unharnessed the horse from the carriage with so much squabbling that July was sure Byron was once again drunk upon rum. July called out to Molly. When there came no reply, she walked to the kitchen.

But the kitchen was empty. The stove was unlit. The jalousies were closed. When Elias mounted the steps on to the veranda, July was upon him. She grabbed him at the shoulders, 'You see Miss Molly?'

And Elias answered, 'Yes.'

'Then where she be?'

Elias, shaking himself from out July's grasp looked puzzled on her as he replied, 'She be gone to England with the missus.'

July had to wait a moment for her breath to return before she asked, 'Did she have pickney?'

'Oh yes,' Elias told her, 'she carried the massa's pickney with her.'

And July roared upon Elias, strong and commanding, telling him to run to Byron—the cart must be got up, a pony harnessed. She must be taken into town and she must be taken now, for she must find her pickney. Now. Quickly. What did he wait upon? Now!

When Elias just stood looking confused upon her, she bashed him about his ear, nearly knocking him down. 'But the boat be sailed,' he told her. 'Me did watch it. Five did sail upon the tide. One big-big sight them sails flapping, and them calling out and . . .' Elias stopped in his musing as July gaped upon him. 'No fear, Miss July,' he went on with a pride intended to calm her, 'it be the massa and missus be taking the pickney to England.' And when July suddenly dropped to sit upon the floor in front of him, he gently asked her, 'But what, Miss July, did you wan' keep that little pickney for your own?'

Part 5

ONLY HIS MAMA CAN rouse my son, Thomas, to quarrel. Let me place you as a guest at our Sunday table so you might find evidence for this judgement. See before you a white cotton cloth upon which sits, between knives and forks, the porcelain dinner plates decorated with delicate pink and canary roses, that Lillian does only allow to escape her display cupboard upon Sunday afternoons.

To your left is Miss May, my son's youngest daughter. Be sure that she is fidgeting—playing with a piece of braid within her fingers, pushing back her chair to look upon her new patent-tipped button shoes, tapping her hand upon the table as she stares through the window. Her sister, Miss Corinne, sits beside her with folded arms and her full mouth drooping with sulk. While across the table Miss Louise, the middle child and quite the darkest of the three, sits making ugly faces at her sisters—widening her black eyes and sticking out her tongue when their mama Lillian, who sits at the other end of the table, is engaged looking elsewhere.

My son Thomas is seated at this table's head—probably still reading some pamphlet or perhaps grinning upon his wife. While your storyteller, who is beside Miss Louise, sits wishing that just this once she might remain peaceful as she waits for the eating to commence, but is forced, as at every meal within this household, to quell the mischief of these three naughty girls by saying, 'Sit still—stop that—be quiet at the table.' Reprimands that their mama and papa should be composing but, alas, never do.

See now, as Miss Essie, our housekeeper, cook and busybody, arrives from the kitchen bearing the food upon a wooden platter. Be sure that what she will serve will be pork . . . again, but do not place your blame with her. Your storyteller did tell Lillian many times that the hog she decide to slay was too big for this family alone.

Reader, you must know as well as I that, if a pig is slaughtered upon this tropical island it must be eaten up soon before the meat does turn renk and wriggle with so many tiny living things that it might journey from the kitchen to your plate without aid. Wait, I tell Lillian, until she has an occasion where more mouths can be fed by that enormous sow. You think she heed me—an old woman? Her husband must suck on pig's foot, she tell me. Her husband desire to chew a pig's cheek. She must boil this pig's bones so her husband might drink his favourite soup. Some was pickled and cured, but it is still five days that we have been eating pork at every meal.

So let us watch now as my son gently commands his family to start nyam. See him place some of the meat within his mouth. Then let us wait while the hot-hot pepper of the scotch bonnet that Miss Essie must use to spice up this meat so no rancid taste does remain, sucks all his breath from out him. See his chest? Watch it jump with hiccup. Then listen as each one of his three daughters start whining with complaint that this meat be too fiery for them to swallow. Even his own mama begins to weep; for I do not have teeth enough to chew meat and must chase this burning substance around my tongue until I might chance to spear it upon those molars that are left. Yet still my son does not think to chastise his wife for the torment we are all suffering. He just hold up his hands and command that it is for Lillian to decide upon these matters.

But let me now arrive at the point of this diversion, for I have very little paper left. Come, on two occasions my son promised to restore my supply with a quarter ream of 'superfine white wove' or some such. Paper is paper, I tell him. And on two occasions, while his hand slapped hard against his forehead, he tell me it was forgot! However, that is not my concern here.

My tale, reader, was at last complete. My pen placed an end dot next to the final word and was laid down to rest. I dozed within my chair for the whole afternoon until the setting sun gradually dusted the room deep pink, without one of my thoughts straying fretful to our July. I even allowed my weary breast to bound with a little excitement, for soon my son would set this tale to printing and I would have not flimsy remembrance but a book to hold.

The last pages of my story I handed to my son, Thomas, when we were both sitting quietly upon the veranda in the place where the sweet orange tree's branches do offer their fruit to any seated there like a gift. Of course Miss May did then run to her papa, fling herself in his lap and pull gently upon his ears until he made promise that—(reader, please pay attention, for I will write these words but have little understanding of them)—the scenery for a photograph likeness that the three girls were to have made in a studio within the town would show them before the ruined castle, and not before the table containing a vase of flowers.

My son who, at first, struggled to remain stern, was soon chuckling like a tickled babe before he cried, 'Yes.' Once Miss May had fled to trouble someone else and all was quiet as it could be within this raucous household, my son was at last free carefully to peruse my ending. Here below, reader, are the very words that my son read that day:

And so our July did have to leave the great house at Amity, which was locked and boarded for the next owner to find. She packed up her belongings into a cloth bag and walked in upon the town. And there she did rent for herself a fine shop. Oh yes. This was not some broken-down stall upon the side of the road from which Miss Clara had once been obliged to hawk her wares. The door to July's shop could be closed and locked. And it was from behind those doors that our July did cook up some of the finest jams and pickles to be found anywhere upon this island. They did not rival Miss Clara's, for Miss Clara's were quite forgot. 'Miss Clara's guava jelly? No. Bring me Miss July's naseberry preserve and do not forget to fill a jug with more of her hot-pepper pickle,' was demanded from this island's whites, coloureds and negroes alike—for all craved them.

And our July did grow so rich and old and happy upon her wit, that she did purchase a little boarding house. Miss Clara's lodging was nearly put from business once Miss July's guest house opened for trade. Naval men and their families and travellers of the highest ranking did lodge with her when visiting within the town. And so often did these good guests return, that her reputation roamed the world and beyond without her. An English gentleman, who did write plenty fine books in England, did tell of Miss July's clean and comfortable boarding house in a small volume. This gentleman (whose name does here escape me) did urge his readers to visit Miss July's establishment should they ever find themselves in closeness to it.

So reader, do not feel pity for the plight of our July, for my tale did not set forth to see her so wounded. And though other books and volumes (wrapped in leather and stamped in gold) might wish you to view her life as worthless, I trust you have walked with her too long and too far to heed that foolishness when it is belched upon you. No. July's tale has the happiest of endings—and you may take my word upon it.

Once my son had completed his reading of the fine style and clever sentiment that you have also perused, he first stared aghast upon me, like his mama had just floated in through the window upon the devil's tail and then he start to laugh. So long did I have to endure his merriment that I had time enough to notice that some of his hair was indeed lost to him, for it was so light and grey upon his head as to appear thin as dust settled upon a table top.

But now, reader, now is the time you must recall those three ill-disciplined girls and Lillian's entirely ignored nasty peppered pork. Then you might have heart enough to grasp the injury your storyteller did feel when my son—finally summoning a scolding spirit—told his old-old mama, 'But this is no good. This will not do. No, no, you must do this again.' For as I did tell earlier, only I can rouse my son to quarrel.

'What be wrong?' asked I.

'Mama, this is not written in truth,' says he.

'It is so true,' says I.

'No, it is not,' replies he.

I will not here repeat the length of this yes-it-is, no-it-is-not argument that was provoked. But know this, if your storyteller had had sufficient paper you, reader, would now be turning, one, two, three, four pages with nothing but my son's back-chat written upon the leaves. There is not a writer in England that must endure such troublesome meddling. . . there is not!

'Mama,' my son finally said, 'you wish your readers to know that after Miss July's baby had been cruelly seized from her by Robert and Caroline Goodwin and taken to England, that she then went on to manage a shop within the town entirely untroubled, and there grew old making first, preserves and pickles, before becoming the mistress of a lodging house?'

'Old and happy, yes,' I told him.

'Then, Mama,' and here he did grin upon me—not with kindness but crafty, like he would soon prick me with reason, as he said, 'Then can you perhaps tell me who was that woman—that half-starved woman— with the stolen chicken under her clothes?'

I had always prayed that my son would never speak of her again. Bewildered by the insolence of this plain chat, I could do nothing but stare wordlessly upon him, while he silently watched me. And we may have stayed within that sullen muteness for another three pages if it was not for Miss Louise. For she did suddenly run in upon the garden, screaming like a flogged runaway, 'Papa, tell her . . . Papa tell her she must not . . . Papa, tell her,' while Miss Corinne chased after her waving a large, hairy-brown, flapping moth within her hand.

One of us, my son or me, did have to warn those two girls sternly that if their skirts got ripped within this horseplay they would have to stitch them themselves. One of us did have to scold them to keep their Sunday petticoats from out the dirt. But I will let my readers guess which of us, my son or me, was finally impelled to break that terrible silence.

So I am at my desk, resting my elbow upon a short pile of 'superfine white wove' paper that my son did eventually remember to supply. My pen—loaded and dripping with ink—is poised above these empty sheets, ready once more to seek out July. My lamp has been trimmed and is no longer smoking. And my tea has been poured. As long as the wind does not disturb me with its howling—for my jalousie does permit any breeze to screech through it as if it be a reed pipe—I will here endeavour to yet again write the final chapter of my tale. But let me first begin by informing my reader that, where you will hear of one fowl flapping within the next part of this tale, your storyteller must share with you a secret—it was, in-matter-of-fact, two stolen fowls. And you may take my word upon it.

CHAPTER 35

⟋

THE JUDGE, PINK OF face and quite sagging with perspiration, had been wiping his sweating brow with a once cooling, but now warm damp cloth for several snatched minutes. The courthouse within the town was so hot upon that day that one of his men of law, fresh from England and dressed entirely in the thick black of justice, had slipped from his chair to collapse in a faint upon the floor to be roused with the splashing of water and the fanning of legal documents. When this judge finally looked up to find our July standing within the dock waiting for her 'larceny of a domestic hen' to be announced, he slowly leaned over to the clerk beside him and said in a loud whisper, 'Is that a woman?'

For this judge believed he was gazing upon no more than a pillar of foul rags. Come, if he had been near enough to whiff the stench of her or close enough to mark the flies that girded her to feed upon her filth, he may have declared her simply shit walking.

Reader, you may recognise a sunlit courthouse room with its pale-blue walls studded with earnest plaques and flags, its wooden panels, benches and tables, bewigged white men in black and important jurors sitting stiffly to attention, but you do not know the July that stands before them in this stifling room. For we have travelled fast to be within this courtroom—perhaps thirty years has passed, or maybe more, since last we met July.

So, please forget the young woman with neat braided hair always wrapped within a clean coloured kerchief. Think not of her mouth with its mischievous turn at the corners where a wry tale or tall-tall truth looked always about to escape it. And do not search for her spirited black eyes. It is time to put that younger July from your mind for another has just walked in. And her face, if the grime was wiped from it, or she was commanded to lift her head, is so pinched with starvation that death's bony skull can be glimpsed beneath it; her skin is as tanned, wrinkled and care-worn as a neglected hide; her hair so matted that it stands in stiff locks; and her gait so stooped that the flimsy tattered rags of the dress she wears appear like a weight for her to carry.

And no seat is offered, so she clings her fingers to the wood of the dock that she might lean against its bulk. A Bible is thrust before her. What must she do? Take it? No, she must place her hand upon it as she speaks her name. For that man—the white man within that big soft chair—must know the name she goes by. But not so hushed. He requires it spoken louder. Yet still he cannot hear when all her breath is used to pronounce it.

The man commanded to listen at her mouth tilts his head so close to hers that she can see white flakes of dead skin entangled within his hair. As he straightens away from her, he puffs out the breath he held so her stench did not overwhelm him and pronounces her name. July, says he. But July who? July who? The big-big man must now know. Again his breath is held as scaly-head man leans forward, but he hears no surname. Red as a goat's testicle his face becomes, waiting for July to respond. But she has not uttered the name Goodwin for too many years and will not speak it now. The accused knows no other name, this gasping man is finally forced to expel.

Then there be a fat-bellied, bewhiskered white man standing erect about the other side of this room behind a desk. He says that she, that negro—and his fleshy finger points steadily across at July—was a squatter upon Unity land.

'Are you living unlawfully upon the land?'

What? She could not hear him.

'Do you live within the boundary of the estate?'

What? How could she reply if she could not hear him?

'Oh, no matter, carry on.'

She has been living upon that land since its ownership passed from Amity to Unity and the boundaries were redrawn, begins this fat man. She was slave to John Howarth who owned Amity, then to his sister Caroline Mortimer. Mrs Mortimer married a Robert Goodwin and the estate was subsequently sold. England is where they now reside, my lord, in England.

Many, many years, the accused has lived upon those backlands. She lives amongst several other of the negroes who used to work the plantation at Amity. Never has she paid any rent, according to the attorney. It is true it is unlevel rough and spent land, useless for cultivation, yet still within the boundary of the estate. But those negroes would not be moved.

This one (and again the fleshy finger points) declares she has no other home but this. Says she had been living upon Amity for all her life. That it was the place of her birth, where her kindred's bones were rested . . . et cetera, et cetera. She believes, as many of the negroes do in their child-like way, my lord, that there is no other world.

How many negroes lived there? Quite a few at first. It was the whole of the negro village from the Amity plantation. They were a blight. And, oh yes, there were several attempts made to have them moved on. The attorney at Unity—a Mr Fielding, my lord, he runs several of the estates in the parish for Sir Salisbury Edwards of Bristol, England, who bought Amity and combined the lands—said that much effort was made to reclaim the area. But never did he use unwarranted brutality, he wishes this court to know, like some Baptist ministers have implied within the press here. Never.

The attorney felt that, at the time, he was within his rights to see the negroes put beyond the land's boundary. But he did not order the lands to be cleared with fire. Those fires were started by the negroes who did not realise how tindered the land had become during the drought of that time. And the militia were sent in only to apprehend those that took part in the prison incident in town.

If the court can recall, several hundred negroes surrounded the prison house to demand release of five or six of the squatters, or settlers, as they insisted they were, who had been charged with trespass and were arrested when the police tried to evict them. The crowd of negroes were singing and making threats that they will see Jamaica become another San Domingo and run all white men from the island. Eventually, in order to free the prisoners, this mob attacked the gaol burning it to the ground.

Very bad business indeed, very bad. But most of the negroes were caught and justice was dealt with a firm hand, as I'm sure the court can recall. This one said she had nothing to do with it but the attorney was never sure—says she's more crafty than most.

How many of them are still living there? Well, less now, as I understand. Many died from sickness—yellow fever mostly. They have been left pretty much alone for several years. And the land there is now very poor, evidently. It hardly yields anything—the odd yellowing banana perhaps—which is why some of them have succumbed of late to starvation. There is still work for them upon the plantation if they will do it, the attorney says. But these negroes, as always, seem to fear that slavery is being brought back; that this island will be sold to the Americas and they will then find themselves again slaves . . . and so on and so on; arguments this court has had to hear too often as justification for wrongdoing. And this one, the accused, who calls herself only July, has never, ever been willing to work.

'Are you willing to work?'

What, what? She still cannot hear him.

'Can you hear me? Can she hear me?'

'Do you hear him?'

What?

'Oh, never mind. Carry on. Let's get to the charge against her. It's so very hot.'

And Constable Campbell is brought forth to stand within the courtroom. Skinny as a broom with a skin pockmarked as a breadfruit. The accused—and now a white bony finger does point across the room to

July—was lying down at the side of the path that runs from town to Unity Pen. He thought her dead, for she was not moving. She was covered with a filthy old shawl. So he kicked her. And he was quite surprised when she began to stir. She yelled several unrepeatable cuss words upon him. He asked her what she was doing. She said that he should mind his business. He repeated the question and this time she replied that she was on her way to market. But it was a very late hour for her to be going to market and she was told so.

Thinking something suspicious about her, the constable asked her to get up from the ground. It was as she was telling him in no uncertain terms to go away, that a fowl was heard clucking underneath her shawl. The constable, at once seeing a bird caught and flapping within her garment, asked her where she got this hen from. The negro replied that she had raised it. When asked to produce the bird from under her shawl so that the constable might inspect it, the accused ran off. By the time the constable had caught up with her, she had no hen under her clothes. She had proceeded to berate the constable—in some of the foulest language the constable had ever had to endure—for making her lose her only chicken. She was then arrested for stealing.

'Did you steal the chicken?'

'No, massa, me did raise it.'

'What did she say? Was it your chicken?'

'Yes, massa, me did raise it, then me did lose it.'

'What did she say?'

'She said, my lord, that she raised the chicken.'

'Yes, but where did she get it?'

'Someone 'pon Allen Pen did give me to raise.'

'What is she saying?'

'Something about Allen Pen. I think she's saying that somebody gave her the fowl to raise.'

'Yes, but are you speaking the truth? Ask her if she is speaking the truth.'

'Me place me hand upon the book and Lord strike me down if me not speak true.'

'What is she saying?'

'She wishes to place her hand upon the Bible to show she is speaking the truth.'

'Was the hen eventually found?'

'No, my lord.'

'Has anyone complained that they are missing a hen?'

'Not up to now, my lord.'

'Has she been in front of us before?'

'Umm, no, no, it does not seem so. I believe this is her first time within a court, my lord.'

'Oh, then let her go. This really is too flimsy a case for jury to hear. Let us get on—it is far too hot.'

Once the judge-man had struck his gavel down so our July might be led out and his next case conducted in, a little commotion began to stir within this hot-hot courtroom. For a man stood up from within the seats upon which the jury sat. But this was not a white man. No. Not a mulatto. Not a quadroon, nor a mustee, and certainly not a mustiphino. It was a negro; a nigger; a black man that stood. A black man raised himself from out the jury. And his voice, as he requested leave to approach the judge's bench, ran about the courtroom genteel and refined as any Englishman.

'Most irregular, most irregular,' came spluttering from the lips of all the white men within this room.

Come, July would not be led from her box—she did cling tighter to its walls for she wished to view this spectacle; a nigger thrown from the court for impersonating a gentleman. For sitting in quiet deceit amid a jury! Stealing a hen—what a puny crime when this tricky man was breathing amongst them. Let her see them chasing him around. The bewigged fat man blundering and puffing within this hunt to grab the nigger-rogue by his toe. The skinny Constable Campbell leaping over chair and table to seize this crafty puff-up black man, shouting, 'Hold up there, hold up there,' just like he pitiful commanded when pursuing her. The judge rising to yell, 'A nigger is escaped in my courtroom. Catch him, catch him. I will see him hanged!' Someone will surely arrive to fire a whip upon this cunning negro's back. Oh, what a fuss-fuss must soon arise!

But this black man was not chased, nor grabbed; no chairs or tables were overturned in his pursuit and no whip was cracked. Approaching the bench with an upright gait, this negro man, with his hands waving gracefully to aid in the reasoning of his enquiry, spoke in a whisper to the judge. True—the judge did lean back a little, his eyebrows raised, as the negro breathed words upon him. But this judge did not command him to be caught and hanged. No. Soon he leaned over to consult his clerk upon this black man's quandary. Eventually the judge shrugged, a you-have-my-permission-to-do-as-you-please gesture upon the negro, who graciously bowed his head to him.

There was no fuss-fuss at all.

'But what of me hen? The constable did make me lose it,' July asked loudly as she was led from the court by the scaly-head man. Come, she had repeated that lie so often she now believed it to be true. But once she was outside and under the hot-hot sun, the constable merely shooed her saying, 'Be off with you and be thankful you're not in shackles. Go on, be off with you.'

Once July had amassed saliva enough to spit upon this man's departing back, she dropped to sit weary upon the ground. How long would she be permitted to rest before some constable or busybody did think to move her? Could she gather her spirit to tread those stony miles back? And which way must this miserable trek to the rough, unlevel spent lands near the plantation that was once named Amity begin? As she considered whether this way up the street or that way down it, would make the right place to start, two shiny black leather shoes stepped to stand before her.

'Are you July of Amity?' an English voice said.

July made no reply but that of a sigh. For she was thinking of the heave she must make to see herself lifted from the ground.

'I know who you are—I have just come from the court,' this English voice carried on.

She had not will enough to cuss, 'So why you bother asking me, nah?

Cha!' for even thinking it, tired her. She just stared upon the black polished shoes, then up the grey trousers to the matching cutaway jacket,
over the stiff collar of the white shirt with its knotted scarlet silk tie,
then gasped. For all at once she was gazing up upon the face of that black
man.

'Are you July?' this man again said, 'once a slave, a house slave at
Amity? Your mistress was Caroline Mortimer?'

'No,' said she, 'Not me.' For there was such certainty within the tone
of his questioning that she was sure this answer would find least trouble
for her.

But the man tipped his head upon her and said, 'But I believe you
are.' Just that. Two times he said it, before leaning down to assist her so
she might rise from the ground. 'I believe you are.' As this man touched
July's arm, she shooed him from it. But without sign of misgiving, the
man raised his hat to her and said, 'My name is Thomas Kinsman. Do
you know me?'

Perhaps if his face had creased to yell like a mewling baby, she may have
known him. Perhaps if he had talked to her of a moonless night, a stony
trail and a red kerchief tied at a pickney's head, she would have begun to
think him familiar. Perhaps if he had conjured an ill-begotten black
pickaninny abandoned upon a stone, and talked of a Baptist manse, of
James Kinsman and of his good-goodly wife Jane, her memory would
have been roused. And then, perhaps, if he had seated himself beside her
to commence the tale of a small negro foundling taken from Jamaica
upon the ship called the *Apolline* to start a new life in England, July may
have recognised this Thomas Kinsman as her son.

And his chronicle might have begun with lengthy, excited description
of a sea voyage; with men dangling high from the ship's masts; a raging
deep-blue ocean drenching foaming water over all aboard; his shivering
body encrusted with a fine layer of salt. But probably not. For Thomas
Kinsman would want you first to know the name of the parish where

the Kinsman family finally rested when they arrived in England. So he would commence his tale with the word Hornsey (that being the parish), before moving on to give you the name and the precise location (perhaps with the aid of some map) of the village of Crouch End.

Then would come the depiction of a small house upon a street named Maynard. (Sometimes he will call this street Mayfield and frown upon his listener for believing it called anything other than this—but then, within the next telling, Maynard would once again appear.) He will want you to understand that this house was much smaller than the one the Kinsmans had occupied in Jamaica, and that its kitchen was set under the same roof as the house. But no servants did scurry and run there; for Jane Kinsman, good-goodly woman that she was, did perform all the duties required for a minister's household with very little help.

There was a fire kept lit within a grange and pots and pans did bubble and boil upon that stove all day long. While within a room called a front room, there was a coal fire. Yes, an open fire within a room where all the sitting and eating, and talking and reading, of his family was done. Sometimes the flames of this fire burned blue, owing to the gas that was given off from the mineral. But any listener would be wise to move Thomas Kinsman away from this fine detail, for his knowledge of coal stuffs could weary you before he has told you of bedtime in this little house. How the three boys—James, Henry and Thomas—every evening did run up the stairs to jump into a cold press-bed, where six fidgeting feet, elbows and knees tussled for warmth before nestling down to lock in sleep.

'Jim, Henry, Black Tom, come out, come out,' Thomas Kinsman will want you to hear—for this was yelled each morning by the ragged gang of children that lived within the rundown houses—the windows blackened with soot—that sat close to their dwelling across the street. He will then have you run with them to ascend a high hill to the road of Mount Pleasant from where you will watch the farm boys ploughing the fields below and follow the line of trees that seemed to stretch out across a dim-dark London to the cathedral of St Paul's.

He will have you strolling with him over to the Crouch Hall estate to walk quietly within the park; to view the wildfowl nesting upon the island in the large lake and sit beneath a drooping willow tree where the water running under the bridge fell frothing for thirty feet; or have you crack the ice upon Cholmeley brook to free the ducks to slip-slide across its surface.

And you will watch him fight the bully-boy, John Smith, and feel him pushing his grimacing face down into the icy snow for calling Thomas Kinsman a savage; and the blood gushing from John Smith's nose will turn that white snow once again into red slush.

And then Thomas Kinsman will see you stand astounded, your mouth agape, as Jacob Walker, leaning upon a freshly whittled stick, saunters into view at the edge of St Mary's churchyard. For here is another negro within this little English village. You will watch as a skinny black man from the Americas, with his greying hair and deep drawling voice, who was servant to a missus in Highgate, presents a grateful and excited Thomas with a gift; the first of the many *Penny Magazines* he gave to his 'little nigger brother' whenever he chanced him.

And be in no doubt that Thomas Kinsman would joy to take you through each page of each edition of every *Penny Magazine* he read, so you too might marvel at the engravings of Goodrich Castle or Highgate Church, or sit engrossed reading of the fertilisation of larvae, or the use of the goat as a wet-nurse.

But you must rest awhile for once Thomas Kinsman starts you upon the journey through his schooldays at the Crouch End Academy, he will demand all your regard as he talks of his lessons in history, geography and arithmetic, Greek, French and Latin. He may even offer to conjugate some Latin verbs for you, but it would be prudent for any listener to refuse politely this proposal; and be thankful that his school books were lost upon the voyage back to Jamaica, for he would have you perusing each and every one.

All these events Thomas Kinsman would willingly impart to any listener; but the story of his life in England does not truly commence until that keen-eyed negro boy—now fourteen, with shoulders that are rest-less to broaden, hair that wishes to sprout in parts never before seen and a voice that craves to pitch low—was bound in apprenticeship to a printer near Fleet Street. James Kinsman signed a deed that tied Thomas to a Mr Linus Gray for seven years—not only for instruction into the trade of print, but also to board within his household for the duration.

For Thomas could no longer remain within the Kinsmans' charge, as liquor had seen them all driven from Crouch End. James Kinsman had declared that he could not minister within a village where the beer shop and the public houses had greater congregation than any Sunday wor-ship. And where the foremost family of the parish shamelessly made their prominence through the distilling of gin.

When James Kinsman had sought to have all dens of inebriation closed down within Hornsey, so the labouring classes might go about their work with clearer heads, a rough and abusive crowd had gathered outside his house in Maynard Street, banging frying pans, pots, kettles, boards, pokers, shovels, to demand that the family depart. And although James Kinsman was forced to leave Hornsey to take up his new ministry in Lewes, in the county of Sussex, the learned, detailed, and very long pamphlet he wrote upon the riotous intoxication to be found within Crouch End remains to this day, unpublished.

But Thomas Kinsman's black eyes will not dim when he recounts this leave-taking. No. Rather, he will place his hands together and thought-fully raise them to his lips while he pronounces slowly, so as to exalt the meaning, that for boys like him—for foundlings—the choice before him for betterment was either employment in service or in trade; and to be a printer, he will say with startling delight, well, ever since he first studied those *Penny Magazines*, to be a printer was his avid wish.

And, before you will realise, you will be standing within a cramped dusty printing office on the south side of Fleet Street in Water Lane, where the dim sunlight from the window shows motes of dust as big as coins gliding through the air. Linus Gray—a skinny, tall man of about two and thirty with a nose so pointed he could spear a fish with it and a jaw square as nobility—was at a desk with his head bowed, perusing several large sheets of paper with the care of a surgeon examining an open wound, as his new apprentice stepped in.

Linus's expression, at first dull and bored, all at once changed upon seeing Thomas. He jumped from his seat laughing and clapping his hands. 'Oh, wait until they see you!' he sang as he skipped around his desk and spun Thomas to examine every angle of him within the dirty light. Linus Gray was so excited to have a negro foundling as his apprentice—a black boy who was born a slave in the West Indies and yet who could conjugate any Latin verb that Linus could bring to mind—that Thomas Kinsman became this man's firm favourite from that day on.

However, when Linus Gray's wife, Susan, first saw the new apprentice who was to lodge with them in their attic room, she screamed. Susan Gray begged her husband not to have a Hottentot board in their house; she thought it bad luck. But Linus ignored her concern and dismissed it with the word, 'fiddlesticks.'

Thomas wrote to James Kinsman to tell that Susan Gray liked him so little and feared him so much that she carried a broom with her when he was about the house so that if Thomas ever approached her she might hold him the length of it from her. James Kinsman, in reply, promised to pray that Thomas would soon come to regard Susan Gray as his mother.

Alone at the top of the Grays' tall narrow house that sat adjacent to the print office, in a room whose sloping roof rendered it no bigger than a cupboard, sitting by the dingy light and feeble heat of two coals that burned in the grate, wrapped in a blanket and wiping the black snot that ran from his nose upon his sleeve—Thomas wept.

And you might see a cloud come into Thomas Kinsman's eye as he recounts those early days in London Town. He may recite for you the prayer he made—the one for the Kinsmans, all of them, to please, please, please, come find him. He may even admit to his listener that he did think to run away. But probably not. Instead, Thomas Kinsman will wave his hand to dismiss your concern. He may even use the word fiddlesticks. For he will not leave his listener to dwell upon sorrow when the print office beckons and he can show you what a good little devil he became.

The print office of Messrs Gray and Co.—a brick house that seemed to lean exhausted upon its neighbour in the middle of Water Lane— became Thomas Kinsman's real home. For he chased up and down its dark winding stairs, ran in and out of the close, overheated rooms, scuttled about the dusty closets, searched the brimming cupboards, as 'Black Tom' was yelled at him from seven in the morning until seven in the evening. People, paper, metal, ink and presses all seemed to demand his devil's care. Every inch of this engorged five-storey house was so hurly-burly that, when in full spurt, the lungs of men competed with the candles' flames for air to breathe—and on long nights, neither burned the colour they should.

Parliament was where Gray and Co. found its work. Porters despatched from that magisterial institution arrived all day laden with colonial papers, reports of committees, election returns, statistics and accounts. Reams and reams of handwritten bluster that passed before Linus Gray's glance, to collate and to folio, to decide upon its worth and to settle upon its price before the four journeymen compositors were commanded to mount their frames to prepare for copy.

Caslon or Garamond or Baskerville is shouted as the compositors search for as many cases of these types as can be found. But never is there enough of those metal letters. The apprentice is charged to clean the ones just used so he can distribute a constant supply, lest a compositor be forced into some fancy spelling for the want of Es. With his uppercase upper and his lowercase lower, the compositor, standing at his frame with his stick held in his hand, like an artist with his palette, looks first to the handwritten copy, before click, click, clicking metal letters into a line. Then, line by line, each page is built up upon a form and the metal words are banged home with a mallet, tightened and spaced with slugs of wood, then locked within this frame by the teeth of quoins. And when the page is set, 'Proof' is yelled at the door.

Up from the basement comes a pressman. Filthy with ink and sweating damp as the paper he carries. He puffs and grunts the form back down four flights of stairs. Here he locks it on to the press—the Albion or the Stanhope (never the Columbian for merely proofing). And the form is inked, the paper is applied, the bed is slid, and the platen is levered down and the proof is printed.

So up the stairs to the top of the house our page now travels, within the hands of the luckless apprentice, for in the closet of the attic, under a sloping roof sit the readers. Three men usually, and the only ones within this series of dark caverns who have ink upon their hands and fingers, but have not been turned black as chimney sweeps by it. And these men scour the printed proof for error, blunder, and misspelling. By daylight or lamplight or a candle's weak glow, these mistakes are found and marked.

Back down the stairs the paper then travels, where the compositor sighs upon the errors that must now be corrected. Then, once amended, 'proof' is yelled again. Three times, this printer's round jig is danced before any form might find itself despatched to press for printing.

And then, down in the basement, the print run starts. On four sturdy iron presses—secured to the floor solid as teeth in a lion's jaw—the pressmen, stripped to the waist, begin their work. When handling paper, a pressman's touch can be gentle as a lady with her skirts. But once these men are printing, once they are caught in the rhythm of inking and sliding and levering, they appear like great goliaths goading a metal beast. And, above them, the readers grab their vibrating ink pots, the compositors steady their clicking letters, Linus Gray weights down his quivering papers, and the devil apprentice upon the stairs, or in a closet, or in a cupboard steadies himself as the whole house upon Water Lane begins to shake under this industry.

⌒

Thomas Kinsman mastered every procedure within this print house; he was accurate at case, strong at press and steadfast at office; but the task upon which he truly excelled beyond all other was as a reader. None queried Linus Gray's boast that his Black Tom was the best reader in the whole of London. None, excepting for one man.

This learned man, this 'scholar of high reputation,' upon becoming aware that the reputed reader at Gray and Co. was indeed a nigger, decided that he would do better to read his pamphlet for error himself.

'Your negro boy,' the scholarly man told Linus with a smile, 'would soon be up to the ears in pumpkins and would only work on it half an hour a day.' And he laughed heartily while continuing, 'I make no claim upon those words, for they are in fact the wisdom of Thomas Carlyle, the Scottish man of letters, in his discourse upon the negro question.'

And fourteen errors that clever man found within his paper; fourteen mistakes upon the first proof sheet; fourteen and it took him only three days to find them. Linus gave the man's proof to his 'negro boy' to read, and within less than half an hour Thomas had found sixty-nine more.

When the 'scholar of high reputation' called to claim his printed pamphlet, Linus summoned the eighteen-year-old Thomas to him. And Thomas Kinsman, standing straight-backed before that learned gentleman said, 'Sir, as the philosopher John Stuart Mill so wisely deduced, if negroes had worked no more than half an hour a day, would the sugar crops have been so considerable?'

As an apprentice, Thomas Kinsman gained a knowledge of the world and the way of it that, for all his education, he had hitherto not known. For Linus Gray was a free-thinker and most of the men that ever worked for him knew it. There was a club for mutual improvement—for which Linus Gray provided the stock of books, drawing materials and papers—that was held in the basement room of a nearby house for any of his workers who wished to join. It cost sixpence to attend (three pennies extra in winter for a coal fire to be lit) and tuppence fine for any who could, but did not turn out.

As the group of seven men met three hundred days of the year from eight o'clock until the hour of eleven, Thomas joined them. For he had no wish to sit lonely in his room every evening, or to spend that time in avoidance of Susan Gray upon the stairs with her broom. And Thomas

Kinsman will eagerly tell you that, within the dark, damp, gloomy close-ness of that basement room, his mind steadily opened, like a bird freshly hatched from its egg that discovers a wide world in which one day it must have the strength to fly.

And, within that nest, Thomas read *Don Quixote*, *Robinson Crusoe*, the works of Dickens—the *Pickwick Papers* and *Oliver Twist*—Wordsworth, Shakespeare, Shelley and many more beside. And the merits or other-wise of this literature was thoroughly discussed. The Bible, that good book, was prodded and poked for any evidence that the stories within the Old and New Testament were based upon truth and not just tales of someone's making.

While Thomas Paine's *The Rights of Man* had each of those working-men present, English and negro, declaring themselves to be fouly wronged by this modern life; for why were there no tax cuts for the poor or subsidies upon education? And in an essay that was applauded by all, Thomas Kinsman wrote how the philosopher, John Locke, stated that there are many things we cannot know, things about which we can only have belief—yet free-thinkers must build their belief upon fact, sci-entific inquiry and logical principles; so how might a free-thinker prove that when, say, looking upon a tree out of a window that the tree still stands outside the window when the free-thinker's back is turned and he can no longer see it? An essay of complete nonsense, as you will agree, reader, and yet Thomas Kinsman will wish you to know that it was awarded a shilling prize!

By the time Thomas Kinsman was twenty-one—his hair sprouted, his voice a deep bass tone and his shoulders mightily broad—he wrote to James Kinsman, eager to declare that he was no more bound to Linus Gray as an apprentice, but employed by him as a journeyman printer. And, he added as no more than an addendum, that he was now also of the deistic belief.

James Kinsman sent in reply a twenty-page letter in which the words heathen, idolater, savage and ingrate played very large part within the message. While the word atheist was repeated so many times that Thomas, in a long reply, explained that although he was no longer of the Baptist faith, he was not a non-believer, not an atheist, but just one who believed in natural religion and a creator God. James Kinsman sent back, in answer, just one page, with the word 'blasphemer' written large upon it.

And now we have reached the point within Thomas Kinsman's story where you will detect some sadness within his eye—but look closer when he tells you that, alas, Susan Gray did pass away, for it may be fancy feigning. Susan Gray died at the age of forty, blaming the Hottentot residing under her roof for blighting her marriage to childlessness and for the invasion of consumption that wasted her away until she weighed little more than a bird. As she lay dead, Linus Gray sobbed at her side with the hysterical abandon of a child; he stopped only to snarl upon her attending priest to keep his cant and humbug to the minimum and then get out.

Indeed, Linus Gray grieved so sorely for his wife that he was never to be the same man again. So crushed was he by her death that he kept himself insensible to the sorrow of it with drink. Not just night upon night, but mornings and afternoons, Thomas Kinsman was required to hunt through the dark lanes and narrow streets in an area between the west Strand and St Paul's in search of Linus. Sometimes, in the tiny rooms of the Cheshire Cheese tavern, Thomas would find Linus lit by a small spur of gas, seated before a hot baked sheep's head or clutching a beer while clumsily toasting a small loaf upon a fork in the fire. He would greet Thomas, earnestly placing his arm about his shoulder to beg him not to think ill of Susan for her actions to him. Or with words that slurred into one another like a fishseller's, he would seek to persuade Thomas that, despite how she treated her negro lodger, despite always wielding that broom upon him, that Susan Gray was a good woman.

At other times Thomas would find Linus, wet and sodden and trembling like a palsied tramp, slumped in an alley within the jumble of narrow courts, snivelling over and over on how he had so disappointed his wife.

Meanwhile within the printing office of Messrs Gray and Co., it was

Thomas Kinsman who did now receive the papers, reports and accounts from the porters from Parliament—who did glance at them, collate and folio them, before deciding upon their worth. And it was Thomas who commanded the compositors to mount their frames to prepare for copy, while Linus Gray, if present at all, drooped dull-eyed and oblivious within his chair.

Susan Gray, in death, soon slipped from being a mortal in Linus Gray's mind and slid into being a saint. And yet in all the years Thomas had lived within the Grays' household, he had witnessed so little affection between the hard-working, sharp-witted Linus and his prim, pious, melancholy wife, as to lead him to the conviction that they had married by some sort of mistake. But her death was to kill Linus Gray too. For he died not a year later, stretched out like a corpse upon her grave within the churchyard—shaking, convulsing and mournfully wailing to the stars above him, 'Forgive me, Susan, forgive me.'

The last will and testament of Linus Gray expressed his wish to be buried alongside his wife within St Bride's churchyard at Fleet Street; for it was a nice, quiet place for his ghost to walk. It also stated that no priest should attend upon his burial, for, it went on, he had no time for such frivolities.

And then, from beyond the grave, Linus Gray could be heard laughing and clapping his hands, 'Oh wait until they hear this, just wait until they hear this,' when his last will and testament went on to state that, in honour of his loyalty and friendship, and in redress for the wrong done to him by his birth and fate, he did devise and bequeath all his real and personal property, whatsoever and wheresoever, unto the negro Thomas Kinsman, so that he may walk within this world as he deserves—as a gentleman.

And you will now wish to know how Thomas Kinsman—suddenly finding himself a man of substance within London Town, a negro gentleman of considerable means, the owner of the printing office and that tall house upon Water Lane—did prosper. How eagerly will you sit forward upon your chair to learn all the detail of his new life amongst English society. How wide might your eyes become in anticipation of this glorious tale of fortune gained. And for a black man!

But alas, you have reached the part in Thomas Kinsman's tale where all those particulars, which had once been gladly imparted in wearying detail, curiously cease. For reasons that must be gleaned only from the pulsing vein upon his head as it throbs and wriggles, Thomas Kinsman does not care to summon that time. He may pull out his watch from within his pocket and declare himself to be late for somewhere. Or he may seek to fill his pipe and beg your leave so he might find his tobacco or a match. Or he may simply wave his hand before his face as if the memory must be batted away then, with rolling eyes or heavy sighs, demand that he be allowed to move on. And he will run to the end of his considerable patience if you are fool enough to insist upon its telling. No. No protestation will have him continue his tale until he has departed from the shores of England. No pleading, nor complaint will start the story again before three silent years have passed and Thomas Kinsman is, once again, back upon the island of Jamaica.

There—standing proud within his new print office upon Water Street, Falmouth, overseeing his three precious Columbian presses, and one Platen secured solid into the floor—is where his tale will once again commence; and no bewildered, nor disappointed look from his listener will have it otherwise.

So, long before you desire it, you will be standing in front of a two-storey, wooden, lime-washed building, girdled within the hubbub of an inquisitive crowd of perspiring negroes, one mangy brown dog, and two fussing goats, admiring the painted sign for Messrs Kinsman & Co. being fastened above the four pillars of this new printing office.

Yet the clamour from outside this works is much greater than any din that comes from within it. The four presses, three frames, the reading closets and the office all lie idle, for no white men of business upon the island would condescend to employ Messrs Kinsman & Co. How does a black boy come to dress and speak like a white gentleman? these English merchants and planters asked while sipping coffee within their clubs. How does a Hottentot with not even one drop of white blood within him find himself a proprietor of a print office? A nigger might composite or work at press or even, with careful instruction become a reader, but no slave-son could ever run a printing establishment of any worth. This broad-nosed, thick-lipped devil does walk too tall, they concluded.

Although the Platen press did sometimes find itself employed when negroes from the dry goods store, the boarding house or the masons did eagerly request their small handbills printed by Messrs Kinsman above all other, it was the volume work from those wealthy white men who owned the wharves, the warehouses, the ships and the plantations that the teeth of his presses wished to bite upon.

So Thomas Kinsman attended St Peter's Church upon Sundays. There those white men, outraged, bemoaning and under duress did have to greet him within a begrudging Christian fellowship. And during the long-long sermons Thomas sketched their faces and wrote their names secretly within a little book as he offered up a prayer to his creator God; 'One,' it began, 'Let just one of these white men of business come with good work—just one—and I will see that the others follow.'

And Thomas will grin to tell you that the Lord then worked in a mysterious way. For, five weeks later, upon a rainy Friday morning, Isaac Cecil Levy, a Jew who had never once attended the church, entered in upon Thomas's office. He required, he said, a press for the first edition of a newspaper he was to publish which was to be called *The Trelawney Mercury*.

And the compositors clicked, the readers read, and the pulling of the presses began. For the next edition Thomas Kinsman proposed to Isaac Levy, that they might print a supplement containing eight extra pages, on which people could pay to place their advertisements. And so *The Trelawney Mercury and Advertiser* was born. And, Thomas will joy to tell you—perhaps with the aid of a column of neat figures—that very profitable did it prove.

Soon newspapers, almanacs, legal blanks, auction catalogues, handbills—official printing of all sorts—flowed in and out of the print office of Messrs Kinsman and Co. upon Water Street. His workers even started a club for their mutual improvement, for which Thomas supplied the books, drawing materials, papers and candles. It met at sundown, cost a half-penny to join, with a farthing fine for any who strolled in so late that, 'Cha, them miss the whole t'ing again.'

With six men compositing, two apprentices, eight at press, five readers, an overseer and clerk in the office, within two years Thomas was required to find bigger premises on which to hang his sign!

So here we have Thomas Kinsman—a gentleman, a printer of high repute, a wealthy black man of commerce who wears shiny shoes and a scarlet tie. When called to do his duty within a jury of the court, as was required of someone of his standing, he sat in quiet fury listening to one of the most feeble, unworthy and unjust cases—where a starving person was to be punished for trying to feed themselves with the food that lives abundant about them—whilst staring upon the most pitiable, begrimed and wretched negro woman he had ever beheld. When, all at once, he began to recall a long-ago essay written by Jane Kinsman concerning a July. A July of Amity. July, once a house servant upon the sugar plantation of Amity. July, a slave girl. July, a slave girl who abandoned her baby to a stone outside a Baptist manse. July! July! And it was then that Thomas Kinsman raised himself slowly from out his seat.

But of course Thomas Kinsman said nothing of any of this on that day that he first stood before his mama. He just tipped his hat and demanded to take July home so he might see her fed.

And that, reader, is what he did.

⁓

When first July beheld the house upon King Street where Thomas Kinsman did reside, she tried to run from that black man in a scarlet tie. She believed his charity to be a trick. He desired a servant to scurry and run. One morsel of meat within her mouth and for ever a broom held in her hand. No, no, no, she would never serve again. But the room he led her into was not the kitchen, nor the outhouse, but a withdrawing room that was lavishly lined with books; from the ceiling to the floor, the solemn hues of leather-bound volumes stamped with gold rippled along every wall of that place. He did not offer her some wobbling broken-down wooden chair upon which to sit, but a fancy padded seat with a soft red cushion about it. And the milk he ordered his servant to bring was handed to her in a glass; and the sweetest, creamiest drink of milk it was that passed July's lips upon that day when Thomas Kinsman first sat down earnestly before her.

His breath was faltering, his fingers fidgeting—with the curve of his nails, his marriage band, his cuff—and his head was bowed when he quietly told July that he believed he was her son. He had longed for this day, but feared it would never come, he said. He had thought her dead. But now he wondered if he was, at last, sitting before the woman who had given birth to him. And then, with nervous searching, he looked upon July's face to seek a response, as he asked if she had once left her pickney upon a stone outside a Baptist manse. It was then that July leaned to one side upon the chair and, for his answer, regurgitated that rich milk to splatter into a pool of curds and whey upon the polished floor.

Yet still my beloved son, Thomas Kinsman, looked upon me kindly. Why, I have never truthfully understood.

But I have lived within my son's household from that day to this. Our first home was within that house in Falmouth where Lillian, my son's very young wife, did attend upon both her husband and me with the flurry of a fusspot. It was there that those three mischievous girls, Louise, Corinne and May, were born—and every day of our lives turned suddenly from peace into raucous mayhem.

But the town of Falmouth soon began to wither. For the sugar that fed and fattened that port lessened with every passing year. It slowly starved. So Thomas Kinsman moved us—his cherished family—to Kingston, where he opened a further printing business. And very profitable it is, too. But do not take my word upon it, go ask my son—he will joy to take you upon a tour of his fine works, if you so desire.

But for me, reader, my story is finally at an end. This long song has come full up to date. It is at last complete. So let me now place that final end dot . . .

Reader, alas my son is not yet finished with me. Must an old woman endure this? Thomas Kinsman is shaking his head once more. No, says he, surely this is not where my tale will end? What of the life lived by July upon those backlands at Amity? He wishes to know of those years betwixt July's stolen pickney and her shuffling starving in upon that courtroom.

So I have just asked him, you wish me to describe how July walked to find those negroes upon the backlands? How she collapsed before them and was tenderly nursed back into this life? Must I show you the trouble that those free negroes had to endure? Should my reader feel the fear of the harassment from planters that came upon that place almost daily? Shall we put out those fires, rebuild the huts, chase mounted white men from out the crops? Would you care to face a loaded pistol with a machete and a hoe? Or perhaps I should enlighten my readers as to how long a little piece of land can last until, lifeless and exhausted, it produces nothing but thistle? Shall I let the earthquakes rattle and the floods pour? Or shall we just sit throughout a drought—parched and dusty as the desiccated earth? Or feel as a fist is pressed into a starving belly so it might be tricked into thinking it is full? Must I find pretty words to describe the yellow fever that took so many? Or perhaps your desire is simply to watch as a large pit is dug for the graves?

All this I asked my son and you know what Thomas Kinsman replied? 'Yes, Mama, yes. We must know of all of this.'

But why must I dwell upon sorrow? July's story will have only the happiest of endings and you must take my word upon it. Perhaps, I told my son, upon some other day there may come a person who would wish to tell the chronicle of those times anew. But I am an old-old woman. And, reader, I have not the ink.

AFTERWORD

I TRUST I WILL be forgiven for this further intrusion upon my mama's story. Although that good woman's tale is at a close, it has left me, her son, with a quandary with which I hope the readers of this book might assist.

Within my mama's careful narration you will recall the story of the second child that was born to her character July. Now, any careful reader of these pages will have realised that my mama's tale, although purporting to be merely a fiction, closely follows the true circumstance of her own life. Therefore the child that was born to July—Emily—was a daughter that my own dear mama did indeed give life to. Emily Goodwin is my half-sister.

However, all trace of Emily Goodwin has been lost. Upon occasion my mama has expressed some curiosity as to what happened to her daughter. She has asked me, for example, whether Emily lives as a white woman in England? Does she reside within a fancy house or is she used as a servant? And upon several occasions my mama has become quite fretful when enquiring of me whether I believe her daughter Emily knows the real circumstances of her birth or remembers her mama? But then the pain of that parting soon causes that dear old woman to put all thought of Emily from out of her mind and feign indifference when any further mention is made of her.

But I have of late been puzzling upon the whereabouts of Emily

Goodwin and the situation under which she now lives. Perhaps she is in England, unaware of the strong family connection she has to this island of Jamaica. She may have children of her own, who have no understanding that their grandmama was born a slave.

So here is where I come to my request. If any readers have information regarding Emily Goodwin—her circumstance, her whereabouts—I would be very obliged to them if they could let me know it. A letter to my print works here in Kingston, addressed to Thomas Kinsman, would always find me. And any news that might allow me to know what happened to my sister would be gratefully received. But here I would also give one word of caution to any wishing to eagerly aid me with this request. In England the finding of negro blood within a family is not always met with rejoicing. So please, do not think to approach upon Emily Goodwin too hastily with the details of this story, for its load may prove to be unsettling.

Thomas Kinsman

ACKNOWLEDGEMENTS

I owe a great deal of thanks to many people for the help, advice, and support that I received during the writing of this novel: Olivia Amiel, Maya Mayblin, Albyn Hall, Catherine Hall, Judy Bastyra, Dorothy Kew, Ele Rickham, Marilyn Delevante, Gad Heuman, Jill Russell, Charles Sweeney, Lola Young, Kate Pullinger, Olive Senior, Patricia Duncker and Sheila Duncker. I would also like to say a big thank-you to all my friends and family (you know who you are) for being so wonderful when times got tough.

As this story is set in Jamaica during the nineteenth century I needed the knowledge of a great many other minds to help transport me to that time and place:

- Henry Bleby, *Death Struggles of Slavery.*

- Compiled and edited by Peter Barber, *Gin and Hell-Fire: Henry Batchelor's Memoirs of a Working Class Childhood in Crouch End 1823–1837.*

- Edited by F. G. Cassidy and R. B. Le Page, *Dictionary of Jamaican English.*

- Mrs Carmichael, *Domestic Manners and Social Customs of the White, Coloured and Negro Populations of the West Indies.*

- Roderick Cave, *Printing and the Book Trade in the West Indies.*

- Bryan Edward, *The History, Civil and Commercial of the British Colonies in the West Indies.*

- Edited with an Introduction by Moira Ferguson, *The History of Mary Prince, A West Indian Slave.* Related by herself.

- Catherine Hall, *Civilising Subjects: Metropole and Colony in the English Imagination 1830–1867.*

- Fernando Henriques, *Family and Colour in Jamaica.*

- Gad Heuman, *Between Black and White: Race Politics and the Free Coloured in Jamaica, 1670–1970.*

- B. W. Higman, *Montpelier Jamaica: A Plantation Community in Slavery and Freedom, 1739–1912.*

- Matthew Lewis, *Journal of a Residence Among the Negroes in the West Indies.*

- Edited by Roderick A. MacDonald, *Between Slavery and Freedom: Special Magistrate John Anderson's Journal of St Vincent during Apprenticeship.*

- Charles Manby Smith, *The Working Man's Way in the World.*

- *Montgomery Ward & Co catalogue no 57 1895 (facsimile).*

- Lady Nugent, *Lady Nugent's Journal.*

- Mrs Seacole (Edited by Ziggi Alexander & Audrey Dewjee), *Wonderful Adventures of Mrs Seacole in Many Lands*.

- Olive Senior, *Encyclopedia of Jamaican Heritage*.

- Raymond T. Smith, *Kinship and Class in the West Indies; A Genealogical Study of Jamaica and Guyana*.

- Anthony Trollope, *The West Indies and the Spanish Main*.

- James Walvin, *Black Ivory: A History of British Slavery*.

- James Walvin, *The Life and Times of Henry Clarke of Jamaica, 1828–1907*.

. . . And of course, the Internet.

I would also like to thank my agent, David Grossman, for his constant care and attention, and my UK editor, Jane Morpeth, for her wisdom. And finally, I am totally indebted to my husband Bill Mayblin not only for being my sensitive and tactful first reader, but also for everything else.